Praise for Jo Nesbø's

The Redeemer

"Full of shocking chance and nuance, unforeseen twists and ice-crystal clear views of Oslo in winter. . . . Nesbø has the prose style . . . to keep a reader entranced." —*The Wall Street Journal*

"A tour de force. . . . So tightly constructed and compelling that it's impossible to put the book down."
—*The Globe and Mail* (Canada)

"A treat. . . . Even when you're positive that the mystery is entirely done and dusted, it invariably turns out that the pragmatic Detective Harry Hole has managed to stay three steps ahead, and there's more to uncover." —*Time Out New York*

"Nesbø is no ordinary writer. . . . A complex story, impossible to second-guess, which proves that greed, lust and a desire for revenge lurk within the saintliest of folk." —*The Sunday Telegraph*

"The search for redemption is on—redemption through violence. The deeply flawed Hole is his familiar self: difficult and disrespectful, brilliant and intuitive. . . . Told in powerful prose, [*The Redeemer*] never fails to grip." —*Publishers Weekly*

JO NESBØ

The Redeemer

Jo Nesbø's books have been translated into forty-seven languages. He has written numerous Harry Hole novels, the latest of which is *Police*, and he is the author of *Headhunters* and several children's books. He has received the Glass Key Award for best Nordic crime novel. He is also a musician, songwriter, and economist and lives in Oslo.

www.jonesbo.com

ALSO BY JO NESBØ

The Redeemer

The Redeemer

JO NESBØ

Translated from the Norwegian by Don Bartlett

VINTAGE CRIME/BLACK LIZARD
Vintage Books
A Division of Random House LLC
New York

FIRST VINTAGE CRIME/ BLACK LIZARD EDITION, SEPTEMBER 2014

Translation copyright © 2013 by Don Bartlett

The Library of Congress has cataloged the Knopf edition as follows:
Nesbø, Jo, date-author.
[Frelseren. English]
The Redeemer / Jo Nesbø ; translated from the Norwegian by Don Bartlett.—
First American Edition.
pages cm
1. Hole, Harry (Fictitious character)—Fiction.
2. Police—Norway—Oslo—Fiction.
3. Murder for hire—Norway—Oslo—Fiction.   4. Oslo (Norway)—Fiction.
5. Mystery fiction.   I. Bartlett, Don, translator.   II. Title.
PT8951.24.E83F7413 2013
839.82'38—dc23   2012047015

Vintage Trade Paperback ISBN: 978-0-307-74298-8
eBook: 978-0-307-59673-4

Book design by Cassandra Pappas

www.weeklylizard.com

Printed in the United States of America
10 9 8 7 6 5

Who is this that comes from Edom, coming from Bozrah, his garments stained crimson? Who is this, in glorious apparel, marching in the greatness of his strength? "It is I, who announce that right has won the day, it is I," says the Lord, "for I am mighty to save."

—ISAIAH, 63:1

PART ONE

Advent

I

The Stars

She was fourteen years old and sure that if she shut her eyes tight and concentrated she could see the stars through the roof.

All around her, women were breathing. Regular, heavy, nighttime breathing. One was snoring, and that was Auntie Sara, who had been given a mattress beneath the open window.

She closed her eyes and tried to breathe like the others. It was difficult to sleep, especially because everything around her was so new and different. The sounds of the night and the forest beyond the window in Østgård were different. The people she knew from the meetings in the citadel and the summer camps were somehow not the same. She was not the same, either. The face and body she saw in the mirror this summer were new. And her emotions, these strange hot and cold currents that flowed through her when the boys looked at her. Or when one of them in particular looked at her. Robert. He was different this year, too.

She opened her eyes again and stared. She knew God had the power to do great things, even allow her to see the stars through the roof. If it was His wish.

It had been a long and eventful day. The dry summer wind had whispered through the corn, and the leaves on the trees danced as if in a fever, causing the light to filter through to the visitors on the field. They had been listening to one of the Salvation Army cadets from the officer-training school talking about his work as a preacher on the Faeroe Islands. He was good-looking and spoke with great sensitivity and passion. But she was preoccupied with shooing away a bumblebee that kept buzzing around her head, and by the time it moved off, the heat had made her drowsy. When the cadet finished, all faces were turned to the territorial commander, David Eckhoff, who had been observing them with his smiling, young eyes, which were actually over fifty years old. He saluted in the Salvation Army manner, with his right hand raised above his shoulder and pointing to the kingdom of heaven, amid a resounding shout of "Hallelujah!" Then he prayed for the cadets' work with the poor and the pariahs to be blessed, and reminded them of the Gospel of Matthew, where it said that Jesus the Redeemer was among them, a stranger on the street, maybe a criminal, without food and without clothing. And that on Judgment Day the righteous, those who had helped the weakest, would have eternal life. It had all the makings of a long speech, but then someone whispered something and he said, with a smile, that Youth Hour was next on the program and today it was Rikard Nilsen's turn.

She had heard Rikard make his voice deeper than it was to thank the commander. As usual, he had prepared what he was going to say in writing and memorized it. He stood up and recited how he was going to devote his life to the fight, to Jesus's fight for the kingdom of God. His voice was nervous, yet monotonous and soporific. His introverted glower rested on her. Her eyes were heavy. His sweaty top lip was moving to form the familiar, secure, tedious phrases. So she didn't react when the hand touched her back. Not until it became fingertips and they wandered down to the small of her back, and lower, and made her freeze beneath her thin summer dress.

She turned and looked into Robert's smiling brown eyes. And she wished her skin were as dark as his so that he would not be able to see her blush.

"Shh," Jon had said.

Robert and Jon were brothers. Although Jon was one year older, many people had taken them for twins when they were younger. But Robert was seventeen now and while they had retained some facial similarities, the differences were clearer. Robert was happy and carefree, liked to tease and was good at playing the guitar, but was not always punctual for services in the citadel, and sometimes the teasing had a tendency to go too far, especially if he noticed others were laughing. Then Jon would often step in. Jon was an honest, conscientious boy who most thought would go to officer-training school and would—though this was never formulated out loud—find himself a girl in the Army. The latter could not be taken for granted in Robert's case. Jon was three-quarters of an inch taller than Robert, but in some strange way Robert seemed taller. From the age of twelve Jon had begun to stoop, as though he were carrying the woes of the world on his back. Both were dark-skinned, good-looking, with regular features, but Robert had something Jon did not have. There was something in his eyes, something black and playful, which she wanted and yet did not want to investigate further.

While Rikard was talking, her eyes were wandering across the sea of assembled familiar faces. One day she would marry a boy from the Salvation Army and perhaps they would both be posted to another town or another part of the country. But they would always return to Østgård, which the Army had just bought and was to be their summer site from now on.

On the margins of the crowd, sitting on the steps leading to the house, was a boy with blond hair stroking a cat that had settled in his lap. She could tell that he had been watching her, but he had looked away just as she noticed. He was the one person here she didn't know, but she did know that his name was Mads Gilstrup, that he was the grandchild of the people who had owned Østgård before, that he was a couple of years older than her and that the Gilstrup family was wealthy. He was attractive, in fact, but there was something solitary about him. And what was he doing here, anyway? He had been there the previous night, walking around with an angry frown on his face, not talking to anyone. She had felt his eyes on her a few times. Everyone looked at her this year. That was new, too.

She was jerked out of these thoughts by Robert taking her hand, putting something in it and saying: "Come to the barn when the general-in-waiting has finished. I've got something to show you."

Then he stood up and walked off, and she looked down into her hand and almost screamed. With one hand over her mouth, she dropped the object into the grass. It was a bumblebee. It could still move, despite not having legs or wings.

At last Rikard finished, and she sat watching her parents and Robert and Jon's parents moving toward the tables where the coffee was. They were both what Army people in their respective Oslo congregations called "strong families," and she knew watchful eyes were on her.

She walked toward the outhouse. Once she was around the corner, where no one could see her, she scurried in the direction of the barn.

"Do you know what this is?" said Robert with the smile in his eyes and the deep voice he had not had the summer before.

He was lying on his back in the hay whittling a tree root with the penknife he always carried in his belt.

Then he held it up and she saw what it was. She had seen drawings. She hoped it was too dark for him to see her blush again.

"No," she lied, sitting beside him in the hay.

And he gave her that teasing look of his, as if he knew

something about her she didn't even know herself. She returned his gaze and fell back on her elbows.

"This is where it goes," he said, and in an instant his hand was up her dress. She could feel the hard tree root against the inside of her thigh and, before she could close her legs, it was touching her underpants. His breath was hot on her neck.

"No, Robert," she whispered.

"But I made it for you," he wheezed in return.

"Stop. I don't want to."

"Are you saying no? To me?"

She caught her breath and was unable either to answer or to scream because at that moment they heard Jon's voice from the barn door: "Robert! No, Robert!"

She felt him relax and let go, and the tree root was left between her clenched thighs as he withdrew his hand.

"Come here!" Jon said, as though talking to a disobedient dog.

With a chuckle Robert got up, winked at her and ran out into the sun to his brother.

She sat up and brushed the hay off her, feeling both relieved and ashamed at the same time. Relieved because Jon had spoiled their crazy game. Ashamed because he seemed to think it was more than that: a game.

Later, during grace before their evening meal, she had looked up straight into Robert's brown eyes and seen his lips form one word. She didn't know what it was, but she had started to giggle. He was crazy! And she was . . . well, what was she? Crazy, too. Crazy. And in love? Yes, in love, precisely that. And not in the way she had been when she was twelve or thirteen. Now she was fourteen and this was bigger. More important. And more exciting.

She could feel the laughter bubbling up inside her now, as she lay there trying to stare through the roof.

Auntie Sara grunted and stopped snoring beneath the window. Something screeched. An owl?

She needed to pee.

She didn't feel like going out, but she had to. Had to walk through the dewy grass past the barn, which was dark and quite a different proposition in the middle of the night. She closed her eyes, but it didn't help. She crept out of her sleeping bag, slipped on some sandals and tiptoed over to the door.

A few stars had appeared in the sky, but they would disappear when day broke in the east in an hour's time. The cool air caressed her skin as she scampered along, listening to the unidentifiable sounds of the night. Insects that stayed quiet during the day. Animals hunting. Rikard said he had seen foxes in the distant copse. Or perhaps the animals were the same ones that were out during the day, but just made different sounds. They changed. Shed their skins, so to speak.

The outhouse stood alone on a small mound behind the barn. She watched it grow in size as she came closer. The strange, crooked hut had been made with untreated wooden boards that had warped, split and turned gray. No windows, a heart on the door. The worst thing about it was that you never knew if anyone was already in there.

And she had an instinct that someone *was* already in there.

She coughed so that whoever was there might signal his presence. A magpie took off from a branch on the edge of the wood. Otherwise all was still.

She stepped up onto the flagstone. Grabbed the lump of wood that passed for a door handle. Pulled it. The black room gaped open.

She breathed out. There was a flashlight beside the toilet seat, but she didn't need to switch it on. She raised the seat lid before closing the door and fastening the door hook. Then she pulled up her nightgown, pulled down her underwear and sat down. In the ensuing silence she thought she heard something. Something that was neither animal nor magpie nor insects shedding skin. Something that moved fast through the tall grass behind the toilet. Then the trickle started and the noise was obscured. But her heart had already started pounding.

When she had finished, she quickly pulled up her underpants and sat in the dark listening. But all she could hear was a faint ripple in the tops of the trees and her blood throbbing in her ears. She waited for her pulse to slow down, then she unhooked the catch and opened the door. The dark figure filled almost the entire doorway. He must have been standing and waiting silently outside on the stone step. The next minute she was splayed over the toilet seat and he stood above her. He closed the door behind him.

"You?" she said.

"Me," he said in an alien, tremulous, husky voice.

Then he was on top of her. His eyes glittered in the dark as he bit her lower lip until he drew blood and one hand found the way under her nightgown and tore off her underwear. She lay there crippled with fear beneath the knife blade that stung the skin on her neck while he kept thrusting his groin into her before he had even got his trousers off, like some crazed, copulating dog.

"One word from you and I'll cut you into pieces," he whispered. And not one word issued from her mouth. Because she was fourteen years old and sure that if she shut her eyes tightly and concentrated she would be able to see the stars through the roof. God had the power to do things like that. If it was His wish.

2

The Visit

He studied his reflected features in the train window. Tried to see what it was, where the secret lay. But he saw nothing in particular, apart from the red neckerchief, just an expressionless face and eyes and hair that, approaching the walls of the tunnels between Courcelles and Ternes, was as black as the eternal night of the métro. *Le Monde* lay in his lap, forecasting snow, but above him the streets of Paris were still cold and deserted beneath impenetrable, low-lying cloud cover. His nostrils flared and drew in the faint but distinct smell of damp cement, human perspiration, hot metal, eau de cologne, tobacco, wet wool and bile, a smell they never managed to wash out of the train seats, or to ventilate.

The pressure created by an oncoming train made the windows vibrate, and the darkness was temporarily banished by the pale squares of light that flashed past. He pulled up the sleeve of his coat and checked his watch, a Seiko SQ50 that he had received as partial payment from a client. There were already scratches on the glass, so he was not sure it was a genuine item. A quarter past seven. It was Sunday evening and the car was no more than half full. He looked around him. People slept on the métro; they always did. On weekdays, in particular. Switched off, closed their eyes and let the daily journey become a dreamless interval of nothing between the red or the blue lines on the métro map, a mute connecting line between work and freedom. He had read about a man who had sat like this for a whole day, eyes closed, to and fro, and it was only when they came to clean the car at the end of the day that they discovered he was dead. Perhaps he had descended into the catacombs for this very purpose, to draw a blue connecting line between life and the beyond in this pale yellow coffin, knowing he would be undisturbed.

As for himself, he was forming a connecting line in the other direction. Back to life. There was this job tonight and then the one in Oslo. The last job. Then he would be out of the catacombs for good.

A dissonant signal screamed before the doors closed in Ternes. They picked up speed again.

He closed his eyes, trying to imagine the other smell. The smell of urinal blocks and hot, fresh urine. The smell of freedom. But perhaps it was true what his mother, the teacher, had said. That the human brain can reproduce detailed images of everything you have seen or heard, but not even the most basic smell.

Smell. The images began to flash past on the inside of his eyelids. He had been fifteen years old, sitting in the corridor of the hospital in Vukovar, listening to his mother repeat the mumbled prayer to Thomas the Apostle, the patron saint of construction workers, to let God spare her husband. He had heard the rumble of the Serbian artillery firing from the river and the screams of those being operated on in the infants' ward, where there were no longer any infants because the women of the town had stopped producing after the siege started. He had worked as an errand boy in the hospital and learned to shut out the noises, the screams and the artillery. But not the smells. And one smell above all others. Surgeons performing an amputation first had to cut through the flesh to the bone, and then, so that patients did not bleed to death, to use something that looked like a soldering iron to cauterize the blood vessels so that they were closed off. The smell of burned flesh and blood was like nothing else.

A doctor came into the corridor and waved him and his mother in. Approaching the bed, he had not dared to look at his father; he had just concentrated on the big brown hand clutching the mattress and trying, as it seemed, to tear it in two. It could have succeeded, for these were the strongest hands in the town. His father was a steel-bender—he was the person who went on building sites when the bricklayers were finished, put his large hands around the ends of the protruding steel used to reinforce the concrete, and with one quick, practiced movement, bent the ends of the steel poles and wove them into each other. He had seen his father working; it looked like he was wringing a cloth. No one had invented a machine that did the job better.

He squeezed his eyes shut as he heard his father scream out in pain and anguish: "Take the boy out!"

"But he asked—"

"Out!"

The doctor's voice: "The bleeding has stopped. Let's get cracking now!" Someone grabbed him under the arms and lifted him. He tried to struggle, but he was so small, so light. And that was when he noticed the smell. Burned flesh and blood.

The last thing he heard was the doctor's voice:

"Saw, please."

The door slammed behind him and he sank down onto his knees and continued to pray where his mother had left off. Save him. Maim him, but save him. God had the power to do things like that. If it was His wish.

He felt someone watching him, opened his eyes and was back in the métro. On the seat opposite was a woman with taut jaw muscles and a weary, distant gaze that moved away when it met his. The second hand on his wristwatch jerked forward as he repeated the address to himself. He felt his pulse. Normal. His head was light, but not too light. He was neither hot nor cold, felt neither fear nor pleasure, neither satisfaction nor dissatisfaction. The train was slowing down. Charles de Gaulle–Étoile. He sent the woman a final glance. She had been studying him, but if she should ever meet him again, maybe even tonight, she still would not recognize him.

He got to his feet and waited by the doors. The brakes gave a low lament. Urinal blocks and urine. And freedom. As impossible to imagine as a smell. The doors slid open.

Harry stepped onto the platform and stood inhaling the warm underground air as he read the address on the slip of paper. He heard the doors close and felt the draft of air on his back as the train set off again. Then he walked toward the exit. An advertisement over the escalator told him there were ways of avoiding colds. "Like hell there are," he coughed, stuffing a hand down the deep pocket of his wool coat and finding the pack of cigarettes under the hip flask and the tin of throat lozenges.

The cigarette bobbed up and down in his mouth as he walked through the glass exit door, leaving the raw, unnatural heat of Oslo's underground behind him, and ran up the steps to Oslo's ultra-natural December darkness and freezing temperatures. Harry instinctively shrank. Egertorget. This small, open square was an intersection between pedestrian streets in the heart of Oslo, if the city could be said to have a heart at this time of the year. Shops were open this Sunday since it was the penultimate weekend before Christmas, and the square was teeming with people hurrying to and fro in the yellow light that fell from the windows of the surrounding modest three-story shops. Harry saw the bags of wrapped presents and made a mental note to buy something for Bjarne Møller, whose last day at Police HQ was tomorrow. Harry's boss and chief protector in the police force for all these years was at long last realizing his plans to reduce his hours, and from next week onward would take over as a so-called senior special investigator at the Bergen police station, which meant in reality that Bjarne Møller could do as he liked until he retired. Cushy setup—but Bergen? Rain and dank mountains. Møller didn't even come from Bergen. Harry had always liked—but not always appreciated—Bjarne Møller.

A man dressed head to toe in a down jacket and trousers slowly waddled past like an astronaut, grinning and blowing frosted breath from round, pink cheeks. Stooped shoulders and closed winter faces. Harry spotted a pallid-faced woman wearing a thin, black leather jacket with holes in the elbows standing by the jeweler's, hopping from one foot to the other as her eyes searched, hoping to find her supplier soon. A beggar, long-haired and unshaven, but well covered in warm, fashionable, youthful clothing, sat in a yoga position, leaning against a lamppost, his head bent forward as if in meditation, with a brown paper cup from a cappuccino bar in front of him. Harry had seen more and more beggars over the last year, and it had struck him that they all looked the same. Even the paper cups were identical, as though it were a secret code. Perhaps they were creatures from outer space quietly taking over his town, his streets. No problem. Feel free.

Harry entered the jeweler's shop.

"Can you fix this?" he said to the young man behind the counter, passing him his grandfather's watch. Harry had been given it when he was a boy in Åndalsnes, the day they had buried his mother. He had almost been frightened, but his granddad had reassured him that watches were the sort of thing you gave away, and Harry should remember to pass it on. "Before it's too late."

Harry had forgotten all about the watch until Oleg visited him in his flat on Sofies Gate and had seen the silver watch in a drawer while he was looking for Harry's Game

Boy. Oleg, who was ten years old, but had long had the measure of Harry at their shared passion—the rather outdated computer game Tetris—was suddenly oblivious to the duel he had been looking forward to, and instead sat fiddling with the watch, trying to make it go.

"It's broken," Harry said.

"Ooof," Oleg answered. "Everything can be repaired."

Harry hoped in his heart of hearts that this contention was true, but he had days when he had severe doubts. Nonetheless, he had wondered in a vague way whether he should introduce Oleg to Jokke & Valentinerne and their album *Everything Can Be Repaired.* However, on reflection, Harry had concluded that Oleg's mother, Rakel, was unlikely to appreciate the connection: her ex-alcoholic lover passing on songs about being an alcoholic, written and sung by a now-dead junkie.

"Can you repair it?" he asked the young man behind the counter. By way of an answer, nimble, expert hands opened the watch.

"Not worth it."

"Not worth it?"

"If you go to an antique shop, they have better-working watches and they cost less than it would to have this fixed."

"Do it anyway," Harry said.

"OK," said the young man, who had already started examining the internal mechanisms and, in fact, seemed pretty pleased with Harry's decision. "Come back on Tuesday."

On leaving the shop Harry heard the frail sound of a single guitar string through an amplifier. It rose when the guitarist, a boy with scraggly facial hair and fingerless gloves, turned one of the tuning keys. It was time for one of the traditional pre-Christmas concerts, when well-known artists performed on behalf of the Salvation Army in Egertorget. People had already begun to gather in front of the band as it took up a position behind the Salvation Army's black

Christmas kettle, a cooking pot that hung from three poles in the middle of the square.

"Is that you?"

Harry turned. It was the woman with the junkie eyes.

"It's you, isn't it? Have you come instead of Snoopy? I need a fix right away. I've—"

"Sorry," Harry interrupted. "It's not me you want."

She stared at him. Leaning her head to one side, she narrowed her eyes, as though appraising whether he was lying to her. "Yep, I've seen you somewhere before."

"I'm a policeman."

She paused. Harry breathed in. There was a delayed reaction, as if the message had to follow detours around scorched neurons and smashed synapses. Then the dull glow of hatred that Harry had been waiting for lit up in her eyes.

"The cops?"

"Thought we had a deal. You were supposed to stay in the square, in Plata," Harry said, looking past her at the vocalist.

"Huh," said the woman, standing straight in front of Harry. "You're not in Narcotics. You're the guy on the TV who killed—"

"Crime Squad." Harry took her by the arm. "Listen, you can get what you want in Plata. Don't force me to drag you into the station."

"Cannot." She tore her arm away.

Harry held up both hands. "Tell me you're not going to do any deals here and I can go. OK?"

She cocked her head. The thin, anemic lips tightened a fraction. She seemed to see something amusing in the situation. "Should I tell you why I can't go to the square?"

Harry waited.

"Because my boy's down there."

He felt his stomach churn.

"I don't want him to see me like this. Do you understand, cop?"

Harry looked into her defiant face as he tried to formulate a sentence. "Merry Christmas," he said, turning his back on her.

Harry dropped his cigarette into the packed brown snow and walked off. He wanted this job off his back. He didn't see the people coming toward him, and, staring down at the blue ice as if they had a bad conscience, they didn't see him, either, as if they, citizens of the world's most generous social democracy, were nonetheless ashamed. *Because my boy's down there.*

On Fredensborgveien, beside Oslo's Deichmanske Public Library, Harry stopped outside the street number that was scrawled on the envelope he was carrying. He leaned back and looked up. The façade was gray and black and had recently been repainted. A graffiti artist's wet dream. Christmas decorations were already hanging from some of the windows like silhouettes against the gentle yellow light in what seemed like warm, secure homes. And perhaps they are indeed that, Harry forced himself to think. "Forced," because you can't be in the police for twelve years without being infected by the contempt for humanity that comes with the territory. But he did fight against it; you had to give him that.

He found the name by the bell, closed his eyes and tried to find the right words. It didn't help. Her voice was still in the way.

"I don't want him to see me like this . . ."

Harry gave up. Is there a right way to formulate the impossible?

He pressed his thumb against the cold metal button, and somewhere inside the building it rang.

* * *

Captain Jon Karlsen took his finger off the button, put the heavy plastic bags down on the pavement and gazed up at the front of the building. The flats looked as if they had been under siege from light artillery. Big chunks of plaster had fallen off and the windows of a burned-out flat on the second floor had been boarded up. At first he had walked right past Fredriksen's blue house; the cold seemed to have sucked all the color out of the buildings and made all the house fronts on Hausmanns Gate the same. It was only when he saw "Vestbredden"—West Bank—scrawled on the wall of a squatters' building that he realized he had walked too far. A crack in the glass of the front door was shaped like a *V. V* for victory.

Jon shivered in his windbreaker and was glad the Salvation Army uniform underneath was made of pure, thick wool. When Jon had gone to be measured for his new uniform after officer-training school, none of the regular sizes had fit him, so he had been issued some material and sent to a tailor, who blew smoke into his face and said apropos of nothing that he rejected Jesus as his personal redeemer. However, the tailor did a good job and Jon thanked him warmly; he was not used to made-to-measure clothes. That was why he had a stoop, it was said. Those who saw him coming up Hausmanns Gate that afternoon might well have thought he was bent over to keep out of the ice-cold December wind that was sweeping icicles and frozen litter along the pavement as the heavy traffic thundered by. But those who knew him said that Jon Karlsen stooped to take the edge off his height. And to reach down to those smaller than him. As he did now, to drop the twenty-krone coin in the brown paper cup held by a filthy, trembling hand next to the doorway.

"How's it going?" Jon asked the human bundle sitting cross-legged on a piece of cardboard in the swirling snow.

"I'm in the line for methadone treatment," the piteous person said in a halting, monotonous voice, as if reciting an ill-rehearsed psalm, while staring at Jon's black-uniformed knees.

"You should go down to our café on Urtegata," Jon said. "Warm up a bit and get some food and . . ."

The rest was drowned out by the roar of the traffic as the lights behind them changed to green.

"No time," the bundle replied. "You wouldn't have a fifty-note, would you?" Jon never ceased to be surprised by drug addicts' unwavering focus. He sighed and thrust a hundred-krone note in the cup.

"See if you can find some warm clothes at Fretex. If not, we've got some new winter jackets at the Lighthouse. You'll freeze to death in that thin denim jacket."

He was resigned to the fact that he was speaking to someone who already knew the gift would be used to buy dope, but so what? It was the same refrain, yet another of the irresolvable moral dilemmas that filled his days.

Jon pressed the bell once again. He saw his reflection in the dirty shop window beside the doorway. Thea said he was a big man. He wasn't big at all. He was small. A small soldier. But when he was finished the little soldier would sprint down Møllerveien, across the Akerselva River, where east Oslo and Grünerløkka started, over Sofienberg Park to 4 Gøteborggata, which the Army owned and rented out to its employees, unlock the door to Entrance B, say hello to one of the other tenants he hoped would assume he was on his way to his flat on the fourth floor. However, he would take the elevator to the fifth, go through the loft space to the A building, make sure the coast was clear, then head for Thea's door and tap out their prearranged signal. And she would open the door and her arms, into which he could creep and thaw out.

Something was trembling.

At first he thought it was the ground, the city, the foundations. He put down the bag and delved into his pocket. His cell phone was vibrating in his hand. The display showed Ragnhild's number. It was the third time today. He knew he could not put it off any longer; he would have to tell her. That he and Thea were getting engaged. When he had found the right words. He put the phone back in his pocket and avoided looking at his reflection. But he made up his mind. He would stop being a coward. He would be frank. Be a big soldier. For Thea, on Gøteborggata. For his father in Thailand. For the Lord above.

"Yes," came the shout from the loudspeaker above the bells.

"Oh, hi. This is Jon."

"Eh?"

"Jon from the Salvation Army." Jon waited.

"What do you want?" the voice crackled.

"I've got some food for you. I thought you might need—"

"Got any cigarettes?"

Jon swallowed and stamped his boots in the snow. "No, I only had enough money for food this time."

"Shit."

It went quiet again.

"Hello?" Jon shouted.

"Yeah, yeah. I'm thinking."

"If you want, I'll come back later."

The mechanism buzzed and Jon quickly pushed open the door. Inside the stairwell there were newspapers, empty bottles and frozen yellow pools of urine. Thanks to the cold weather Jon did not have to brave the pervasive, bittersweet stench that filled the hallway on milder days.

He tried to walk without making much noise, but his footsteps reverberated on the stairs anyway. The woman standing in the doorway and waiting for him was ogling the bags. To avoid looking him in the eye, Jon thought. She had that same bloated, swollen face that came with many years of addiction, was overweight and wore a filthy white T-shirt under her bathrobe. A stale smell emanated from the door.

Jon stopped on the landing and put down the bags. "Is your husband in, too?"

"Yes, he's in," she said in mellifluous French.

She was good-looking. High cheekbones and large, almond-shaped eyes. Narrow, bloodless lips. And well dressed. At any rate, the part of her he could see through the crack in the door was well dressed.

Instinctively, he adjusted his red neckerchief.

The security lock between them was made of solid brass and attached to a heavy oak door without a nameplate. While standing outside the building on Avenue Carnot and waiting for the concierge to open the door, he had noticed that everything seemed new and expensive, the door furniture, the bells, the cylinder locks. And the fact that the pale-yellow façade and the white shutters were covered in an unsightly, dirty layer of black pollution served to emphasize the established and solid nature of this district of Paris even more. Original oil paintings hung in the hallway.

"What do you want?"

The eyes and the intonation were neither friendly nor unfriendly, but contained perhaps a smidgen of skepticism because of his terrible French pronunciation.

"A message, madame."

She hesitated. But acted as expected in the end.

"All right. Could you wait here, please, and I'll get him?"

She shut the door and the lock fell into position with a well-oiled click. He stamped his feet. He ought to learn to speak better French. His mother had force-fed him English in the evenings, but she had never sorted out his French. He stared at the door. French underwear. French letter. Good-looking.

He thought about Giorgi. Giorgi of the white smile was one year older than he was, so twenty-eight now. Was he still as good-looking? Blond and small and pretty like a girl? He had been in love with Giorgi, in the unprejudiced, unconditional way that only children can fall in love.

He heard steps coming from inside. A man's steps. Someone fiddling with the lock. A blue connecting line between work and freedom, from here to soap and urine. The snow would come soon. He prepared himself.

The man's face appeared in the doorway.

"What the fuck do you want?"

Jon lifted the plastic bags and ventured a smile. "Fresh bread. Smells good, doesn't it."

Fredriksen laid a large brown hand on the woman's shoulder and pushed her away. "All I can smell is Christian blood . . ." It was said with clear, sober diction, but the washed-out irises in the bearded face told a different story. The eyes tried to focus on the shopping bags. He looked like a large, powerful man who had shrunk inside. His skeleton and even his cranium had become smaller inside the skin that drooped, three sizes too big, from the malevolent face. Fredriksen ran a grubby finger over the fresh cuts along the bridge of his nose.

"You're not going to preach now, are you?"

"No, actually I wanted—"

"Oh, come on, soldier. You want something back for this, don't you? My soul, for example."

Jon shivered in his uniform. "It's not me who deals with souls, Fredriksen. But I can arrange for food, so—"

"Oh, you can manage a little sermon first."

"As I said—"

"A sermon!"

Jon stood looking at Fredriksen.

"Give us a sermon with that wet little cunt-hole of yours!" Fredriksen yelled. "A sermon so that we can eat with a good conscience, you condescending Christian bastard. Come on, get it over with. What's God's message today?"

Jon opened his mouth and closed it again. Swallowed. Tried again, and this time his vocal cords responded. "The message is that He gave His only son, who died . . . for our sins."

"You're lying!"

"No, I'm afraid I'm not," Harry said, observing the terrified face of the man in the doorway in front of him. There was a smell of lunch and a rattle of cutlery in the background. A family man. A father. Until now. The man scratched his forearm and gazed at a spot above Harry's head as if someone were there. The scratching made an unpleasant rasping noise.

The rattle of cutlery had stopped. The shuffle of feet came to a halt behind the man and a small hand was placed on his shoulder. A woman's face with large red eyes peeped out.

"What is it, Birger?"

"This policeman has something to tell us," Birger said in a monotone.

"What?" the woman said looking at Harry. "Is it about our son? Is it about Per?"

"Yes, Fru Holmen," Harry said and saw the fear steal into her eyes. He searched for the impossible words. "We found him two hours ago. Your son is dead."

He had to look away.

"But he . . . he . . . where . . . ?" Her eyes jumped from Harry to the man, who kept scratching his arm.

Won't be long before he draws blood, Harry thought, and cleared his throat. "In a container by the harbor. What we feared. He's been dead for a good while."

Birger Holmen seemed to lose his balance, staggered

backward into the lit hallway and grabbed a coatrack. The woman stepped forward and Harry saw the man fall to his knees behind her.

Harry breathed in and shoved his hand inside his coat. The metal hip flask was ice-cold against his fingertips. He found what he was looking for and pulled out an envelope. He hadn't written the letter, but knew the contents all too well. The brief official notification of death, stripped of all the verbiage. The bureaucratic act of pronouncing death.

"I'm sorry, but it's my job to give you this."

"Your job to do what?" said the small, middle-aged man with the exaggerated *mondaine* French pronunciation characteristic not of the upper classes but of those who strive to belong. The visitor studied him. Everything matched the photograph in the envelope, even the mean-spirited tie knot and the loose red smoking jacket.

He didn't know what this man had done wrong. He doubted it had been physical, because despite the irritation in his expression, his body language was defensive, almost anxious, even in the doorway to his own home. Had he been stealing money, embezzling? He could be the type to work with figures. But not the big sums. His attractive wife notwithstanding, he looked more like the kind who helped himself to small change here and there. He might have been unfaithful, might have slept with the wife of the wrong man. No. As a rule, short men with above-average assets and wives much more attractive than themselves were more concerned with her infidelity. The man annoyed him. He slipped his hand into his pocket.

"This," he said, resting the barrel of a Llama Mini-Max, which he had bought for just three hundred euros, on the taut brass door chain, "is my job."

He pointed the silencer. It was a plain metal tube, made by a gunsmith in Zagreb, and screwed to the barrel. The black duct tape lashed around where the two parts met was to make it airtight. Of course, he could have bought a so-called quality silencer for over a hundred euros, but why? No one could silence the sound of a bullet breaking the sound barrier, of the hot gas meeting the cold air and the mechanical metal parts striking each other. Pistols with silencers that sounded like popcorn under a lid were pure Hollywood.

The explosion was like the crack of a whip. He pressed his face against the narrow opening.

The man in the photo was gone; he had fallen backward without a sound. The hall was dark, but in the wall mirror he saw the sliver of light from the door and his magnified eye framed in gold. The dead man lay on a thick burgundy carpet. Persian? Perhaps he had had money, after all?

Now he had a little hole in his forehead.

He looked up and met the eyes of the wife. If she was his wife. She was standing in the doorway of another room. Behind her, a large yellow Oriental lamp. She had her hand in front of her mouth and was staring at him. He gave a brief nod. Then he carefully closed the door, put the gun back in his shoulder holster and began to walk down the stairs. He never used the elevator when he was making his getaway. Or rented cars or motorbikes or anything else that could malfunction. And he didn't run. He didn't talk or shout; the voice could be identified.

The getaway was the most critical part of the job, but also the part he loved best. It was like flying, a dreamless nothing.

The concierge, a woman, had come out of her flat on the ground floor and watched him in bewilderment. He whispered an *Au revoir, madame,* but she glared back in silence. When she was questioned by the police in an hour's time, they would ask her for a description. And she would oblige. A man, normal appearance, medium height. Twenty years old. Or thirty, perhaps. Not forty, anyway, she thought.

He emerged into the street. The low rumble of Paris, like thunder that never came any closer, but never stopped, either. He discarded his Llama Mini-Max in a garbage can he had chosen for the purpose beforehand. Two new, unfired guns from the same manufacturer awaited his return in Zagreb. He had been given a bulk-purchase discount.

When the airport bus passed Porte de la Chapelle half an hour later, on the highway between Paris and Charles de Gaulle, the air was full of snowflakes. They settled on the scattered strands of pale-yellow straw pointing stiffly upward to the gray sky.

After checking in for his flight and going through security, he went straight to the men's restroom. He stood at the end of the line of white bowls, unbuttoned and sprayed the white urinal blocks at the bottom of the bowl. He closed his eyes and concentrated on the sweet smell of paradichlorobenzene and the lemon fragrance enhancer from the J & J Chemicals Company. The connecting line to freedom had one stop left. He rolled the name on his tongue. *Os-lo.*

3

The Bite

In the red zone on the sixth floor of Police HQ, the concrete-and-glass colossus with the largest concentration of police in Norway, Harry sat back in his chair in Room 605. This was the office that Halvorsen—the young policeman Harry shared the thirty square feet with—liked to call the Clearing House. And that Harry, when Halvorsen had to be taken down a peg or two, called In-House Training.

But at this moment Harry was on his own, staring at the wall where the window might have been if the Clearing House had such a thing.

It was Sunday; he had written the report and could go home. So why didn't he? Through the imaginary window he saw the fenced-off harbor in Bjørvika, where fresh snow lay like confetti on the green, red and blue containers. The case had been solved. Per Holmen, a young heroin addict, had had enough of life and had taken his final shot inside a container. From a gun. No external signs of violence, the gun down by his side. As far as the undercover boys knew, Per Holmen did not owe any money. When dealers execute junkies with debts, they don't usually try to camouflage it as something else. Quite the contrary. A cut-and-dried case of suicide, then. So why waste the evening ferreting around a grim, windblown container terminal, where all he would find was more sorrow and grief?

Harry looked at his wool coat hanging on the coatrack. The small hip flask in the inside pocket was full. And untouched since he'd gone to the liquor store in October, bought a bottle of his worst enemy, Jim Beam, and filled his flask before emptying the rest down the sink. Since then he had carried the poison on him, a bit like the way Nazis kept cyanide pills in the soles of their shoes. Why bother with such a stupid idea? He didn't know. He didn't have to know. It worked.

Harry looked at the clock. Almost eleven. At home he had a much-used espresso machine and a DVD he had put by for just such an evening as this. *All About Eve*, Mankie-wicz's 1950 masterpiece with Bette Davis and George Sanders.

He took an internal reading. And knew it was going to be the harbor.

Harry had turned up the lapels of his coat and stood with his back to the north wind that blew right through the tall fence in front of him and formed snowdrifts around the containers on the inside. The harbor area and the large, empty expanses looked like a desert at night.

The enclosed container terminal was illuminated, but the lampposts swayed in the gusting wind and the metal boxes piled up in twos or threes cast shadows over the streets. The particular one Harry had his eye on was red and represented something of a color clash with the orange police tape. But it was a great refuge on a December night in Oslo, with almost identical measurements and the same level of comfort as the holding cells at Police HQ.

The report by the Crime Scene Unit—though it was hardly a unit, numbering one detective and one technician—said the container had stood empty for a while. Unlocked.

The site watchman had explained that they didn't bother much about locking empty containers since the area was fenced off and, furthermore, under surveillance. Nevertheless a drug addict had got in. Per Holmen, he supposed, had been one of the many who had hung out around Bjørvika, which was a mere stone's throw from the junkies' supermarket in Plata. Perhaps the watchman had turned a blind eye to their using the containers as a place to stay? Perhaps he knew that in so doing he had saved the odd life or two?

There was no lock on the container, but there was a big, fat padlock on the gate in the fence. Harry regretted that he hadn't called from HQ to say he was coming. If there were any guards here, he couldn't see them.

Harry checked his watch. Deliberated and surveyed the top of the fence. He was in good shape. Better than in a long time. He hadn't touched alcohol since the catastrophe last summer, and he had been training on a regular basis in the police gym. More than regular. Before the snow came, he had broken Tom Waaler's old steeplechase record in Økern. A few days later Halvorsen had cautiously asked if all the training had anything to do with Rakel. Because his impression was that they weren't seeing each other anymore. Harry had explained to the young officer in a curt yet clear way that they might share an office but they did not share a private life. Halvorsen had shrugged, asked who else Harry talked to and had his assumption confirmed when Harry got up and marched out of Room 605.

Nine feet. No barbed wire. Easy. Harry caught hold of the fence as high as he could, put his feet against the fence post and straightened up. Right arm up, then left, hung with arms outstretched until his feet got a grip. Caterpillar movements. He swung himself over to the other side.

He raised the bolt and pulled open the door of the container, took out his solid black army flashlight, ducked under the police tape and went in.

It was eerily quiet inside; sound seemed to have been

frozen, too. Harry switched on the flashlight and shone it inside the container. In the cone of light he could see the chalk outline on the floor where they had found Holmen. Beate Lønn, the young head of Krimteknisk, the Forensics department, in the new building on Brynsalléen, had shown him the pictures. Holmen had been sitting with his back to the wall with a hole in his right temple and the gun on his right. Very little blood. That was the advantage of shots to the head. The only one. The gun fired ammunition of a modest caliber, so the entry wound was small and there was no exit wound. Forensics would find the bullet in the skull, where it would have bounced around like a pinball and pulped what Per Holmen had once thought with, made this decision with and at the end ordered his forefinger to press the trigger with.

"Incomprehensible," his colleagues tended to say when they discovered young people who had chosen to take their own lives. Harry assumed they said that to protect themselves, to reject the whole idea of it. If not, he didn't understand what they meant by its being incomprehensible.

All the same, that was the word he himself had used this afternoon, standing at the entrance and looking down the hallway at Holmen's father on his knees, his back bent, shaking with sobs. And since Harry had had no words of comfort to say about death, God, redemption, life afterward or the sense of it all, he had just mumbled the same feeble: "Incomprehensible . . ."

Harry switched off the flashlight and put it in his coat pocket; the darkness closed in around him.

He thought of his own father. Olav Hole, the retired teacher and widower living in a house in Oppsal. Of how his eyes lit up when Harry, or Sis, visited him once a month and how the light slowly faded as they drank coffee and talked about things of little import. Anything of meaning had pride of place in a photo on the piano she had once played. Olav Hole did almost nothing now. Read his books. About countries and empires he would never see, and in fact no longer had any desire to see, since she could not join him. "The greatest loss of all," he said on the few occasions they talked about her. And what Harry was thinking about now was what Olav Hole would call the day they went to tell him his son was dead.

Harry left the container and walked toward the fence. Grabbed hold of it with his hands. Then there was one of those strange moments of sudden total silence, when the wind catches its breath to listen or change its mind and all that is heard is the reassuring rumble of the town in the winter darkness. That, and the sound of wind-borne paper scraping against the pavement. But the wind had dropped. It wasn't paper—it was steps. Quick, light steps. Lighter than footsteps.

Paws.

Harry's heart accelerated out of control and, facing the fence, he bent his knees lightning-quick. And straightened up. Only afterward would it occur to him what had made him so frightened. It was the silence, and the fact that he heard nothing in this silence, no growling, no signs of aggression. As though whatever it was out there in the dark did not want to frighten him. Quite the contrary. It was hunting him. Had Harry known much about dogs, he might have been aware that there was one kind of dog that never growls, neither when it is frightened nor when it attacks: the male of the black Metzner species. Harry stretched his arms upward and was bending his knees again when he heard the change in rhythm and then silence, and he knew it had launched itself. He pushed upward.

The claim that you don't feel pain when terror has pumped the blood full of adrenaline is, at best, somewhat less than accurate. Harry let out a yell when the teeth of the large, lean dog gripped the flesh of his right leg and sank

farther and farther in until finally they were pressing on
the sensitive tissue membrane around the bone. The wire
fence sang, gravity pulled at them both, but in sheer desperation Harry managed to hang on. By normal standards
he would have been safe by now. Because any other dog
weighing as much as a mature black Metzner would have let
go. But a black Metzner has teeth and jaw muscles that can
crush bone—hence its alleged reputation as a relative of the
bone-devouring speckled hyena. So it hung there, bolted to
Harry's leg by two canine teeth set backward in the upper
jaw and one in the lower jaw, which stabilized the bite. It
had broken the second canine in the lower jaw on a steel
prosthesis when it was just three months old.

Harry managed to put his left elbow over the edge of
the fence and tried to drag them both up, but the dog had
one paw in the wire. With his right hand he groped for his
coat pocket, found it and then grabbed the rubber shaft of
the flashlight. He looked down, and for the first time saw
the animal. The black eyes in the equally black face had a
dull sheen. Harry swung the flashlight. It hit the dog on
the head right between its ears and so hard that he heard a
crunch. He raised the flashlight and struck again. Hitting
the sensitive snout. Struck out in desperation at the eyes,
which still had not blinked. He lost hold of the flashlight
and it fell to the ground. The dog was still hanging from his
leg. Soon Harry would not have the strength to hold on to
the fence. He did not want to think about what might happen then, but was unable to stop himself.

"Help!"

Harry's feeble cry was carried away on the wind that had
sprung up again. He changed grip and felt a sudden urge
to laugh. Surely it couldn't all end like this? Being found
in a container terminal with his throat savaged by a guard
dog? Harry took a deep breath. The jagged points from the
wire netting were digging into his armpit; his fingers were
wilting fast. He was seconds away from letting go. If only

he had a weapon. If only he had had a bottle instead of the hip flask, he could have smashed it and used it to stab with.

The hip flask!

Summoning his last strength, Harry reached inside his coat and pulled out the flask. He stuffed the spout into his mouth, clenched his teeth on the metal top and twisted. The top loosened and he held it between his teeth as the whisky filled his mouth. A shock ran through his body. Christ. He pressed his face against the fence, forcing his eyes closed, and the distant lights of the Plaza and Opera hotels became white stripes in all the darkness. With his right hand he lowered the flask until it was above the dog's red jaws. Then he spat out the top and the whisky, mumbled, "*Skål*," and emptied the flask. For two long seconds the black doggy eyes stared up at Harry in total perplexity as the brown liquid gurgled and trickled down Harry's leg into the open jaws. The animal relinquished its hold. Harry heard the smack of living flesh on bare pavement. Followed by a kind of death rattle and low whimpering, then the scratching sound of paws, and the dog was swallowed up by the dark from which it had emerged.

Harry swung his legs over the fence. He rolled up his trouser leg. Even without the flashlight he knew the evening was going to be spent in the emergency room and not watching *All About Eve*.

Jon lay with his head in Thea's lap and his eyes closed, enjoying the regular drone of the TV. It was one of these series she liked so much. *King of the Bronx*. Or was it *The King of Queens*?

"Have you asked your brother if he would do your shift in Egertorget?" Thea asked.

She had placed a hand over his eyes. He could smell the sweet fragrance of her skin, which meant that she had just given herself a shot of insulin.

"Which shift?" Jon asked.

She snatched away her hand and stared at him in disbelief. Jon laughed. "Relax. I spoke to Robert ages ago. He agreed."

She gave a groan of resignation. Jon grabbed her hand and put it back over his eyes.

"I didn't say it was your birthday, though," he said. "If I had, I'm not sure he would have agreed."

"Why not?"

"Because he's crazy about you, and you know it."

"That's what you say."

"And you don't like him."

"That's not true!"

"Why do you always go stiff whenever I mention his name, then?"

She laughed out loud. Must have been something in the Bronx. Or Queens.

"Did you get a table at the restaurant?" she asked.

"Yes."

She smiled and squeezed his hand. Then she furrowed her brow. "I've been thinking. Someone might see us there."

"From the Army? Out of the question."

"What if they do?"

Jon didn't answer.

"Perhaps it's time we went public," she said.

"I don't know," he said. "Isn't it best to wait until we're absolutely sure that—"

"Aren't you sure, Jon?"

Jon moved her hand and looked up at her in dismay: "Thea, please. You know very well that I love you above all else. That's not the point."

"What is the point, then?"

Jon sighed and sat up beside her. "You don't know Robert, Thea."

She gave a wry smile. "I've known him since we were tiny, Jon."

Jon squirmed. "Yes, but there are things you don't know.

You don't know how angry he can get. He takes after Dad. He can be dangerous, Thea."

She leaned back against the wall and stared into the air.

"I suggest we defer it for a while." Jon wrung his hands. "Out of consideration for your brother, too."

"Rikard?" she said, surprised.

"Yes. What would he say if you, his own sister, announced your engagement to me right now?"

"Ah, I see what you mean. Since you're both competing for the head-of-admin job?"

"You know very well that the High Council sets great store by high-ranking officers having a respectable officer as their spouse. It's obvious that the right thing to do from a tactical point of view would be to announce my marriage to Thea Nilsen, the daughter of Frank Nilsen, the commander's right hand. But would it be morally right?"

Thea chewed her bottom lip. "Why is this job so important to you and Rikard?"

Jon shrugged. "The Army has paid our way through officer-training school and four years for an economics degree at a school of management. I suppose Rikard thinks the way I do. You have a duty to apply for Salvation Army jobs seeking your qualifications."

"Maybe neither of you will get it. Dad says no one under thirty-five has ever been appointed head of admin."

"I know." Jon sighed. "Don't tell anyone, but actually I would be relieved if Rikard got the job."

"Relieved?" Thea said. "You? You've had the responsibility for all the rental property in Oslo for over a year now."

"That's right, but the head of admin has all of Norway, Iceland and the Faeroes. Did you know that the Army's property company owns over two hundred and fifty plots, with three hundred buildings in Norway alone?" Jon patted himself on the stomach and stared at the ceiling with a familiar, concerned expression. "I saw my reflection in a shop window today and it struck me how small I am."

Thea did not seem to have heard. "Someone told Rikard that whoever gets the job will be the next territorial commander."

Jon laughed out loud. "I definitely do not want that."

"Don't fool around, Jon."

"I'm not fooling around, Thea. You and I are much more important. I'm saying I'm not interested in the admin job, so let's announce our engagement. I can do other important work. Lots of the corps need economists, too."

"No, Jon," Thea said, horrified. "You're the best we've got. You have to be employed where we need you most. Rikard is my brother, but he doesn't have . . . your intelligence. We can wait until the decision has been made to tell them about the engagement."

Jon shrugged.

Thea looked at the clock. "You'll have to leave before twelve today. In the elevator yesterday Emma said she had been worried about me because she had heard my door open and close in the middle of the night."

Jon swung his legs onto the floor. "I don't understand why we bother living here."

She sent Jon a reproving glance. "At least we can take care of each other here."

"Right." He sighed. "We take care of each other. Good night, then."

She wriggled over to him and slipped her hand up his shirt and, to his surprise, he could feel that her hand was sweaty, as if she had been clenching it or squeezing something. She pressed herself against him and her breathing began to quicken.

"Thea," he said. "We mustn't . . ."

She went rigid. Then she sighed and took her hand away.

Jon was amazed. So far Thea had not exactly come on to him—more the opposite; she had seemed anxious about physical contact. And he valued that modesty. She had seemed reassured after their first date, when he had quoted the statutes and said, "The Salvation Army considers abstinence before marriage a Christian ideal." Even though many thought there was a difference between "ideal" and "command," which the statutes used when referring to tobacco and alcohol, he saw no reason to break a promise to God because of nuances.

He gave her a hug, stood up and went to the bathroom. Locked the door behind him and turned on the tap. Let the water run over his hands as he regarded the smooth surface of molten sand reflecting the face of a person who to all outward appearances ought to be happy. He had to call Ragnhild. Get it over with. Jon took a deep breath. He *was* happy. It was just that some days were harder than others.

He dried his face and went back to her.

The waiting area of Oslo's emergency room at 40 Storgata was bathed in harsh, white light. There was the usual human menagerie at this time of day. A trembling drug addict stood up and left twenty minutes after Harry arrived. As a rule they couldn't sit still for longer than ten. Harry could understand that. He still had the taste of whisky in his mouth; it had stirred up his old friends, who heaved and tugged at the chains below. His leg hurt like hell. And the trip to the harbor had yielded—like 90 percent of all police work—nothing. He promised himself he would keep the appointment with Bette Davis next time.

"Harry Hole?"

Harry looked up at the man in the white coat in front of him.

"Yes?"

"Could you come with me?"

"Thank you, but I think it's her turn," Harry said, nodding toward a girl with her head in her hands in the row of chairs opposite.

The man leaned forward. "It's the second time she's been here this evening. She'll survive."

Harry limped down the corridor after the doctor's white coat and into a narrow examining room with a desk and a plain bookshelf. He saw no personal items.

"I thought you police had your own medicine men," the coat said.

"Fat chance. Usually we don't even get priority in the line. How do you know I'm a policeman?"

"Sorry. I'm Mathias. I was on my way through the waiting room and spotted you."

The doctor smiled and reached out his hand. He had regular teeth, Harry saw. So regular you could have suspected him of wearing dentures, if the rest of his face had not been as symmetrical, clean and square. The eyes were blue, with tiny laugh lines around them, and the handshake firm and dry. Straight out of a doctor novel, Harry thought. A doctor with warm hands.

"Mathias Lund-Helgesen," the man added, taking stock of Harry.

"I realize you think I should know who you are," Harry said.

"We've met before. Last summer. At a garden party at Rakel's place." Harry went rigid at the sound of her name on someone else's lips.

"Is that right?"

"That was me," Mathias Lund-Helgesen gabbled in a low voice.

"Mm." Harry gave a slow nod. "I'm bleeding."

"I understand." Lund-Helgesen's face wrapped itself in grave, sympathetic folds.

Harry rolled up his trouser leg. "Here."

"Aha." Lund-Helgesen assumed a somewhat bemused smile. "What is it?"

"A dog bite. Can you fix it?"

"Not a lot to fix. The bleeding will stop. I'll clean the

wounds and put something on it." He bent down. "Three wounds, I can see, judging by the teeth marks. And you'd better get a tetanus shot."

"It bit right through to the bone."

"Yes, it often feels like that."

"No, I mean, its teeth did go . . ."

Harry paused and exhaled through his nose. He had just realized that Mathias Lund-Helgesen thought he was drunk. And why shouldn't he? A policeman with a torn coat, a dog bite, a bad reputation and alcohol on his breath. Was that what he would say when he told Rakel that her ex had turned to drink again?

". . . right through," Harry finished.

4

The Departure

"Trka!"

He sat up in bed with a start, hearing the echo of his voice between the bare white hotel walls. The telephone on his bedside table rang. He snatched at the receiver.

"This is your wake-up call . . ."

"Hvala," he said, although he knew it was only a recorded voice. He was in Zagreb. He was going to Oslo today. To the most important job. The final one.

He closed his eyes. He had been dreaming again. Not about Paris, not about any of the other jobs; he never dreamed about them. It was always about Vukovar, always about the autumn, about the siege.

Last night he had dreamed about running. As usual, he had been running in the rain, and as usual, it had been the same evening they sawed off his father's arm in the infants' ward. Four hours later his father had died, even though the doctors had pronounced the operation a success. They said his heart had just stopped beating. And then he had run away from his mother, into the dark and the rain, down to the river, with his father's gun in his hand, to the Serbian positions, and they had sent up flares and shot at him and he hadn't cared and he'd heard the smack of the bullets into the ground, which had disappeared beneath his feet, and he had fallen into the huge bomb crater. The water had swallowed him up, swallowed all sound, and it was quiet and he had kept running under the water, but he got nowhere. As he'd felt his limbs stiffening and sleep numbing him, he had seen something red moving in all the blackness, like a bird beating its wings in slow motion. When he had come to he was wrapped in a wool blanket and a naked lightbulb was swinging to and fro as Serbian artillery pounded them, and small lumps of earth and plaster had fallen into his eyes and mouth. He spat, and someone had stooped down and told him that Bobo, the captain himself, had saved his life in the water-filled crater. And pointed to a bald man standing by the steps of the bunker. He had been wearing a uniform with a red cloth tied around his neck.

He opened his eyes again and looked at the thermometer he had put on the bedside table. The temperature in the room had not risen above sixty degrees since November, even though in reception they maintained that the heat was fully on. He got up. He had to hurry; the airport bus would be outside the hotel in half an hour.

He stared into the mirror over the basin and tried to visualize Bobo's face. But it was like the northern lights; little by little it faded as he stared. The telephone rang again.

"*Da, Majka.*"

After shaving, he dried himself and dressed in haste. He took out one of the two metal boxes he kept in the safe and opened it. A Llama Mini-Max subcompact, which could hold seven bullets—six in the magazine plus one in the chamber. He disassembled the weapon and divided the parts into the four small, purpose-designed hiding places under the reinforced corners of the suitcase. If customs officers stopped him and checked his suitcase, the reinforced metal pieces would hide the gun parts. Before leaving, he checked that he had his passport and the envelope with the ticket that she had given him, the photograph of the target and the information he needed for when and where. It was due to happen tomorrow night at seven in a public place. She had told him this job was riskier than the previous one. Nevertheless, he was not afraid. Now and then he wondered whether the ability to be afraid had been lost along with his father's amputated arm that night. Bobo had said you cannot survive for long if you are not frightened.

Outside, Zagreb had just woken up, snow-free, gray with mist, its face drawn and haggard. He stood in front of the hotel entrance, thinking that in a few days' time they would be going to the Adriatic, a little place with a little hotel, off-peak prices and a bit of sun. And talking about the new house.

The bus to the airport should have been here by now. He peered into the mist. The way he had that autumn, crouching beside Bobo and trying in vain to see something behind the white smoke. His job had been to run messages they didn't dare send over the radio link, as the Serbs were tuned to the frequency and didn't miss a thing. And since he was so small, he could run through the trenches at full speed without having to duck. He had told Bobo he wanted to attack tanks.

Bobo had shaken his head. "You're a messenger. These messages are important, sonny. I've got men to take care of the tanks."

"But they're frightened. I'm not frightened."

Bobo had raised an eyebrow. "You're only a little kid."

"If bullets find me here rather than out there, I don't get any older. And you said yourself that if we don't stop the tanks, they'll take the town."

Bobo had given him a searching look.

"Let me think about it," he said in the end. So they had sat in silence, scanning the white screen without being able to distinguish between autumn mist and smoke from the ruins of the burning town. Then Bobo had cleared his throat: "Last night I sent Franjo and Mirko to the gap in the embankment where the tanks come out. The mission was to hide and attach mines to the tanks as they rolled past. You know how that worked out?"

He had nodded again. He had seen the bodies of Franjo and Mirko through the binoculars.

"If they'd been smaller, they might have been able to hide in the hollows in the ground," Bobo said.

The boy had wiped away the snot from under his nose with a hand.

"How do I fix the mines to the tanks?"

At the crack of dawn on the following day he had wriggled back to his own lines, shaking with cold and covered in mud. Behind him, on the embankment, lay two destroyed Serbian tanks with smoke belching out of the open hatches. Bobo had dragged him down into the trench and shouted in triumph: "To us a little redeemer is born!"

And that same day, when Bobo had dictated the message to be radioed to HQ in the town, he was given the code name that would follow him until the Serbs occupied and razed his hometown to ashes, killing Bobo, massacring doctors and patients at the hospital, imprisoning and torturing any who offered resistance. It was a bitter paradox of a name. Given to him by the one person he had not been able to save. *Mali spasitelj.* The little redeemer.

A red bus emerged out of the sea of mist.

The meeting room in the red zone on the sixth floor buzzed with low conversation and muted laughter as Harry approached, and he saw that he had timed his arrival well. Too late to mingle, eat cake and exchange the jokes and jibes with colleagues that men resort to when they have to say good-bye to someone they appreciate. On time for the presents and the speeches laden with too many pompous words men feel emboldened to use when they are in front of an audience and not in private.

Harry took stock of the crowd and found the three faces

he could rely on to be friendly. His departing boss, Bjarne Møller. Officer Halvorsen. And Beate Lønn. He did not make eye contact with anyone and no one tried with him. Harry was under no illusions about his popularity in Crime Squad. Møller had once said there was only one thing people disliked more than a sullen alcoholic, and that was a tall, sullen alcoholic. Harry was six feet and four inches of sullen alcoholic, and the fact that he was a brilliant detective mildly worked in his favor, but no more than that. Everyone knew that had it not been for Bjarne Møller's protective wing, Harry would have been off the force years ago. And now that Møller was going, everyone also knew that the top brass were just waiting for him to step out of line. Paradoxically, what was protecting him now was the same thing that stamped him as an eternal outsider: the fact that he had brought down one of their own. The Prince: Tom Waaler, an inspector in Crime Squad, one of the men behind the extensive gun-running operation in Oslo for the last eight years. Tom Waaler had ended his days in a pool of blood in the basement of a residential apartment tower in Kampen. In a brief ceremony in the cafeteria three weeks later the chief superintendent had, through clenched teeth, acknowledged Harry's contribution to cleaning up their own ranks. And Harry had thanked him.

"Thank you," he had said, running his eyes across the assembled officers to check if anyone's met his. In fact, he had meant to restrict his speech to these two words, but the sight of averted faces and sardonic smiles had whipped up a sudden fury in him, and he had added: "I guess this will make it a little more difficult for someone to give me the boot now. The press might believe that the person in question is doing it out of fear that I will be after him as well."

And then they had looked at him. In disbelief. He had continued nevertheless.

"No reason to gape, guys. Tom Waaler was an inspector with us in Crime Squad and dependent on his position to do what he was doing. He called himself the Prince and, as you know . . ." Here Harry had paused while his gaze moved from face to face, stopping at the chief superintendent's. "Where there's a prince, there's usually a king."

"Hello, old boy. Lost in thought?" Harry looked up. It was Halvorsen.

"Thinking about kings," Harry mumbled, taking the cup of coffee that the young detective passed him.

"Well, there's the new guy," Halvorsen said, pointing.

By the table of presents there was a man in a blue suit talking to the chief superintendent and Bjarne Møller.

"Is that Gunnar Hagen?" Harry said after taking a sip of coffee. "The new PAS?"

"They're not a Politiavdelingssjef anymore, Harry."

"No?"

"POB. Politioverbetjent. They changed the names of the ranks more than four months ago."

"Is that so? I must have been sick that day. Are you still a police officer?"

Halvorsen smiled.

The new POB seemed agile, and younger than the fifty-three years it said he was in the memo. More medium-tall than tall, Harry noticed. And lean. The network of defined muscles in his face, around the jaw and down his neck suggested an ascetic lifestyle. His mouth was straight and firm and his chin stuck out in a way you could designate either determined or protruding. The little hair Hagen had was black and formed half a wreath around his pate; however, it was so thick and compact you might be forgiven for thinking the new POB had a rather eccentric choice of hairstyle. At any rate, the enormous, demonic eyebrows boded well for the growing conditions of his body hair.

"Straight from the military," Harry said. "Perhaps he'll introduce reveille."

"He was supposed to have been a good cop before switching pastures."

"Judging from what he wrote about himself in the memo, you mean?"

"Nice to hear you being so positive, Harry."

"Me? I'm always anxious to give new people a fair chance."

"*A* being the operative word," Beate said, joining them. She flicked her short blond hair to the side. "I thought I saw you limping as you came in, Harry."

"Met an overexcited guard dog down at the container terminal last night."

"What were you doing there?"

Harry studied Beate before answering. The job of head at Brynsalléen had been good for her. And it had been good for Krimteknisk, too. Beate had always been a competent professional, but Harry had to admit he hadn't seen obvious leadership qualities in the self-effacing, shy young girl when she joined the Robberies Unit after police-training college.

"Wanted to take a look at the container where Per Holmen was found. Tell me—how did he get into the area?"

"Cut the lock with wire cutters. They were beside him. And you? How did you get in?"

"What else did you find?"

"Harry, there is no suggestion that this is—"

"I'm not saying there is. What else?"

"What do you think? Tools of the trade, a dose of heroin and a plastic bag containing tobacco. You know, they poke the tobacco out of the butts they pick up. And not one krone, of course."

"And the Beretta?"

"The serial number has been removed, but the file marks are familiar. A gun from the days of the Prince."

Harry had noticed that Beate refused to let the name Tom Waaler pass her lips.

"Mm. Have the results for the blood sample arrived?"

"Yep," she said. "Surprisingly clean—hadn't shot up

recently, anyway. So conscious and capable of killing himself. Why do you ask?"

"I had the pleasure of communicating the news to the parents."

"Ooooh," Lønn and Halvorsen said in unison. It was happening more and more often, even though they had been a couple for just two years.

The chief superintendent coughed and the gathering turned toward the table of presents as the chatter subsided.

"Bjarne has requested permission to say a word or two," the chief superintendent said, rocking on his heels and pausing for effect. "And permission was granted."

Chuckles all around. Harry noticed Bjarne Møller's tentative smile in the direction of his superior officer.

"Thank you, Torleif. And thank you and the chief constable for my farewell present. And a special thank-you to all of you for the wonderful picture you have given me."

He pointed to the table.

"Everyone?" Harry whispered to Beate.

"Yes. Skarre and a couple of others collected the money."

"I didn't hear anything about that."

"They might have forgotten to ask you."

"Now I'll distribute a few presents of my own," Møller said. "From the deceased's estate, so to speak. First of all, there is this magnifying glass."

He held it up in front of his face and the others laughed at the ex-PAS's distorted features.

"This goes to a girl who is every bit as good a detective and police officer as her father was. Who never takes the credit for her work, but prefers to let us shine in Crime Squad. As you know, she has been the subject of research by brain specialists as she is blessed with the very rare fusiform gyrus, which allows her to remember every single face she has seen."

Harry saw Beate blush. She didn't like the attention,

least of all concerning this exceptional skill, which meant she was still being used to identify grainy images of ex-cons on bank-robbery videos.

"I hope that you won't forget this face," Møller said, "even though you won't see it for a while. And if you have cause to doubt, you can use this."

Halvorsen nudged Beate in the back. When Møller gave her a hug as well as the magnifying glass and the audience applauded, even her forehead went a fiery red.

"The next heirloom is my office chair," Bjarne said. "You see, I found out that my successor, Gunnar Hagen, has put in for a new one in black leather with a high back and other features."

Møller sent a smile to Hagen, who did not return it, but gave a brief nod.

"The chair goes to an officer from Steinkjer who, ever since he came here, has been banished to an office with the biggest troublemaker in the building. And forced to sit on a defective chair. Junior, I think it's time."

"Yippee," Halvorsen said.

Everyone turned and laughed, and Halvorsen laughed in return.

"And, to conclude, a technical aid for someone who is very special to me. He has been my best investigator and my worst nightmare. To the man who always follows his nose, his own agenda and—unhappily for those of us who try to get you to turn up on time for morning meetings—his own watch." Møller took a wristwatch from his jacket pocket. "I hope this will make you work in the same time frame as the others do. Anyway, I have more or less set it to Crime Squad clocks. And, well, there was a lot between the lines there, Harry."

Scattered applause as Harry went forward to receive the watch with a plain black leather strap. The brand was unfamiliar to him.

"Thanks," Harry said.

The two tall men embraced.

"I put it two minutes fast so that you're in time for what you thought you would miss," Møller whispered. "No more warnings. Do what you have to."

"Thanks," Harry repeated, thinking Møller was holding him for a bit too long. He reminded himself he had to leave the present he had brought with him from home. Fortunately, he had never got around to ripping off the plastic cover of *All About Eve*.

5

The Lighthouse

Jon found Robert in the backyard of Fretex, the Salvation Army shop on Kirkeveien.

He was leaning against the door frame with his arms crossed, watching the guys carrying garbage bags from the truck into the shop's storeroom. They were blowing white speech bubbles, which they filled with swear words in a variety of dialects and languages.

"Good catch?" Jon asked.

Robert shrugged. "People happily give away their whole summer wardrobe so that they can buy new clothes next year. But it's winter clothes we need now."

"Your guys use colorful language. Paragraph-twelve types—doing social work instead of prison?"

"I counted up yesterday. We've now got twice as many volunteers doing a stretch as we have people who have turned to Jesus."

Jon smiled. "Untilled fields for missionaries. Just a question of getting started."

Robert called to one of the guys, who threw him a pack of cigarettes. Robert put a coffin nail between his lips, no filter.

"Take it out," Jon said. "Soldier's vows. You could be dismissed."

"I wasn't thinking of lighting it, bro. What do you want?"

Jon shrugged. "To talk."

"What about?"

Jon chuckled. "It's normal for brothers to talk now and then."

Robert nodded and picked flakes of tobacco off his tongue. "When you say *talk*, you usually mean you're going to tell me how to lead my life."

"Come on."

"What is it, then?"

"Nothing! I was wondering how you were."

Robert took out the cigarette and spat in the snow. Then he peered up into the high, white cloud cover.

"I'm fucking sick of this job. I'm fucking sick of the flat. I'm fucking sick of the shriveled-up, hypocritical sergeant major running the show here. If she weren't so ugly I would"—Robert grinned—"fuck the old pruneface stupid."

"I'm freezing," Jon said. "Can we go in?"

Robert walked ahead into the tiny office and sat on a chair squeezed between a cluttered desk, a narrow window with a view of the backyard and a red and yellow flag with the Salvation Army's emblem and motto, "Blood and Fire." Jon lifted a heap of papers, some yellowing with age, off a wooden chair he knew Robert had pinched from the Majorstuen Corps's room next door.

"She says you're a malingerer," Jon said.

"Who?"

"Sergeant Major Rue." Jon grimaced. "Pruneface."

"So she called you. Is that how it is?" Robert poked around in the desk with his pocketknife, then burst out: "Oh, yes, I forgot. You're the new admin boss, the boss of the whole shebang."

"No decision has been made yet. It might well be Rikard."

"Whatever." Robert carved two semicircles in the desk to form a heart. "You've said what you came to say. Before you get lost, can I have the five hundred for your shift tomorrow?"

Jon took the money from his wallet and laid it on the desk in front of his brother. Robert stroked the blade of the knife against his chin. The black bristles rasped. "And I'll remind you of one more thing."

Jon knew what was coming and swallowed. "And what's that?"

Over Robert's shoulder he could see it had begun to snow, but the rising heat from the houses around the back-yard made the flimsy white flakes stand still in the air out-side the window, as though listening.

Robert placed the point of the knife in the center of the heart. "If I find you even once in the vicinity of you-know-who . . ." He put his hand around the shaft of the knife and leaned forward. His body weight forced the blade into the dry wood with a crunch. "I'll destroy you, Jon. I swear I will."

"Am I interrupting?" came a voice from the door.

"Not at all, Fru Rue," Robert said, as sweet as pie. "My brother was just about to leave."

The chief superintendent and the new POB, Gunnar Hagen, stopped talking when Bjarne Møller came into his office. Which of course was no longer his.

"Well, do you like the view?" Møller asked in what he hoped was a cheery tone. And added: "Gunnar." The name felt strange on his tongue.

"Mm, Oslo is always a sad sight in December," Gunnar Hagen said. "But we'll have to see whether we can sort that out, too."

Møller felt an urge to ask what he meant by "too," but stopped when he saw the chief superintendent give a nod of approval.

"I was giving Gunnar the lowdown on the people around here. In all confidence, you understand."

"Ah, yes—you two know each other from before."

"Yes, indeed," said the chief superintendent. "Gunnar and I have known each other ever since we were cadets at what used to be called police school."

"It said in the memo that you do the Birkebeiner race every year," Møller said, turning to Gunnar Hagen. "Did you know that the chief superintendent does, too?"

"Oh, yes, indeed." Hagen looked over at the chief superintendent with a smile. "Sometimes Torleif and I go together. And try to outdo each other in the final spurt."

"Well, what do you know," Møller said, amused. "So if the Chief had been on the appointment board, he could have been accused of cronyism."

The chief superintendent gave a dry chuckle and shot an admonitory glance at Bjarne Møller.

"I was telling Gunnar about the man you so generously presented with a watch."

"Harry Hole?"

"Yes," Gunnar Hagen said. "I know he's the man who killed an inspector in connection with that stupid smuggling business. Tore the man's arm off in an elevator, I heard. And now he's also under suspicion of leaking the case to the press. Not good."

"First of all, the 'stupid smuggling business' was a gang of pros, with offshoots in the police, who flooded Oslo with cheap handguns for years," Bjarne Møller said, trying in vain to keep the irritation out of his voice. "A case that Hole, despite the resistance here in HQ, solved unaided, thanks to many years of painstaking police work. Second, he killed Waaler in self-defense and it was the elevator that tore off his arm. And, third, we have no evidence whatsoever regarding who leaked what."

Gunnar Hagen and the chief superintendent exchanged glances.

"Be that as it may," the chief superintendent said, "he's someone you'll have to keep an eye on, Gunnar. From what I gather, his girlfriend left him recently. And we know that men with Harry's bad habits are extra susceptible to relapses. Which, of course, we cannot accept, however many cases he's solved in this unit."

"I'll keep him in line," Hagen said.

"He's an inspector," Møller said, closing his eyes. "Not rank and file. Not very big on being kept in line, either."

Gunnar Hagen nodded slowly as his hand went up through his thick wreath of hair.

"When is it you begin in Bergen . . ." Hagen lowered his hand. "Bjarne?"

Møller guessed his name sounded just as strange on the other man's tongue.

Harry wandered down Urtegata and could see by the footwear of the people he met that he was getting close to the Lighthouse. The guys in Narcotics used to say that no one did more for the identification of addicts than the Army-Navy surplus stores. Because sooner or later military footwear ended up on junkies' feet via the Salvation Army. In the summer it was blue sneakers; in the winter, like now, the junkie's uniform was black military boots together with a green plastic bag containing a Salvation Army–packed lunch.

Harry swung through the door with a nod to the guard wearing the Salvation Army hoodie.

"Anything?" the guard asked.

Harry patted his pockets. "Nothing."

A sign on the wall said all alcohol had to be handed in at the door and given back when leaving. Harry knew they had given up on drugs and the equipment. No junkie would hand that in.

Harry entered, poured himself a cup of coffee and sat on the bench by the wall. Fyrlyset, the Lighthouse, was the Army's café, the new millennium's version of the soup kitchen, where the needy were given free snacks and coffee.

A cozy, well-lit room—the only difference between this and the usual cappuccino bar was the clientele. Ninety percent of drug users were male. They ate slices of white bread with Norwegian brown or white cheese, read the newspapers and had quiet conversations around the tables. It was a free zone, a chance to thaw out and take a breather from the search for the day's fix. Although undercover police dropped by now and again, there was a tacit agreement that no arrests would be made inside.

A man sitting next to Harry had frozen into a deep bow. His head hung down over the table and in front of him black fingers held a cigarette paper. There were a few butts scattered around.

Harry noticed the uniformed back of a mini-woman changing burned-down candles on a table with four picture frames. Inside three of them were individual photographs; inside the fourth was a cross and a name on a white background. Harry stood up and walked over.

"What are they?" he asked.

Perhaps it was the slim neck or the grace of the movement, or the smooth, raven-black, almost unnatural, shiny hair that made Harry think of a cat even before she had turned around. The impression was reinforced by the small face with the disproportionately broad mouth and the pertest of noses possible, like those the characters in Harry's Japanese comics had. But, more than anything else, it was the eyes. He couldn't put his finger on why, but something about them was not right.

"November," she answered.

She had a calm, deep, gentle alto voice that made Harry wonder if it was natural or a way of speaking she had acquired. He had known women who did that, who changed their voices the way they changed clothes. One voice for home use; one for first impressions and social occasions; and one for nighttime intimacies.

"What do you mean?" Harry asked.

"Our November crop of deaths."

Harry looked at the photos and he realized what she meant.

"Four?" he said in a low voice. In front of the pictures was a letter written with an unsteady hand in penciled capitals.

"On average one customer dies a week. Four is not out of the ordinary. Our remembrance day is on the first Wednesday of every month. Is there anyone you . . . ?"

Harry shook his head. "*My dearest Geir*," the letter began. No flowers.

"Is there anything I can help you with?" she asked.

It struck Harry that she may not have had any other voices in her repertoire, just this deep, warm tone.

"Per Holmen . . ." Harry started, not knowing quite how to finish.

"Poor Per, yes. We'll have a remembrance day for him in January."

Harry nodded. "First Wednesday."

"That's it. And you're very welcome to come, brother."

This "brother" was enunciated with such unforced ease, like an underplayed and hence almost unarticulated appendix to the sentence. For a moment Harry almost believed her.

"I'm a detective," Harry said.

The difference in height between them was so great that she had to crane her neck to see him clearly.

"I've seen you before, I think, but it must be years ago."

Harry nodded. "Maybe. I've been here once or twice, but I haven't seen you."

"I'm part-time here. Otherwise I'm at the Salvation Army headquarters. And you work in the drugs division?"

Harry shook his head. "Murder investigations."

"Murder. But Per wasn't murdered . . . ?"

"Can we sit down for a moment?"

She hesitated and looked around.

"Busy?" Harry asked.

"Not at all—it's unusually quiet. On a normal day we serve eighteen hundred slices of bread. But today's dole day."

She called one of the boys behind the counter, who agreed to take over. Harry caught her name at the same time: Martine. The head of the man with the empty cigarette paper had been ratcheted down a few more notches.

"There are a couple of things that don't check out," Harry said after sitting down. "What sort of person was he?"

"Hard to say," she said. Harry's quizzical expression produced a sigh. "When you've been on drugs for so many years, like Per, the brain is so destroyed that it's hard to see a personality. The urge to get high is all-pervasive."

"I know that, but I mean . . . to people who knew him well . . ."

"Can't help, I'm afraid. You can ask Per's father how much of his son's personality was left. He came down here a couple of times to collect him. In the end, he gave up. He said Per had started to threaten them at home, because they locked away all their valuables when he was around. He asked me to keep an eye on the boy. I said we would do our best, but we couldn't promise miracles. And we didn't, of course . . ."

Harry observed her. Her face expressed nothing more than the usual social worker's resignation.

"It must be hell," Harry said, scratching his leg.

"Yes, you have to be an addict yourself to understand it."

"To be a parent, I was thinking."

Martine didn't answer. A man in a torn quilted jacket had come to the neighboring table. He opened a transparent plastic bag and emptied out a pile of dry tobacco that must have come from hundreds of cigarette butts. It covered the cigarette paper and the black fingers of the man sitting there.

"Merry Christmas," the man mumbled, and departed with a junkie's old-man gait.

"What doesn't check out?" Martine asked.

"The blood specimen shows almost no toxins," Harry said.

"So?"

Harry looked at the man next to him. He was desperately trying to roll a cigarette, but his fingers would not obey. A tear ran down his brown cheek.

"I know a couple of things about getting high," Harry said. "Do you know if he owed money to anyone?"

"No." Her answer was curt. So much so that Harry already knew the answer to his next question.

"But you could maybe—"

"No," she interrupted, "I cannot make inquiries. Listen, these are people no one cares about, and I am here to help them, not to persecute them."

Harry gave her a searching look. "You're right. I apologize for asking, and it won't happen again."

"Thank you."

"Just one last question?"

"Come on."

"Would you . . ." Harry hesitated, wondering if he was about to commit a blunder. "Would you believe me if I said I did care?"

She angled her head and studied Harry. "Should I?"

"Well, I'm investigating a case everyone thinks is the cut-and-dried suicide of a person no one cared about."

She didn't answer.

"It's good coffee." Harry got up.

"You're welcome," she said. "And may God bless you."

"Thank you," Harry said, feeling, to his surprise, the lobes of his ears flush.

On his way out he stopped in front of the guard in the hoodie and turned, but she had gone. The man offered Harry the green plastic bag with the packed lunch, but he turned it down, pulled his coat tighter around him and went out into the streets, where he could already see the sun making its blushing retreat into the Oslo Fjord. He walked toward the Akerselva. In the area known as Eika a man was standing erect in a snowdrift with the sleeve of a quilted jacket rolled up and a needle hanging from his forearm. He smiled as he looked straight through Harry and the frosty mist over Grønland.

Halvorsen

Pernille Holmen seemed even smaller sitting in her arm-chair on Fredensborgveien, her large, red-rimmed eyes staring at Harry. In her lap she held a glass-framed photo-graph of her son.

"He was nine here," she said.

Harry had to swallow. Partly because no smiling nine-year-old in a life jacket looks as if he imagines he will end up in a container with a bullet through his head. And partly because the photo reminded him of Oleg, who could for-get himself and call Harry "Pappa." Harry wondered how long it would take him to call Mathias Lund-Helgesen "Pappa."

"Birger, my husband, used to go out in search of Per if he had been missing for a few days," she said. "Even though I asked him to stop. I couldn't stand having Per here any longer."

Harry repressed his thought, *Why not?*

Birger Holmen was at the undertaker's, she had explained, when Harry came by unannounced.

She sniffled. "Have you ever shared a house with some-one who has an addiction?"

Harry didn't answer.

"He stole everything in sight. We accepted it. That is, Birger accepted it. He's the loving one of us two." She pulled her face into a grimace, which Harry interpreted as a smile.

"He defended Per in everything. Right up to this autumn. Until Per threatened me."

"Threatened you?"

"Yes, threatened to kill me." She looked down at the photo and rubbed the glass as though it had become unclear. "Per rang the bell one morning and I refused to let him in. I was on my own. He wept and begged, but we had played that game before, so I was hard. I went back into the kitchen and sat down. I don't know how he got in, but all of a sudden there he was—standing in front of me with a gun."

"The same gun he—"

"Yes. Yes, I think so."

"Go on."

"He forced me to unlock the cupboard where I kept my jewelry. That is, the little I had left. He had already taken most of it. Then he was off."

"And you?"

"Me? I had a breakdown. Birger came and took me to hospital." She sniffled. "Where they wouldn't even give me any more pills. They said I'd had enough."

"What kind of pills were they?"

"What do you think? Tranquilizers. Enough! When you have a son who keeps you awake at night because you're frightened he'll return . . ." She paused and pressed a clenched fist against her mouth. Tears were in her eyes. Then she whispered in such a low voice that Harry struggled to catch the words: "Sometimes you don't want to live any longer."

Harry cast his eyes down to his notepad. It was blank.

"Thank you," he said.

*   *   *

"One night, sir. Is that correct?" asked the female receptionist at the Scandia Hotel by Oslo Central Station, without looking up from the reservation on the computer screen.

"Yes," the man before her answered.

She had made a mental note that he was wearing a light-brown coat. Camel hair. Or imitation.

Her long red nails scurried across the keyboard like frightened cockroaches. Imitation camels in wintry Norway. Why not? She had seen pictures of camels in Afghanistan, and her boyfriend had written that it could be just as cold there as here.

"Will you be paying by cash or credit card, sir?"

"Cash."

She pushed the registration form and a pen over the counter to him and asked to see his passport.

"No need," he answered. "I'll pay now."

He spoke English almost like a Brit, but there was something about the way he articulated consonants that made her think of Eastern Europe.

"I still have to see your passport, sir. International regulations."

He nodded in acknowledgment, passed her a smooth thousand-krone note and his passport. Republika Hrvatska? Probably one of the new countries in the East. She gave him his change, put the note in the cash box and reminded herself to check it against the light when the hotel guest had gone. She endeavored to maintain a certain style, although she had to concede that for the moment she was working at one of the city's less sophisticated hotels. And this particular guest did not look like a swindler, more like a . . . well, what did he look like, in fact? She gave him the plastic card and the spiel about floor, elevator, breakfast and checkout times.

"Will there be anything else, sir?" she warbled, confident that her English and service attitude were too good for this hotel. Before very long she would move to somewhere better. Or—if that was not possible—trim her approach.

He cleared his throat and asked where the nearest telephone booth was.

She explained that he could call from his room, but he shook his head. She had to think. The rise in cell-phone use had meant that most phone booths in Oslo had been removed, but she thought there was still one close by, in Jernbanetorget, the square outside the station. Although it was only a hundred yards away, she took out a little map, marked it and gave him directions. As they did in the Radisson and Choice hotels. Peering up to see whether he had understood, she was confused for a moment, without quite knowing why.

"It's us against the rest of the world, Halvorsen!"

Harry shouted his regular morning greeting as he burst into their shared office.

"Two messages," Halvorsen said. "You've got to report to the new POB's office. And a woman called asking for you. Stunning voice."

"Oh?" Harry slung his coat in the direction of the coatrack. It landed on the floor.

"Wow," Halvorsen exclaimed without thinking. "At last you're over it, aren't you?"

"I beg your pardon?"

"You're chucking clothes at the coatrack again. And saying, 'It's us against the rest of the world!' You haven't done either since Rakel dumped—"

Halvorsen shut up as he saw his colleague's warning expression.

"What did the lady want?"

"To pass on a message. Her name is . . ." Halvorsen searched through the yellow Post-its in front of him. "Martine Eckhoff."

"Don't know her."

"Works at the Lighthouse."

"Aha!"

"She said she'd been making inquiries. And that no one had heard anything about Per Holmen having any debts."

"Mm. Perhaps I should call and check if there was anything else."

"Oh? OK. Fine."

"All right? Why are you looking so cheated?" Harry bent down for his coat, but instead of hanging it up, he put it on. "Do you know what, Junior? I have to go out again."

"But the POB—"

"—will have to wait."

The gate to the container terminal was open, but there was a sign on the fence prohibiting access and directing vehicles to the parking lot outside. Harry scratched his bad leg, glanced at the long, open expanse between the containers and drove in. The watchman's office was a low building much like a workman's shed that had been extended at regular intervals over the last thirty years. Which was not that far from the truth. Harry parked in front of the entrance and covered the remaining yards at a quick walk.

The watchman leaned back in his chair, silent, his hands behind his head, chewing on a matchstick, while Harry explained why he was there. And what had happened the night before.

The matchstick was the only thing moving in the watchman's face, but Harry thought he detected the hint of a grin as he told him about the altercation with the dog.

"Black Metzner," the watchman said. "A cousin of the Rhodesian ridgeback. Lucky to get it imported. Great guard dog. And quiet, too."

"I noticed."

The matchstick jumped in amusement. "The Metzner is a hunter, so it sneaks up. Doesn't want to frighten the prey."

"Are you saying the animal intended to . . . er, eat me?"

"Depends what you mean by eat."

The watchman did not go into any details, just stared at Harry with a blank expression. The interwoven hands framed the whole of his head, and Harry was thinking that he had either unusually big hands or an unusually small head.

"So you didn't see or hear anyone at the time we are assuming Per Holmen was shot?"

"Was shot?"

"Shot himself. Anything?"

"Guard stays indoors in the winter. And the Metzner is quiet, as I said."

"Isn't that impractical? That it doesn't raise an alarm, I mean?"

The watchman shrugged. "It gets the job done. And we don't have to go out."

"It didn't catch Per Holmen when he slipped in."

"It's a big area."

"But later?"

"The body, you mean? Bah. That was frozen, wasn't it? And the Metzner's not so crazy about dead things. It likes fresh meat."

Harry shuddered. "In the police report it says you'd never seen Holmen down here before."

"That's right."

"I've just been to see his mother and she lent me this family photo." Harry put the picture on the watchman's desk. "Could you take a look and swear to me that you have never seen this person before?" The watchman lowered his gaze. Rolled the matchstick to the corner of his mouth to answer, then paused. The hands moved from behind his head and he picked up the photo. Studied it at length.

"I made a mistake. I have seen him. He was here in the summer. It wasn't so easy to recognize the . . . what was in the container."

"I can appreciate that."

When Harry went to leave a few minutes later, he

opened the door a crack at first and checked. The watch-man grinned.

"It's locked up during the day. And anyway, a Metzner's teeth are narrow. The wound heals fast. I've been thinking about buying a Kentucky terrier. Jagged teeth. Bites chunks out of you. You were lucky, Inspector."

"Well," Harry said, "you'd better warn Fido that a lady is on her way and she'll give him something else to bite."

"What?" Halvorsen asked, carefully maneuvering the car past a snowplow.

"Something soft," Harry said. "Kind of clay. Afterward Beate and her team will put the clay in plaster, let it set and, bingo, you've got a model of a dog's jaw."

"Right. And that's supposed to prove that Per Holmen was murdered?"

"No."

"I thought you said—"

"I said that's what I need to prove that it was murder. The missing link in the chain of evidence."

"I see. And what are the other links?"

"The usual. Motive, murder weapon and opportunity. Turn right here."

"I don't know. You said your suspicions were based on Holmen using wire cutters to break into the container ter-minal?"

"I said that was what made me wonder. To be precise, I wondered how a heroin addict so out of his skull that he has to look for refuge in a container would be alert enough to make sure he had wire cutters to get through the gate. Then I had a closer look at the case. You can park here."

"What I don't understand is how you can claim that you know who the guilty party is."

"Work it out, Halvorsen. It's not difficult, and you have all the facts."

"I hate it when you do this."

"I only want you to be good."

Halvorsen cast a glance at his older colleague to see if he was joking. They got out of the car.

"Aren't you going to lock up?" Harry asked.

"The lock froze last night. The key broke in it this morning. How long have you known who the guilty person is?"

"Awhile."

They crossed the street.

"Knowing *who* is in most cases the easy part. It's the obvious candidate. The husband. The best friend. The guy with a record. And never the butler. That's not the problem; the problem is proving what your head and your gut have been telling you for ages." Harry pressed the bell beside HOLMEN. "And that's what we're going to do now. Find the little piece that changes apparently unconnected information into a perfect chain of evidence."

A voice crackled "*Ja*" over the speaker.

"Police here, Harry Hole. Can we . . . ?" The lock buzzed.

"It's all a question of moving fast," Harry said. "Most murder cases are solved in the first twenty-four hours or not at all."

"Thanks. I've heard that one before," Halvorsen said.

Birger Holmen stood waiting for them at the top of the stairs.

"Come in," he said and led them into the living room. A bare Christmas tree stood by the door to the French balcony, waiting to be decorated.

"My wife is sleeping," he said before Harry could ask.

"We'll whisper," Harry said.

Birger Holmen gave a sad smile. "She won't wake up." Halvorsen sent Harry a quick glance.

"Mm," the inspector said. "Taken a tranquilizer?"

Birger Holmen nodded. "The funeral's tomorrow."

"Yes, of course—that's a strain. Well, thank you for lend-ing me this." Harry put a photograph on the table. It was of Per Holmen seated, with his mother and father standing on either side. Protected. Or, depending on how you saw it, surrounded. A silence ensued as no one said a word. Birger Holmen scratched his forearm through his shirt. Halvorsen wriggled forward in his chair, then moved back.

"Do you know much about drug addiction, Herr Holmen?" Harry asked without looking up.

Birger Holmen frowned. "My wife has taken one sleeping pill. That doesn't mean—"

"I'm not talking about your wife. You may be able to save her. I'm talking about your son."

"Depends what you mean by *know*. He was hooked on heroin. It made him unhappy." He was going to say something else, but paused. He examined the picture on the table. "It made us all unhappy."

"I don't doubt that. But if you had known anything about drug addiction, you would have known that it takes precedence over everything else."

Birger Holmen's voice trembled with indignation. "Are you saying I don't know that, Inspector? Are you saying . . . my wife was . . . he . . ." But tears had crept into his voice. "His own mother . . ."

"I know," Harry whispered. "But drugs come before mothers. Before fathers. Before life." Harry breathed in. "And before death."

"I'm exhausted, Inspector. What do you want?"

"Tests show there were no drugs in his blood when he died. So he was in a bad state. And when heroin addicts are like this, the need for redemption is so strong that you can threaten your own mother with a gun to get it. And redemption is not a shot in the head, but in the arm, the neck, the groin or any other place you can still find a fresh vein. Your son was found with his kit and a bag of heroin in his pocket, Herr Holmen. He can't have shot himself. Drugs take precedence, as I said, over everything. Also—"

"Death." Birger Holmen still had his head in his hands, but his voice was quite distinct. "So you think my son was killed? Why?"

"I was hoping you could tell us."

Birger Holmen did not answer.

"Was it because he threatened her?" Harry asked. "Was it to give your wife peace of mind?"

Holmen raised his head. "What are you talking about?"

"My guess is you hung around Plata waiting. And when he turned up, you followed him after he had bought his fix. You took him down to the container terminal, as he sometimes went there when he had nowhere else."

"How am I supposed to know that?! This is outrageous. I—"

"Of course you knew. I showed this photo to the watchman, who recognized the person I was asking about."

"Per?"

"No, you. You were there this summer asking if you could search the containers for your son."

Holmen stared at Harry, who went on: "You had it all planned. Wire cutters to get in and an empty container, which was an appropriate place for a drug addict to end his life, where no one could hear or see you shoot him. With the gun you knew Per's mother could testify was his."

Halvorsen studied Birger Holmen and held himself in readiness, but Holmen showed no signs of making any kind of move. He breathed heavily through his nose and scratched his forearm while staring into space.

"You can't prove any of this." He said this in a resigned tone, as if it were a fact he regretted.

Harry made a conciliatory gesture. In the ensuing silence they could hear loud barking from down in the street.

"It won't stop itching, will it," Harry said. Holmen stopped scratching at once.

"Can we see what itches so much?"

"It's nothing."

"We can do it here or down at the station. Your choice, Herr Holmen." The barking increased in intensity. A dog sled, here, in the middle of the city? Halvorsen had a feeling there was going to be an explosion.

"Fine," Holmen whispered, unbuttoning the cuff and pushing up his sleeve.

There were two small sores with scabs on them. The skin around them was red and inflamed.

"Turn your arm around," Harry ordered. Holmen had a matching sore underneath.

"They itch like hell, dog bites, don't they," Harry said. "Especially after ten to fourteen days, when they begin to heal. A doctor down at the emergency room told me that I had to try to stop scratching. You should have done that, too, Herr Holmen."

Holmen gazed at his sores without seeing them. "I should have?"

"The skin is punctured in three places. We can prove that a particular dog down at the container terminal bit you—we have a model of its jaw. Hope you managed to defend yourself."

Holmen shook his head. "I didn't want . . . I just wanted her to feel free."

The barking in the street came to a sudden end.

"Are you going to confess?" Harry asked, signaling to Halvorsen, who thrust a hand into his inside pocket. Without finding pen or paper. Harry rolled his eyes and gave him his own notepad.

"He said he was so low," Holmen said, "that he couldn't go on. That now he really wanted to give up. So I searched around and found him a room in the Salvation Army hostel. A bed and three meals a day for twelve hundred kroner a month. And he was promised a place in the methadone project. There was just a couple of months to wait. But then I heard nothing from him, and when I called the hostel, they said he had absconded without paying the rent, and . . . well, then he turned up here again. With the gun."

"And you decided then and there?"

"He was a goner. I had already lost my son. And I couldn't let him take her with him."

"How did you find him?"

"Not in Plata. He was down in Eika and I said I would buy the gun off him. He was carrying it and showed it to me. Wanted the money on the spot. But I said I didn't have enough money. He should meet me at the gate at the back of the container terminal the next evening. You know, in fact I'm glad you have . . . I . . ."

"How much?" Harry interrupted.

"What?"

"How much did you have to pay?"

"Fifteen thousand kroner."

"And . . ."

"He came. It turned out he didn't have any ammunition for the weapon. Never did, he said."

"But you must have had an inkling that would be the case, and it's a standard caliber, so you bought some?"

"Yes."

"Did you pay him first?"

"What?"

"Forget it."

"You have to understand it wasn't only Pernille and me who suffered. For Per every day was a prolongation of his suffering. My son was a dead person waiting for . . . for someone to stop his heart that would not stop beating. A . . . a . . ."

"Redeemer."

"Yes, that's it. A redeemer."

"But that's not your job, Herr Holmen."

"No, it's God's job." Holmen bowed his head and mumbled something.

"What?" asked Harry.

Holmen raised his head, but his eyes were staring into empty space. "If God doesn't do His job, though, someone else has to do it."

On the street, a brown dusk had descended around the yellow lights. Even in the middle of the Oslo night the darkness was never total when snow had fallen. Noises were wrapped in cotton and the creaking of snow underfoot sounded like distant fireworks.

"Why don't we take him with us?" Halvorsen asked.

"He's not going anywhere. He has something to tell his wife. We'll send a car in a couple of hours."

"Bit of an actor, isn't he?"

"Eh?"

"Well, wasn't he sobbing his guts out when you brought him the news of his son's death?"

Harry shook his head in resignation. "You've got a lot to learn, Junior."

Annoyed, Halvorsen kicked at the snow. "Enlighten me, O Wise One."

"Committing a murder is such an extreme act that many repress it. They can walk around with it like a kind of half-forgotten nightmare. I have seen that several times now. It's when others say it out loud that they realize it is not just something that exists in their head. It *did* happen."

"Right. A cold fish, anyway."

"Didn't you see the man was crushed? Pernille Holmen was probably right when she said that her husband was the loving one."

"Loving? A murderer?" Halvorsen's voice quivered with indignation.

Harry laid a hand on the detective's shoulder. "Think about it. Isn't it the ultimate act of love? Sacrificing your only son?"

"But—"

"I know what you're thinking, Halvorsen. But you'll just have to get used to the idea. This is the type of moral paradox that will fill your days."

Halvorsen pulled at the unlocked car door, but it was frozen fast. In a sudden bout of fury, he heaved, and it came away from the rubber with a ripping noise.

They got in, and Harry watched as Halvorsen twisted the ignition key and pinched his forehead hard with the other hand. The engine roared into life.

"Halvorsen . . ." Harry started.

"Anyway, the case is solved and the POB is bound to be happy," Halvorsen shouted, pulling out in front of a truck with its horn blaring. He held up an outstretched finger to the mirror. "So let's smile and celebrate a little." He lowered his hand and continued to pinch at his forehead.

"Halvorsen . . ."

"What's up?" he barked.

"Park the car."

"What?"

"Now."

Halvorsen pulled over to the curb, let go of the steering wheel and focused ahead through vacant eyes. In the time they had been with Holmen, the ice flowers had crept up the windshield like a sudden attack of fungus. Halvorsen wheezed as his chest rose and fell.

"Some days this is a shit job," Harry said. "Don't let it get to you."

"No," Halvorsen said, breathing even harder.

"You are you, and they are them."

"Yes."

Harry placed a hand on Halvorsen's back and waited. After a while he felt his colleague's breathing calm down.

"Tough guy," Harry said.

Neither of them spoke as the car crawled its way through the afternoon traffic toward Grønland.

7

Anonymity

He stood at the highest point of Oslo's busiest pedestrian street, named after the Swedish-Norwegian king, Karl Johan. He had memorized the map he had been given at the hotel and knew that the building he saw in silhouette to the west was the Royal Palace and that Oslo Central Station was at the eastern end.

He shivered.

High up a house wall the sub-zero temperature shone out in red neon, and even the slightest current of air felt like an Ice Age penetrating his camel-hair coat, which, until then, he had been very happy with; he had bought it in London for a song.

The clock beside the temperature gauge showed 7:00. He started walking east. The omens were good. It was dark, there were lots of people about and the only surveillance cameras he saw were outside banks and directed at their respective cash machines. He had already excluded the subway for his getaway because of the combination of too many cameras and too few people. Oslo was smaller than he had imagined.

He went into a clothing shop, where he found a blue wool hat for 49 kroner and a wool jacket for 200, but changed his mind when he saw a thin raincoat for 120. While he was trying on the raincoat in a changing room he discovered that the urinal blocks from Paris were still in his suit jacket pocket, crushed and ground into the material.

The restaurant was several hundred yards down the pedestrian walkway, on the left-hand side. He registered at once that there was no cloakroom attendant. Good—that made things easier. He entered the dining area. Half full. Good sight lines; he could see all the tables from where he stood. A waiter came over and he reserved a window table for six o'clock the following day.

Before leaving, he checked the bathroom. There were no windows. So the only other exit was through the kitchen. OK—nowhere was perfect, and it was improbable that he would need an alternative way out.

He left the restaurant, looked at his watch and started to walk toward the station. People avoided eye contact. A small town, but it still had the cool aloofness of a capital city. Good.

He checked his watch again as he stood on the platform for the express train to the airport. Six minutes from the restaurant. Trains left every ten minutes and took nineteen. In other words, he could be on the train at 7:20 and in the airport by 7:40. The direct flight to Zagreb left at 9:10 and the ticket was in his pocket. Bought on special offer from SAS.

Satisfied, he walked out of the new rail terminal, down a staircase, under a glass roof that had obviously been the old departure hall, but where there were now shops, and out into the open square. Jernbanetorget, as it was called on the map. In the middle there was a tiger twice the size of life, frozen in mid-stride, between tram rails, cars and people. But he couldn't see a phone booth anywhere, as the receptionist had said. At the end of the square, by a shelter, there was a throng of people. He went closer. Several of them had stuck their hoodie-covered heads together and were talking. Perhaps they came from the same place, or they were neighbors waiting for the same bus. It reminded him of something else, though. He spotted things changing hands, skinny men hurrying away with their backs bent into the freezing wind. And he knew what the things were. He had seen heroin deals taking place in Zagreb and other European towns, but nowhere as openly as here. Then he realized what it reminded him of. The gatherings of people he himself had been part of after the Serbians had withdrawn. Refugees.

Then a bus did come. It was white and stopped just short of the shelter. The doors opened, but no one got on. Instead a young woman came out, wearing a uniform he recognized at once. The Salvation Army. He slowed down.

She went over to one of the women and helped her onto the bus. Two men followed.

He stopped and looked up. A coincidence, he thought. That was all. He turned around. And there, at the bottom of a small clock tower, he saw three telephones.

Five minutes later he had called Zagreb and told her everything was looking good.

"The final job," he had repeated.

And Fred had told him that his Blue Lions, Dinamo Zagreb, were leading 1–0 against Rijeka at Maksimar Stadium at halftime.

The conversation had cost him five kroner. The clocks on the tower showed 7:25. The countdown had started.

The group met in the hall belonging to Vestre Aker Church.

The snowdrifts were high on both sides of the gravel path leading to the small brick building on the slope beside the cemetery. Fourteen people were seated in a bare meeting hall, with plastic chairs piled up against the walls and a long table in the middle. If you had stumbled into the room, you might have guessed it was a general assembly of some cooperative, but nothing about the faces, age, sex or clothes revealed what kind of community this was. The harsh light was reflected in the windowpanes and on the linoleum floor. There was a low mumbling and fidgeting with paper cups. A bottle of Farris mineral water hissed as it was opened.

At seven o'clock on the dot the chattering stopped as a hand at the end of the table was raised and a little bell rang. Eyes turned to a woman in her mid-thirties. She met them with a direct, fearless gaze. She had narrow, severe lips softened with lipstick, long, thick, blond hair held in place with a clip and large hands that, at this moment, were resting on the table, exuding calm and confidence. She was elegant, meaning she had attractive features but not the grace that would qualify her for what Norwegians termed "sweet." Her body language betokened control and strength, which was underlined by the firm voice that filled the chilly room the next minute.

"Hi, my name is Astrid and I'm an alcoholic."

"Hi, Astrid!" the gathering answered in unison.

Astrid bent the spine of the book in front of her and began to read.

"The only requirement for AA membership is a desire to stop drinking."

She went on, and around the table the lips of those who knew the Twelve Traditions moved by rote. In the breaks, when she paused for breath, you could hear the church choir practicing on the floor above.

"Today the theme is the First Step," Astrid said, "which runs thus: We admit we are powerless over alcohol, and that our lives have become unmanageable. I can begin, and I will be brief, since I consider myself finished with the First Step."

She drew breath and gave a laconic smile.

"I've been dry for seven years, and the first thing I do when I wake up is to tell myself I'm an alcoholic. My children don't know this. They think Mommy used to get very drunk and stopped drinking because she got so angry when she drank. My life requires an appropriate measure of truth and an appropriate measure of lies to find its equilibrium. I may be going to pieces, but I take one day at a time and avoid the first drink, and at present I'm working on the Eleventh Step. Thank you."

"Thank you, Astrid," came the response from the assembled members, followed by clapping as the choir sang its praises from the second floor.

She nodded to her left, to a tall man with cropped blond hair.

"Hi, my name is Harry," said the man in a gravelly voice. The fine network of red veins on his large nose bore witness to a long life out of the ranks of the sober. "I am an alcoholic."

"Hi, Harry."

"I'm new here. This is my sixth meeting. Or seventh. And I haven't finished the First Step. In other words, I know I'm an alcoholic, but I think I can contain my alcoholism. So there is a kind of contradiction in my sitting here. But I came here because of a promise I made to a psychologist, a friend, who has my best interests at heart. He claimed that if I could stand all the chat about God and the spiritual stuff for the first weeks, I would find out it works. Well, I don't know if anonymous alcoholics can help themselves, but I am willing to try. Why not?" He turned to the left to signal that he had finished. But before the clapping could get under way, it was interrupted by Astrid.

"This is the first time you've said anything at our meetings, Harry. So that's nice. But perhaps you'd like to tell us a little more while you're at it."

Harry looked at her. The others did, too, since pressuring anyone in the group was a clear breach of protocol. Her eyes held his. He had felt them on him in the earlier meetings, but had returned her gaze only once. However, then he had given her the full treatment, a searching look from top to toe and back again. Actually, he had liked what he saw, but what he liked best was when he returned to the top and her face was a great deal redder. And at the next meeting he had been invisible.

"No, I wouldn't, thank you," Harry said. Tentative applause.

Harry observed her out of the corner of his eye while his neighbor was talking. After the meeting she asked him where he lived and offered him a lift. Harry hesitated while the choir on the floor above rose in pitch in their eulogy of the Lord.

An hour and a half later they were each smoking a cigarette in silence and watching the smoke add a blue tinge to the bedroom darkness. The damp sheets on Harry's narrow bed were still warm, but the cold in the room had made Astrid pull the thin white duvet right up to her chin.

"That was wonderful," she said.

Harry didn't answer. He was thinking it probably wasn't a question.

"I came," she said. "The first time together. That's not—"

"So your husband's a doctor?" Harry said.

"That's the second time you've asked, and the answer is still yes."

Harry nodded. "Can you hear that sound?"

"Which sound?"

"The ticking. Is it your watch?"

"I don't have a watch. It must be yours."

"Digital. Doesn't tick."

She placed a hand on his hip. Harry slipped out of bed. The freezing-cold linoleum burned the soles of his feet. "Would you like a glass of water?"

"Mmm."

Harry went into the bathroom and looked into the mirror as he ran the water. What was it she had said? She could see loneliness in his eyes? He leaned forward, but all he could see was a blue iris around small pupils and deltas of veins in the whites. When Halvorsen found out he had split up with Rakel, he said Harry should find solace in other women. Or, as he so poetically put it, screw the melancholy out of his soul. However, Harry had neither the energy nor the will. Because he knew that any woman he touched would turn into Rakel. And that was what he needed to forget, to get her out of his blood, not some sexual methadone treatment.

But he might have been wrong and Halvorsen might have been right. Because it had felt good. It *had* been wonderful. And instead of the empty feeling you got from trying to quench one desire by satisfying another, he felt his batteries recharged. And relaxed at the same time. She had taken what she needed. And he liked the way she had done it. Perhaps it could be as easy as this for him, too?

He moved back a step and studied his body in the mirror. He had become leaner in the last year. There was less fat on him, but fewer muscles. He had begun to resemble his father. As one would expect.

He went back to bed with a large glass, which they shared. Afterward she snuggled up to him. Her skin was clammy and cold at first, but she soon began to warm him up.

"Now you can tell me," she said.

"Tell you what?" Harry watched the smoke coil into a letter.

"What's her name? Because it is a *she*, isn't it?" The letter dissolved. "She's the reason you came to us."

"Might be."

Harry observed the glow eat away at the cigarette as he talked. A little at first. The woman beside him was a stranger, it was dark and the words rose and melted away, and he thought this is what it must be like to sit in a confessional. To unburden yourself. Or to share problems with others, as AA called it. So he continued. He told her about Rakel, who had thrown him out of the house over a year ago because she thought he was obsessed with the hunt for a mole in the police force, the Prince. And about Oleg, her son, who had been snatched from his bedroom and used as a hostage when Harry finally got within shooting distance of the Prince. Oleg had coped well, considering the circumstances of the kidnapping and the fact that he had witnessed Harry killing the kidnapper in an elevator in Kampen. It was worse for Rakel. Two weeks later, when she was *au fait* with all the details, she had told him she could not have him in her life. Or, to be more precise, Oleg's life.

Astrid nodded. "She left you because of the harm you had done to them?"

Harry shook his head. "Because of the harm I had not done to them. Yet."

"Oh?"

"I said the case was closed, but she maintained I was obsessed, that it would never be closed as long as they were still out there." Harry stubbed his cigarette out in the ashtray on the bedside table. "And if it wasn't them, I would find others. Other people who could hurt them. She said she could not take that responsibility."

"Sounds like she's obsessed."

"No." Harry smiled. "She's right."

"Really? Would you care to amplify?"

Harry shrugged. "Submarines . . ." he started, but was stopped by a violent coughing fit.

"What did you say about submarines?"

"She said that. That I was a submarine. Going down into the cold, murky depths where you can't breathe and coming up to the surface once every second month. She didn't want to keep me company down there. Reasonable enough."

"Do you still love her?"

Harry was not sure he liked the direction this problem-sharing was taking. He took a deep breath. In his head he was playing the rest of the last conversation he'd had with Rakel.

His own voice, low, as it tends to be when he is angry or frightened: "Submarine?"

Rakel: "I know it's not a very good image, but you understand . . ."

Harry holds up his hands: "Of course. Excellent image. And what is this . . . doctor? An aircraft carrier?"

She groans: "He has nothing to do with this, Harry. It's about you and me. And Oleg."

"Don't hide behind Oleg now."

"Hide . . ."

"You're using him as a hostage, Rakel."

"I'm using him as a hostage? Was it me who kidnapped Oleg and put a gun to his temple so that you could slake your thirst for revenge?"

The veins on her neck are standing out and she screams so loud her voice becomes ugly—someone else's; she hasn't the vocal cords to support such fury. Harry leaves and closes the door gently, almost without a sound, behind him.

He turned to the woman in his bed. "Yes, I love her. Do you love your husband, the doctor?"

"Yes."

"So why this?"

"He doesn't love me."

"Mm. So now you're taking your revenge?"

She looked at him in surprise. "No. I'm lonely. And I like you. The same reasons you're here, I would think. Did you hope it was more complicated?"

Harry chuckled. "No. That'll do fine."

"Why did you kill him?"

"Who?"

"Are there more? The kidnapper, of course."

"That's not important."

"Maybe not, but I would like to hear you tell me"—she put her hand between his legs, cuddled up to him and whispered in his ear—"the details."

"I don't think so."

"I think you're mistaken."

"OK, but I don't like . . ."

"Oh, come on!" she hissed with irritation and gave his member a good, firm squeeze. Harry looked at her. Her eyes sparkled blue and hard in the dark. She put on a hasty smile and added in a sugary-sweet tone: "Just for me."

Outside the bedroom, the temperature continued to fall, making the roofs in Bislett creak and groan while Harry told her the details and felt her stiffen, then take her hand away and in the end whisper she had heard enough.

After she had left, Harry stood listening in his bedroom. To the creaking. And the ticking.

Then he bent over the jacket he had thrown to the floor, with all the other clothes, in their stampede through the front door into the bedroom. He found the source in his pocket: Bjarne Møller's parting gift. The watch glass glinted.

He put it in the bedside-table drawer, but the ticking followed him all the way into dreamland.

He wiped the superfluous oil off the gun parts with one of the hotel's white towels.

The traffic outside reached him as a regular rumble, drowning out the tiny TV in the corner with its mere three channels, a grainy picture and a language he assumed was Norwegian. The girl in reception had taken his jacket and promised that it would be cleaned by early the following morning. He lined up the parts of the gun on a newspaper. When they had all been dried, he assembled the gun, pointed it at the mirror and pulled the trigger. There was a smooth click and he felt the movement of the steel components travel along his hand and arm. The dry click. The mock execution.

That was how they had tried to crack Bobo.

In November 1991, after three months of nonstop siege and bombardment, Vukovar had finally capitulated. The rain poured down as the Serbs marched into town. Along with the remnants of Bobo's unit, numbering around eighty weary and starving Croatian prisoners of war, he had been commanded to stand in line before the ruins of what had been the town's main street. The Serbs had told them not to move and had withdrawn into their heated tent. The rain had whipped down, making the mud froth. After two hours the first men began to fall. When Bobo's lieutenant left the line to help one of those who had collapsed in the mud, a young Serbian private—just a boy—came out of the tent and shot the lieutenant in the stomach. Thereafter no one stirred; they watched the rain obliterate the mountain ridges around them and hoped the lieutenant would soon stop screaming. He began to cry, but then he heard Bobo's voice behind him: "Don't cry." And he stopped.

Morning turned to afternoon and it was dusk when an open jeep arrived. The Serbs in the tent rushed out and saluted. He knew the man in the passenger seat had to be the commanding officer—"the rock with the gentle voice," as he was called. In the back of the jeep sat a man in civilian clothing with a bowed head. The jeep halted right in front of their unit, and since he was in the first row, he heard the commanding officer ask the civilian to look at the prisoners of war. He recognized the civilian at once when he reluctantly raised his head. He was from Vukovar, the father of a boy at his school. The father scanned the lines of men, reached him, but there was no sign of recognition and he moved on. The commander sighed, stood up in the jeep and yelled over the rain, not using the gentle voice: "Which of you goes under the code name of 'the little redeemer'?"

No one in the unit moved.

"Are you frightened to step forward, *mali spasitelj*? You, who blew up twelve of our tanks and deprived our women of their husbands and made Serbian children fatherless?"

He waited.

"I thought so. Which of you is Bobo?" Still no one moved.

The commander looked at the civilian, who pointed a trembling finger at Bobo in the second row.

"Come forward," the commander shouted.

Bobo walked the few steps to the jeep and the driver, who had got out and was standing beside the vehicle. When Bobo stood to attention and saluted, the driver knocked his cap into the mud.

"We have been given to understand on the radio that the little redeemer is under your command," the commander said. "Please point him out to me."

"I've never heard of any redeemer," Bobo said.

The commander raised his gun and struck him. A red stream of blood issued from Bobo's nose.

"Quick. I'm getting wet and food is ready."

"I am Bobo, a captain in the Croatian ar—"

The commander nodded to the driver, who snatched Bobo's hair and turned his face to the rain, washing the blood from his nose and mouth down into the red neckerchief.

"Idiot!" said the commander. "There is no Croatian army here, just traitors! You can choose to be executed right now or save us time. We'll find him whatever happens."

"And you'll execute us whatever happens," Bobo groaned.

"Of course."

"Why?"

The commander went through the motions of loading his gun. Raindrops fell from the gun stock. He placed the barrel against Bobo's temple. "Because I'm a Serbian officer. And a man has to respect his work. Are you ready to die?"

Bobo shut his eyes; raindrops hung from his eyelashes.

"Where is the little redeemer? I'll count to three, then I'll shoot. One . . ."

"I am Bobo—"

"Two!"

"—captain in the Croatian army. I—"

"Three!"

Even in the pouring rain the dry click sounded like an explosion.

"Sorry—I must have forgotten to load the magazine," the commander said.

The driver passed the commander a magazine. He thrust it into the handle, loaded and raised the pistol again.

"Last chance! One!"

"I . . . my . . . unit is—"

"Two!"

"—the first infantry battalion in . . . in—"

"Three!"

Another dry click. The father in the backseat sobbed.

"Goodness me! Empty magazine. Shall we try it with some of those nice shiny bullets in?"

Magazine out, new one in, load.

"Where is the little redeemer? One!"

Bobo mumbled the Lord's Prayer: "*Oče naš* . . ."

"Two!"

The skies opened, the rain beat down with a roar as though in a desperate attempt to stop what they were doing. He couldn't stand it anymore, the sight of Bobo; he opened his mouth to scream that he was the little redeemer, he was the one they wanted, not Bobo, just him, they could have his blood. But at that moment Bobo's gaze swept across and past him and he could see the wild, intense prayer in it, saw him shake his head. Then Bobo's body jerked as the bullet cut the connection between body and soul, and he saw his eyes snuff out and life drain away.

"You," shouted the commander, pointing to one of the men in the first row. "Your turn. Come here!"

The young Serbian officer who had shot the lieutenant ran over.

"There's some shooting up at the hospital," he shouted.

The commander swore and waved to the driver. The next moment the engine started with a roar and the jeep vanished in the gloom. But not before he had told them there was no reason for the Serbs to worry. There were no Croatians in the hospital in a position to shoot. They didn't have any weapons.

They had left Bobo where he lay, facedown in the black mud. And when it was so dark that the Serbs in the tent could no longer see them, he crept forward, bent over the dead captain, loosened the knot and took the red neckerchief.

8

The Mealtime

It was eight o'clock in the morning, and the day that would go down as the coldest December 16 in Oslo in twenty-four years was still as dark as night. Harry left the police station after going to Gerd and signing out the key to Tom Waaler's flat. He walked with upturned coat collar, and when he coughed the sound seemed to disappear into cotton padding, as though the cold had made the air heavy and dense.

People in the early-morning rush hurried along the sidewalks. They couldn't get indoors quickly enough, whereas Harry took long, slow steps, bracing his knees in case the rubber soles of his Doc Martens didn't grip the packed ice.

When he let himself into Tom Waaler's centrally positioned bachelor flat, the sky behind Ekeberg Ridge was growing lighter. The flat had been sealed off in the weeks following Waaler's death, but the inquiry had not thrown up any leads pointing to other potential arms smugglers. At least that was what the chief superintendent had said when he informed them that the case would be given a lower priority because of "other pressing investigative tasks."

Harry switched on the light in the living room and once again noticed that dead people's homes had a silence all their own. On the wall in front of the gleaming black leather furniture hung an enormous plasma TV with three-foot-high speakers on each side, part of the surround-sound system in the flat. There were a lot of pictures on the walls with blue cubelike patterns. Rakel called it ruler-and-compass art.

He went into the bedroom. Gray light filtered through the window. The room was tidy. On the desk there was a computer screen, but he couldn't see a tower anywhere. They must have taken it away to check it for evidence. However, he hadn't seen it among the evidence at HQ. Although, of course, he had been denied access to the case. The official explanation was that he was under investigation by SEFO, the internal-affairs division, for the murder of Waaler. Yet he could not get the idea out of his head that someone was not happy about every stone being turned over.

Harry was about to leave the bedroom when he heard it: The deceased's flat was no longer quiet.

A sound, a distant ticking, made his skin tingle and the hairs stand up on his arm. It came from the closet. He hesitated. Then he opened the closet door. On the floor inside was an open cardboard box, and he at once recognized the jacket Waaler had been wearing that night in Kampen. At the top, in the jacket, a wristwatch was ticking. The way it had after Tom Waaler had punched his arm through the window in the elevator door, into the elevator where they were, and the elevator had started moving and had cut off his arm. Afterward they had sat in the elevator with his arm between them, waxlike and lifeless, a severed limb off a mannequin, with the bizarre difference that this one was wearing a watch. A watch that ticked, that refused to stop, but was alive, as in the story Harry's father had told him when he was small, the one where the sound of the dead man's beating heart would not stop and in the end drove the killer insane.

It was a distinct ticking sound, energetic, intense. The kind of sound you remember. It was a Rolex watch. Heavy and in all probability exorbitantly expensive.

Harry slammed the closet door. Stamped his way to the front door, creating an echo against the walls. Rattled the keys loudly when he locked up and hummed in frenzied fashion until he was in the street and the blissful traffic noise drowned out everything else.

At three o'clock shadows were already falling on 4 Kommandør T. I. Øgrims Plass, and lights had started to come on in the windows of the Salvation Army headquarters. By five o'clock it was fully dark, and the mercury had dropped to 5° F. A few stray snowflakes fell on the roof of the funny little car Martine Eckhoff sat waiting in.

"Come on, Daddy," she mumbled as she glanced anxiously at the battery gauge. She was not sure how the electric car—which the Army had been presented with by the royal family—would perform in the cold. She had remembered everything before locking the office: had entered information about upcoming and canceled meetings of the various corps on the home page, revised the duty rosters for the soup bus and the boiling pot in Egertorget, and checked the letter to the office of the prime minister about the annual Christmas performance at Oslo Concert Hall.

The car door opened, and in came the cold and a man with thick white hair beneath his uniform cap and the brightest blue eyes Martine had seen. At any rate, on anyone over sixty. With some difficulty he arranged his legs in the cramped footwell between seat and dashboard.

"Let's go," he said, brushing snow off the emblem that told everyone he was the highest-ranking Salvation Army officer in Norway. He spoke with the cheeriness and effortless authority that are natural to people who are used to their commands being obeyed.

"You're late," she said.

"And you're an angel." He stroked her cheek with the

outside of his hand and his blue eyes were bright with energy and amusement. "Let's hurry now."

"Daddy . . ."

"One moment." He rolled down the car window. "Rikard!"

A young man was standing in front of the entrance to the citadel, which was beside, and under the same roof as, the headquarters. He was startled and rushed over to them at once, knock-kneed, with his arms pressed into his sides. He slipped and almost fell, but flapped his arms and regained balance. On reaching the car, he was already out of breath.

"Yes, Commander."

"Call me David, like everyone else, Rikard."

"All right, David."

"But not every sentence, please."

Rikard's eyes jumped from Commander David Eckhoff to his daughter, Martine, and back again. He ran two fingers across his perspiring top lip. Martine had often wondered how it was that someone could sweat so much in one particular area regardless of weather and wind conditions, but especially when he sat next to her during a church service, or anywhere else, and whispered something that was supposed to be funny and might have been just that, had it not been for the poorly disguised nervousness, the rather too intense nearness—and, well, the sweaty top lip. Now and then, when Rikard was sitting close to her and all was quiet, she heard a rasping sound as he ran his fingers across his mouth. Because, in addition to producing sweat, Rikard Nilsen also produced stubble, an unusual abundance of stubble. He could arrive at headquarters in the morning with a face like a baby's bottom, but by lunch his white skin would have taken on a blue shimmer, and she had often noticed that when he came to meetings in the evening he had shaved again.

"I'm teasing you, Rikard." David Eckhoff smiled.

Martine knew there was no bad intention behind them, these games of her father's, but sometimes he seemed unable to see that he was bullying people.

"Oh, right," Rikard said, forcing a laugh. He stooped. "Hello, Martine."

"Hello, Rikard," Martine said, pretending to be concentrating on the battery gauge.

"I wonder whether you could do me a favor," the commander said. "There is so much ice on the roads now and the tires on my car don't have studs. I should have changed them, but I have to go to the Lighthouse—"

"I know," Rikard said with zeal. "You have a lunch meeting with the minister for social affairs. We're hoping for lots of press coverage. I was talking to the head of PR."

David Eckhoff gave him a patronizing smile. "Good to hear you keep up, Rikard. The point is that my car is here in the garage and I would like to have studded tires put on by the time I return. You know—"

"Are the tires in the trunk?"

"Yes. But only if you have nothing more pressing going on. I was about to call Jon. He said he could—"

"No, no," Rikard said, shaking his head vigorously. "I'll fix them right away. Trust me, er . . . David."

"Are you sure?"

Rikard looked at the commander, bewildered. "That you can trust me?"

"That you don't have anything more pressing?"

"I'm sure. This is a good job. I like working on cars and . . . and . . ."

"Changing tires?"

Rikard swallowed and nodded as the commander beamed.

As he wound up the window and they turned out of the square, Martine said that she thought it was wrong of him to exploit Rikard's obliging nature.

"Subservience, I suppose you mean," her father answered. "Relax, my dear—it's a test, nothing more."

"A test? Of selflessness or fear of authority?"

"The latter," the commander said with a chortle. "I was talking to Rikard's sister, Thea, and she happened to tell me that Rikard is struggling to finish the budget for tomorrow's deadline. If so, he should make that a priority and leave this to Jon."

"And then? Perhaps Rikard is being kind."

"Yes, he is kind, and clever. Hardworking and serious. I want to be sure he has the backbone and the courage that an important post in management requires."

"Everyone says Jon will get the post."

David Eckhoff looked down at his hands with an imperceptible smile.

"Do they? By the way, I appreciate your standing up for Rikard."

Martine did not take her eyes off the road, but felt her father's eyes on her as he continued: "Our families have been friends for many years, you know. They're good people. With a solid foundation in the Army."

Martine took a deep breath to suppress her irritation.

The job required one bullet.

Nevertheless, he pushed all the cartridges into the magazine. First of all, because the weapon was in perfect balance only when the magazine was full. And because it minimized the chances of a malfunction. Six in the magazine plus one in the chamber.

Then he put on the shoulder holster. He had bought it secondhand, and the leather was soft and smelled salty, acrid, from skin, oil and sweat. The gun lay flat, as it should. He stood in front of the mirror and put on his jacket. It could not be seen. Bigger guns were more accurate, but this

was not a case of precision shooting. He put on his raincoat.
Then the coat. Shoved the cap in his pocket and groped for
the red neckerchief in his inside pocket.

He looked at his watch.

"Backbone," said Gunnar Hagen. "And courage. These are
the qualities I seek above all else in my inspectors."

Harry didn't answer. He didn't consider it a question.
Instead, he looked around the office where he had sat so
often, like now. But apart from the familiar scenario of
POB-tells-inspector-what's-what, everything had changed.
Gone were Bjarne Møller's piles of paper, the Donald Duck
comics squeezed between legal documents and police regulations on the shelf, the big photograph of the family and
the even bigger one of a golden retriever the children had
been given and long forgotten about, since it had been dead
for nine years, but which Bjarne was still grieving over.

What remained was a cleared desk with a monitor and a
keyboard, a small silver pedestal with a tiny white bone and
Gunnar Hagen's elbows, on which he was leaning at this
very moment while eyeballing Harry from under his great
thatched eyebrows.

"But there is a third quality I prize even higher, Hole.
Can you guess what it is?"

"No," Harry said in an even monotone.

"Discipline. Di-sci-pline."

The POB's division of the word into syllables suggested
to Harry that he was in for a lecture on its etymology. However, Hagen stood up and began to strut to and fro with his
hands behind his back, a sort of marking-out of territory
that Harry had always found vaguely risible.

"I'm having this face-to-face conversation with everyone
in the section to make it clear what my expectations are."

"Unit."

"I beg your pardon?"

"We've never been called a section. Even though your rank used to be known as 'Section Head,' PAS. Just for your information."

"Thank you for drawing that to my attention, Inspector. Where was I?"

"Di-sci-pline."

Hagen bored his eyes into Harry, who didn't turn a hair. So the POB resumed his strutting.

"For the last ten years I have been a lecturer at the military academy. My area of specialty was the war in Burma. It may surprise you to hear that it has great relevance for my job here, Hole."

"Well." Harry scratched his leg. "You can read me like an open book, boss."

Hagen ran his forefinger over the window frame and studied the result with displeasure. "In 1942, a mere hundred thousand Japanese soldiers conquered Burma. Burma was twice the size of Japan and at that time occupied by British troops who were superior in numbers and firepower." Hagen raised his grubby forefinger. "But there was one area where the Japanese were superior, and this made it possible for them to beat the British and the Indian mercenaries: discipline. When the Japanese marched on Rangoon, they walked for forty-five minutes and slept for fifteen. Slept on the road wearing their backpacks and their feet pointing toward their destination. So that they didn't walk into the ditch or in the wrong direction when they woke up. Direction is important, Hole. Do you understand?"

Harry had an inkling of what was to come. "I understand that they made it to Rangoon, boss."

"They did. All of them. Because they did what they were told. I have just been told that you signed out the keys to Tom Waaler's flat. Is that correct, Hole?"

"I took a look, boss. For therapeutic reasons."

"I hope so. That case is buried. Snooping around Waaler's flat is not only wasted time, it also contravenes the orders you were given by the Chief and now by me. I don't think I need to spell out the consequences of refusing to obey orders. I might mention, however, that Japanese officers shot soldiers who drank water outside drinking times. Not out of sadism, but because discipline is about excising the tumors at the outset. Am I making myself clear, Hole?"

"As clear as . . . well, something that is very clear, boss."

"That's all for now, Hole." Hagen sat down on his chair, took a piece of paper from the drawer and started to read with a passion, as though Harry had already left the office. And looked up in surprise when he saw Harry was still sitting in front of him.

"Anything else, Hole?"

"Mm, I was wondering. Didn't the Japanese lose the war?"

Gunnar Hagen sat staring vacantly at the document long after Harry had gone.

The restaurant was half full. As it had been the day before. He was met at the door by a young, good-looking waiter with blue eyes and blond curls. He was so like Giorgi that for a moment he stood there entranced. And, on seeing the smile on the waiter's lips broaden, realized that he had given himself away. He took off his raincoat in the cloakroom and felt the waiter's eyes on him.

"Your name?" the waiter asked.

He mumbled his answer.

The waiter ran a long, thin finger down the page of the reservations book. It stopped.

"I've got my finger on you now," the waiter said, and the blue eyes held his gaze until he felt himself blushing.

It didn't seem to be an exclusive restaurant, but unless his ability to do mental arithmetic had abandoned him, the prices on the menu were beyond belief. He ordered pasta and a glass of water. He was hungry. And his heartbeat was calm and regular. The other people in the restaurant were talking, smiling and laughing as though nothing could happen to them. It had always surprised him that it was not visible, that he did not have a black aura or that a chill—perhaps a stench of decay—did not radiate off of him.

Or, to be precise, that no one else noticed.

Outside, the town hall clock chimed its three notes six times.

"Nice place," Thea said, looking around. The restaurant had uncluttered views and their table gave on to the pedestrian walkway outside. From hidden speakers there was the barely audible murmur of meditative New Age music.

"I wanted it to be special," Jon said, studying the menu. "What would you like to eat?"

Thea ran a quick eye down the single page. "First I need something to drink."

Thea drank a lot of water. Jon knew it was connected with diabetes and her kidneys.

"It's not so easy to choose," she said. "Everything looks good, doesn't it?"

"But we can't have everything on the menu."

"No . . ."

Jon swallowed. The words had just come out. He peeked up at her. Thea obviously hadn't noticed.

All of a sudden she raised her head. "What did you mean by that?"

"By what?" he asked in a casual manner.

"Everything on the menu. You were trying to say something. I know you, Jon. What's up?"

He shrugged. "We agreed that before we get engaged, we would tell each other everything, didn't we?"

"Yes."

"Are you sure you've told me everything?"

She sighed, resigned. "I am sure, Jon. I have not been with anyone. Not . . . in *that* way."

But he could see something in her eyes, something in her expression he had not seen before. A muscle twitching beside her mouth, a darkening of her eyes, like an aperture closing. And he could not stop himself. "Not even with Robert?"

"What?"

"Robert. I can remember you two flirting the first summer in Østgård."

"I was fourteen years old, Jon!"

"So?"

At first she stared at him in disbelief. Then she seemed to churn inside; she closed up and cut him off. Jon grabbed her hand in both of his, leaned forward and whispered, "Sorry, sorry, Thea. I don't know what came over me. I . . . Can we forget I asked?"

"Have you made up your minds?"

Both of them looked up at the waiter.

"Fresh asparagus as a starter," Thea said, passing him the menu. "Chateaubriand with porcini mushrooms for the main course."

"Good choice. May I recommend a hearty, well-priced red wine we just got in?"

"You may, but water is fine," she said with a radiant smile. "Lots of water." Jon looked at her. Admired her ability to hide her emotions.

When the waiter had gone, Thea directed her gaze at Jon. "If you're finished interrogating me, what about yourself?"

Jon gave a thin smile and shook his head.

"You never did have a girlfriend, did you?" she said. "Not even at Østgård."

"And do you know why?" Jon said, placing his hand on hers.

She shook her head.

"Because I fell in love with one girl that summer," Jon said and regained her full attention. "She was fourteen years old. And I have been in love with her ever since."

He smiled and she smiled, and he could see she had reemerged from her hiding place, come over to where he was.

"Nice soup," said the minister for social affairs, turning to Commander David Eckhoff. But loud enough for the assembled press corps to hear.

"Our own recipe," the commander said. "We published a cookbook a couple of years ago we thought might be of . . ."

At a signal from her father, Martine approached the table and placed the book beside the minister's tureen.

". . . some use if the minister desired a good, nutritious meal at home."

The few journalists and photographers to turn up at the Lighthouse café chuckled. Otherwise attendance was sparse, a couple of elderly men from the hostel, a teary lady in a cape and a junkie who was bleeding from the forehead and trembling like an aspen leaf in dread of going up to the Field Hospital, the treatment room on the second floor. It was not very surprising there were so few people; the Lighthouse was not usually open at this time. However, a morning visit had not fit into the minister's schedule, so he did not see how full it normally was. The commander explained all of this. And how efficiently it was run and how much it cost. The minister nodded at intervals as, duty-bound, he put a spoonful of soup into his mouth.

Martine checked her watch. A quarter to seven. The minister's secretary had said seven o'clock. They had to go.

"That was delicious," the minister said. "Do we have time to talk to anyone here?"

The secretary nodded.

Playing to the gallery, Martine thought. Of course they have time to talk—that's why they are here. Not to apportion funds—they could have done that over the phone—but to invite the press and show a minister for social affairs moving among the needy, eating soup, shaking hands with junkies and listening with empathy and commitment.

The press aide signaled to the photographers that they could take photos. Or, to be more precise, that she wanted them to take photos.

The minister got to his feet and buttoned up his jacket as he scanned the room. Martine wondered how he would view his three options: the two elderly men looked like typical occupants of an old folks' home and would not serve the purpose: MINISTER MEETS DRUG ADDICTS, or PROSTITUTES, or something like that. There was something deranged about the injured junkie, and you can have too much of a good thing. But the woman . . . she seemed like a normal citizen, someone you could identify with and would like to help, especially if you heard her heartrending story first.

"Do you appreciate being able to come here?" the minister asked, reaching out with his hand.

The woman looked up at him. The minister said his name.

"Pernille . . ." the woman began, but was interrupted by the minister.

"Christian name's fine, Pernille. The press is here, you know. They would like a picture. Is that OK with you?"

"Holmen," the woman said, sniffling into her handkerchief. "Pernille Holmen." She pointed to the table where a candle burned in front of one of the photographs. "I'm here to commemorate my son. Would you mind please leaving me in peace?"

Martine stood at the woman's table while the minister plus retinue swiftly withdrew. She noted that they went for the two old men, after all.

"I'm sorry about what happened to Per," Martine said in

a low voice. The woman peered up with a face swollen from crying. And from pills, Martine guessed.

"Did you know Per?" she whispered.

Martine preferred the truth. Even when it hurt. Not because of her upbringing, but because she had discovered it made life easier in the long run. In the strangled voice, however, she could hear a prayer. A prayer for someone to say that her son was not only a drug-addicted robot, one less burden for society now, but a person someone could say he had known, been friends with, maybe even liked.

"Fru Holmen," Martine said with a gulp, "I knew him and he was a fine boy."

Pernille Holmen blinked twice and said nothing. She was trying to smile, but her attempts turned into grimaces. She just managed to say, "Thank you," before the tears began to flow down her cheeks.

Martine saw the commander waving to her from the table. Nevertheless, she sat down.

"They . . . they took my husband, too," Pernille Holmen sobbed.

"What?"

"The police. They say he did it."

As Martine left Pernille Holmen, she was thinking about the tall blond policeman. He had seemed so decent when he said he cared. She could feel her anger mounting. Also her confusion. Because she could not understand why she should be so angry at someone she didn't know. She looked at her watch. Five minutes to seven.

Harry had made fish soup. A Findus bag mixed with milk and supplemented with fish pudding. And French bread. All bought at Niazi, the little grocery store that his neighbor from the floor below, Ali, ran with his brother. Beside the soup plate on the sitting-room table was a large glass of water.

Harry put a CD into the machine and turned up the volume. Emptied his head and concentrated on the music and the soup. Sound and taste. That was all.

Halfway into the soup and the third track the telephone rang. He had decided to let it ring. But at the eighth ring he got up and turned down the music.

"Harry."

It was Astrid. "What are you doing?" She spoke in a low voice, but there was still an echo. He guessed she had locked herself into the bathroom at home.

"Eating and listening to music."

"I have to go out. Not far from you. Plans for the rest of the evening?"

"Yes."

"And they are?"

"Listening to more music."

"Hm. You make it sound like you don't want company."

"Maybe."

Pause. She sighed. "Let me know if you change your mind."

"Astrid?"

"Yes?"

"It's not you. OK? It's me."

"You don't need to apologize, Harry. If you're laboring under the illusion that this is vital for either of us, I mean. I just thought it could be nice."

"Another time, perhaps."

"Like when?"

"Like another time."

"Another time, another life?"

"Something like that."

"OK. But I'm fond of you, Harry. Don't forget that."

When he had put down the phone, Harry stood without moving, unable to take in the sudden silence. Because he was so astonished. He had visualized a face when Astrid rang. The astonishment was not because he had seen a face, but the fact that it was not Rakel's. Or Astrid's. He sank into the chair and decided not to spend any more time reflecting. If this meant that the medicine of time had begun to work and that Rakel was on her way out of his system, it was good news. So good that he didn't want to complicate the process.

He turned up the volume on his stereo and emptied his head.

He had paid the bill. He dropped the toothpick in the ashtray and looked at his watch. Three minutes to seven. The shoulder holster rubbed against his pectoral muscle. He took the photograph from his inside pocket and gave it a final glance. It was time.

None of the other customers in the restaurant—not even the couple at the neighboring table—took any notice of him as he got up and went to the restroom. He locked himself into one of the stalls, waited for a minute without succumbing to the temptation of checking that the gun was loaded. He had learned that from Bobo. If you got used to the luxury of double-checking everything, you would lose your sharpness.

The minute had passed. He went to the cloakroom, put on his raincoat, tied the red neckerchief and pulled the cap down over his ears. Opened the door onto Karl Johans Gate.

He hurried up to the highest point in the street. Not because he was in a rush, but because he had noticed that was how people walked here—the tempo that ensured you didn't stand out. He passed the garbage can on the lamppost where he had decided the day before that the gun would be dropped on the way back. In the middle of the busy pedestrian street. The police would find it, but it didn't matter. The point was that they didn't find it on him.

He could hear the music long before he was there.

A few hundred people had gathered in a semicircle in front of the musicians, who were finishing a song as he arrived. A bell pealed during the applause, and he knew he was on time. Inside the semicircle, on one side and in front of the band, a black cooking pot hung from three wooden sticks, and beside it the man in the photograph. In fact, street lamps and two flashlights were all the light they had, but there was no doubt. Especially since he was wearing the Salvation Army uniform coat and cap.

The vocalist shouted something into the microphone and people cheered and clapped. A flash went off as they started up again. Their playing was loud. The drummer raised his right hand high in the air every time he hit the snare drum.

He maneuvered his way through the crowd until he was standing about nine feet from the Salvation Army man and had checked that his back was clear. In front of him stood two teenage girls exhaling chewing-gum breath into the freezing air. They were smaller than he was. He had no particular thoughts in his head, he didn't hurry, he did what he had come to do, without any ceremony: took out the gun and held it with a straight arm. It reduced the distance to six feet. He took aim. The man by the cooking pot blurred into two. He relaxed and the two figures merged back into one.

"*Skål*," Jon said.

The music oozed out of the speakers like viscous cake batter.

"*Skål*," said Thea, obediently lifting her glass to his.

After drinking, they gazed into each other's eyes and he mouthed the words *I love you*.

She lowered her eyes with a blush, but smiled.

"I've got a little present for you," he said.

"Oh?" The tone was playful, coquettish.

He put his hand in his jacket pocket. Beneath the cell phone he could feel the hard plastic of the jeweler's box against his fingertips. His heart beat faster. Lord above, how he had looked forward to, yet dreaded, this evening, this moment.

The phone began to vibrate.

"Anything the matter?" Thea asked.

"No, I . . . sorry. I'll be back in a sec."

In the bathroom he took out the phone and read the display. He sighed and pressed the green button.

"Hi, sweetie. How's it going?"

The voice was jokey, as though she had just heard something funny that had made her think of him and then called, on an impulse. But his log showed six missed calls.

"Hi, Ragnhild."

"Weird sound. Are you—?"

"I'm in a bathroom. At a restaurant. Thea and I are here for a meal. We'll have to talk another time."

"When?"

"A . . . another time." Pause.

"Aha."

"I should have called you, Ragnhild. There's something I have to tell you. I'm sure you know what." He breathed in. "You and I, we can't—"

"Jon, it's almost impossible to hear what you're saying." Jon doubted that was true.

"Can I see you tomorrow night at your place?" Ragnhild said. "Then you can tell me?"

"I'm not free tomorrow night. Or any other—"

"Meet me at the Grand for lunch, then. I can text you the room number."

"Ragnhild, not—"

"I can't hear you. Call me tomorrow, Jon. Oh, no—I'm in meetings all day. I'll call you. Don't switch your cell off. And have fun, sweetie."

"Ragnhild?"

Jon read the display. She had hung up. He could go outside and call back. Get it over with. Now that he had started. That would be the proper thing to do. The wise thing to do. Give it the coup de grâce, kill it off.

They were standing opposite each other now, but the man in the Salvation Army didn't appear to see him. His breathing was calm, his finger on the trigger, then he slowly increased the pressure. And it flashed through his mind that the soldier showed no surprise, no shock, no terror. On the contrary, the light of understanding seemed to cross his face, as though the sight of the pistol gave him the answer to something he had been wondering about. Then there was a bang.

If the shot had coincided with the bang on the snare drum, the music might have drowned it out, but, as it was, the explosion made many turn around and look at the man in the raincoat. At his gun. And they saw the Salvation Army soldier, who now had a hole in the peak right under the *A* of his cap, fall backward as his arms swung forward like a puppet's.

Harry jerked in his chair. He had fallen asleep. The room was still. What had woken him? He listened, but all he could hear was the low, reassuringly even rumble. No, there was another sound there, too. He strained to hear. There it was. The sound was almost inaudible, but now that he had identified it, it rose in magnitude and became clearer. It was a low ticking sound.

Harry remained in his chair with closed eyes.

Then a sudden fury surged through him, and without thinking, he had marched into the bedroom, opened the bedside-table drawer, snatched Møller's wristwatch, opened the window and hurled it into the dark with as much force as he could muster. He heard the watch hit first the wall of the adjacent building and then the icy pavement in the street.

He slammed the window shut, fastened the catches, went back to the sitting room and turned up the volume. So loud that the speaker membranes vibrated in front of his eyes, the treble was wonderfully bright in his ears and the bass filled his mouth.

The crowd had turned away from the band and looked at the man lying in the snow. His cap had rolled away and come to a halt in front of the singer's mike stand while the musicians, who still had not realized what had happened, continued to play.

The two girls standing closest to the man in the snow retreated. One of them started to scream.

The vocalist, who had been singing with her eyes shut, opened them and discovered she no longer had the audience's attention. She turned and caught sight of the man in the snow. Her eyes sought a guard, an organizer, a gig manager, anyone who could deal with the situation, but this was just an ordinary street concert. Everyone was waiting for everyone else and the musicians kept playing.

Then there was a movement in the crowd and people cleared a path for the woman elbowing her way through.

"Robert!"

The voice was rough and hoarse. She was pale and wore a thin black leather jacket with holes in the sleeves. She staggered through to the lifeless body and fell on her knees beside him.

"Robert?"

She placed a skinny hand against his throat. Then she turned to the musicians.

"Stop playing, for Christ's sake."

One after another, the members of the band stopped playing.

"The man's dying. Get hold of a doctor. Quick!"

She put her hand back on his neck. Still no pulse. She

had experienced this many times before. Sometimes it was fine. As a rule it wasn't. She was confused. This couldn't be an overdose; a Salvation Army soldier wouldn't be doing drugs, would he? It had started to snow and the snowflakes were melting on his cheeks, the closed eyes and the half-open mouth. He was a good-looking young man. And she thought now—with his face relaxed—he looked like her own boy when he was asleep. Then she discovered the single red stripe going down from the tiny black hole in his head, across the forehead and temple and into his ear.

A pair of arms grabbed her and lifted her away while someone else bent over the young man. She caught a last glimpse of his face, then the hole, and it occurred to her with a sudden painful certainty that this fate was awaiting her boy, too.

He walked at a fast pace. Not too fast; he wasn't fleeing. Looked at the backs in front of him, spotted someone hurrying and followed in his wake. No one had tried to stop him. Of course they hadn't. The report of a gun makes people stand back. The sight of it makes them run away. And in this case most had not even absorbed what was going on.

The final job.

He could hear that the band was still playing.

It had started to snow. Great. That would make people look down to protect their eyes.

A few hundred yards down the street he saw the yellow station building. He experienced a feeling that he had from time to time, that everything was floating, that nothing could happen to him, that a Serbian T-55 tank was no more than a slow-moving iron monster, blind and deaf, and that his town would be standing when he returned home.

Someone was standing where he was going to drop the gun.

The clothes looked new and fashionable, apart from the

blue sneakers. But the face was lacerated and scorched, like a blacksmith's. And the man, or the boy, or whatever he was, looked as if he were there to stay. He had stuffed his entire right arm into the opening of the green garbage can.

Without slowing down, he checked his watch. Two minutes since he had fired the shot and eleven minutes to the departure of the train. And he still had the weapon on him. He walked past the garbage can and continued in the direction of the restaurant.

A man came toward him, staring. But didn't turn after they had passed each other.

He headed for the restaurant door and pushed it open.

In the cloakroom area a mother was bent over a boy, fiddling with a zipper on a jacket. Neither of them looked at him. The brown camel-hair coat was hanging where it should be, the suitcase underneath. He took both into the men's restroom, locked himself into one of the two stalls again, took off his raincoat, put the hat in the pocket and put on the camel-hair coat. Even though there were no windows, he could hear the sirens outside. Many sirens. He cast around him. Must get rid of the gun. There wasn't a great deal of choice. He stood on the toilet seat, stretched up to the white ventilation gap in the wall and tried to push the gun in there, but there was a grid inside.

He stepped back down. He was breathing hard now, and getting hot inside his shirt. Eight minutes to the train. He could take a later one, of course; that wasn't critical. What was critical was that five minutes had passed and he still hadn't got rid of the weapon, and she always said that anything over four minutes was an unacceptable risk.

Naturally, he could leave the gun on the floor, but they always worked on the principle that the gun should not be found before he was safe.

He left the stall and went to the sink. Washed his hands while his eyes scrutinized the deserted room. *Upomoć!* And stopped at the soap container over the sink.

*   *   *

Jon and Thea left the restaurant on Torggata with arms entwined.

Thea let out a scream as she slipped on the ice under the treacherous new snow. She almost dragged Jon down with her, but he saved them at the last minute. Her bright laughter pealed in his ears.

"You said yes!" he shouted to the sky and felt the snow-flakes melting on his face. "You said yes!"

A siren rang out in the night. Several sirens. The sounds came from the direction of Karl Johans Gate.

"Should we go and see what the fuss is?" Jon asked, taking her hand.

"No, Jon," said Thea, with a frown.

"Yes, come on, let's!"

Thea dug her feet into the ground, but the slippery soles couldn't find any purchase. "No, Jon."

But Jon just laughed and pulled her after him like a sled.

"No, I said!"

The sound of her voice was enough to make Jon let go at once. He looked at her in surprise.

She sighed. "I don't want to see a fire right now. I want to go to bed. With you."

Jon studied her face. "I am so happy, Thea. You have made me so happy." He couldn't hear what she replied. Her face was buried in his jacket.

PART TWO

The Redeemer

9

The Snow

The snow falling on Egertorget was stained yellow by the floodlights of the Crime Scene Unit.

Harry and Halvorsen stood outside the bar 3 Brødre, watching the spectators and the media pushing against the police barriers. Harry took the cigarette out of his mouth and gave a cough, throaty and moist. "Lots of press," he said.

"They were here in no time," Halvorsen said. "Only a stone's throw from their offices, of course."

"Juicy number. Murder in the midst of the Christmas scramble on Norway's most famous street. A victim everyone has seen: the guy standing by the Salvation Army pot. While a well-known band is performing. What more can they ask for?"

"An interview with celebrity investigator Harry Hole?"

"We'll stay here for the moment," Harry said. "What was the time of the murder?"

"A little after seven."

Harry looked at his watch. "That's almost an hour ago. Why didn't anyone call me before?"

"Dunno. I got a call from the POB a little before seven-thirty. I thought you would be here when I arrived . . ."

"So you called me on your own initiative?"

"Well, you're, like, the inspector, after all."

"Like," Harry mumbled, flicking the cigarette to the ground. It melted its way through the light covering of snow and vanished.

"All the evidence will soon be under a foot of snow," Halvorsen said. "Typical."

"There won't be any evidence," Harry said.

Beate was walking toward them with snow in her blond hair. Holding a small plastic bag between her fingers with an empty casing inside.

"Wrong," Halvorsen said to Harry with a triumphant smile.

"Nine-millimeter," Beate said, grimacing. "Most common ammo around. And that's all we've got."

"Forget what you have or haven't got," Harry said. "What was your first impression? Don't think, speak."

Beate smiled. She knew Harry now. First, intuition, then the facts. Because intuition provides facts, too; it's all the information the crime scene gives you, but which the brain cannot articulate right away.

"Not a great deal. Egertorget is the busiest square in Oslo. Hence we had an extremely contaminated scene even though we arrived twenty minutes after the man was killed. But it seems professional. The doctor is looking at the victim now—it looks like he was hit by one bullet. Right in the forehead. Pro. Yes, that's my instinct."

"Working by instinct, are we, Inspector?"

All three turned around to the voice behind them. It was Gunnar Hagen. He was wearing a green military jacket and a black wool cap. The smile was visible only at the corners of his mouth.

"We try anything that works, boss," Harry said. "What brings you here?"

"Isn't this where it happens?"

"In a way."

"Bjarne Møller preferred the office, I gather. As for me,

I believe that a leader should be in the field. Was more than one shot fired? Halvorsen?"

Halvorsen flinched. "Not according to the witnesses we've spoken to."

Hagen stretched the fingers of his gloves. "Description?"

"A man." Halvorsen's eyes flitted between the POB and Harry. "That's all we know so far. People were watching the band and the whole thing happened very quickly."

Hagen sniffed. "In a crowd like this someone must have got a good look at the gunman."

"You would think so," Halvorsen said. "But we don't know for certain where the man was standing."

"I see." Again the tiny smile.

"He was standing in front of the victim," Harry said. "Distance of six feet, maximum."

"Oh?" Hagen and the other two turned to Harry.

"Our gunman knew that if you want to kill someone with a small-caliber weapon, you shoot him in the head," Harry said. "Since he fired only one shot, he was sure of the result. Ergo, he must have been standing so close that he could see the hole in the forehead and know that he hadn't failed. If you examine his clothes, you should be able to find a fine gunshot residue that will prove what I am saying. Maximum six feet."

"Closer to five," Beate said. "Most guns eject the shell casing to the right, but not very far. This was found trampled into the snow four feet nine inches from the body. And the dead man had singed woolen threads on his coat sleeve."

Harry studied Beate. It was not primarily her innate ability to distinguish faces he appreciated, but her intelligence, zeal and the idiotic notion they shared: that the job they did was important.

Hagen stamped his feet in the snow. "Well done, Lønn. But who on earth would shoot a Salvation Army officer?"

"He wasn't an officer," Halvorsen said. "Just a normal soldier. Officers are permanent; soldiers are volunteers or work on contracts." He flipped open his notepad. "Robert Karlsen. Twenty-nine years old. Single, no children."

"Not without enemies, it seems," Hagen said. "Or what do you say, Lønn?"

Beate didn't look at Hagen, but at Harry, as she answered: "It might not have been directed at the individual."

"Oh?" Hagen smiled. "Who else could it have been directed at?"

"The Salvation Army, perhaps."

"What makes you think that?"

Beate shrugged.

"Controversial views," Halvorsen said. "Homosexuality. Women priests. Abortion. Perhaps some fanatic or other . . ."

"The theory has been noted," Hagen said. "Show me the body."

Both Beate and Halvorsen sent Harry a quizzical look. Harry nodded toward Beate.

"Jeez," Halvorsen said when Hagen and Beate had gone. "Is the POB intending to take over the investigation?"

Harry, his eye on the cordon where the media photographers were lighting up the winter darkness with their flashes, rubbed his chin, deep in thought. "Pro," he said.

"What?"

"Beate said the perp was a pro. So let's start there. What's the first thing a pro does after a murder?"

"Makes his escape?"

"Not necessarily. But at any rate he gets rid of anything that can link him to the shooting."

"The weapon."

"Right. I want all repositories, containers, garbage cans and backyards in a five-block radius of Egertorget checked. Now. Request uniformed backup, if necessary."

"OK."

"And get all the videocassettes from surveillance cameras in shops in the area from before seven o'clock to well after."

"I'll get Skarre to do that."

"And one more thing. *Dagbladet* also has a hand in organizing the street concerts, and they write articles about them. Check whether their photographer took any pictures of the spectators."

"Of course. I hadn't thought of that."

"Send the photos to Beate for her to take a look. And I want all the detectives assembled in the meeting room in the red zone at ten tomorrow. Will you contact them?"

"Yes."

"Where are Li and Li?"

"They're questioning witnesses at the station. A couple of girls were standing next to him when he fired."

"OK. Ask Ola to make a list of family and friends of the victim. That's where we'll start to see if there are any obvious motives."

"I thought you said this was the work of a pro?"

"We have to keep several balls in the air at once, Halvorsen. And start looking wherever it seems promising. Family and friends are easy to find, as a rule. Eight out of ten murders are committed—"

"By someone who knows the victim." Halvorsen sighed.

They were interrupted by someone calling Harry Hole. They turned in time to see the press bearing down on them through the snow.

"Showtime," Harry said. "Point them to Hagen. I'm headed for the station."

The suitcase had been checked in with the airline and he was walking toward security. He was in high spirits. The final job was done. He was in such a good mood that he decided to run the gauntlet. The woman at security nodded her head when he took the blue envelope from his inside pocket to show his ticket.

"Cell phone?" she asked.

"No." He put the envelope on the table between the X-ray machine and the metal detector while taking off his camel-hair coat, discovered he was still wearing his neckerchief, removed it and put it in the pocket, placed the coat in the tray the official gave him and walked through the detector, watched by two additional pairs of alert eyes. Including the man screening his coat, and the one at the end of the conveyor belt, he counted five security people whose sole job it was to make sure he didn't take anything with him that could be used as a weapon on board the plane. On the other side of the detector, he put on his coat and went back to collect his ticket on the table. No one stopped him, and he walked past the officials. That is how easy it would have been to smuggle a knife blade through in the envelope. He emerged into the large departure hall. The first thing that struck him was the view from the enormous panoramic window. There wasn't one. The snow had drawn a white curtain in front of the scene outside.

Martine sat bent over the steering wheel as the windshield wipers swished the snow away.

"The minister was positive," David Eckhoff said with satisfaction. "Very positive."

"You already knew that," Martine said. "People like that don't come for soup and invite the press if they're going to say no. They want to be re-elected."

"Yes," Eckhoff said with a sigh. "They have to be re-elected." He looked out the window. "Good-looking boy, Rikard, isn't he?"

"You're repeating yourself, Daddy."

"He just needs a bit of guidance to be a really good man for us." Martine drove down to the garage under the headquarters and pressed the remote control. The steel doors jolted open. They rumbled in and the studded tires crunched over the concrete floor of the empty parking garage.

Beneath one of the roof lights, beside the commander's blue Volvo, stood Rikard, wearing overalls and gloves. But it wasn't him she was looking at. It was the tall blond man standing next to him; she recognized him instantly.

She parked alongside the Volvo, but sat in the car searching for something in her bag while her father got out. He left the door open and she heard the policeman say:

"Eckhoff?" The sound echoed off the walls.

"That's right. Anything I can help you with, young man?"

The daughter recognized the voice her father had assumed. The friendly but authoritative commander's voice.

"My name is Inspector Harry Hole, Oslo district. It's about one of your employees. Robert . . ."

Martine could feel the policeman's eyes on her as she got out of the car.

". . . Karlsen," Hole went on, turning back to the commander.

"A brother," David Eckhoff said.

"I beg your pardon?"

"We like to think of our colleagues as members of a family."

"I see. In that case, I am afraid I have to announce a death in the family, Herr Eckhoff."

Martine felt her chest constrict. The policeman waited to let it sink in before continuing: "Robert Karlsen was shot dead in Egertorget at seven o'clock this evening."

"Good God," her father exclaimed. "How?"

"All we know is that an unidentified person in the crowd shot him and fled the scene."

Her father shook his head in disbelief. "But . . . but at seven o'clock, you say? Why . . . why haven't I been told until now?"

"Because there are routine procedures in cases like these and we inform relatives first. I regret to say we have not been able to get hold of them."

Martine realized from the detective's factual, patient response that he was accustomed to people reacting to news of bereavement with that kind of irrelevant question.

"I understand," Eckhoff said, blowing out his cheeks and then releasing the air through his mouth. "Robert's parents don't live in Norway anymore, but you must have contacted his brother, Jon."

"He's not at home, and he isn't answering his cell phone. I was told he might be here at headquarters, working late. However, the only person I've met is this young man." He nodded toward Rikard, who was standing there with glazed eyes like a dejected gorilla, arms limp, hanging down by his sides and capped off with enormous specialist gloves, sweat gleaming from his blue-black top lip.

"Any idea where I can find the brother?" the policeman asked. Martine and her father looked at each other and shook their heads.

"Any idea who would want to take Robert Karlsen's life?" Again, they shook their heads.

"Well, now you know. I need to get going, but we would like to come back to you with more questions tomorrow."

"Of course, Inspector," the commander said, straightening up. "But before you go, might I ask you for more details about what has happened?"

"Send me a text. I have to go."

Martine watched her father's face change color. Then she turned toward the policeman and met his gaze.

"I apologize," he said. "Time is an important factor in this phase of the investigation."

"You . . . you could try my sister's place. Thea Nilsen." All three of them turned to Rikard. He gulped. "She lives in the Army building on Gøteborggata."

The policeman nodded. He was about to go when he turned back to Eckhoff.

"Why don't the parents live in Norway?"

"It's a long story. They lapsed."

"Lapsed?"

"They abandoned their faith. People brought up in Army ways often find it difficult when they choose a different path."

Martine observed her father. But not even she—his daughter—could detect the lie in his granite features. The policeman moved off, and she felt the first tears flow. After the sound of his footsteps had faded away, Rikard cleared his throat. "I put the summer tires in the trunk."

By the time the announcement finally came over Gardermoen Airport's PA system, he had already guessed:

"Due to weather conditions, the airport has been temporarily closed." Matter-of-fact, he said to himself. Like an hour before, when the first announcement was made about the delay due to snow.

They had waited while the snow laid thick blankets over the aircraft outside. He had kept an unconscious eye on uniformed personnel. They would be uniformed at an airport, he imagined. And when the woman in blue behind the counter by Gate 42 lifted the microphone, he could see it written all over her face. The flight to Zagreb was canceled. She was apologetic. Said it would depart at 10:40 the following morning. There was a collective but muted groan from the passengers. She went on that the airline would cover the cost of the train back to Oslo and a room at the SAS hotel for transit passengers and those traveling on a return ticket.

Matter-of-fact, he thought once more, as the train flew through the blackened night landscape. It stopped just once before Oslo, at an assortment of houses on white terrain. A dog sat shivering under one of the benches on the platform as the snow drifted in cones of light. It looked like Tinto, the playful stray that had run around the neighborhood in Vukovar when he was small. Giorgi and a couple of the other older boys had given it a leather collar inscribed NAME:

TINTO; OWNER: SVI ("Everyone"). No one had wished Tinto any harm. No one. Sometimes that wasn't enough.

Jon had moved to the end of the room that was not visible from Thea's front door while she went to open it. It was Emma, the neighbor: "I'm so sorry, Thea, but this man needs to get hold of Jon Karlsen as a matter of urgency."

"Jon?"

A man's voice: "Yes. I've been informed that I might be able to find him at this address with a Thea Nilsen. There were no names downstairs by the bells, but this lady has been very helpful."

"Jon here? I don't know how—"

"I'm from the police. My name is Harry Hole. It's about Jon's brother."

"Robert?"

Jon stepped toward the door. A man of his height with bright-blue eyes looked at him from the doorway. "Has Robert done something wrong?" he asked, trying to ignore the neighbor, who was standing on tiptoes to see over the policeman's shoulder.

"We don't know," the man said. "May I come in?"

"Please do," Thea said.

The detective stepped inside and closed the door in the neighbor's disappointed face. "I'm afraid it's bad news. Perhaps you ought to sit down."

The three of them sat around a coffee table. It was like a punch to the stomach, and Jon's head shot forward in automatic response to what the policeman told him.

"Dead?" he heard Thea whisper. "Robert?"

The policeman cleared his throat and continued talking. The words seemed like dark, cryptic, barely comprehensible sounds to Jon. All the time he was listening to the detective explaining the circumstances, he was focusing on one point. On Thea's half-open mouth and sparkling lips, moist, red. Her breathing came in short, rapid pants. Jon didn't notice that the policeman had stopped speaking until he heard Thea's voice:

"Jon? He asked you a question."

"Sorry. I . . . what did you say?"

"I know this is a difficult time, but I was wondering whether you know of anyone who might have wished to kill your brother."

"Robert?" Everything around Jon seemed to be happening in slow motion, even the shake of his head.

"Right," the policeman said, without making a note on the pad he had just produced. "Is there anything in his job or private life that might have made him enemies?"

Jon heard his own inappropriate laughter. "Robert's in the Salvation Army," he said. "Our enemy is poverty. Material and spiritual. It's rare for any of us to be killed."

"Mm. That's the job. What about private life?"

"What I said applied to both job and private life."

The policeman waited.

"Robert was kind," Jon said and heard his voice starting to disintegrate. "Loyal. Everyone liked Robert. He . . ." His voice thickened and stopped.

The policeman looked around the room. He didn't seem comfortable with the situation, but he waited. And waited.

Jon kept swallowing. "He could be a little wild now and then. A bit . . . impulsive. Some may have considered him a little cynical. But that was the way he was. Deep down, Robert was a harmless boy."

The policeman turned to Thea and looked down at his notes. "You're Thea Nilsen, sister of Rikard Nilsen, I gather. Does this tally with your impression of Robert Karlsen?"

Thea shrugged. "I didn't know Robert so well. He . . ." She had crossed her arms and avoided Jon's gaze. "He never hurt anyone, as far as I am aware."

"Did Robert ever say anything that might suggest he was in conflict with anyone?"

Jon shook his head hard, as though there were something inside he was trying to get rid of. Robert was dead. Dead.

"Did Robert owe any money?"

"No. Yes. Me. A little."

"Sure he didn't owe anyone else money?"

"What do you mean?"

"Did Robert take drugs?"

Jon stared at the policeman in horror, then replied: "No, he did not."

"How can you know for sure? It's not always—"

"We work with drug addicts. We know the symptoms. And Robert didn't take drugs. OK?"

The policeman nodded and took notes. "Sorry, but we have to ask these things. Naturally, we cannot exclude the possibility that the man who fired the gun was insane and Robert was an arbitrary victim. Or—since the Salvation Army soldier standing by the Christmas pot is a symbol—that the killing was directed against your organization. Are you aware of anything that would support the latter theory?"

As though synchronized, the two young people shook their heads.

"Thank you for your help." The policeman stuffed the notepad in his coat pocket and stood up. "We haven't been able to find a telephone number or address for your parents . . ."

"I'll take care of that," Jon said, staring into empty space. "Are you quite sure?"

"Sure about what?"

"That it is Robert?"

"Yes, I'm afraid so."

"But that's all you're sure about," Thea burst out. "Otherwise you know nothing."

The policeman paused in front of the door and considered her comment.

"I think that's a fairly accurate summary of the situation," he said.

At two o'clock in the morning the snow stopped. The clouds that had been hanging over the town like a heavy black stage curtain were drawn to one side and a large yellow moon made its appearance. The temperature beneath the naked sky began to fall again, making house walls creak and groan.

10

The Doubter

The seventh day before Christmas Eve broke with such freezing temperatures that people on the streets of Oslo felt they were being squeezed by a steel glove as they hurried in silence, focused on one thing: to arrive and escape its icy grip.

Harry was sitting in the meeting room in the red zone at Police HQ listening to Beate Lønn's demoralizing report while trying to ignore the newspapers in front of him on the table. They all had the murder on the front page; they all had a grainy photo of a winter-dark Egertorget, with references to two or three pages of articles inside the paper. *Verdens Gang* and *Dagbladet* had managed to cobble something together that, with a little goodwill, might be termed portraits of Robert Karlsen, based on random, hasty conversations with friends and acquaintances. "A nice guy." "Always willing to lend a hand." "Tragic." Harry had read through them with a fine-toothed comb, but was unable to find anything of value. No one had contacted the parents, and *Aftenposten* was the only newspaper to run a quotation from Jon: "Incomprehensible" was the brief caption under a picture of a man with a bewildered expression and tousled hair in front of the Army apartments on Gøteborggata. The article was written by an old friend of Harry's, Roger Gjendem.

Harry scratched his thigh through a tear in his jeans, thinking he ought to have put on some long johns. On arriving for work at seven-thirty he had gone to Hagen to ask him who was leading the investigation. Hagen had looked at him and replied that he, together with the chief superintendent, had decided that Harry would lead it. Until further notice. Harry had not asked for an elaboration of what "until further notice" meant; he nodded and left.

From ten o'clock onward twelve detectives from Crime Squad plus Beate Lønn and Gunnar Hagen, who had wanted to "come along for the ride," had sat in discussion.

And Thea Nilsen's assessment from the previous evening was as accurate as before.

First of all, they had no witnesses. None of those who had been in Egertorget had seen anything of value. The closed-circuit TV footage was still being checked, but so far nothing had been found. None of the employees they had spoken to in the shops and restaurants on Karl Johans Gate had noticed anything unusual, and no other witnesses had come forward. Beate, who had been sent pictures of the spectators by *Dagbladet* the night before, had reported back that they were either close-ups of smiling girls or panning shots that were too indistinct to get a decent look at facial characteristics. She had magnified sections of the latter, highlighting the audience in front of Robert Karlsen, but she hadn't spotted a weapon or anything else that would identify the person they were searching for.

Second, they had no forensic evidence, except that the ballistics expert at Krimteknisk had established that the projectile that had penetrated Robert Karlsen's head in fact matched the empty casing they had found.

And, third, they didn't have a motive.

Beate Lønn finished and Harry turned it over to Magnus Skarre.

"This morning I spoke to the boss of the Fretex shop on Kirkeveien where Robert Karlsen worked," said Skarre, whose surname, with fate's usual impish sense of humor, meant "to roll your *r*'s," and indeed he did. "She was devastated and said Robert was a person everyone liked, full of charm and good cheer. She conceded he could be a bit unpredictable, not turning up for work on the odd occasion, but she could not imagine he would have any enemies."

"Same comments from those I've interviewed," said Halvorsen. During the discussion Gunnar Hagen had sat with his hands folded behind his head, watching Harry with a tiny expectant smile, as though he were at a magic show and waiting for Harry to pull a rabbit out of a hat. But there was nothing. Apart from the usual suspects. The theories.

"Guesses?" Harry said. "Come on. You're allowed to make asses of yourselves. After this meeting is over, permission is withdrawn."

"Shot down in full view of everyone, in one of Oslo's busiest areas," Skarre said. "There's only one line of business that does this kind of thing. This is a professional hit job to deter others who don't pay their drug debts."

"Well," said Harry, "none of the undercover guys in Narcotics has seen or heard of Robert Karlsen. He's clean. No priors, nothing. Has anyone here heard of drug addicts who have never been arrested?"

"Forensics didn't find any illegal substances in the blood samples," Beate said. "Nor was there any mention of needle marks or other indications."

Hagen cleared his throat and the others turned around. "A Salvation Army soldier would not be involved in that sort of thing. Go on." Harry noticed red patches developing on Magnus Skarre's forehead. Skarre was short and stocky, an ex-gymnast, with smooth brown hair and a side part. He was one of the youngest detectives, an arrogant and ambitious arriviste who in many ways was reminiscent of a young Tom Waaler. But without Waaler's very special intelligence and talent for police work. In the last year, however, Skarre's self-confidence had evaporated somewhat, and Harry had begun to think it was not impossible that they would make a decent policeman out of him after all.

"On the other hand, Robert Karlsen had an experimental bent," Harry said. "And we know that addicts can serve their sentences in Fretex shops. Curiosity and accessibility are a bad combination."

"Exactly," Skarre said. "And when I asked the lady in Fretex whether Robert was single, she said she thought so. Even though there had been a foreign girl in a couple of times asking after him, but she seemed too young. She guessed the girl came from somewhere in the former Yugoslavia. Bet you she's Kosovar Albanian."

"Why's that?" Hagen asked.

"Kosovar Albanian. Drugs."

"Whoa there," clucked Hagen, rocking back on his chair. "That sounds like gross prejudice, young man."

"Right," Harry said. "And our prejudices solve cases. Because they are not based on lack of knowledge, but on actual facts and experience. In this room we reserve the right to discriminate against everyone, regardless of race, religion or gender. Our defense is that it is not exclusively the weakest members of society who are discriminated against."

Halvorsen grinned. He had heard this rule before.

"Homosexuals, true believers and women are, from a statistical point of view, more law-abiding than heterosexual men between eighteen and sixty. But if you are female, lesbian and a Kosovar Albanian with religious convictions, the chances that you are drug-dealing are nevertheless a lot higher than for a fat, Norwegian-speaking, male chauvinist pig with tattoos all over his forehead. So if we have to choose—and we do—we bring in the Albanian woman for questioning first. Unfair to law-abiding Kosovar Albanians? Of course. But since we work with probabilities and limited resources, we cannot afford to ignore knowledge wherever we find it. If experience had taught us that an unexpectedly high percentage of those we arrested at customs at Gard-ermoen Airport were wheelchair users smuggling drugs in their orifices, we would put on rubber gloves, drag them out of their chairs, and finger-fuck every single one of them. We just keep our mouths shut about that sort of thing when we talk to the press."

"Interesting philosophy, Hole." Hagen checked around to gauge the reaction among the others, but the closed faces told him nothing. "Well, back to the case."

"OK," Harry said. "We'll continue where we left off, searching for the murder weapon, but the area will be increased to a radius of six blocks. We'll continue questioning witnesses and take a trip around the shops that were closed last night. We won't waste any more time on closed-circuit TV footage. Let's wait until we have something specific to look for. Li and Li, you have the address of Robert Karlsen's flat and the search warrant. Gørbitz Gate, isn't it?"

Li and Li nodded.

"Check out his office as well. You may find something of interest there. Bring any correspondence and hard disks here from both places so that we can see who he's been in contact with. I have spoken to Kripos, who contacted Inter-pol today to find out if there are similar cases in Europe. Halvorsen, you're coming with me to the Salvation Army headquarters later. Beate, I would like a few words with you after the meeting. Get going!"

Scraping of chairs and shuffling of feet.

"One moment, gentlemen!"

Silence. They looked at Gunnar Hagen.

"I can see that some of you are coming to work in ragged jeans and items of clothing advertising what I assume is the Vålerenga soccer team. The previous boss may have approved of that, but I do not. The press will be following us with Argus eyes. From tomorrow I want to see clothing that is whole and intact and does not display advertising slo-gans. The general public is out there and we want to be seen as neutral public servants. And I would ask all of you with the rank of inspector or above to remain."

As the room emptied, Harry and Beate stayed behind.

"I'm going to draw up a document for all inspectors in the unit, instructing them to carry weapons, starting next week," Hagen said.

Harry and Beate both looked at him incredulously.

"The war is heating up out there," Hagen said, raising his chin. "We have to get used to the idea that weapons will be a necessity in the police force of the future. And then high-ranking officers will have to set an example and show the way. A weapon must not be an unfamiliar item but a normal tool of the trade like a cell phone or a computer. OK?"

"Well," Harry said, "I don't have a firearms license."

"I assume you're joking," Hagen said.

"I missed the test last autumn and had to hand in my gun."

"I'll issue a license. I have the authority to do that. You'll find a requisition order in your mailbox here and you can pick the weapon up. No one will be exempt. That's all."

Hagen departed.

"He's out of his mind," Harry said. "What the hell do we need guns for?"

"Time to patch our jeans and buy a gun belt then, eh?" Beate said with a glint of amusement in her eyes.

"Mm. I wouldn't mind a look at the pictures *Dagbladet* took of Egertorget."

"Help yourself." She passed him a yellow folder. "May I ask you something, Harry?"

"Goes without saying."

"Why did you do that?"

"Do what?"

"Why did you defend Magnus Skarre? You know he's a racist and you didn't mean one iota of what you said about discrimination. Is it to irritate the new POB? Or make sure you're really unpopular from day one?"

Harry opened the envelope. "You'll get the photos back later."

He stood by the window of the Radisson SAS Hotel on Holbergs Plass, looking out over the white, frozen town at the break of day. The buildings were low and modest; it was strange to think this was the capital of one of the richest countries in the world. The Royal Palace was an anonymous yellow construction, a compromise between a pietistic democracy and a penniless monarchy. Through the branches of the naked trees he glimpsed a large balcony. The King must have addressed his subjects from there. He raised an imaginary rifle to his shoulder, closed one eye and took aim. The balcony blurred into two.

He had dreamed about Giorgi.

The first time he had met Giorgi he had been crouching by a whimpering dog. The dog was Tinto, but who was this boy with blue eyes and blond curly hair? Working together, they had managed to get Tinto into a wooden box and carry it to the town vet, who lived in a gray two-room brick house in an overgrown apple orchard down by the river. The vet had diagnosed dental problems and said he was no dentist. Besides, who would pay for an aging stray that would soon lose the rest of its teeth? It would be better to put it to sleep now to avoid the pain and a slow death by starvation. But then Giorgi had started crying. High-pitched, heartrending, almost melodic crying. And when the vet had asked why he was crying, Giorgi had said perhaps the dog was Jesus, because his father had told him that Jesus walked among us, was one of the humblest of us, well, maybe even a poor, pathetic dog that no one would give either shelter or food. With a shake of his head, the vet had called the dentist. After school he and Giorgi had gone back to see a tail-wagging Tinto, and the vet had shown them the fine black fillings in the dog's mouth.

Although Giorgi was in the grade above him, they had

played together a few times after that. But it lasted just a few weeks because the summer vacation had begun. And when school started up again in the autumn, Giorgi seemed to have forgotten him. At any rate, he ignored him as though wanting nothing to do with him.

He had forgotten about Tinto, but he never forgot Giorgi. Several years later, though, during the siege, he had come across an emaciated dog in the ruins at the southern end of the town. It had trotted over to him and licked his face. It had lost its leather collar, and it was only when he saw the black fillings that he had realized it was Tinto.

He checked his watch. The bus to take them to the airport would arrive in ten minutes. He grabbed his suitcase, threw a last glance around the room to make sure he hadn't forgotten anything. Paper rustled as he pushed open the door. He looked down the corridor and saw the same newspaper lying outside several of the rooms. The picture of the crime scene on the front page met his eyes. He bent down and picked up the thick newspaper bearing a name in illegible Gothic script.

While he was waiting for the elevator, he tried to read, but although some of the words somehow reminded him of German, he understood next to nothing. Instead, he flicked through to the pages referred to on the front. At that moment the elevator doors opened, and he decided to put the large, unwieldy newspaper in the garbage can between the two elevators. But the elevator was empty, so he kept it, pressed the ground floor and concentrated on the pictures. His eye was caught by the text beneath one of the pictures. At first he didn't believe what he was reading. But as the elevator jolted into action he realized something with such horrible certainty that he went dizzy for a second and had to support himself against the wall. The newspaper almost fell out of his hand, and he didn't see the elevator doors opening in front of him.

When, at last, he did look up, he was staring into the

darkness, and he knew he was in the basement and not in reception, which for some strange reason was floor one in this country.

He stepped out of the elevator, and the doors closed behind him. In the dark he sat down and tried to think clearly. Because this upset all his plans. The airport bus left in eight minutes. That was all the time he had to make a decision.

"I'm trying to look at some pictures here," Harry said in desperation.

Halvorsen peered up from his desk opposite Harry's. "Be my guest."

"Stop snapping your fingers, then. Why do you do that?"

"This?" Halvorsen looked at his fingers, snapped them and, a little abashed, laughed. "It's just an old habit."

"Oh, yes?"

"My dad was a fan of Lev Yashin, the Russian goalkeeper in the sixties." Harry waited for him to go on.

"My dad wanted me to be the goalie at the Steinkjer club. So when I was small he used to snap his fingers between my eyes. Like this. To harden me, so that I wouldn't be afraid of shots at goal. Apparently, Yashin's father had done the same. If I didn't blink, I got a sugar cube." The words were followed by a moment of total silence in the office.

"You're kidding," Harry said.

"No. Nice brown sugar."

"I meant the snapping. Is it true?"

"Absolutely. He did it all the time. During mealtimes, when we were watching TV, even when my pals were there. In the end I started doing it to myself. I wrote 'Yashin' on all my schoolbags and carved his name into my desk. Even now I always use it as my password on computer programs or anything that needs one. Despite knowing that I am being manipulated. Do you understand?"

"No. Did the snapping help?"

"Yes, I'm not afraid of shots coming at me."

"So you . . ."

"No. Turned out I had no ball sense."

Harry pinched his top lip between two fingers.

"Can you see anything in the pictures?" Halvorsen asked.

"Not when you're sitting there snapping your fingers. And talking."

Halvorsen gave a slow shake of the head. "Shouldn't we be on our way to the Salvation Army headquarters?"

"When I've finished. Halvorsen!"

"Yes?"

"Do you have to breathe so . . . *weirdly*?"

Halvorsen clamped his mouth shut and held his breath. Harry's eyes shot up and back down again. Halvorsen thought he caught a hint of a smile. But he wouldn't have put money on it. Now the smile was gone, replaced by a deep furrow in the inspector's brow.

"Come take a look at this, Halvorsen."

Halvorsen walked around the desks. There were two photographs in front of Harry, both of the crowds in Egertorget.

"Can you see the man with the wool hat and neckerchief at the side?" Harry pointed to a grainy face. "He's right in line with Robert Karlsen on the very edge of the band, isn't he?"

"Yes . . ."

"But look at this picture. There. The same hat and the same neckerchief, but now he's in the middle, right in front of the band."

"Is that so strange? He must have moved to the middle to hear and see better."

"But what if he did that in reverse order?" Halvorsen didn't answer, so Harry went on. "You don't change a place at the front for somewhere by the speaker where you can't see the band. Unless you have a good reason."

"To shoot someone?"

"Cut the flippancy."

"OK, but you don't know which photo was taken first. I bet he moved to the middle."

"How much?"

"Two hundred."

"Done. Look at the light under the lamppost. It's in both photos." Harry passed Halvorsen a magnifying glass. "Can you see any difference?"

Halvorsen nodded slowly.

"Snow," Harry said. "On the photo with him at the side it's snowing. When it started in the evening, yesterday, it didn't stop until well into the night. So that photo was taken later. We'll have to call that Wedlog guy from *Dagbladet*. If he was using a digital camera with an internal clock, he may have the precise time the photo was taken."

Hans Wedlog, from *Dagbladet*, was one of those who swore by single-lens reflex cameras and rolls of film. Hence, as far as the timing of individual photos was concerned, he had to disappoint the inspector.

"OK," Hole said. "Did you cover the concert last night?"

"Yes, Rødberg and I do all the street-music stuff."

"If you use rolls of film, you must have crowd shots lying around somewhere, right?"

"Yes, I do. And I wouldn't if I used a digital camera. They would have been deleted already."

"That's what I was wondering. I was also wondering whether you would do me a favor."

"Yes?"

"Could you check your film from the day before yesterday to see if you can find a guy with a wool hat and a black raincoat? And a neckerchief. We're poring over one of your photos right now. Halvorsen can scan it in and send it to you if you're near a computer."

Harry could hear from Wedlog's voice that he had reservations. "I can send you the photos, no problem, but checking them sounds like police work, and as a press guy I don't want to get any lines crossed here."

"We're a little short on time, I'm afraid. Would you like a photo of the police suspect or not?"

"Does that mean you would let us print it?"

"Yep."

Wedlog's voice warmed up. "I'm in the lab now, so I can check right away. I took loads of pictures of the crowd, so there's hope. Five minutes." Halvorsen scanned the photo in and sent it, and Harry drummed his fingers while they waited.

"What makes you so sure he was there the evening before?" Halvorsen asked.

"I'm not sure of anything," Harry said. "But if Beate is right and he is a pro, he would have done a reconnoiter, and preferably at a time when conditions were as similar to those of the planned hit as possible. And there was a street concert the day before."

The five minutes came and went. Eleven minutes later the phone rang.

"Wedlog here. Sorry—no wool hats and no black raincoats. And no neckerchief."

"Fuck," Harry said, loud and clear.

"Apologies. Should I send them over so that you can check them for yourself? I had the lights focused on the audience that night. You'll have a better view of the faces."

Harry hesitated. It was important to decide how time was allocated, especially in these critical first twenty-four hours.

"Send them and we'll look at them later," Harry said, on the verge of giving Wedlog his email address. "By the way, better if you send them to Lønn at Krimteknisk. She's got a thing about faces. Perhaps she can see something." He gave Wedlog the address. "And I don't want my name mentioned, OK?"

"Course not. It'll be an 'anonymous source in the police force.' Nice to do business with you."

Harry put down the receiver and nodded to a wide-eyed Halvorsen. "OK, Junior, let's head for the Salvation Army headquarters."

Halvorsen glanced over at Harry. The inspector was unable to conceal his impatience as he scanned the bulletin board and the announcements about visiting preachers, music rehearsals and duty rosters. At length the uniformed, gray-haired receptionist was finished with incoming phone calls and turned to them with a smile.

Harry told her the purpose of their visit in swift, concise terms. She nodded as though she had been expecting them, and gave them directions.

They didn't speak as they waited for the elevator, but Halvorsen could see the beads of sweat on the inspector's brow. He knew Harry didn't like elevators. They got out on the fifth floor and Halvorsen followed Harry at a canter through the yellow corridors, which culminated in an open office door. Harry came to such an abrupt halt that Halvorsen almost crashed into him.

"Hello there," Harry said.

"Hi," said a woman's voice. "Is it you again?"

Harry's sizable figure filled the doorway and prevented Halvorsen from seeing who was speaking, but he noted the change in Harry's voice. "Indeed it is. The commander?"

"He's waiting for you. Just go in."

Halvorsen followed Harry through the small anteroom, with a quick nod to a small girl-woman behind a desk. The walls of the commander's office were decorated with wooden shields, masks and spears. On the well-stacked bookshelves were carved African figures and pictures of what Halvorsen supposed were the commander's family.

"Thank you for seeing us at such short notice, Herr Eck-hoff," Harry said. "This is Officer Halvorsen."

"Tragic thing," said Eckhoff, who had got up from behind his desk and indicated two chairs with his hand. "The press has been on our backs all day. Let me hear what you have so far."

Harry and Halvorsen exchanged glances.

"We don't wish to go public with it yet, Herr Eckhoff."

The commander's eyebrows sank menacingly close to his eyes. Halvorsen released a silent sigh and prepared himself for yet another of Harry's cockfights. But then the commander's eyebrows shot back up.

"Forgive me, Inspector Hole. Occupational hazard. As the commanding officer here, I sometimes forget that not everyone reports to me. How can I help?"

"In a nutshell, I was wondering whether you could imagine any potential motives for what has happened."

"Hm. Of course, I have thought about this. It's difficult to see any causes. Robert was a mess, but a nice boy. Quite different from his brother."

"Jon isn't nice?"

"He's not a mess."

"What sort of messes was Robert involved in?"

"Involved? You're suggesting things of which I know nothing. I meant that Robert had no direction in his life, unlike his brother. I knew their father well. Josef was one of our best officers. But he lost his faith."

"You said it was a long story. Would it be possible to have a short version?"

"Good question." The commander heaved a heavy sigh and gazed out the window. "Josef was working in China at the time of floods. Few there had heard about Our Lord, and they were dying like flies. No one, according to Josef's interpretation of the Bible, would be saved unless they received Jesus; they would burn in hell. He was distributing medicines in the Hunan Province. The floodwaters were full of Russell's vipers and many people had been bitten. Even though Josef and his team had taken a whole chest of serum with them, they tended to arrive too late because this snake has a hemotoxic venom that dissolves artery walls and makes victims bleed from the eyes, ears and all other orifices, killing them within one to two hours. I was myself witness to the effects of this venom when I was working as a missionary in Tanzania and saw people bitten by boom-slangs. A terrible sight."

Eckhoff closed his eyes for a moment.

"However, in one of the villages, Josef and his nurse were giving penicillin to twins who both had pneumonia. While they were doing this, the father came in. He had just been bitten by a Russell's viper in the water on the rice paddy. Josef Karlsen had one dose of serum left, which he asked the nurse to load into a syringe and give to the man. In the meantime Josef went outside to evacuate as he, like many others, had stomach cramps and diarrhea. While he was crouching in the floodwater he was bitten in the tes-ticles and screamed so loudly that everyone knew what had happened. When he returned to the house, the nurse said the Chinese heathen refused to let her inject him because if Josef had also been bitten, he wanted Josef to have the serum: If Josef was allowed to live, he reasoned, he could save many children's lives, and he was only a farmer who didn't even have a farm anymore."

Eckhoff took a breath.

"Josef said he was so frightened he didn't even consider rejecting the offer, and told the nurse to give him the injec-tion at once. Afterward he began to cry while the Chinese farmer tried to console him. After he'd finally pulled him-self together he asked the nurse to inquire whether the Chi-nese heathen had heard of Jesus. She didn't even have time to pose the question because the farmer's trousers started to run red with blood. He died within seconds."

Eckhoff watched them as though waiting for the story to sink in. A trained preacher's pause for effect, thought Harry.

"So the man is burning in hell now?"

"According to Josef's understanding of the Bible, yes. However, Josef has renounced religion now."

"So that was the reason he lost his faith and left the country?"

"That was what he told me."

Harry nodded and spoke to the notepad he had taken out: "So now Josef Karlsen will burn because he was unable to accept . . . er, the paradox about faith. Have I understood correctly?"

"You're moving into a difficult area for theologians, Hole. Are you a Christian?"

"No. I'm a detective. I believe in proof."

"Which means?"

Harry sneaked a look at his watch and hesitated before giving a rapid answer, delivered in flat intonation.

"I have problems with a religion that says faith in itself is enough for a ticket to heaven. In other words, that the ideal is your ability to manipulate your own common sense to accept something your intellect rejects. It's the same model of intellectual submission that dictatorships have used throughout time, the concept of a higher reasoning without any obligation to discharge the burden of proof."

The commander nodded. "A considered objection, Inspector. And of course you are not the first to have made it. Nevertheless, there are a great many far more intelligent people than you or I who believe. Is that not a paradox to you?"

"No," Harry said. "I meet a lot of people who are more intelligent than me. Some of them kill for reasons neither you nor I can fathom. Do you think Robert's murder might have been directed against the Salvation Army?"

The commander's instinctive reaction was to sit bolt upright in his chair. "If you think this is the action of a politically motivated group, I doubt it. The Salvation Army line has always been to remain neutral in political matters. And we have been pretty consistent in this. We didn't even come out with a public condemnation of the German occupation during the Second World War. We went about our work as before."

"Congratulations," Halvorsen commented drily, and received a warning glare from Harry.

"The one invasion we have given our blessing to is that of 1888," Eckhoff said, undaunted, "when the Swedish Salvation Army decided to occupy Norway, and we had the first soup station in the poorest working-class district of Oslo. Where your Police HQ is situated now, you know."

"No one bears a grudge against you for that, I would imagine," Harry said. "It seems to me that the Salvation Army is more popular than ever."

"Well, yes and no," Eckhoff said. "We enjoy the trust of the Norwegian people. We can feel that. But recruitment is so-so. This autumn there were only eleven cadets at the officer-training school in Asker, although the residence hall has room for sixty. And since it is our policy to adhere to a conservative interpretation of the Bible on issues such as homosexuality, it goes without saying that we are not popular in all quarters. We will catch up, we will—we're just a little slower than our more liberal counterparts. But do you know what? I think in our changing times it doesn't matter so much if some things move a little slower." He smiled at Halvorsen and Harry in a way that suggested they had expressed agreement. "Anyway, younger personnel will take over. With a younger view of things, I assume. At the moment we are about to appoint a new chief of administration and some very young candidates have applied." He placed a hand on his stomach.

"Was Robert one of them?" Harry asked.

The commander shook his head with a smile. "I can say with confidence he was not. But his brother, Jon, is.

The appointee will have control over considerable sums of money, among them all our properties, and Robert was not the type you would give that kind of responsibility. He hadn't been to the officer-training school, either."

"Are the properties the ones on Gøteborggata?"

"We have many. Our own employees live on Gøteborggata while other places, such as on Jacob Aalls Gate, are used to house refugees from Eritrea, Somalia and Croatia."

"Mm." Harry looked at his notepad, slapped the pen down on the arm of the chair and stood up. "I think we've taken up enough of your time, Herr Eckhoff."

"Oh, it wasn't so much. After all, this is a matter that concerns us." The commander followed them to the door.

"May I ask you a personal question, Hole?" the commander asked. "Where have I seen you before? I never forget a face, you see."

"Maybe on the TV or in the paper," Harry said. "There was a great deal of fuss about me in connection with the murder of a Norwegian national in Australia."

"No, I forget those faces. I must have seen you in the flesh."

"Can you go and get the car?" Harry said to Halvorsen. When Halvorsen had gone, Harry turned to the commander.

"I don't know, but the Army helped me once," he said. "Picked me up off the street one winter's day when I was so drunk that I couldn't look after myself. The soldier who found me wanted to call the police at first, since he thought they could do the job better. However, I explained that I worked for the police and that would mean the sack. So he took me down to the Field Hospital, where I was given an injection and allowed to sleep. I owe you all a big debt of gratitude."

David Eckhoff nodded. "Well, I thought it was something like that, though I didn't want to say. And, as far as the gratitude is concerned, I think we should forget it for the time being. We will be indebted to you if you find the person who killed Robert. God bless you and your work, Hole."

Harry nodded and walked into the anteroom, where he remained for a moment, gazing at Eckhoff's closed door.

"You're very similar," Harry said.

"Oh?" came the woman's deep voice. "Was he severe?"

"I mean in the photograph."

"Nine years old," said Martine Eckhoff. "You did well to recognize me."

Harry shook his head. "By the way, I meant to get in touch. I wanted to talk to you."

"Oh?"

Harry could hear how that sounded and hastened to add: "About Per Holmen."

"Is there anything to talk about?" she replied with an indifferent shrug of her shoulders, although the temperature of her voice had fallen. "You do your job and I do mine."

"Maybe. But I . . . well, I wanted to say it was not quite the way it may have looked."

"And how did it look?"

"I told you I cared about Per Holmen. And ended up ruining what was left of his family. That's what my job is like sometimes."

She was going to answer when the telephone rang. She lifted the receiver and listened.

"Vestre Aker Church," she replied. "Sunday the twenty-first, at twelve o'clock. Yes."

She put down the phone.

"Everyone will be going to the funeral," she said, flicking through paperwork. "Politicians, clergy and celebs. Everyone wants a chunk of us in our hour of sorrow. The manager of one of our new singers phoned to say his client could sing at the funeral."

"Well," Harry said, wondering what he was going to say, "it's—"

But the telephone rang again so he didn't find out. He knew it was time for a quick exit, nodded and walked toward the door.

"I've put Ole down for Wednesday in Egertorget," he heard her say behind him. "Yes, for Robert. So the question is whether you can do the soup bus with me tonight."

In the elevator he cursed under his breath and rubbed his face with his hands. Then he let out a desperate laugh. The way you laugh at terrible clowns.

Robert's office seemed, if possible, even smaller today. And just as chaotic. The Salvation Army flag dominated, next to the icy patterns on the window, and the pocketknife was stuck in the desk beside a pile of papers and unopened envelopes. Jon was sitting at the desk letting his gaze wander across the walls. It stopped at a picture of Robert and himself. When was that taken? In Østgård, of course, but which summer? In the photograph Robert was trying to remain serious, but couldn't restrain a smile. His smile seemed unnatural, forced.

Jon had read the newspapers today. It was unreal, although he knew all the details, as if it were all about someone else and not Robert.

The door opened. Outside stood a tall blond woman in a military-green pilot's jacket. Her mouth was narrow and bloodless, her eyes hard and neutral, her features expressionless. Behind her stood a red-haired squat man with a round, boyish countenance and the type of grin that seems to be etched into some people's faces. They greet all news with it, good or bad.

"Who are you?" asked the woman.

"Jon Karlsen." When he saw the woman's eyes become even harder he went on. "I'm Robert's brother."

"My apologies," the woman said in a monotone, coming

into the room and proffering her hand. "Toril Li, police officer with Crime Squad." Her hand was bone-hard, but warm. "This is Officer Ola Li."

The man nodded and Jon returned the nod.

"We're sorry about what happened," the woman said. "But since this is a murder case, we have to seal off this room."

Jon continued nodding while his eyes found their way back to the photo on the wall.

"I'm afraid that means we have to . . ."

"Oh, yes, of course," Jon said. "Sorry—I'm not quite with it."

"Entirely understandable," Toril Li replied with a smile. Not a broad, heartfelt smile, but a small, friendly one, appropriate for the situation. Jon was thinking that the police must have experience of this kind of thing, working with murders and so on. Like priests. Like his father.

"Have you touched anything?" she asked.

"Touched? No, why would I do that? I've been sitting in the chair." Jon got up and, without knowing why, pulled the knife out of the desk, folded it and put it in his pocket.

"It's all yours," he said, leaving the room. The door was closed quietly behind him. He had reached the stairs when he realized it was an idiotic thing to do, to walk off with the knife, and he turned to take it back. Outside the closed door, he heard the woman laughing. "My goodness, what a shock that gave me! He's the spitting image of his brother. At first I thought I was seeing a ghost."

"They don't look at all similar," said the man.

"You've only seen a photo . . ."

A terrible thought struck Jon.

Flight SK-655 to Zagreb took off from Gardermoen Airport, at 10:40 on the dot, banked left over Lake Hurdal and set a course south, toward the navigation tower in Aalborg,

Denmark. Since it was an unusually cold day the atmospheric layer known as the tropopause had sunk so low that the McDonnell Douglas MD-81 was already climbing through it when they were over central Oslo. And since planes in the tropopause leave vapor trails in the sky, he would have seen—if he had looked up from where he was standing and shivering by the phone booths in Jernbanetorget—the plane he had a ticket for.

He had left his bag in a luggage locker in Oslo Central Station. Now he needed a hotel room. And he had to complete the job. And that meant he had to have a gun. But how to get hold of one in a town where you don't have a single contact?

He listened to the woman in directory assistance explaining in singsong Scandinavian English that there were seventeen entries in the Oslo telephone book for people under the name of Jon Karlsen and she was afraid that she could not give him all of them. However, yes—she could give him the number for the Salvation Army.

The lady at Salvation Army headquarters said they had a Jon Karlsen, but he was not at work today. He told her he wanted to send him a Christmas present. Did she have his home address?

"Let me see. Four Gøteborggata, post number oh-five-six-six. Nice that someone is thinking about him, poor thing."

"Poor thing?"

"Yes, his brother was shot dead yesterday."

"Brother?"

"Yes, in Egertorget. It's in today's paper."

He thanked her for her help and hung up.

Something touched him on the shoulder and he whirled around.

It was the paper cup that explained what the young man wanted. True, the denim jacket was a little grubby, but he was clean-shaven, had a modern hairstyle, substantial clothes and an open, alert gaze. The young man said something, but when he demonstrated with a shrug that he didn't speak Norwegian, the young man broke into perfect English:

"I'm Kristoffer. I need money for a room tonight. Or else I'll freeze to death."

It sounded like something he had learned in a marketing course, a brief and concise message plus his name, to add an effective emotional immediacy. The request came with a broad smile.

He shook his head and made to go, but the beggar stood in front of him with the cup. "Come on, mister. Haven't you ever had to sleep on the street, frozen, dreading the night?"

"As a matter of fact I have." For one crazy moment he felt like telling him he had hidden in a water-filled foxhole for four days waiting for a Serbian tank.

"Then you know what I'm talking about, mister."

He answered with a slow nod. Stuffed his hand in his pocket, took out a note and gave it to Kristoffer without looking. "You'll sleep on the street anyway, won't you?"

Kristoffer pocketed the money, nodded and said with an apologetic smile: "Have to make my medicine the priority, mister."

"Where do you usually sleep?"

"Down there." The junkie pointed and he followed the long, slim forefinger. "Container terminal. They're going to build an opera house there in the summer." Kristoffer flashed another broad smile. "And I love opera."

"Isn't it a little cold there now?"

"Tonight it might have to be the Salvation Army. They always have a free bed in the hostel."

"Do they?" He studied the boy. He looked well groomed, and his smile revealed a set of shining white, even teeth. Nevertheless he smelled decay. As he listened, he thought he could hear the crunching of a thousand jaws, of flesh being consumed from inside.

11

The Croatian

Halvorsen sat patiently behind the steering wheel, waiting for the car with the Bergen license plate in front of him. Its wheels spun around on the ice as the driver pressed the accelerator to the floor. Harry was talking to Beate on his cell phone.

"What do you mean?" Harry shouted to drown out the noise of the racing engine.

"It doesn't look like it's the same person in these two pictures," Beate repeated.

"It's the same wool hat, same raincoat and same neckerchief. It must be the same person."

She didn't answer.

"Beate?"

"The faces are unclear. There's something strange. I'm not quite sure what. Maybe something to do with the light."

"Mm. Do you think we're on a wild-goose chase?"

"I don't know. His position in front of Karlsen tallies with the technical evidence. What's all that noise?"

"Bambi on ice. See you."

"Hang on!" Harry hung on.

"There's one more thing," Beate said. "I looked at the other pictures, from the day before."

"Yeah?"

"I can't see any faces that match, but there is one small detail. There's a man wearing a yellowish coat, maybe a camel-hair coat. He's got a scarf . . ."

"Mm. A neckerchief, you mean?"

"No, it looks like an ordinary wool scarf, but it's tied in the same way as he—or they—ties the neckerchief. The right-hand side sticks up from the knot. Have you seen it?"

"No."

"I've never seen anyone tie a scarf in that way before," Beate said.

"Email me the pictures and I'll take a look."

The first thing Harry did upon getting back to the office was to print out Beate's pictures.

When he went to the print room to collect them, Gunnar Hagen was already there.

Harry nodded, and the two men stood in silence, watching the gray machine spitting out sheet after sheet.

"Anything new?" Hagen asked at length.

"Yes and no," Harry replied.

"The press are on my back. Would be good if we had something to give them."

"Ah, yes, I almost forgot to say, boss: I tipped them off that we were looking for this man." Harry took one of the printouts from the pile and pointed to the man with the neckerchief.

"You did what?" Hagen said.

"I tipped off the press. To be exact, *Dagbladet*."

"Without going through me?"

"Routine number, boss. We call them constructive leaks. We say the information is from an anonymous source in the police so that the newspaper can pretend they have been doing serious investigative journalism. They like that, so they give it more column space than if we had asked them to publish pictures. Now we can get some help from the general public to identify the man. And everyone is happy."

"I'm not, Hole."

"I'm genuinely sorry to hear that then, boss," Harry said, and underlined the genuineness with a concerned expression.

Hagen glared at him with his upper and lower jaw moving sideways in opposite directions, in a kneading motion that reminded Harry of a ruminant.

"And what is so special about this man?" Hagen said, snatching the printout from Harry.

"We're not quite sure. Maybe there are many of them. Beate Lønn thinks they . . . well, tie the neckerchief in a particular way."

"That's a cravat knot." Hagen took another look. "What about it?"

"What did you say it was, boss?"

"A cravat knot."

"Do you mean a tie knot?"

"A Croat knot, man."

"What?"

"Isn't this basic history?"

"I'd be grateful if you would enlighten me, boss."

Hagen placed his hands behind his back. "What do you know about the Thirty Years' War?"

"Not enough, I suppose."

"During the Thirty Years' War, before he marched into Germany, Gustav Adolf, the Swedish king, supplemented his disciplined but small army with what were reckoned to be the best soldiers in Europe. They were the best because they were considered totally fearless. He hired Croat mercenaries. Did you know that the Norwegian word *krabat* comes from Swedish and its original meaning was *Croat*, in other words, a fearless maniac?"

Harry shook his head.

"Although the Croatians were fighting in a foreign country and had to wear King Gustav Adolf's uniform, they were allowed to retain a marker to distinguish them from the others: the cavalry neckerchief. It was a neckerchief the Croatians tied in a special way. The item of clothing was adopted and developed further by the French, but they kept the name, which became *cravate*."

"*Cravate*. Cravat."

"Exactly."

"Thank you, boss." Harry took the last printout of the pictures off the paper tray and studied the man with the scarf Beate had identified. "You may just have given us a clue."

"We don't need to thank each other for doing our jobs, Hole." Hagen took the rest of the printouts and marched out.

Halvorsen peered up as Harry raced into the office.

"Got a lead," Harry said. Halvorsen sighed. This phrase tended to mean loads of work and nothing to show for it.

"I'm going to call Alex in Europol," Harry said.

Halvorsen knew Europol was Interpol's little sister in The Hague, set up by the EU, after the terrorist attacks in Madrid in 1998, to focus specifically on international terror and organized crime. What he didn't know was why this Alex was often willing to help Harry when Norway was not in the EU.

"Alex? Harry, from Oslo. Could you check something out for me, please?" Halvorsen listened to Harry asking Alex in his jerky but effective English to search the database for offenses committed by suspected international criminals in Europe over the last ten years. Search words: "contract killing" and "Croatian."

"I'll wait," Harry said, and waited. Then, in surprise,

"That many?" He scratched his chin, then asked Alex to add "gun" and "nine-millimeter" to the search.

"Twenty-three hits, Alex? Twenty-three murders with a Croatian as the suspect? Jesus! Well, I know that wars create professional hit men, but nevertheless. Try 'Scandinavia.' Nothing? OK, do you have any names, Alex? None? Hang on a sec."

Harry looked at Halvorsen as though hoping for a few timely words, but Halvorsen just shrugged.

"OK, Alex," Harry said. "One last attempt."

He asked him to add "red neckerchief" or "scarf" to the search. Halvorsen could hear Alex laughing on the line.

"Thanks, Alex. Talk to you soon." Harry put down the receiver.

"Well?" said Halvorsen. "Lead gone up in smoke?"

Harry nodded. He had slumped a few notches lower in his chair, but then straightened up with a start. "We have to think along new lines. What have we got? Nothing? Great—I love blank sheets of paper."

Halvorsen remembered Harry had once said that what separates a good detective from a mediocre one is the ability to forget. A good detective forgets all the times his gut instinct lets him down, forgets all the leads he has believed in that led nowhere. And pitches in, naïve and forgetful again, with undiminished enthusiasm.

The telephone rang. Harry snatched at the receiver. "Harr—" But the voice at the other end was already in full flow.

Harry got up from behind the desk and Halvorsen could see the knuckles on his hand around the receiver going white.

"Wait, Alex. I'll ask Halvorsen to take notes."

Harry held his hand over the receiver and called to Halvorsen: "He tried one last time for fun. Dropped 'Croatian,' 'nine-millimeter' and the other things, and searched under 'red scarf.' Found Zagreb in 2000 and 2001. Munich in 2002 and Paris in 2003."

Harry went back to the phone. "This is our man, Alex. No, I'm not sure, but my gut is. And my head says that two murders in Croatia are not a coincidence. Do you have any further details Halvorsen can jot down?"

Halvorsen watched Harry gape in astonishment.

"What do you mean, *no description*? If they remembered the scarf, they must have noticed other things. What? Normal height? Is that all?"

Harry shook his head as he listened.

"What's he saying?" Halvorsen whispered.

"Wide discrepancies between statements," Harry whispered back. Halvorsen noted down "discrepancies."

"Yes, great—email me the details. Well, thanks for now, Alex. If you find anything else, such as a suspected haunt or something like that, give me a buzz, OK? What? Ha-ha. Right, I'll send you a copy of me and my wife."

Harry hung up and noticed Halvorsen's quizzical stare.

"Old joke," Harry said. "Alex thinks all Scandinavian couples make private porn films."

Harry dialed another number, discovered while he was waiting for an answer that Halvorsen was still looking at him and sighed. "I've never even been married, Halvorsen."

Magnus Skarre had to shout to be heard over the coffee machine, which appeared to be suffering from a serious lung condition. "Perhaps there are a number of hit men from a hitherto-unknown gang who wear red scarves as a kind of uniform."

"Bullshit," drawled Toril Li, taking her place in the coffee line behind Skarre. She was holding an empty mug with the slogan THE WORLD'S BEST MOM.

Ola Li gave a little chuckle. He took a seat by the table

inside the kitchenette, which functioned as a cafeteria for the Crime and Vice squads.

"Bullshit?" said Skarre. "It could be terrorism, couldn't it? Holy war against the Christians? Muslims. Then all hell would be let loose. Or perhaps it's *los dagos*. They wear red scarves, don't they?"

"They prefer to be called Spaniards," said Toril Li.

"Basques," said Halvorsen, sitting at the table across from Ola Li.

"Eh?"

"The running of the bulls. San Fermin in Pamplona. The Basque country."

"ETA!" shouted Skarre. "Shit—why didn't we think of them before?!"

"You should write film scripts," Toril Li said. Ola Li was laughing out loud now, but said nothing, as usual.

"And you two should stick to bank robbers on Rohypnol," Skarre mumbled, referring to the fact that Toril Li and Ola Li, who were neither married nor related, had come from the Robberies Unit.

"There's just the little detail that terrorists tend to claim responsibility," Halvorsen said. "The four cases we received from Europol were *hits*, and then it all went quiet afterward. And the victims have generally been involved in something or other. Both the victims in Zagreb were Serbs who had been acquitted of war crimes, and the one in Munich had been threatening the hegemony of a local baron involved in people smuggling. And the guy in Paris was a pedophile with two previous convictions."

Harry Hole wandered in with a mug in his hand. Skarre, Li and Li filled their cups and, instead of sitting down, ambled off. Halvorsen had noticed that Harry had that effect on colleagues. The inspector sat down, and Halvorsen saw the troubled furrow in his brow.

"Soon be twenty-four hours," Halvorsen said.

"Yes," said Harry, staring into his still-empty mug.

"Is anything the matter?"

Harry paused. "I don't know. I called Bjarne Møller in Bergen. To get some constructive ideas."

"What did he say?"

"Not a great deal. He sounded . . ." Harry searched for the word. "Lonely."

"Isn't his family with him?"

"They were supposed to follow."

"Trouble?"

"Don't know. I don't know anything."

"What's bothering you, then?"

"He was drunk."

Halvorsen knocked his mug of coffee and spilled it. "Møller? Drunk at work? You're kidding."

Harry didn't answer.

"Maybe he wasn't well or something like that?" Halvorsen added.

"I know what a drunken man sounds like, Halvorsen. I have to go to Bergen."

"Now? You're leading a murder investigation, Harry."

"I'll be there and back in a day. You hold the fort in the meantime."

Halvorsen smiled. "Are you getting old, Harry?"

"Old? What do you mean?"

"Old and human. That's the first time I've heard you give the living priority over the dead."

The instant Halvorsen saw Harry's face he was filled with regret. "I didn't mean . . ."

"That's fine," Harry said, standing up. "I want you to get hold of the passenger lists of all flights to and from Croatia over the last few days. Ask the police at Gardermoen Airport whether you need a prosecutor to make an application. Should you need a court order, pop over to the court and get it on the spot. When you have the lists, call Alex in Europol and ask him to check the names for us. Say it's for me."

"And you're sure he can help?"

Harry nodded. "In the meantime Beate and I will go have a chat with Jon Karlsen."

"Oh?"

"So far, all we've heard about Robert Karlsen is pure Disney. I think there's more."

"Why aren't you taking me along?"

"Because Beate, unlike you, knows when people are lying."

He breathed in before tackling the steps up to the restaurant called Biscuit.

The difference from the previous evening was that there were almost no people around. But the same waiter was leaning against the door to the dining room. The one with the Giorgi curls and the blue eyes.

"Hello there," said the waiter. "I didn't recognize you."

He blinked twice, caught unawares by the fact that it meant he *had* been recognized.

"But I recognized the coat," the waiter said. "Very stylish. Is it camel hair?"

"I hope so," he stammered with a smile.

The waiter laughed and placed a hand on his arm. He didn't see a trace of fear in the man's eyes and concluded the waiter was without suspicions. And hoped that meant the police had not been here and therefore had not found the gun.

"I don't want to eat," he said. "I just want to use the bathroom."

"The bathroom?" repeated the waiter, and he saw the blue eyes scanning his. "You came here to use the bathroom? Really?"

"A quick visit," he said, swallowing. The waiter's presence made him uneasy.

"A quick visit," repeated the waiter. "I see."

The men's room was empty and smelled of soap. But not freedom.

The smell of soap was even stronger when he flipped up the lid of the soap dispenser. He rolled up his sleeve and thrust his hand down into the cold green mush. For an instant a thought shot through his mind: that they had changed soap dispensers. But then he felt it. Slowly he fished it out, and the soap dripped long, green fingers on the white porcelain basin. After a rinse and a little oil, the gun would be fine. And he still had six bullets in the magazine. He hurriedly rinsed the gun and was about to put it in his coat pocket when the door opened.

"Hello again," the waiter whispered with a big smile. But the smile went rigid when he caught sight of the gun.

He slipped it into his pocket, mumbled a good-bye and forced his way past the waiter in the narrow doorway. He felt rapid breathing against his face and the other man's erection on his thigh.

It was only when he was out in the cold again that he became aware of his heart. It was pounding. As though he had been frightened. The blood streamed through his body, making him feel warm and light.

Jon Karlsen was on his way out as Harry arrived on Gøteborggata.

"Is it that late?" Jon asked with a glance at his watch, confused.

"I'm a little early," Harry said. "My colleague will be along in a moment."

"Do I have time to buy some milk?" He was wearing a thin jacket and his hair was combed.

"By all means."

The corner shop was on the other side of the street, and while Jon was rummaging for the change to buy a quart of low-fat milk, Harry studied the lavish selection of Christmas decorations between the toilet paper and the cereal boxes. Neither of them commented on the newspaper stand by the cash desk on which the Egertorget murder screamed out at them in bold capitals. The front page of *Dagbladet* carried a blurred, grainy crop of Wedlog's picture of the crowd, with a red circle around the head of the person with the scarf and the headline: POLICE SEEK THIS MAN.

They went out and Jon stopped in front of a beggar with red hair and a seventies goatee. He searched long and hard in his pocket until he found something he could drop in the brown paper cup.

"I don't have much to offer you," Jon said to Harry. "And, to tell the truth, the coffee has been standing in the percolator for a while. Probably tastes like tar."

"Great—that's just how I like it."

"You, too?" Jon Karlsen gave a pale smile. "Ow!" Jon held his head and turned to the beggar. "Are you throwing money at me?" he asked in astonishment.

The beggar snorted into his beard in annoyance and shouted in a clear voice: "Legal tender only, thank you!"

Jon Karlsen's flat was identical to Thea Nilsen's. It was clean and tidy, but the interior still bore the unmistakable signs of bachelorhood. Harry drew three quick assumptions: that the old but well-looked-after furniture came from the same place as his, namely Elevator, the second-hand shop on Ullevålsveien; that Jon had not been to the art exhibition the solitary poster on the sitting-room wall was advertising; and that more meals were eaten bent over the low table in front of the TV than in the place provided in the kitchenette. On the almost-empty bookshelf there was a photograph of a man in a Salvation Army uniform looking out into space with an authoritative air.

"Your father?" Harry asked.

"Yes," Jon answered, taking two mugs from the kitchen cupboard and pouring from a stained brown coffee jug.

"You look very similar."

"Thank you," said Jon. "I hope that's true." He brought the mugs in and deposited them on the coffee table next to the fresh carton of milk. Harry was going to ask how his parents had taken the news of Robert's death, but changed tack.

"Let's begin with the hypothesis," Harry said, "that your brother was killed because he had done something to someone. Tricked them, borrowed money from them, insulted them, threatened them, hurt them or whatever. Your brother was a good guy; everyone says that. And that's what we tend to hear in murder cases. People like to emphasize the good sides. Most of us have dark sides, though. Don't we?"

Jon nodded, although Harry was unable to decide whether this was a sign of agreement or not.

"What we need is some light shed on Robert's dark sides."

Jon stared, uncomprehending.

Harry cleared his throat. "Let's start with money. Did Robert have any financial problems?"

Jon shrugged. "No. And yes. He didn't exactly live in style so I can't imagine he had incurred huge debts, if that's what you mean. By and large he borrowed from me, if he needed money, I think. By borrowing I mean . . ." Jon's smile was wistful.

"What sort of sums are we talking about?"

"Not big ones. Apart from this autumn."

"How much?"

"Er . . . thirty thousand."

"For what purpose?"

Jon scratched his head. "He had a project, but wouldn't expand on it. Just said he would need to travel abroad. I would find out, he said. Yes, I thought it was quite a lot of money, but I live cheaply and I don't have a car. And for once he seemed so enthusiastic. I was curious about what it was, but then . . . well, then this happened."

Harry took notes. "Mm. What about Robert's darker sides, as a person?"

He waited. Studied the coffee table and let Jon sit and think while the vacuum of silence took effect, the vacuum that sooner or later always elicited something: a lie, a despairing digression or, in the best-case scenario, the truth.

"When Robert was young he was . . ." Jon ventured, then stopped. Harry, motionless, said nothing.

"He lacked . . . inhibition."

Harry nodded, without looking up. Gave encouragement, without disturbing the vacuum.

"I used to dread what he might be up to. He was so violent. There seemed to be two people inside him. One was the cold, controlled investigative type who was curious about . . . what should I say? Reactions. Feelings. Suffering, too, perhaps. That sort of thing."

"Can you give me any examples?" Harry asked.

Jon swallowed. "Once when I came home he said he had something to show me in the laundry room in the cellar. He had put our cat in a small empty aquarium, where Dad had kept guppies, and stuffed the end of the garden hose in under a wooden lid on the top. Then he turned the tap on full. Things moved so fast that the aquarium was almost full before I managed to remove the lid and rescue the cat. Robert said he wanted to see how the cat would react, but now and then I have wondered whether it was in fact me he was observing."

"Mm. If he was like that, it's strange no one mentioned it."

"Not many people knew that side of Robert. I suppose it was partly my own fault. From the time we were small I had to promise Dad I would keep an eye on Robert so that he didn't get into any real trouble. I did what I could. Robert's behavior was, as I said, not out of control. He could be hot and cold at the same time, if you understand. So only those closest to him had a sense of Robert's . . . other sides. Well, and the occasional frog." Jon smiled. "He launched them into the air in helium balloons. When Dad caught him, Robert said it was so sad to be a frog and never be able to get a bird's-eye view. And I . . ." Jon stared into space and Harry could see his eyes becoming moist. "I started to laugh. Dad was furious, but I couldn't help myself. Robert could make me laugh like that."

"Mm. Did he grow out of this?"

Jon shrugged. "To be honest, I don't know everything Robert has been doing in recent years. Since Mom and Dad moved to Thailand, Robert and I have not been so close."

"Why's that?"

"That sort of thing often happens between brothers. There doesn't have to be any reason."

Harry didn't answer, just waited. A door slammed in the hallway.

"There were a few incidents with girls," Jon said.

The distant sound of ambulance sirens. An elevator with a metallic hum. Jon breathed out with a sigh. "Young girls."

"How young?"

"I don't know. Unless Robert was lying, they must have been very young."

"Why would he lie?"

"As I said, I think he liked to see how I would react."

Harry stood up and went over to the window. A man was ambling across Sofienberg Park along a path that looked like an uneven brown line drawn by a child on a white piece of paper. To the north of the church was a small enclosed cemetery for the Jewish community. Ståle Aune, the psychologist, had once told him that hundreds of years ago the whole park had been a cemetery.

"Was he violent toward any of these girls?" Harry asked.

"No!" Jon's exclamation echoed among the bare walls. Harry said nothing. The man had left the park and was crossing Helgesens Gate toward their building.

"Not as far as I know," Jon said. "And if he had told me he had been, I wouldn't have believed him."

"Do you know any of the girls he met?"

"No. He never stayed with them for long. As a matter of fact there was just one girl I know he was serious about."

"Oh?"

"Thea Nilsen. He was obsessed with her when we were young boys."

"Your girlfriend?"

Jon gazed thoughtfully into his coffee cup. "You would think I could keep away from the one girl my brother had made his mind up he would have, wouldn't you? And God knows I have wondered why."

"And?"

"All I know is that Thea is the most fantastic person I've ever met." The hum of the elevator came to a sudden stop.

"Did your brother know about you and Thea?"

"He found out that we had met a couple of times. He had his suspicions, but Thea and I have been trying to keep it a secret."

There was a knock at the door.

"That'll be Beate, my colleague," Harry said. "I'll get it."

He turned over his notepad, placed his pen parallel to it and walked the few steps to the front door. He struggled for a few seconds until he realized it opened inward. The face he met was as surprised as his own, and for a moment they stood looking at each other. Harry noticed a sweet, perfumed smell, as if the other person used a strong aromatic deodorant.

"Jon?" the man asked tentatively.

"Of course," Harry said. "Sorry—we were expecting someone else. One moment."

Harry went back to the sofa. "It's for you."

The instant he flopped down into the soft cushion, it struck Harry that something had happened, right now in the last few seconds. He checked that his pen was still parallel with the pad. Untouched. But there was something; his brain had detected something he couldn't place.

"Good evening?" he heard Jon say behind him. Polite, reserved form of address. Rising intonation. The way you greet someone you don't know. Or when you don't know what they want. There it was again. Something happened, something grated. There was something about him. He had used Jon's first name when he asked after him, but it was obvious Jon didn't know him.

"What message?" Jon said.

Then it clicked into place. The neck. The man was wearing something around his neck. A neckerchief. The cravat knot. Harry put both hands on the coffee table to lever himself up, and the cups went flying as he screamed: "Shut the door!"

But Jon stood staring through the doorway, as if hypnotized. He stooped to listen.

Harry stepped back one pace, jumped over the sofa and sprinted for the door.

"Don't—" Jon said.

Harry aimed and launched himself. Then everything seemed to stop. Harry had experienced it before, when the adrenaline kicks in and changes your perception of time. It was like moving in water. And he knew it was too late. His right shoulder hit the door, his left Jon's hip and his eardrum received the sound waves of the exploding gunpowder and a bullet leaving a gun.

Then came the bang. The bullet. The door slamming into the frame and locking. Jon hitting the cupboard and the kitchen unit. Harry swiveled onto his side and looked up. The door handle was being pressed down.

"Fuck," Harry whispered, getting to his knees. The door was shaken hard, twice.

Harry grabbed Jon's belt and dragged him, lifeless, over the parquet floor to the bedroom.

There was a scratching sound outside the door. Then another bang. Splinters flew from the middle of the door, one of the cushions on the sofa jerked, a column of grayish-black down rose to the ceiling and the carton of low-fat milk began to gurgle. A jet of milk described a weak white arc onto the table.

The damage a nine-millimeter projectile can do is underrated, thought Harry, turning Jon onto his back. One drop of blood ran from a hole in his forehead.

Another bang. The tinkle of glass.

Harry flipped his cell out of his pocket and punched in Beate's number.

"OK, OK—don't hassle me. I'm coming," Beate answered after the first ring. "I'm outsi—"

"Listen," Harry interrupted. "Radio all patrol cars to get here now. With their sirens blaring. Someone is outside the flat peppering us with lead. And you keep away. Received?"

"Received. Stay on the line."

Harry put the cell on the floor in front of him. Scraping sound against the wall. Could he hear them? Harry sat motionless. The scraping came nearer. What kind of walls were they? A bullet that could go through an insulated front door would have no problems with a stud wall of plasterboard and fiberglass. Even nearer. It stopped. Harry held his breath. And that was when he heard: Jon was breathing.

Then a sound rose from the general rumble of city noise and it was music to Harry's ears. A police siren. Two police sirens.

Harry listened for scraping. Nothing. Make a run for it, he prayed. Beat it. And was heard. The sound of footsteps down the corridor and the stairs.

Harry lay back on the cold parquet floor and stared at the ceiling. There was a draft coming from under the door. He closed his eyes. Nineteen years. Christ. Nineteen years until he could go into retirement.

12

Hospital and Ashes

In the shop window he saw the reflection of a police car pulling up in the street behind him. He kept walking, forcing himself not to run—as he had a few minutes ago, when he raced down the stairs from Jon Karlsen's flat, came out onto the pavement and almost knocked over a young woman with a cell phone in her hand, and sprinted across the park, westward, to the busy streets where he was now.

The police car was moving at the same speed as he was. He saw a door, opened it and had the impression he had stepped into a film. An American film with Cadillacs, bolo ties and young Elvises. The music on the speakers sounded like an old hillbilly record running at three times the speed and the bartender's suit looked like it had been lifted from the LP cover.

He was looking around the surprisingly full but tiny bar area when he noticed that the bartender was talking to him.

"Sorry?"

"A drink, sir?"

"Why not? What have you got?"

"Well, a slow comfortable screw, maybe. Though you look as if you could do with a whisky from the Orkneys."

"Thank you."

A police siren rose and fell. The heat in the bar was causing the sweat to stream out of his pores now. He tore off his neckerchief and stuffed it in his coat pocket. He was glad of the tobacco smoke, which camouflaged the smell of the gun in his coat pocket.

He was given a drink and found a seat by the wall facing the window.

Who had the other person in the room been? A friend of Jon Karlsen? A relative? Or someone Karlsen shared the flat with? He took a sip of the whisky. It tasted of hospital and ashes. And why did he ask himself such stupid questions? Only a policeman could have reacted in the way he did. Only a policeman could have called for help with such speed. And now they knew who his target was. That would make his job much harder. He would have to consider retreat. He took another sip.

The policeman had seen his camel-hair coat.

He went to the bathroom, moved the gun, neckerchief and passport into his jacket pockets and shoved the coat into the trash can beneath the sink. On the pavement outside, rubbing his hands and shivering, he surveyed the street in both directions.

The final job. The most important. Everything depended on it.

Easy does it, he said to himself. They don't know who you are. Go back to the beginning. Think constructively.

Nevertheless, he couldn't repress the thought running through his mind: Who was the man in the flat?

"We don't know," Harry said. "All we know is that he might have been the same man who killed Robert."

He tucked in his legs so that the nurse could roll the empty bed past them down the narrow corridor.

"M-might have been?" Thea Nilsen stuttered. "Are

there several of them?" She sat slightly forward, holding the wooden seat of the chair tightly as though she were afraid of falling off.

Beate Lønn leaned over and placed a comforting hand on Thea's knee. "We don't know. The most important thing is that it went well. The doctor says he has a concussion—that's all."

"Which *I* gave him," Harry said. "Along with the edge of the kitchen unit, which made a small hole in his forehead. The bullet missed. We found it in the wall. The second bullet came to rest in the milk carton. Just imagine. *Inside* the milk carton. And the third in the kitchen cupboard between the currants and . . ."

Beate sent Harry a glance that he guessed was supposed to say that right now Thea would hardly be interested in ballistic idiosyncrasies.

"Anyway. Jon is fine, but he was out cold for a bit, so the doctors are keeping him under observation for the time being."

"All right. Can I go in and see him now?"

"Of course," Beate said. "We would like you to take a look at these pictures first, though. And tell us if you have seen any of these men before." She took three photos out of a folder and gave them to Thea. The photos of Egertorget had been blown up so much that the faces seemed like mosaics of black and white dots.

Thea shook her head. "This is difficult. I can't even see any differences between them."

"Neither can I," Harry said. "But Beate is a specialist in facial recognition, and she says they're two different people."

"I *think* they are," Beate corrected him. "In addition, I was almost knocked over by him as he came running out of the building on Gøteborggata. And to me he didn't look like either of these people in the pictures."

Harry was taken aback. He had never heard Beate express doubt about this sort of thing before.

"Good God," Thea whispered. "How many do you think there really are?"

"Don't worry," Harry said. "We have a guard outside Jon's room."

"What?" Thea stared at him wide-eyed, and Harry realized it had not even occurred to her that Jon could be in danger at Ullevål Hospital. Until now. Amazing.

"Come on—let's go see how he is," Beate suggested in a friendly tone. Yes, thought Harry. And leave this idiot to sit and ponder the concept of "people management."

He turned at the sound of running footsteps from the other end of the corridor.

It was Halvorsen slaloming between patients, visitors and nurses in clattering clogs. Breathless, he pulled up in front of Harry and handed him a sheet of paper with streaky black writing on it and that shiny quality that told Harry it was from Crime Squad's fax machine.

"A page from the passenger lists. I tried to call you—"

"Cells have to be switched off here," Harry said. "Anything interesting?"

"I got the passenger lists, no problem. And mailed them to Alex, who got on them right away. A couple of the passengers have small blemishes on their records, but nothing that would raise suspicion. But there was one thing that was a bit odd . . ."

"Oh?"

"One of the passengers came to Oslo two days ago and had a return flight that should have left yesterday, but was postponed until today. Christo Stankic. He never showed up. That's odd because he had a cheap ticket and it isn't valid for other flights. On the list he is given as a Croatian national, so I asked Alex to check the national register in Croatia. Now, Croatia isn't a member of the EU either, but since they're dead set on joining, they're very cooperative as far as—"

"Come to the point, Halvorsen."

"Christo Stankic doesn't exist."

"Interesting." Harry scratched his chin. "Although Stankic may not have anything to do with our case."

"Of course."

Harry studied the name on the list. Christo Stankic. It was just a name. But a name that would have to be in the passport the airline would ask to see at check-in, since the name was on the passenger list. The same passport that hotels would ask to see.

"I want all the hotel guest lists in all of Oslo checked," Harry said. "Let's see if any of them have put up Christo Stankic over the last two days."

"I'll get on it right away."

Harry straightened up and sent Halvorsen a nod he hoped contained what he wanted to say. That he was pleased with him.

"I'm off to my psychologist," Harry said.

The psychologist, Ståle Aune, had his office on the part of the street called Sporveisgata where there was no *sporvei*, or tramline, but its pavements did showcase an interesting selection of walks: the confident, bouncy walk of the keep-fit housewives at the SATS fitness studio, the cautious walk of the guide-dog owners from the Institute for the Blind and the careless gait of the down-at-heel but undeterred clientele from the hospice for drug users.

"So this Robert Karlsen liked girls under the age of consent," Aune said, having hung his tweed jacket over the back of the chair and forced his double chin down toward his bow tie. "That can be caused by many things, of course, but I gather he grew up in a pietistic Salvation Army environment. Is that correct?"

"Yes," said Harry, looking up at the well-stocked but chaotic bookshelves of his personal and professional adviser.

"But isn't it a myth that you become perverted from growing up in closed, strict, religious communities?"

"No," Aune said. "Christian sects are over-represented as far as the sexual assault you mention is concerned."

"Why's that?"

Aune pressed his fingertips together and smacked his lips with glee. "If one is punished or humiliated in one's childhood or adolescence by, for example, one's parents, for exhibiting a natural sexuality, what happens is that one represses this part of one's personality. Normal sexual maturation comes to a grinding halt, and sexual preferences find a deviant outlet, so to speak. At an adult age many try to return to a period in their lives when they were allowed to be natural, to find a release for their sexuality."

"Like wearing diapers."

"Yes. Or playing with excrement. I remember a case in California about a senator who—"

Harry coughed.

"Or, at an adult age, they go back to what is known as a *core event*," Aune continued. "Which is often the last time they were successful in their sexual endeavors, that is, the last time sex worked for them. And it might be a teenage infatuation, or sexual contact of some kind, that went undiscovered or unpunished."

"Or a sexual assault?"

"Right. A situation when they were in control and therefore felt powerful, the very opposite of humiliation. And so they spend the rest of their lives seeking to re-create that situation."

"It can't be that easy being a sexual molester, then."

"Indeed not. Many were beaten black and blue for being found with a pornographic magazine in their teens and showing a quite normal, healthy sexuality. But if you wish to maximize the chances of a person becoming a sexual abuser, give him a violent father, an invasive or sexually importu-

nate mother and an environment in which the truth is suppressed and the lusts of the flesh are rewarded with hellfire."

Harry's cell bleeped. He pulled it out and read the text
from Halvorsen. A Christo Stankic had stayed at the Scandia Hotel by Oslo Central Station the night before the murder.

"What's AA like?" Aune asked. "Is it helping you to
abstain?"

"Well," Harry said, getting up, "yes and no."

A scream jolted him back into reality.

He turned and looked into a pair of saucer eyes and a
black hole of an open mouth a few inches from his face. The
child pressed its nose against the glass partition in Burger
King's playroom before falling backward onto the carpet of
red, yellow and blue plastic balls with a gleeful squeal.

He wiped the remains of ketchup from his mouth, emptied his tray into the garbage and rushed out onto Karl
Johans Gate. Tried to huddle up into the thin suit jacket,
but the cold was merciless. He decided to buy a new coat
as soon as he had got himself a decent room in the Scandia
Hotel.

Six minutes later he walked through the doors of the
hotel lobby and lined up behind a couple who were obviously checking in. The female receptionist cast a fleeting
glance at him without any sign of recognition. Then she
bent over the new guests' papers while speaking in Norwegian. The woman turned to him. A blonde. Attractive,
he noticed. Even if in a plain kind of way. He smiled back.
That was as much as he managed. Because he had seen her
before. Just a few hours ago. Outside the building on Gøteborggata.

Without moving from the spot, he inclined his head and
put his hands in his jacket pockets. The grip on the gun was
firm and reassuring. Taking great care, he raised his head,

spotted the mirror behind the receptionist and stared. But the image blurred, became double. He closed his eyes, took a deep breath and opened them again. The tall man gradually came into focus. The shorn skull, the pale skin with the red nose, the hard, pronounced features that were at variance with the sensitive mouth. It was him. The second man in the flat. The policeman. He took stock of the reception area. They were the only people around. And, as though to remove the last shadow of doubt, he heard two familiar words amid all the Norwegian. *Christo Stankic.* He forced himself to remain calm. How they had managed to trace him he had no idea, but the consequences were beginning to dawn on him.

The blond woman was given a key by the receptionist, grabbed what looked like a toolbox and walked toward the elevator. The tall man said something to the receptionist and she made a note. Then the policeman turned around and their eyes met for an instant before the cop headed for the exit.

The receptionist smiled, articulated a rehearsed, friendly Norwegian phrase and sent him an inquiring look. He asked her if she had a nonsmoking room on the top floor.

"Let me see, sir." She tapped away on the keyboard.

"Excuse me. The man you were talking with—wasn't he the policeman whose photo has been in the newspapers?"

"I don't know." She smiled.

"Think it was. He's famous—what's his name again . . . ?"

She glanced down at her notebook. "Harry Hole. Is he famous?"

"Harry Hole?"

"Yes."

"Wrong name. I must have made a mistake."

"I have one free room. If you want it, you'll have to fill in this card and show your passport. How would you like to pay?"

"How much is it?"

She told him the price.

"Sorry." He smiled. "Too expensive."

He left the hotel and went into the railway station, headed for the restroom and locked himself in a stall. There he sat, trying to organize his thoughts. They had the name. So he had to find some accommodation where he would not have to show his passport. And Christo Stankic could forget about booking a plane, boat or train or even crossing a national border. What was he going to do? He would have to call Zagreb and talk to her.

He strolled into the square outside the station. A numbing wind swept the open area as, with chattering teeth, he kept an eye on the public telephones. A man was leaning against the white hot-dog vehicle in the middle. He was wearing a quilted down jacket and trousers and resembled an astronaut. Was he imagining it, or was the man keeping the phones under surveillance? Could they have traced his calls and now be waiting for him to return? No, impossible. He hesitated. If they were tapping the phones, there was a chance he might give her away. He made up his mind. The call could wait. What he needed now was a room with a bed and a heater. They would want cash at the kind of place he was looking for now, and he had spent his last money on the hamburger.

Inside the high concourse, between the shops and the platforms, he found a cash machine. He took out his Visa card, read the English instructions telling him to keep the magnetic strip to the right, and went to put the card in the slot. His hand stopped. The card was made out in the name of Christo Stankic, too. It would be in a database and somewhere an alarm would go off. He returned the card to his wallet. He sauntered through the concourse. The shops were closing. He didn't even have enough money to buy a warm jacket. A security guard was giving him the once-over. He stumbled into Jernbanetorget again. A northerly wind was sweeping through the square. The man by the hot-dog stand was gone. But there was another by the tiger sculpture.

"I need some money for a place to sleep tonight."

He didn't need to know any Norwegian to understand what the man was asking him for. It was the same young junkie he had given money to earlier in the day. Money he was in dire need of now. He shook his head and cast a glance at the shivering collection of junkies by what he had at first taken to be a bus stop. The white bus had arrived.

Harry's chest and lungs ached. The good ache. His thighs burned. The good burn.

When he was stuck on a case he sometimes did what he was doing now—he went down to the basement fitness room at Police HQ and cycled. Not because it made him think better, but because it made him stop thinking.

"They said you were here." Gunnar Hagen mounted the stationary bike beside him. The tight yellow T-shirt and the cycling shorts emphasized rather than covered the muscles in the POB's lean, almost ravaged body. "What program are you on?"

"Number nine," Harry panted.

Hagen regulated the height of the saddle while standing on the pedals and then punched in the necessary settings on the cycle's computer. "I gather you've had quite a dramatic day today."

Harry nodded.

"I'll understand if you want to apply for sick leave," Hagen said. "After all, this is peacetime."

"Thank you, but I'm feeling pretty fresh, boss."

"Good. I've just spoken to Torleif."

"The chief super?"

"We need to know how the case is going. There have been phone calls. The Salvation Army is popular, and influential people in town would like to know whether we'll clear the case up before Christmas. Peace and Yuletide goodwill and all that stuff."

"The politicians coped fine with six fatal ODs in their Yuletide last year."

"I was asking for an update on the case, Hole." Harry could feel the sweat stinging his nipples.

"Well, no witnesses have come forward despite the photos in *Dagbladet* today. And Beate Lønn says that the photos suggest we are not dealing with one killer, but at least two. And I share her opinion. The man at Jon Karlsen's flat was wearing a camel-hair coat and a neckerchief, and the clothes match those of the man in Egertorget the evening before the murder."

"Only the clothes?"

"I couldn't see his face very well. And Jon Karlsen can't remember a great deal. One of the residents has admitted she let an Englishman in to leave a Christmas present outside Jon Karlsen's door."

"Right," said Hagen. "But we'll keep the theory about several killers to ourselves. Go on."

"There's not much more to say."

"Nothing?"

Harry checked the speedometer as, with calm determination, he stepped up the pace to twenty miles an hour.

"Well, we have a false passport belonging to a Croatian, a Christo Stankic, who was not on the Zagreb plane today and should have been. We found out he had been staying at the Scandia Hotel. Lønn examined his room for DNA. They don't have so many guests staying so we hoped the receptionist would recognize the man from our photos."

"And?"

"Afraid not."

"What is our basis for thinking this is our man, then?"

"The false passport," Harry said, stealing a glimpse at Hagen's speedometer. Twenty-five miles an hour.

"And how will you find him?"

"Well, names leave traces in the information age and we have alerted all our standard contacts. If anyone bearing the name of Christo Stankic sets foot in a hotel, buys a plane ticket or uses a credit card, we will know at once. According to the receptionist he had asked where he could find a telephone booth, and she directed him to Jernbanetorget. Telenor is going to send us a list of outgoing calls over the last two days from the public phones there."

"So all you have is a Croatian with a false passport who didn't turn up for his flight," Hagen said. "You're stuck, aren't you?"

Harry didn't answer.

"Try thinking laterally," Hagen said.

"Right, boss," Harry drawled.

"There are always alternatives," Hagen said. "Have I told you about the Japanese platoon and the cholera outbreak?"

"Don't think I've had the pleasure, boss."

"They were in the jungle north of Rangoon and kept bringing up everything they ate and drank. They were getting dehydrated, but the leader refused to lie down and die, so he ordered them to empty their morphine syringes and use them to inject themselves with the water from their canteens."

Hagen increased his tempo and Harry listened in vain for any signs of breathlessness.

"It worked. But after a few days the only water they had left was a barrel teeming with mosquito larvae. Then the second in command suggested sticking the syringes in the flesh of the fruit growing around them and injecting it into the bloodstream. In theory, fruit juice is ninety percent water anyway, and what did they have to lose? It saved the platoon, Hole. Imagination and courage."

"Imagination and courage," wheezed Hole. "Thanks, boss."

He pedaled for all he was worth and could hear the

crackle of his own breathing, like fire through an open stove door. The speedometer showed twenty-six. He glanced over at the POB's. Thirty. Breathing? Even.

Harry was reminded of a sentence from a two-thousand-year-old book he had been given by a bank robber, *The Art of War*: "Choose your battles." And he knew this was one battle he should withdraw from. Because he would lose, whatever he did.

Harry slowed down. The speedometer showed twenty. To his surprise, he didn't feel frustration, just weary resignation. Perhaps he was growing up, perhaps he was finished with being the idiot who lowered his horns and attacked anyone waving a red rag? Harry snatched a sidelong glance. Hagen's legs were going like pistons now, and the smooth layer of sweat on his face glistened in the white light from the lamp.

Harry dried his sweat. Took two deep breaths. Then went for it again. The wonderful pain returned in seconds.

13

The Ticking

Every so often Martine thought that the square in Plata had to be the basement staircase to hell. Nevertheless, she was terrified by rumors going around that in spring the City Council's Welfare Committee was going to abandon the plan that allowed the open trading of drugs. The overt argument put forward by opponents of Plata was that the area attracted young people to drugs. Martine's opinion was that anyone who thought that the life you saw played out in Plata could be attractive either had to be crazy or had never set foot there.

The covert argument was that this terrain, demarked by a white line in the pavement next to Jernbanetorget, disfigured the image of the city. And was it not a glaring admission of failure in the world's most successful—or at least richest—social democracy to allow drugs and money to exchange hands openly in the very heart of the capital?

Martine agreed with that: that there had been a failure. The battle for a drug-free society had been lost. On the other hand, if you wanted to prevent drugs from gaining further ground it was better for the drug dealing to take place under the ever-watchful eyes of surveillance cameras than under bridges along the Akerselva and in dark backyards along Rådhusgata and the southern side of Akershus

Fortress. And Martine knew that most people whose work was in some way connected with Narco-Oslo—the police, social workers, street preachers and prostitutes—all felt the same way: that Plata was better than the alternatives.

But it was not a pretty sight.

"Langemann!" she shouted to the man standing in the darkness outside their bus. "Don't you want any soup tonight?"

But Langemann sidled away. He had probably bought his fix and was off to inject it.

She concentrated on ladling soup for a Mediterranean type in a blue jacket when she heard chattering teeth beside her and saw a man dressed in a thin suit jacket awaiting his turn. "Here you are," she said, pouring out his soup.

"Hello, sweetie," came a rasping voice.

"Wenche!"

"Come over and thaw out a poor wretch," said the aging prostitute with a hearty laugh, and embraced Martine. The smell of the damp skin and body that undulated against the tight-fitting leopard-pattern dress was overwhelming. But there was another smell, one she recognized, a smell that had been there before Wenche's broadside of fragrances had overpowered everything else.

They sat down at one of the empty tables.

Although some of the foreign working girls who had flooded the area in the last year also used drugs, it was not as widespread as among their homegrown rivals. Wenche was one of the few Norwegians who did not indulge. Furthermore, in her words, she had begun to work more from home with a fixed clientele, so the intervals between visits with Martine had lengthened.

"I'm here to look for a girlfriend's son," Wenche said. "Kristoffer. I'm told he's on shit."

"Kristoffer? Don't know him."

"Aaah!" She dismissed it. "Forget it. You've got other things on your mind, I can see."

"Do I?"

"Don't fib. I can see when a girl's in love. Is it him?"

Wenche nodded toward the man in the Salvation Army uniform with a Bible in one hand who had just sat down next to the man in the thin suit jacket.

Martine puffed out her cheeks. "Rikard? No, thank you."

"Sure? His eyes have been trailing you ever since I arrived."

"Rikard is all right," she said with a sigh. "At any rate he volunteered for this shift at short notice. The person who should have been here is dead."

"Robert Karlsen?"

"Did you know him?"

Wenche answered with a heavy-hearted nod, then brightened up again. "But forget the dead and tell Mommy who you're in love with. It's about time, by the way."

Martine smiled. "I didn't even know I was in love."

"Come on."

"No, this is too silly. I—"

"Martine," said another voice.

She peered up and saw Rikard's imploring eyes.

"The man sitting there says he has no clothes, no money and nowhere to stay. Do you know if the hostel has any free spots?"

"Call them and ask," Martine said. "They do have some winter clothes."

"Right." Rikard didn't move, even though Martine was facing Wenche. She didn't need to look up to know that his top lip was sweaty.

Then he mumbled a thanks and went back to the man in the suit jacket.

"Tell me," Wenche urged in a whisper.

Outside, the northerly wind had lined up its small-caliber artillery.

*   *   *

Harry walked along with his sports bag over his shoulder, narrowing his eyes against the wind, which was making the sharp, almost invisible snowflakes embed small pinpricks in the cornea. As he passed Blitz, the squatters' property on Pilestredet, his cell rang. It was Halvorsen.

"There have been two calls to Zagreb in the last two days from the phones in Jernbanetorget. Same number both times. I called the number and got through to a hotel receptionist. Hotel International. They couldn't tell me who had called from Oslo or who this person was trying to contact. Nor had they heard of anyone named Christo Stankic."

"Hm."

"Should I follow up?"

"No." Harry sighed. "We'll let it go until something tells us this Stankic might be interesting. Switch off the light before you go and we'll talk tomorrow."

"Hang on!"

"I'm not going anywhere."

"There's more. The uniformed officers received a call from a waiter at Biscuit. He said he was in the restroom this morning and bumped into one of the customers—"

"What was he doing there?"

"I'll come to that. You see, the customer had something in his hand—"

"I mean the waiter. Restaurant employees always have their own restrooms."

"I didn't ask," Halvorsen said, becoming impatient. "Listen. This customer was holding something green and dripping."

"Sounds like he should see a doctor."

"Very funny. The waiter swore it was a gun covered in soap. The lid of the soap dispenser was off."

"Biscuit," Harry repeated as the information sank in. "That's on Karl Johan."

"Two hundred yards from the crime scene. I bet a crate of beer that's our gun. Er . . . sorry, I bet—"

"By the way, you still owe me two hundred kroner. Give me the rest of the story."

"Here comes the best part. I asked for a description. He couldn't give me one."

"Sounds like the refrain in this case."

"Except that he recognized the guy by his coat. A very ugly camel-hair coat."

"Yes!" Harry shouted. "The guy with the scarf in the photo of Egertorget the night before Karlsen was shot."

"Incidentally, the waiter figured it was imitation. And he sounded like he knew about that sort of thing."

"What do you mean?"

"You know. The way they speak."

"Who are 'they'?"

"Hello! Poofs. Whatever. The man with the gun was through the door and gone. That's all I have so far. I'm on my way to Biscuit to show the waiter the photos now."

"Good," said Harry.

"What are you wondering?"

"Wondering?"

"I'm getting to know your ways, Harry."

"Mm. I was wondering why the waiter didn't phone the police right away this morning. Ask him, OK?"

"In fact, I was intending to do just that, Harry."

"Of course you were. Sorry."

Harry hung up, but five minutes later his cell rang again.

"What did you forget?" Harry asked.

"What?"

"Oh, it's you, Beate. Well?"

"Good news. I've finished at the Scandia Hotel."

"Did you find any DNA?"

"Don't know yet. I've got a couple of hairs that might belong to the maid or a previous guest. But I did get the ballistics results half an hour ago. The bullet in the milk carton at Jon Karlsen's place comes from the same weapon as the bullet we found in Egertorget."

"Mm. That means the theory about several gunmen is weakened."

"Yes. And there's more. The receptionist at the Scandia Hotel remembered something after you left. This Christo Stankic had a particularly ugly piece of clothing. She reckoned it was a kind of imitation—"

"Let me guess. Camel-hair coat?"

"That's what she said."

"We're in *business*," Harry yelled, so loud that Blitz's graffiti-covered wall sent an echo around the deserted downtown street.

Harry hung up and called Halvorsen back.

"Yes, Harry?"

"Christo Stankic is our man. Give the description of the camel-hair coat to the uniforms and the Ops Room and ask them to alert all patrol cars." Harry smiled at an old lady tripping and scraping along with spiked cleats attached to the bottom of her fashionable ankle boots. "And I want twenty-four-hour surveillance of telecommunications so we know if anyone calls Hotel International in Zagreb from Oslo. And which number they call from. Talk to Klaus Torkildsen at Telenor, Oslo region."

"That's wiretapping. We need a warrant for that, and it can take days."

"It's not wiretapping. We just need the address of the incoming call."

"I'm afraid Telenor won't be able to tell the difference."

"Tell Torkildsen you've spoken to me. OK?"

"Can I ask why he would be willing to risk his job for you?"

"Old story. I saved him from being beaten to a pulp in the precinct a few years back. Tom Waaler and his pals. You know what it's like when flashers are brought in."

"So he's a flasher?"

"Now retired. Happy to exchange services for silence."

"I see."

Harry hung up. They were on the move now, and he no longer felt the northerly wind or the onslaught of snow needles. Now and then the job gave him moments of unalloyed pleasure. He turned and walked back to Police HQ.

In the private room at Ullevål Hospital Jon felt the phone vibrate against the sheet and grabbed it at once. "Yes?"

"It's me."

"Oh, hi," he said, without quite managing to conceal his disappointment.

"You sound as if you were hoping it was someone else," Ragnhild said in the rather too-cheerful tone that betrays a wounded woman.

"I can't say much," Jon said, glancing at the door.

"I wanted to say how awful the news about Robert is," Ragnhild said. "And I feel for you."

"Thank you."

"It must be painful. Where are you, actually? I tried to call you at home."

Jon didn't answer.

"Mads is working late, so if you want I can walk over to your place."

"No, thanks, Ragnhild—I'll manage."

"I was thinking about you. It's so dark and cold. I'm afraid."

"You're never afraid, Ragnhild."

"Sometimes I am." She put on her sulky voice. "There are so many rooms here, and there is no one around."

"Move to a smaller house, then. I have to hang up now. We're not allowed to use cell phones here."

"Wait! Where are you, Jon?"

"I've got a slight concussion. I'm in the hospital."

"Which hospital? Which department?"

Jon was taken aback. "Most people would have asked how I got the concussion."

"You know I hate not knowing where you are."

Jon visualized Ragnhild marching in with a large bunch of roses during visiting time the next day. And Thea's questioning looks, first at her and then at him.

"I can hear the sister coming," he whispered. "I have to hang up." He pressed the OFF button and stared at the ceiling until the phone had played its fanfare and the display was extinguished. She was right. It *was* dark. But *he* was the one who was afraid.

Ragnhild Gilstrup stood by the window with her eyes closed. Then she looked at her watch. Mads had said he had work to do for the board meeting and would be late. He had started saying things like that in recent weeks. Before, he had always given her a time and arrived on the dot, sometimes even a little early. Not that she wanted him home earlier, but it was somewhat odd. Somewhat odd—that was all. Just as it was odd that all the calls had been itemized on the last landline bill. And she had not requested any such thing. But there it was: five pages with much too much information. She should have stopped calling Jon, but she couldn't. Because he had that look. That Johannes look. It wasn't kind or clever or gentle or anything like that. But it was a look that could read whatever she thought before she had got as far as thinking it herself. That saw her as she was. And still liked her.

She opened her eyes again and surveyed the one-and-a-half-acre site of unsullied nature. The view reminded her of boarding school in Switzerland. The reflection off the snow shone into the large bedroom and covered the ceiling and walls in a bluish-white light.

She was the one who had insisted on building here, high above the city—well, in the forest, in fact. It would make her feel less enclosed and restricted, she had said. And her husband, Mads Gilstrup, who had imagined that the city was the restriction she was referring to, had gladly spent some of the money he possessed on the construction. The extravagance had cost him twenty million kroner. When they moved in, Ragnhild felt as though she were moving from a cell to a prison yard. Sun, air and room. Yet still confined. Like at boarding school.

At times—like this evening—she wondered how she had ended up here. Her external circumstances could be summed up as follows: Mads Gilstrup was heir to one of Oslo's great fortunes. She had met him while in college outside Chicago, Illinois, where they had both studied business administration at a middling university that, by virtue of being American, bestowed greater prestige than its counterparts in Norway. And anyway, American colleges were a lot more fun. Both came from wealthy families, but his was wealthier. While his family consisted of five generations of shipowners with old money, her family was peasant stock, whose money still bore the whiff of printer's ink and farmed fish. They had lived in the interstices between agricultural subsidies and wounded pride until her father and uncle had sold their tractors and gambled their capital on a small fish farm in the fjord outside their sitting-room window on the southernmost, windblown coastline of Vest-Agder. The timing had been perfect, competition minimal and the price per pound astronomical, and in the course of four lucrative years they became multimillionaires. The house on the crag was demolished and replaced by a virtual chateau, bigger than the barn and boasting eight bay windows and a double garage.

Ragnhild had just turned sixteen when her mother sent her from one crag to another crag: Aron Schüster's private school for girls, twenty-nine hundred feet above sea level in a Swiss town with a train station, six churches and a beer hall. The official reason was that Ragnhild was to learn French, German and art history, subjects that were considered useful as the price per pound of farmed fish was still hitting record levels.

The real reason for her exile, however, was of course her boyfriend, Johannes. Johannes of the warm hands, Johannes of the gentle voice and the look that could read whatever she thought before she had got as far as thinking it. Johannes, the country clod, who was going nowhere. Everything changed after Johannes. She changed after Johannes.

At Aron Schüster's private school she was freed from the nightmares, the guilt and the smell of fish, and learned all that young girls need to acquire a husband of their own or higher status. And with the inherited survival instinct that had enabled her to survive on the crag in Norway, she had slowly but surely buried the Ragnhild whose mind Johannes had read so well and become the Ragnhild who was going places, who did her own thing and would not be held back by anyone, least of all by upper-class French girls or spoiled Danish brats who sniggered in corners at the futile attempts of girls like Ragnhild to be anything but provincial or vulgar.

Her little revenge was to seduce Herr Brehme, the young German teacher with whom they were all infatuated. The teachers lived in a building facing the pupils' dorm and she simply crossed the cobbled square and knocked on the door of his little room. She visited him four times. And four nights she click-clacked her way back across the cobblestones, her heels echoing off the walls of both buildings.

Rumors started up, and she did little or nothing to stop them. When the news broke that Herr Brehme had resigned and hastily taken up a teaching post in Zurich, Ragnhild had beamed a smile of triumph at all the grief-stricken faces of the young girls in her class.

After the final year of school in Switzerland, Ragnhild returned home. Home at last, she thought. But then Johannes's eyes were there again. In the silver fjord, in the shadows of the verdigris forest, behind the shiny black windows of the chapel or in the cars that flashed past, leaving a cloud of dust that made your teeth crunch and was bitter to the taste. When the letter from Chicago arrived, with the offer of a place to study business administration—four years for a BA, five for an MA—she went to Daddy to ask him to transfer the tuition money without delay.

It was a relief to go. A relief to be the new Ragnhild once again. She was looking forward to forgetting, but to do that she needed a project, a goal. In Chicago she found that goal: Mads Gilstrup.

She anticipated that it would be simple. After all, she had the theoretical and practical grounding to seduce upper-class boys. And she was good-looking. Johannes and several others had said that. Above all, it was her eyes. She had been blessed with her mother's light-blue irises, surrounded by unusually white sclera, which science had proven attracted the opposite sex, signaling robust health and hearty genes. For that reason Ragnhild was seldom seen wearing sunglasses. Unless she had planned the effect it created by taking them off at an especially favorable moment.

Some said she looked like Nicole Kidman. She understood what they meant. Beautiful in a stiff, severe way. Perhaps that was the reason: the severity. Because when she had tried to engineer some contact with Mads Gilstrup in the hallways or the campus cafeteria, he had behaved like a frightened wild horse, averted his eyes, tossed his bangs back and trotted off to a safe area.

In the end she staked everything on one card.

The evening before one of the many silly annual and, apparently, traditional parties, Ragnhild had given her roommate money for a new pair of shoes and a hotel room in town and spent three hours in front of the mirror. For once she arrived early at the party. Because she knew Mads Gilstrup went to all parties early in order to pre-empt potential rivals.

He stuttered and stammered, barely daring to look into her eyes—light-blue irises and clear sclera notwithstanding—and even less down the plunging neckline she had arranged with such care. She had come to the conclusion—contrary to her previous opinion—that confidence did not necessarily come with money. Later she was to conclude that the reason for Mads's bad self-image lay at the door of his brilliant, demanding, weakness-hating father, who was unable to grasp why he had not been granted a son more in his own mold.

But she did not give up, and she dangled herself like bait in front of Mads Gilstrup. It was so obvious she was making herself accessible that she noticed the girls she called friends, and vice versa, were standing with their heads together in a huddle. When it came down to it, they were all herd animals. Then—after six American lagers and a growing suspicion that Mads Gilstrup was homosexual—the wild horse ventured out into open terrain, and two lagers later they left the party.

She let him mount her, but in her best friend's bed. After all, it had cost her an expensive pair of shoes. And when, three minutes later, Ragnhild wiped him off with her roommate's homemade crocheted bedspread, she knew she had lassoed him. Harness and saddle would follow in good time.

After their studies they traveled home as an engaged couple, Mads Gilstrup to administer his portion of the family fortune in the secure knowledge that he would never have to be tested in any rat race. His job consisted of finding the right advisers.

Ragnhild applied for and got a job with a trust manager, who had never heard of the mediocre university, but had heard of Chicago, and liked what he heard. And saw. He was not so brilliant, but he was demanding and found a soulmate in Ragnhild. Thus, after quite a short spell, she was removed from the intellectually overdemanding work as a share analyst and put behind a screen and telephone on one of the tables in the "kitchen," as they called the traders' room. This was where Ragnhild Gilstrup (she had changed her name to Gilstrup as soon as they were engaged because it was "more practical") came into her own. If it was not enough to *advise* brokerages' own and, one presumed, professional, investors to buy Opticum, she could purr, flirt, hiss, manipulate, lie and cry. Ragnhild Gilstrup could caress her way up a man's legs—and, if pushed, a woman's—in a way that shifted shares with far greater efficacy than any of her analyses had done. Her greatest quality, however, was her supreme understanding of the most important motivation of the equity market: greed.

Then one day she became pregnant. And, to her surprise, she found herself considering an abortion. Until then she had really believed she wanted children, or one, anyway. Eight months later she gave birth to Amalie. She was filled with such happiness that she repressed the memory of her thoughts of abortion. Two weeks later Amalie was taken to the hospital with a high fever. Ragnhild could see that the doctors were uneasy, but they couldn't tell her what was wrong with her child. One night Ragnhild had considered praying to God, but then dismissed the idea. The next night, at eleven o'clock, little Amalie died of pneumonia. Ragnhild locked herself indoors and cried for four successive days.

"Cystic fibrosis," the doctor had told her in private. "It's genetic and means that either you or your husband is a carrier of the disease. Do you know if anyone has had it in your family or his? It may manifest itself in frequent asthma attacks or something similar."

"No," Ragnhild had answered. "And I assume you're aware of client confidentiality."

The period of grieving was managed with professional help. After a couple of months she was able to talk to people again. When summer came they went to the Gilstrups' chalet on the west coast of Sweden and tried for another child. But one evening Mads found his wife crying in front of the bedroom mirror. She said this was her punishment because she had wanted an abortion. He comforted her, but when his tender caresses became bolder she pushed him away and said that would be the last time for a good while. Mads thought she meant having children, and agreed right away. He was therefore disappointed—disconsolate—to find that she meant she wanted a break from the act itself. Mads Gilstrup had acquired a taste for mating and particularly appreciated the self-esteem he felt when giving her what he interpreted as small but distinct orgasms. Nevertheless, he accepted her explanation as the reaction to grieving and hormonal changes after childbirth. Ragnhild didn't think she could tell him that from her side the last two years had been a duty, or that the last remnants of pleasure she had been able to work up for him had disappeared in the delivery room, when she had peered up into his stupid, gaping, terror-stricken face. And when he had cried with happiness and dropped the scissors just as he was supposed to cut the victory tape for all new fathers, she had felt like walloping him. Nor did she think she could tell him that, as far as the mating department was concerned, for the last year she and her less-than-brilliant boss had been meeting each other's demanding needs.

Ragnhild was the only stockbroker in Oslo to have been offered a full partnership as she left for maternity leave. To everyone's surprise, however, she resigned. She had been offered another job: managing Mads Gilstrup's family fortune.

She explained to her boss on the farewell night that she thought it was time that brokers schmoozed with her, and not vice versa. She didn't breathe a word about the real reason: that, sad to say, Mads Gilstrup had been unable to manage the sole task he had been entrusted with, that of finding good advisers, and that the family fortune had shrunk at such an alarmingly rapid rate that Ragnhild and her father-in-law, Albert Gilstrup, had both intervened. That was the last time she met her boss. A few months later she heard he had taken sick leave after years of struggling with asthma.

Ragnhild didn't like Mads's social circle and she noticed that Mads didn't, either. But they still went to the parties they were invited to, since the alternative—ending up outside the clique of people who meant or owned anything—was even worse. It was one thing to spend time with pompous, complacent men who, deep in their hearts, felt that their money gave them the right to be so; however, their wives, or the "bitches," as Ragnhild labeled them in secret, were quite another. The chattering, shopaholic, health-freak housewives with tits that looked so genuine, not to mention the tans, although those were genuine, since they and their children had just returned from two weeks in St. Tropez "relaxing," away from au pairs and noisy work-men who never finished swimming pools and new kitchens. They talked with unfeigned concern about how bad the shopping had been in Europe over the last year, but otherwise their horizons didn't stretch farther than skiing in Slemdal or swimming in Bogstad, both near Oslo, and at a pinch, Kragerø, in the south. Clothes, face-lifts and exercise machines were the wives' topics of conversation, since that was the means to holding on to their rich, pompous husbands, which of course was their sole real mission here on earth.

When Ragnhild thought like that she could surprise herself. Were they so different from her? Maybe the difference was that she had a job. Was that why she couldn't stand their smug faces at the coffee shop in Vinderen when they complained about all the welfare abuse and tax evasion in what they, with a slight sneer, called "society"? Or was there another reason? Because something had happened. A revolution. She had begun to care for someone other than herself. She hadn't felt that since Amalie. Or Johannes.

The whole thing had started with a plan. Share values had continued to tumble, thanks to Mads's unfortunate investments, and something drastic had to be done. It wasn't just a question of shifting assets to funds with a lower risk; debts had accumulated that had to be covered. In short, they needed to make a financial coup. Her father-in-law had launched the idea. And it really did smack of a coup, or to be more precise, a robbery. Not a robbery of a well-guarded bank, but of old ladies. The lady in question was the Salvation Army. Ragnhild had gone through their property portfolio, which was nothing short of impressive. That is, the properties were not in very good condition, but their potential and location were excellent. Above all, those in central Oslo, and especially those in Majorstuen. The accounts of the Salvation Army had demonstrated at least two things to her: They needed money, and the properties were hugely undervalued. In all probability they were not aware of the assets they were sitting on; she very much doubted the decision-makers in the organization were the sharpest knives in the drawer. In addition, it was perhaps the perfect time to buy, since the real estate market had fallen at the same time as share prices, and other leading indicators had begun to point upward again.

One telephone call later she had arranged a meeting.

It was a wonderful spring day as she drove up to the Salvation Army headquarters.

Commander David Eckhoff received her, and within three seconds she had seen through the joviality. Behind it she saw a domineering leader of the herd, the kind she was so talented at manipulating, and she thought to herself: This could go well. He led her into a meeting room with waffles, sensationally bad coffee and one older and two younger colleagues. The older one was the chief administrator, a lieutenant colonel who was on the verge of retiring. The first of the two younger ones was Rikard Nilsen, a timid young man similar, at first glance, to Mads Gilstrup.

But that recognition was nothing compared with the shock she received when greeting the other young man. He shook hands with a tentative smile and introduced himself as Jon Karlsen. It wasn't the tall, stooped figure, nor the open, boyish face, nor the warm voice, but the eyes. He looked straight at her. Inside her. The way *he* had done. They were Johannes's eyes.

For the first part of the meeting, while the chief administrator accounted for the turnover of the Norwegian Salvation Army, amounting to just under a billion kroner, of which a significant contribution was rental income from the 230 plots the Army owned, she sat in a trancelike state, trying to stop herself from staring at the young man. At his hair, at his hands resting on the table in total serenity. At his shoulders, which didn't quite fill the black uniform, a uniform that Ragnhild had, from her childhood, associated with old men and women, who, despite not believing in life before death, sang to three-chord songs with a smile. She must have thought—without really thinking—that the Salvation Army was for those who couldn't gain a foothold anywhere else, the simple ones, the lackluster and the blockheads no one else wanted to play with but who knew that in the Army there was a community where even they could meet the requirements: singing backup.

When the chief administrator was finished, Ragnhild thanked him, opened the folder she had brought with her and passed a single sheet of paper over to the commander.

"This is our offer," she said. "It will become clear which properties we're interested in."

"Thank you," said the commander, studying the document.

Ragnhild tried to read the expression on his face. But knew it didn't mean much. A pair of reading glasses lay untouched on the table in front of him.

"Our specialist will have to do the calculations and make

a recommendation," the commander said with a smile, and passed the document on. To Jon Karlsen. Ragnhild noticed the twitch in Rikard Nilsen's face.

She pushed a business card across the table to Jon Karlsen.

"If anything is unclear, just give me a ring," she said, and felt his eyes on her like a physical caress.

"Thank you for talking to us, Fru Gilstrup," Commander Eckhoff said, clapping his hands. "We promise to give you an answer in the course of . . . Jon?"

"Not too long."

The commander gave a jovial smile. "Not too long."

All four of them accompanied her to the elevator. No one said anything while they waited.

As the elevator doors slid open she half leaned toward Jon and said in a low voice: "Any time at all. Use my cell number."

She had tried to catch his eye to feel it again, but had failed. On the way down in the elevator, alone, Ragnhild Gilstrup had felt her blood pumping in sudden, painful bursts and she had started to tremble uncontrollably.

Three days passed before he called to say no. They had assessed the offer and concluded they didn't want to sell. Ragnhild made an impassioned defense of the price and pointed out that the Salvation Army's position in the property market was vulnerable, the properties were not being run in a professional manner, that they were losing money with the low rents and that the Army should diversify their investments. Jon Karlsen listened without interrupting.

"Thank you," he said when she was finished, "for examining the case with such thoroughness, Fru Gilstrup. And, as an economist, I don't disagree with what you say. But—"

"But what? The calculations are unambiguous . . ." She had heard the breathy excitement in her voice.

"But there is a human dimension."

"Human?"

"The tenants. Human beings. Old people who have lived there all their lives, retired Army soldiers, refugees, human beings who need security. They are my human dimension. You'll throw them out to fix up the flats and rent or sell at a profit. The calculations are—as you yourself said—unambiguous. That's your all-consuming economic dimension, and I accept it. Do you accept mine?"

She caught her breath.

"I . . ." she started.

"I would be very happy to take you to meet some of these people," he said. "Then you might understand better."

She shook her head. "I would like to clear up a few misunderstandings as far as our intentions are concerned," she said. "Are you busy Thursday evening?"

"No, but—"

"Let's meet at Feinschmecker at eight."

"What is Feinschmecker?"

She had to smile. "A restaurant in Frogner. Let me put it this way: The taxi driver will know where it is."

"If it's in Frogner, I'll ride my bike."

"Fine. See you."

She called a meeting with Mads and her father-in-law and reported back on the outcome.

"Sounds like the key is this adviser of theirs," said Albert Gilstrup. "If we can get him on our side, the properties are ours."

"But I'm telling you he's not interested in any price we would pay."

"Oh, yes, he is," said the father-in-law.

"No, he isn't!"

"Not to the Salvation Army, he isn't. He can wave his moral flag there as much as he likes. We have to appeal to his personal greed."

Ragnhild shook her head. "Not to this person's. He . . . he's not the kind to do that."

"Everyone has his price," Albert Gilstrup said with a sad

smile, wagging his forefinger from side to side, like a metronome, in front of her face.

"The Salvation Army grew out of pietism, and pietism was the practical person's approach to religion. That's why pietism was such a hit in the unproductive north: bread first, then a prayer. I propose two million."

"Two million?" Mads Gilstrup gasped. "For . . . recommending that they sell?"

"Providing that there's a sale, of course. No cure, no pay."

"That's still an insane sum of money," the son protested.

The father-in-law answered without a glance: "The only thing that's insane is that we have managed to decimate a family fortune at a time when everything else has gone up."

Mads Gilstrup opened his mouth like an aquarium fish, but nothing came out.

"This adviser of theirs won't have the stomach to negotiate the price if he thinks the first offer is too low," the father-in-law said. "We have to knock him out with the first punch. Two million. What do you say, Ragnhild?"

Ragnhild nodded slowly, concentrating on something outside the window because she couldn't bring herself to look at her husband, who sat with bowed head in the shadow beyond the reading lamp.

Jon Karlsen was already at the table waiting when she arrived. He seemed smaller than she remembered, but perhaps that was because he had swapped his uniform for a sack of a suit she assumed had been bought in Fretex. Or he looked as though he felt lost in the fashionable restaurant. He knocked over the flower vase as he stood up to greet her. They rescued the flowers in a joint operation and laughed. Afterward they talked about a variety of things. When he asked her if she had any children, she just shook her head.

Did he have any children? No. Right, but maybe he had . . . ? No, not that, either.

The conversation moved over to the properties owned by the Salvation Army, but she noticed he was arguing without the usual spark. He wore a polite smile and sipped his wine. She increased the offer by 10 percent. He shook his head, still smiling, and complimented her on the necklace she knew contrasted well with her skin.

"A present from my mother," she lied without effort. Thinking it was her eyes he was admiring. The light-blue irises with the clear sclera.

Between main course and dessert she threw in the offer of a personal emolument of two million. She was spared looking into his eyes because he was studying his wineglass, silent, suddenly white-faced.

At length, he asked, in a whisper: "Was this your idea?"

"Mine and my father-in-law's." She noticed she was short of breath.

"Albert Gilstrup?"

"Yes. Apart from us two and my husband no one will ever know about this. We would have as much to lose if this came out as . . . er, as you."

"Is it something I've said or done?"

"I beg your pardon?"

"What made you and your father-in-law think I would agree to a handful of silver?"

He looked up at her and Ragnhild could feel the blush spreading across her face. She couldn't remember blushing since her adolescence.

"Shall we drop the dessert?" He took the napkin from his lap and put it on the table beside the dinner plate.

"Take your time and think before you answer, Jon," she stammered. "For your own good. This can give you the chance to realize some dreams."

The words grated and jarred even in her ears. Jon signaled to the waiter for the bill.

"And what dreams are they? The dream of being a corrupt servant, a miserable deserter? Driving around in a fine car while everything you're trying to achieve as a person lies in ruins around you?" The fury in his voice was making it quiver. "Is that the kind of dream you have, Ragnhild Gilstrup?"

She was unable to answer.

"I must be blind," he said. "Because do you know what? When I met you I thought I saw . . . an altogether different person."

"You saw me," she whispered, sensing the onset of trembling, the same as she had experienced in the elevator.

"What?"

She cleared her voice. "You saw me. And now I've offended you. I am so sorry."

In the ensuing silence she felt herself sinking through hot and cold layers of water.

"Let's put all this behind us," she said as the waiter approached and took the card she had held up in one hand. "It's not important. Not for either of us. Would you like to walk with me in Frogner Park?"

"I . . ."

"Please?"

He looked at her in astonishment. Or did he?

How could those eyes—that saw everything—be astonished? Ragnhild Gilstrup looked down now from her window in Holmenkollen at a dark square below. Frogner Park. That was where the insanity had all started.

It was past midnight, the soup bus was parked in the garage and Martine felt pleasantly exhausted, but also blessed. She was standing on the pavement in front of the hostel on the dark, narrow street of Heimdalsgata, waiting for Rikard, who had gone to fetch the car, when she heard the snow crunch behind her.

"Hi."

She turned and felt her heart stop as she saw the silhouette of a tall figure towering under the solitary streetlight.

"Don't you recognize me?"

One heartbeat. Two. Then three and four. She had recognized the voice.

"What are you doing here?" she asked, hoping her voice
would not reveal how frightened she had been.

"I found out you were working on the bus this evening
and that it was parked here at midnight. There has been
a development in the case, as they say. I've been doing a
bit of thinking." He stepped forward and the light fell on
his face. It was harder, older than she remembered. Strange
how much you can forget in twenty-four hours. "And I have
a couple of questions."

"Which couldn't wait?" she asked with a smile, and saw
that her smile had made the policeman's face soften.

"Are you waiting for someone?" Harry asked.

"Yes, Rikard is going to drive me home."

She looked at the bag the policeman was carrying over
his shoulder. It had JETTE written on one side, but looked
too old and worn to be the fashionable retro model.

"You should get yourself a couple of new insoles for the
sneakers you've got in there," she said, pointing.

He eyed her in astonishment.

"You don't need to be Jean-Baptiste Grenouille to recognize the smell," she added.

"Patrick Süskind," he said. *"Perfume."*

"A policeman who reads," she said.

"A Salvation Army soldier who reads about murder," he
said. "Which leads us back to the reason for my being here,
I'm afraid."

A Saab 900 drove up and stopped. The window was lowered without a sound.

"Ready to go, Martine?"

"Just a moment, Rikard." She turned to Harry. "Where
are you going?"

"Bislett. But I prefer—"

"Rikard, is it all right if Harry joins us as far as Bislett? You live there, too, don't you?"

Rikard stared out into the dark before replying with a drawled "Of course."

"Come on," Martine said, passing a hand to Harry. Harry sent her a look of surprise.

"Slippery shoes," she whispered, grabbing his hand. She could feel that his hand was warm and dry, and it automatically squeezed hers as if he were afraid she would fall that instant.

Rikard drove with care, his eyes jumping from mirror to mirror as though expecting an ambush from behind.

"Well?" said Martine from the front seat.

Harry cleared his throat. "Someone tried to shoot Jon Karlsen today."

"What?" cried Martine.

Harry met Rikard's eyes in the mirror.

"Had you already heard?" Harry asked.

"No," Rikard said.

"Who . . . ?" Martine started.

"We don't know," Harry said.

"But . . . both Robert and Jon. Has this got something to do with the Karlsen family?"

"I think they were only after one of them," Harry said.

"What do you mean?"

"The gunman postponed his trip home. He must have discovered he had shot the wrong man. Robert wasn't the intended target."

"Robert hadn't—"

"That's why I had to talk to you. I think you can tell me whether my theory is right or not."

"Which theory?"

"That Robert died because he was unlucky enough to take Jon's shift in Egertorget."

Martine swiveled around and looked in alarm at Harry.

"You have the duty roster," Harry said. "When I first went to see you, I noticed the roster hanging from the board in reception. Where everyone could see who was on duty that night in Egertorget. It was Jon Karlsen."

"How . . . ?"

"I popped in after going to the hospital and checked. Jon's name was there. But Robert and Jon swapped shifts after the list was typed up, didn't they?"

Rikard turned up Stensberggata toward Bislett.

Martine chewed her lower lip. "Shifts are changed all the time, and if people arrange switches I don't always find out."

Rikard drove down Sofies Gate.

Martine's eyes widened. "Ah, now I remember! Robert called to tell me they had swapped, so I didn't need to do anything. That must be why I didn't think of it. But . . . but that means that . . ."

"Jon and Robert are very similar," Harry said. "And in uniform . . ."

"And it was dark and snowing . . ." Martine said in a hushed voice, as though to herself.

"What I wanted to know is if anyone had called you to ask about the roster. And about that evening, in particular."

"Not as far as I can remember," Martine said.

"Can you think about it? I'll call you tomorrow."

"OK," said Martine.

Harry held her eyes and in the light from the street lamp again he noticed the irregularities in her pupils.

Rikard pulled over to the curb.

"How did you know?" Harry asked.

"Know what?" Martine asked with alacrity.

"I was asking the driver," Harry said. "How did you know I live here?"

"You said," Rikard answered. "I know my way around. As Martine said, I live in Bislett, too."

Harry stood on the pavement watching the car drive away.

It was obvious the young man was besotted. He had driven here first so that he could be alone with Martine for a few minutes. To talk to her. To have the requisite peace and quiet when you have something to say, to make it clear who you are, to unburden your soul, to find out about yourself and all the stuff that is part of being young, and with which, he was happy to say, he had finished. All for a kind word, a hug and the hope of a kiss before she went. To beg for love the way that infatuated idiots do. Of all ages.

Harry ambled toward the front door as his hand instinctively searched for the keys in his trouser pocket, and his mind searched for something that was repelled every time he came close. And his eyes sought something he struggled to hear. It was a tiny sound, but at this late hour Sofies Gate was quiet. Harry looked down at the piles of snow left by the plows today. It sounded like a cracking noise. Melting. Impossible; it was three degrees below zero.

Harry put the key in the lock.

And he could hear it was not a melting sound. It was ticking. He turned slowly and scrutinized the snowdrifts. A glint. Glass. Harry walked back, bent down and picked up the watch. The glass on Møller's present was as shiny as the surface of water. Not a scratch. And the time was accurate to the second. Two minutes ahead of his watch. What was it Møller had said? So that he would be in time for what he thought he would miss.

The Darkness

The electric radiator in the recreation room of the hostel banged as though someone were throwing pebbles at it. The hot air quivered above the brown burn marks on the burlap wallpaper, which sweated nicotine, glue and the greasy smell of those who had lived here and moved on. The sofa material scratched him through his trousers.

Despite the dry, crackling heat from the radiator, he was trembling as he watched the news on the TV set attached to the wall bracket. He recognized the pictures of the square, but understood nothing of what they were saying. In the other corner an old man was sitting in an armchair smoking thin hand-rolled cigarettes. When there was so little left that they were burning his black fingertips he quickly produced two matchsticks from a box, trapped the cigarette end between them and inhaled until he burned his lips. A decorated lopped-off top end of a spruce tree stood on a table in the corner, attempting to glitter.

He thought about the Christmas dinner in Dalj.

It was two years after the end of the war and the Serbs had withdrawn from what once had been Vukovar. The Croatian authorities had packed them into the Hotel International in Zagreb. He had asked lots of people if they knew where Giorgi's family had ended up, and one day he had met another refugee who knew that Giorgi's mother had died during the siege and that he and his father had moved to Dalj, a small border town not far from Vukovar. On December 26 he caught the train to Osijek and then from there to Dalj. He talked to the conductor, who confirmed that the train would go on to Borovo, the terminal, and would be back in Dalj by six-thirty. It was two o'clock when he alighted in Dalj. He asked for directions to the address, which was a low apartment building as gray as the town. He went into the hallway, found the door and before ringing said a silent prayer that they would be at home. His heart was pounding fast as he heard light footsteps inside.

Giorgi opened the door. He hadn't changed much. Paler, but the same blond curls, blue eyes and heart-shaped mouth that had always made him think of a young god. The smile in his eyes was gone, however, like a broken lightbulb.

"Don't you recognize me, Giorgi?" he asked after a while. "We lived in the same town; we went to the same school."

Giorgi furrowed his brow. "Did we? Wait. The voice. You must be Serg Dolac. Of course, you were the fast runner. Jesus, how you've changed. But it's great to see people we knew in Vukovar. They've all gone."

"Not me."

"No, not you, Serg."

Giorgi embraced him and held him for such a long time that he could feel the heat beginning to tremble through his frozen body. Then he led him into the flat.

It was dark in the sparsely furnished sitting room as they sat talking about all the things that had happened, and all the people they had known in Vukovar and where they were now. When he asked whether Giorgi remembered Tinto the dog, Giorgi gave him a rather perplexed smile.

Giorgi said his father would be home soon. Did Serg want to stay and eat?

He looked at his watch. The train would be at the station in three hours.

The father was very surprised to meet a visitor from Vukovar.

"This is Serg," Giorgi said. "Serg Dolac."

"Serg Dolac?" the father asked, scrutinizing him. "Yes, there's something familiar about you. Hm. Didn't I know your father? No?"

Darkness fell, and after taking their places at the table, the father gave them large white napkins and loosened his red neckerchief and tied the napkin around his neck. The father said grace, made the sign of the cross and inclined his head to the only picture in the room, a framed photo of a woman.

As Giorgi and his father took their cutlery, he bowed and intoned:

"Who is this that comes from Edom, coming from Bozrah, his garments stained crimson? Who is this, in glorious apparel, marching in the greatness of his strength? 'It is I, who announce that right has won the day, it is I,' says the Lord, 'for I am mighty to save.'"

The father eyed him in astonishment. Then he passed him the dish with the large, pale pieces of meat.

The meal continued in silence. The wind made the thin windows groan.

After the meat, there was dessert. *Palacinka*, thin pancakes filled with jam and chocolate spread over the top. He hadn't had one since he was a child in Vukovar.

"Take another, dear Serg," the father said. "It's Christmas."

He checked his watch. The train would leave in half an hour. It was time. He cleared his throat, put down the napkin and stood up. "Giorgi and I have been talking about all the people we remember from Vukovar, but there is one person we haven't spoken about yet," he said.

"I see," the father said, mystified, and smiled. "Who is that, Serg?" The father had turned his head a little and viewed him with one eye, as though trying to identify something he could not put his finger on.

"His name was Bobo."

He could see in Giorgi's father's eyes that now he knew. He might have been waiting for this moment. He heard his voice resound between the bare walls. "You were sitting in the jeep and pointed him out to the Serbian commanding officer." He swallowed. "Bobo died."

The room went still. The father put down his cutlery. "It was war, Serg. We all have to die." He said this with composure. Almost resignation.

The father and Giorgi were motionless as he took the gun from the waistband of his trousers, pointed it across the table and fired. The explosion was brief and dry, and the father's body jerked as the chair legs scraped against the floor. The father lowered his head and stared at the hole in the napkin hanging in front of his chest. Then it was sucked into his chest as the blood spread like a red flower over the white cloth.

"Look at me," he ordered, and the father automatically raised his head. The second shot made a tiny black hole in his forehead, which fell forward, hitting the plate of *palacinka* with a soft thud.

He turned to Giorgi, who was staring open-mouthed, a red line running down his cheek. It took him a second to realize that this was jam from his father's *palacinka*. He stuffed the pistol into the waistband of his trousers.

"You'll have to shoot me, too, Serg."

"I don't have any scores to settle with you." He walked out of the sitting room and took the jacket hanging by the door.

Giorgi followed. "I'll get even with you! I'll find you and kill you, if you don't kill me!"

"And how will you find me, Giorgi?"

"You cannot hide. I know who you are."

"Do you? You think I'm Serg. But Serg Dolac had red hair and was taller than me. And I'm not a fast runner, Giorgi. But let's just be happy you don't recognize me, Giorgi. It means I can spare your life."

Then he leaned forward, kissed Giorgi hard on the mouth, opened the door and left.

The newspapers had written about the murder, but the police had never looked for anyone. And three months later, one Sunday, his mother told him about a Croatian who had visited her to ask for help. The man had been unable to pay much, but he had collected some money from the family. A Serbian who had tortured his brother during the war had been found living nearby. And someone had mentioned something about the one they called the little redeemer.

The old man burned his fingertips on the thin cigarette and swore aloud.

He stood up and went to reception. Behind the boy on the other side of the glass partition was the red flag of the Salvation Army.

"Could I use the phone, please?"

The boy scowled at him. "If it's a local call, yes."

"It is."

The boy pointed to a narrow office behind him, and he entered. Sat down at the desk and contemplated the telephone. He thought of his mother's voice. How concerned and frightened it could be, and gentle and warm at the same time. It was like an embrace. He stood up, closed the door to reception and punched in the number of Hotel International. She wasn't there. He didn't leave a message. The door opened.

"You're not allowed to close the door," the boy said. "OK?"

"OK. Sorry. Do you have a telephone directory?"

The boy rolled his eyes, pointed to a thick book beside the phone and left.

He found Jon Karlsen at 4 Gøteborggata, and dialed the number.

Thea Nilsen contemplated the ringing telephone.

She had locked herself in Jon's flat with the key he had given her. They said there was a bullet hole somewhere. She had searched and found it in the cupboard door.

The man had tried to shoot Jon. To kill him. The thought made her strangely agitated. Not frightened at all. At times she thought she would never be frightened again, not like that, not about that, not about dying.

The police had been here, but they hadn't spent much time looking. No clues apart from the bullets, they had said.

In the hospital she had listened to Jon breathing in and out as he gazed at her. He had looked so helpless there in the large hospital bed. As though all she had to do was place a pillow over his face and he would be dead. And she had liked that, seeing him weak. Perhaps the schoolteacher in Hamsun's *Victoria* was right: For some women the need to feel sympathy made them hate their strong, healthy men and in secret they wished their husbands were cripples and dependent on their kindness.

But now she was alone in his flat and the telephone was ringing. She looked at her watch. It was the middle of the night. No one would call now. No one with honest intentions. Thea was not afraid to die. But she was afraid of this. Was it her, the woman Jon thought she knew nothing about?

She took two paces toward the phone. Paused. The fourth ring. It would stop after five. She hesitated. Another ring. She surged forward and picked up the receiver.

"Yes?"

It was quiet for a moment at the other end. Then a man spoke in English. "Sorry for calling so late. My name is Edom. Is Jon there?"

"No," she said with relief. "He's in the hospital."

"Ah, yes, I heard about what happened today. I'm an old friend and would like to visit him. Which hospital is he in?"

"Ullevål."

"Ullevål."

"Yes. I don't know what the department is called in English—it's *Neurokirurgisk* in Norwegian. But there's a policeman sitting outside the room and he won't let you in. Do you understand what I'm saying?"

"Understand?"

"My English . . . it's not very . . ."

"I understand perfectly. Thank you very much."

She put down the receiver and stood thinking for a long time. Then she resumed her search. They had said there were several bullet holes.

He told the boy in reception at the hostel that he was going for a walk and handed him the room key.

The boy glanced at the clock on the wall showing a quarter past twelve and told him to keep the key. He explained that he was going to lock up and go to bed soon, but the room key also opened the front door.

The cold assaulted him as soon as he was outside, biting and scratching. He lowered his head and began to stride out with purpose. This was risky. Definitely risky. But he had to do it.

Ola Henmo, the production manager at Hafslund Energi, sat in the control room at the load dispatch center in Montebello, Oslo, thinking how great it would be to smoke while keeping an eye on the forty screens scattered around the room. During the day there were twelve people in here, but at night just three. They usually sat at their own workstations, but tonight the cold outside seemed to have driven them around one desk in the middle of the room.

Geir and Ebbe were arguing about horses, as always, and the recent racing results. For eight years they had been doing that, and it had never occurred to them to place separate bets.

Ola was more concerned about the substation on Kirkeveien between Ullevålsveien and Sognsveien.

"Thirty-six percent overload on T-One. Twenty-nine percent on T-Two to T-Four," he said.

"Christ, the way people are stoking up out there," Geir said. "Are they frightened of freezing to death? It's nighttime. Why don't they snuggle up under the duvet? Sweet Revenge in the third? Are you out of your mind?"

"Folks don't turn down the heating because of that," Ebbe said. "Not in this country. They chuck money out the window."

"It's going to end in tears," Ola said.

"No, it won't," Ebbe said. "We'll just pump up more oil."

"I'm thinking about T-One," Ola said, pointing to the screen. "It's on six hundred and eighty amps now. Full capacity is five hundred nominal load."

"Relax," Ebbe managed to get in, a second before the alarm went off.

"Oh, shit," Ola said. "There she blows. Check the list and call the guys on duty."

"See," Geir said. "T-Two's down, too. And T-Three just went."

"Bingo!" shouted Ebbe. "Should we have a bet on whether T-Four—"

"Too late. She just blew," Geir said.

Ola ran his eye over the small-scale map. "OK." He sighed. "Power's gone in lower Sogn, Fagerborg and Bislett."

"Bet you I know what's happened!" Ebbe said. "A thousand on cable sleeving."

Geir screwed up one eye: "Meter transformer. And five hundred's enough."

"Cut that out now," Ola growled. "Ebbe, call the fire station. I bet there's a fire up there."

"Agreed," Ebbe said. "Two hundred?"

When the light went out in the hospital room the darkness was so total that Jon's first thought was that he had gone blind. The optic nerve must have been damaged in the collision and the effect was only apparent now. But then he heard shouting from the corridor, made out the outline of the window and realized that the electricity was down.

He heard the chair scrape outside and the door swung open.

"Hello, are you there?" a voice said.

"Yes," Jon answered at a higher pitch than he had intended.

"I'll just walk around and see what has happened. Don't go anywhere, OK?"

"No, but . . ."

"Yes?"

"Don't they have an emergency generator?"

"I think they're for operating rooms and surveillance cameras."

"I see . . ."

Jon listened to the policeman's footsteps fading away as he stared at the green illuminated exit sign over the door. The sign reminded him of Ragnhild again. That had also started in the dark. After eating, they had gone for a walk in pitch-black Frogner Park and stood in the deserted square by the monolith, looking eastward toward downtown. And he had told her the story about how Gustav Vigeland, the singular artist from Mandal, had made it a condition of his decorating the park with sculptures that the park should be extended so that the monolith would be symmetrical in relation to the surrounding churches, and the main gate directly facing Uranienborg Church. When the City Council representative had explained that they could not move the park, Vigeland had demanded that the churches be moved.

She had just looked at him with a serious expression while he was talking, and it had run through his mind that this woman was so strong and intelligent that she frightened him.

"I'm frozen," she had said, shivering under her coat.

"Perhaps we should go back . . ." he had started, but then she had placed her hand behind his head and turned her face up to his. She had the most unusual eyes he had ever seen. Light blue, almost turquoise, surrounded by a whiteness that made her wan skin take on color. And he had done what he always did; he stooped and bent down. Then her tongue was in his mouth, hot and wet, an insistent muscle, a mysterious anaconda that wound its way around his tongue and searched for a grip. He had felt the heat through the thick wool material of the suit trousers from Fretex when her hand came to rest with impressive accuracy.

"Come on," she had whispered in his ear, putting one foot on the fence, and he had looked down and caught a glimpse of white skin where the stockings finished before tearing himself away.

"I can't," he had said.

"Why not?" she had groaned.

"I've made a vow. To God."

And she had scrutinized him, puzzled at first. Then her eyes had filled with water, and she had begun to cry quietly and rested her head against his chest, saying she never thought she would ever find him again. He had not understood what she meant, but had stroked her hair, and that was how it all started. They always met in his flat and always after she had taken the initiative. At first she made a few halfhearted attempts to make him break his chastity vows, but then she seemed to be happy for them to lie next to each other on the bed and just caress and be caressed. Now and then, for reasons he did not understand, she could become desperate and say he must never leave her. They didn't speak much, but he had a feeling that their abstinence bound her closer to him. Their meetings had come to a sudden end when he met Thea. Not so much because he didn't want to meet her, but because Thea had wanted to exchange spare keys with Jon. She had said it was a question of trust, and he hadn't been able to come up with a riposte.

Jon turned in bed and shut his eyes. He wanted to dream now. Dream and forget. If that was possible. Sleep was on its way when he felt a draft in the room. As an instinctive reaction, he opened his eyes and rolled over. In the pale-green light from the exit sign he saw that the door was closed. He peered into the shadows as he held his breath and listened.

Martine stood in the darkened window of her flat on Sorgenfrigata, which had also been blacked out by the power cut. Nevertheless, she could still make out the car down below. It looked like Rikard's.

Rikard had not tried to kiss her when she got out of the car. He had just looked at her with puppy eyes and said he was going to be the new chief administrator. There had been signals. Positive signals. It would be him. There had been a strange stiffness in his expression when he had asked her if she thought so, too.

She had said he would make a good chief administrator and went to open the door handle while waiting for his touch. But it hadn't come. And then she was out.

Martine sighed, picked up the cell phone and dialed the number she had been given.

"Speak." Harry Hole's voice sounded quite different on the phone. Or perhaps it was because he was at home; maybe this was his home voice.

"It's Martine," she said.

"Hi." It was impossible to hear if he was pleased or not.

"You asked me to give some thought to whether I could

remember anyone calling or asking about the duty roster," she said. "About Jon's shift."

"Yes?"

"I've thought about it."

"And?"

"No one." Long pause.

"Did you call to tell me that?" His voice was warm and rough. As though he had been asleep.

"Yes. Shouldn't I have done that?"

"Yes, yes, of course. Thank you very much for your help."

"Not at all."

She closed her eyes and waited until she heard his voice again.

"Did you . . . get home all right?"

"Mm. There's a blackout here."

"Here, too," he said. "It'll be back soon."

"What if it isn't?"

"What do you mean?"

"Will we be cast into chaos?"

"Do you think about that sort of thing a lot?"

"From time to time. I think civilization's infrastructure is much more fragile than we like to believe. What do you think?"

He paused for a long time before answering. "Well, I think all the systems we rely on can short-circuit and hurl us into deepest night, where laws and regulations no longer protect us, where the cold and beasts of prey rule, and everyone has to try to save his own skin."

"That," she said, when no more was forthcoming, "was not very suitable for helping little girls get off to sleep. I think you're a real dystopian, Harry."

"Of course. I'm a policeman. Good night."

He had put down the receiver before she had a chance to formulate an answer.

*   *   *

Harry crept back under the duvet and gazed at the wall.

The temperature had plummeted in his flat.

Harry thought about the sky outside. About Åndalsnes. About his grandfather. And his mother. The funeral. And the prayer she had whispered at night in her gentle, gentle voice: "A mighty fortress is our God." But in the weightless moment before sleeping he thought of Martine and her voice, which was still in his head.

The TV in the sitting room came to life with a groan and began to hiss. The lightbulb in the corridor came back on and cast light through the open bedroom door and onto Harry's face. But by then he was already asleep.

Twenty minutes later Harry's telephone rang. He thrust open his eyes and swore. Shuffled, shivering, into the hallway and lifted the receiver.

"Speak. Softly."

"Harry?"

"Just about. What's up, Halvorsen?"

"Something's happened."

"Something, or a lot?"

"A lot."

"Fuck."

15

The Raid

Sail stood shivering on the path beside the Akerselva. To hell with the Albanian bastard! Despite the cold, the river was ice-free and black and reinforced the darkness under the plain iron bridge. Sail was sixteen years old and had come from Somalia with his mother when he was twelve. He had started selling hash when he was fourteen, and heroin last spring. Now Hux had let him down again, and he couldn't risk standing here all night with his goods and no trade. Ten fixes. If he had been eighteen he could always have gone down to Plata and sold them there. But the cops hauled in underage dealers at Plata. Their territory was here, along the river. Most of them were young boys from Somalia selling to customers who either were underage, too, or had other reasons not to be seen at Plata. Fuck Hux—he needed the cash desperately!

A man came walking down the footpath. It wasn't Hux—that was for sure; he was still limping after the B gang had beaten him up for selling diluted amphetamines. As if there were anything else. And he didn't look like an undercover cop, either. Or a junkie, even though he was wearing the type of blue coat he had seen many junkies wear. Sail looked around. They were alone.

When the man was close enough Sail stepped out of the shadow of the bridge. "Wanna fix?"

The man gave a brief smile, shook his head and made to walk on. However, Sail had positioned himself in the middle of the path. He was big for his age. For any age. And his knife was, too. A Rambo *First Blood* with a hollow handle containing a compass and fishing line. It cost around a thousand kroner at the Army shop but he had got it for three hundred from a pal.

"Do you want to buy or just pay up?" Sail asked, holding the knife so that the grooved blade reflected the pale light from the street lamp.

"Excuse me?"

Foreignerspeak. Not Sail's strongest suit.

"Money." Sail heard his voice rising. He always got so angry when he robbed people; he didn't know why. "Now."

The foreigner nodded and held up his left hand in defense while calmly moving his right inside his jacket. Then he withdrew his hand with lightning speed. Sail did not have time to react; he whispered a "shit" as he realized he was staring down the muzzle of a gun. He wanted to run, but the black metal eye seemed to have frozen his feet to the ground.

"I . . ." he began.

"Run," said the man. "Now."

And Sail ran. Ran with the cold, damp air from the river burning in his lungs and the lights from the Plaza and the Post House jumping up and down on his retinas, ran until the river flowed out into the fjord and he could run no farther, and he screamed at the fences around the container terminal that one day he would kill them all.

A quarter of an hour had passed since Harry had been awoken by Halvorsen's call. The police car pulled up by the curb at Sofies Gate and Harry slid onto the backseat beside his colleague. He mumbled an "Evening" to the uniformed policemen in the front.

The driver, a hefty fellow with a closed police face, drove off quietly.

"Put your foot down," said the pale young pimply policeman in the passenger seat.

"How many are there of us?" Harry peered at his watch.

"Two cars plus this one," Halvorsen said.

"So six plus us two. I don't want any blue lights. We'll try to do this in a calm manner. You, me, a uniform and a gun will perform the arrest. The other five will cover potential escape routes. Are you carrying a weapon?"

Halvorsen slapped his chest pocket.

"That's good because I'm not," Harry said.

"Don't you have your firearms license yet?"

Harry leaned forward between the front seats. "Which of you would most like to join us in arresting a professional hit man?"

"Me!" was the instant response from the young man in the passenger seat.

"Then it's you," Harry said to the driver, nodding slowly to the mirror. Six minutes later they had parked at the bottom of Heimdalsgata in Grønland and were studying the front door where Harry had been standing earlier in the evening.

"So our man in Telenor was sure?" Harry asked.

"Yep," Halvorsen said. "Torkildsen says an internal number in the hostel tried to call the Hotel International about fifty minutes ago."

"Can't be a coincidence," Harry said, opening the car door. "This is Salvation Army territory. I'll take a look around. Be back in a minute."

When Harry returned, the driver was sitting with a machine gun in his lap, an MP5, which recent regulations allowed patrol cars to carry locked in the trunk.

"You don't have anything more discreet?" Harry asked.

The man shook his head. Harry turned to Halvorsen. "And you?"

"Just a sweet little Smith and Wesson thirty-eight."

"You can borrow mine," said the young policeman in the passenger seat with gusto. "Jericho nine forty-one. Real power. Same as the police in Israel use to blow off the heads of the Arab scum."

"Jericho?" Harry echoed. Halvorsen could see his eyes had narrowed.

"I'm not going to ask where you got hold of that gun. But I think I should inform you that in all probability it comes from a gang of gun smugglers. Led by your former colleague Tom Waaler."

The policeman in the passenger seat turned around. His blue eyes vied with his fiery pimples for brightness. "I remember Tom Waaler. And do you know what, Inspector? Most of us think he was a good guy."

Harry swallowed and looked out the window.

"Most of you are wrong," Halvorsen said.

"Give me the radio," Harry said.

He passed on quick, efficient instructions to the other drivers. Said where he wanted each car without mentioning street names or buildings that could be identified by the regular radio audience: crime correspondents, crooks and nosey parkers who picked up the frequency and doubtless already knew that something was brewing.

"Let's get going," Harry said, turning to the passenger seat. "You stay here and keep in contact with the Ops Room. Call us on your colleague's walkie-talkie if there is anything. OK?"

The young man shrugged.

Only after Harry had rung three times at the front door of the hostel did a boy come shuffling out. He opened the door a little and peered at them through sleepy eyes.

"Police," Harry said, rummaging in his pocket. "Shit.

Looks like I've left my ID at home. Show him yours, Halvorsen."

"You can't come in here," the boy said. "You know that."

"This is murder, not drugs."

"Eh?"

The boy was looking with big eyes over Harry's shoulder at the policeman who had raised his MP5. Then he opened the door and stepped back without even noticing Halvorsen's ID.

"Do you have a Christo Stankic here?" Harry asked. The boy shook his head.

"A foreigner with a camel-hair coat, maybe?" Halvorsen asked as Harry slipped behind the reception desk and opened the guest register.

"The only foreigner we have here is one they brought from the soup bus," the boy stuttered. "But he didn't have a camel-hair coat. Just a suit jacket. Rikard Nilsen gave him a winter jacket from our store."

"Did he make a call from here?" Harry called from behind the desk.

"He used the phone in the office behind you."

"Time?"

"About eleven-thirty."

"Matches the call to Zagreb," Halvorsen murmured.

"Is he in?" Harry asked.

"Don't know. He took the key with him and I've been asleep."

"Do you have a master key?"

The boy nodded, unhooked a key from the bunch he had attached to his belt and put it in Harry's outstretched hand.

"Room number?"

"Twenty-six. Up the stairs. At the end of the corridor."

Harry had already set off. The uniformed policeman followed close behind with both hands on the machine gun.

"Stay in your room until this is over," Halvorsen said

to the boy as he pulled out his Smith & Wesson revolver, winked and patted him on the shoulder.

He unlocked the door and noted that reception was unmanned. Natural enough. As natural as a police car occupied by a policeman parked farther up the street. After all, he had just discovered firsthand that this was a criminal area.

He trudged up the stairs, and as he rounded the corner of the corridor he heard a crackle he recognized from the bunkers in Vukovar—a walkie-talkie.

He glanced up. At the end of the corridor, by the door to his room, stood two men in plain clothes and one uniformed policeman holding a machine gun. Right away he recognized one of the plainclothes men, the one with his hand on the doorknob. The uniformed policeman raised the walkie-talkie and spoke quietly into it.

The other two were facing him. It was too late to retreat.

He nodded to them, stopped in front of Room 22 and shook his head as if to show his despair at the increasing criminality in the neighborhood while pretending to rummage through his pockets for his room key. From the corner of his eye he watched the policeman from the reception line at the Scandia Hotel push open the door to the room without a sound, closely followed by the other two.

As soon as they were out of sight he went back down the way he had come. Took the stairs in two strides. He had noted all the exits—as he always did—when he arrived in the white bus earlier in the evening. For an instant he wondered about the door leading into the backyard, but it was too obvious. Unless he was very much mistaken, they would have placed a policeman there. His best chance was the main entrance. He walked out and turned left, straight toward the police car. On that route there was only one of them. If he managed to slip past he could go down to the river and the darkness.

"Fuck, fuck, fuck!" Harry shouted, on finding the room empty.

"Maybe he's gone out for a walk," Halvorsen said.

They both turned to the driver. He hadn't said anything, but the walkie-talkie on his chest was speaking. "It's the same guy I saw going in a moment ago. Now he's coming out again. He's coming toward me." Harry breathed in. There was a particular perfumed smell in the room that he vaguely recognized.

"That's him," Harry said. "He tricked us."

"That's him," the driver said into the microphone, running after Harry, who was already out the door.

"Fantastic. I've got him," the radio crackled. "Out."

"No!" Harry shouted as they stormed down the corridor. "Don't try to stop him. Wait for us!"

The driver repeated the order into the mike, but received a wordless hiss in response.

He saw the door of the police car open and a young uniformed officer step out under the streetlight with a gun.

"Halt!" shouted the man, standing with legs apart and the gun pointed at him. Inexperienced, he thought. There was almost fifty yards of darkened street between them, and, unlike the young mugger under the bridge, this policeman was not canny enough to wait until the victim's escape routes were cut off. For the second time that night he took out his Llama Mini-Max. And instead of making off, he began to run straight toward the policeman.

"Halt!" repeated the police officer.

The distance had shrunk to thirty yards. Twenty yards. He raised his gun and shot.

People tend to overestimate the chances of hitting another person at distances over ten yards. On the other hand, they often underestimate the psychological effect of the sound, of the explosion combined with the pinging of lead against something close by. When the bullet hit the car windshield, which went white, then collapsed, the same thing happened to the policeman. He went white and sank to his knees as his fingers tried to cling to the too-heavy Jericho 941.

Harry and Halvorsen arrived on Heimdalsgata at the same time.

"There," Halvorsen said.

The young policeman was still on his knees beside the car with his gun pointing to the sky. But farther up the street they caught sight of the back of the blue coat they had seen in the corridor.

"He's running toward Eika," Halvorsen said.

Harry turned to the driver, who had joined them.

"Give me the MP-Five."

The officer passed Harry the weapon. "It isn't . . ."

But Harry had already started running. He heard Halvorsen behind him, but the rubber soles of his Doc Martens gave him a better purchase on the blue ice. The man in front of him had a long lead; he had already rounded the corner to Vahls Gate, which skirted the park. Harry held the machine gun in one hand and concentrated on breathing while trying to run with an efficient use of movement. He slowed down and got the gun into a shooting position before arriving at the corner. Tried not to think too much as he stuck out his head and looked to the right.

There was no one waiting for him.

No one to be seen on the street, either.

But a man like Stankic would hardly have been stupid enough to run into any of the backyards, which were rat traps, with their locked gates. Harry peered into the park, where the large white surface of snow reflected the lights of the surrounding buildings. Wasn't something moving over there? Sixty, seventy yards away, a figure making slow headway through the snow. Blue jacket. Harry sprinted across the road, took off and sailed over the snowdrift and plunged into it, sinking up to his waist in fresh snow.

"Fuck!"

He had dropped the machine gun. The figure ahead of him turned, then struggled forward. Harry's hand searched for the gun as he watched Stankic feverishly fighting his way through the loose snow, which wouldn't allow him to gain a foothold. His fingers met something hard. There. Harry pulled out the weapon and heaved himself up. Got one leg out, stretched it as far as he could, rolled over, pulled the other leg, stretched it out. After thirty yards the lactic acid was burning in his thigh muscles, but the distance between them had shrunk. The other man was almost on the footpath and out of the mass of snow. Harry gritted his teeth and managed to speed up. He put the distance at fifteen yards. Close enough. Harry dropped onto his stomach in the snow and set up the weapon. Blew the snow off the sights, released the safety catch, selected the lever for single-fire mode and waited until the man had reached the cone of light from the street lamp by the footpath.

"Police!" Harry didn't appreciate the comical side of the next word until he had shouted it: "Freeze!"

The man ahead continued to plow his way through. Harry squeezed the trigger.

"Halt or I'll shoot!"

The man was only five yards from the path now.

"I'm aiming at your head," Harry shouted. "And I won't miss."

Stankic dived forward, grabbed the lamppost with both hands and pulled himself out of the snow. Harry had the blue jacket in his sights. Held his breath and did what he had been taught, to overrule the impulse in the cerebellum, which, with the logic of evolution, says you should not kill anyone of your kind; he concentrated on technique, on not pushing or jerking the trigger. Harry felt the spring mechanism give and heard a metallic click, but there was no recoil against his shoulder. A malfunction? Harry fired again. Another click.

The man stood up with a flurry of snow around him, stepped onto the path and stamped his feet. He turned and watched Harry. Harry didn't move. The man stood with his arms hanging down by his sides. Like a sleepwalker, thought Harry. Stankic raised his hand. Harry saw the gun and knew he was helpless where he lay. Stankic's hand continued up to his forehead in an ironic salute. Then he pivoted and set off at a run up the path.

Harry closed his eyes and felt his heart pounding against the inside of his ribs.

By the time he had fought his way through to the path, the man had long been swallowed up by the darkness. Harry slid out the magazine of the MP5 and checked. As he thought. In a sudden bout of fury he hurled the weapon in the air, and it rose like an ugly black bird in front of the Plaza before falling and landing with a gentle splash in the black water beneath him.

When Halvorsen arrived, Harry was sitting in the snow with a cigarette between his lips.

Halvorsen was bent double, holding his knees, his chest heaving. "Christ, you can run," he wheezed. "Gone?"

"Vanished," Harry said. "Let's go back."

"Where's the MP-Five?"

"Didn't you just ask me that?"

Halvorsen looked at Harry and decided not to dig any further.

Two police cars stood in front of the hostel with their blue lights flashing. A crowd of shivering men with long lenses protruding from their chests thronged outside the front door, which was obviously locked. Harry and Halvorsen walked down Heimdalsgata. Halvorsen was finishing a conversation on his cell phone.

"Why do I always think of a line for a porn film when I see that?" Harry said.

"Journalists," Halvorsen said. "How did they get wind of this?"

"Ask the whelp on the walkie-talkie," Harry said. "My guess is he let the cat out of the bag. What did they say in the Ops Room?"

"They're sending all available patrol cars to the river at once. The Uniformed Division is sending a dozen guys on foot. What do you think?"

"He's good. They'll never find him. Call Beate and ask her to come."

One of the journalists had spotted them and came over. "Well, Harry?"

"You're up late, Gjendem."

"What's going on?"

"Not a great deal."

"Oh? I see someone has shot out the windshield of one of your police cars."

"Who says someone didn't hit it with a stick?" Harry said, with the journalist still trotting after him.

"The officer sitting in there. He says he was shot at."

"Christ, I'd better have a word with him," Harry said. "Excuse me, gentlemen!"

The throng moved aside with grudging reluctance and Harry knocked on the front door. There was a clicking and buzzing of cameras and flashes.

"Is there any connection between this and the murder in Egertorget?" one of the journalists shouted. "Is the Salvation Army involved?"

The door opened a crack and the driver's face came into view. He stepped back, and Harry and Halvorsen pushed through. They walked through reception, where the young policeman was sitting in a chair staring into space with vacant eyes while a colleague crouched in front of him, speaking in a low voice.

On the floor above, the door to Room 26 was still open.

"Touch as little as possible," Harry said to the driver. "Beate Lønn's sure to want fingerprints and DNA."

They cast around, opened cupboard doors and peeked under the bed.

"Jeez," Halvorsen said. "Not a single thing. The guy had only what he was standing up in."

"He must have had a suitcase or something to bring the gun into the country," Harry said. "He may have got rid of it, of course. Or put it somewhere for safekeeping."

"There aren't that many luggage-storage places in Oslo anymore."

"Think."

"Right. The luggage room in one of the hotels where he was staying. The lockers in Oslo Central Station, of course."

"Follow the line of thought."

"Which line?"

"He's out there now and has a bag somewhere."

"He might need it now, yes. I'll call Ops and get someone sent to Scandia and the station and . . . what was the other hotel that had Stankic on their lists?"

"Radisson SAS on Holbergs Plass."

"Thank you."

Harry turned to the driver and asked if he wanted to go out and have a cigarette. They went down and out the back door. On the snow-covered handkerchief of a garden in the quiet backyard an old man was standing and smoking while contemplating the dirty yellow sky, oblivious of their presence.

"How's your colleague?" Harry asked, lighting both of their cigarettes.

"He'll survive. Sorry about the reporters."

"It's not your fault."

"Yes, it is. When he called me on the radio he said some-one had entered the hostel. I should have drilled things like that into him."

"There were a couple of other things you should have concerned yourself with."

The driver's eyes shot up. And blinked twice, in quick succession. "I apologize. I tried to warn you, but you ran off."

"OK. But why?"

The glow of the cigarette lit up, red and reproachful, as the driver sucked hard. "Most criminals give up the second they have an MP-Five pointing at them."

"That wasn't what I asked."

The muscles in his jaw tensed and relaxed. "It's an old story."

"Mm." Harry regarded the policeman. "We've all got old stories to tell. That doesn't mean we can put colleagues' lives at risk with empty magazines."

"You're right." The man dropped the half-smoked ciga-rette and it disappeared into the fresh snow with a hiss. He took a deep breath. "And you won't get into any trouble for it, Hole. I'll confirm your report."

Harry shifted his weight. Studied his cigarette. He put the policeman's age at about fifty. There weren't so many of them left in patrol cars. "The old story, is it one I would like to hear?"

"You've heard it before."

"Mm. A kid?"

"Twenty-two, no priors."

"Killed?"

"Paralyzed from the chest down. I hit him in the stom-ach, but the bullet went right through."

The old man coughed. Harry looked across. He was holding the cigarette between two matches.

In reception the young officer was still sitting on the

chair, being comforted. Harry motioned with his head for the sympathetic colleague to withdraw and sank down onto his haunches.

"Trauma counseling doesn't help," Harry said to the wan young man. "Get yourself together."

"Eh?"

"You're frightened because you think you were a shot away from dying. You weren't. He wasn't aiming at you. He aimed at the car."

"Eh?" the whelp repeated in the same monotone.

"This guy's a pro. He knows that if he shot a policeman, he wouldn't have a hope of getting away. He fired to frighten you."

"How do you know . . . ?"

"He didn't fire at me, either. You tell yourself that and you'll be able to sleep. And don't go to a psychologist; there are other people who need them." Harry's knees gave a nasty crack as he stood up. "And remember that higher-ranked officers are by definition cleverer than you. So next time, follow orders, OK?"

His heart was beating like a hunted animal's. A gust of wind caught the lamps hanging from the thin wires above the street and his shadow danced across the pavement. He wished he could take longer strides, but because of the ice's slippery surface he had to keep his legs beneath him as much as possible.

It must have been the telephone call to Zagreb from the office that had led the police to the hostel. And it had happened at such speed! As a result he would not be able to call her. He heard a car coming from behind and had to force himself not to turn around. Instead he listened. So far it hadn't braked. It passed by, followed by a rush of air and a flurry of powdery snow that settled on the tiny strip of neck not covered by the blue jacket, the jacket that the policeman had seen him wearing and meant he was no longer invisible. He had considered discarding the jacket, but a man in a shirt would not only look suspicious but would also freeze to death. He glanced at his watch. There were quite a few hours before the town came to life, before cafés and shops where he could find refuge were open. He had to find somewhere before then. A bolt-hole, a place where he could keep warm and rest until day broke.

He walked by a dirty yellow house front covered with graffiti. His eye was caught by one word painted there. VESTBREDDEN. The West Bank? A bit farther up the street a man was bent double in front of an entrance. From a distance it looked like he was resting his head against a door. As he came closer he saw that the man was holding his finger on a bell.

He stopped and waited. This might be his salvation.

A voice crackled from the speaker above the bell and the stooped figure straightened up, swayed and started yelling furiously by way of answer. His reddened, booze-battered skin hung off his face like the folds on a Shar-Pei dog. The man stopped, and the echoes between the houses died away in the night-still town. There was a low electric buzz and, with some difficulty, he shifted his center of gravity forward, pushed open the door and staggered in.

The door began to close, and his reactions were lightning fast. Too fast. His foot slipped on the blue ice and he just managed to slap down the palms of his hands on the burning cold surface before the rest of his body hit the pavement. He scrambled up again, saw that the door was on the verge of snapping shut, charged forward, stuck out his foot and felt the weight of the door trap his ankle. He sneaked inside and stood listening. Shuffling feet. Which seemed to stop before painfully resuming. Knocking. A door opened and a woman's voice screamed something in this weird singsong language of theirs. Then it came to an abrupt end, as though someone had cut her throat. After a few seconds of silence he heard a low whine, the noise children make when they are getting over the shock of hurting themselves. Then the door upstairs banged again and it was quiet.

He let the door close behind him. Among the trash under the stairs were a couple of newspapers. In Vukovar they had put paper in their shoes, since it insulated and absorbed moisture. His frosty breath was still visible, but for the time being he was safe.

Harry sat in the office behind the reception desk of the hostel, with the receiver against his ear, as he tried to visualize the flat he was calling. He saw photos of friends stuck to the mirror above the telephone. Smiling, in a party mood, maybe on a trip abroad. Girlfriends, mainly. He saw a flat with simple furnishings but cozy. Words of wisdom on the fridge door. Che Guevara poster in the bathroom. Did people still do that?

"Hello?" said a sleepy voice.

"It's me again."

"Daddy?"

Daddy? Intake of breath and Harry felt himself blush. "The policeman."

"Oh, yes." Stifled laughter. Bright and deep at the same time.

"Sorry to wake you, but we—"

"That doesn't matter."

There was one of those pauses Harry had wanted to avoid.

"I'm at the hostel," he said. "We've been trying to arrest a suspect. The receptionist says you and Rikard Nilsen brought him here earlier this evening."

"The poor man without any outdoor clothes?"

"Yes."

"What's he done?"

"We suspect he killed Robert Karlsen."

"My God!"

Harry noticed she pronounced these two words with equal stress.

"If it's all right with you, I'll send an officer over to talk to you. In the meantime perhaps you might try to remember what he said."

"OK, but can't it . . . ?" Pause.

"Hello?" Harry said.

"He said nothing," she said. "Just like war refugees. You can see it in the way they move. Like sleepwalkers. As if they're on autopilot. As if they're already dead."

"Mm. Did Rikard talk to him?"

"Maybe. Do you want his number?"

"Please."

"One moment."

She was right. Harry thought about the man getting up from the snow. How it had fallen off him, the limp arms and the blank face, like the zombies rising from graves in *Night of the Living Dead*.

Harry heard a cough and spun around in his chair. In the office doorway stood Gunnar Hagen and David Eckhoff.

"Are we disturbing you?" Hagen asked.

"Come in," Harry said.

The two men came in and sat down on the other side of the desk.

"We'd like a report," Hagen said.

Before Harry could ask who he meant by "we," Martine's voice was back with the number. Harry jotted it down.

"Thank you," he said. "Good night."

"I was wondering—"

"I've got to go," Harry said.

"Uh-huh. Good night."

He put down the receiver.

"We came as fast as we could," Martine's father said. "This is awful. What happened?"

Harry looked at Hagen.

"Tell us," Hagen said.

Harry gave them the bare bones of the failed arrest, described the bullet hitting the car and the chase through the park.

"But if you were so close and had an MP-Five with you, why didn't you shoot him?" Hagen asked.

Harry cleared his throat, but waited. He observed Eck-hoff.

"Well?" Hagen said with incipient irritation in his voice.

"It was too dark," Harry said.

Hagen contemplated his inspector before responding. "So he was out walking at the time you were entering his room. Any idea why a gunman would be outdoors when it's four degrees below and the middle of the night?" The POB lowered his voice. "I assume you have round-the-clock protection for Jon Karlsen."

"Jon?" said David Eckhoff. "But he's at Ullevål Hospital."

"I have an officer posted outside his room," Harry said, hoping his voice gave an impression of the kind of control he wished he had. "I was about to check that everything was all right."

The first four notes of "London Calling" by The Clash reverberated around the bare walls of the corridor in the neurosurgical ward of Ullevål Hospital. A man with flat hair and a bathrobe, walking with a drip on a stand, sent the police guard a reproachful glance as he passed. The guard was answering his cell phone, against hospital regulations.

"Stranden."

"Hole here. Anything to report?"

"Not much. There's an insomniac wandering the corridors. Shifty-looking, but seems harmless enough."

The man with the drip continued on his rounds with a sniff.

"Anything earlier this evening?"

"Yep. Spurs got trounced by Arsenal at White Hart Lane. And there was a blackout."

"And the patient?"

"Not a peep."

"Have you checked that everything is OK?"

"Apart from hemorrhoids, everything seemed fine."

Stranden listened to the ominous silence. "Just a joke. I'll go and check right away. Stay on the line."

The room smelled sugary. Sweets, he assumed. The light from the corridor swept across the room and went as the door closed behind him, but he could make out a face on the pillow. He went closer. It was quiet in here. Too quiet. As though sound were missing. One sound.

"Karlsen?"

No reaction.

Stranden coughed and repeated the name a bit louder. "Karlsen."

It was so quiet that Harry's voice on the phone rang out loud and clear. "What's up?"

Stranden put the phone to his ear. "He's sleeping like a baby."

"Sure?"

Stranden observed the face on the pillow. And realized that was what was bothering him. Karlsen *was* sleeping like a baby. Grown men tend to make more noise. He leaned over the face to listen to his breathing.

"Hello!" Harry Hole's shout on the cell phone sounded distant. "Hello!"

16

The Refugee

The sun warmed him and the slight breeze across the sand dunes made the grass ripple and nod in appreciation. He must have been swimming because the towel beneath him was wet. "Look," said his mother, pointing. He shaded his eyes and scanned the gleaming, unbelievably blue Adriatic Sea. And there he saw a man wading toward land with a big smile. It was his father. Behind him, Bobo. And Giorgi. A small dog was swimming beside him with its tiny tail upright like a mast. While he was watching them, many more rose from the sea. Some he knew very well. Like Giorgi's father. Others were familiar, like a face in a doorway in Paris. The features were distorted beyond recognition, grotesque masks grimacing at him. The sun disappeared behind a cloud and the temperature plummeted. The masks started shouting.

He woke to a searing pain in his side and opened his eyes. He was in Oslo. On the floor under the stairs in an entrance hall. A figure stood over him, mouth open wide, shouting something. He recognized one word, which was almost the same as in his own language: *narkoman*.

Then the figure, a man in a short leather jacket, took a step back and lifted his foot. The kick hit him on his sore side and he rolled over in pain. There was another man behind the one wearing the jacket, laughing and holding his nose. The leather jacket pointed to the door.

He eyed the two of them. Put his hand on his jacket pocket and felt it was wet. And that he still had the gun. There were two bullets left in the magazine. But if he threatened them with the gun there was a chance they would alert the police.

The leather jacket yelled and raised his hand.

He held his arm over his head in defense and staggered to his feet. The man holding his nose opened the door with a grin and kicked his backside on the way out.

The door snapped shut behind him and he heard the two men stomping up the stairs. He looked at his watch. Four o'clock in the morning. It was still dark and he was frozen to the marrow. And wet. He could feel with his hand that the back of his jacket was saturated and his trouser legs soaked. He stank of piss. Had he pissed on himself? No, he must have been lying in it. A pool. On the floor. Frozen piss that he had thawed with his body heat.

He stuffed his hands in his pockets and began to jog down the road. The cars passing by didn't bother him anymore.

The patient mumbled "Thank you," and Mathias Lund-Helgesen closed the door after him and flopped down into his office chair. Yawned and looked at the clock. Six. An hour to go before the morning shift took over. Before he could go home. A few hours' sleep and then up to Rakel's. Right now she was probably lying under the duvet in the large timber-clad house in Holmenkollen. He still hadn't found the right tone with the boy, but it would come. It usually did for Mathias Lund-Helgesen. It wasn't that Oleg disliked him; it was more that the boy had formed too strong a link with the predecessor. The policeman. Odd how a child could elevate an obviously disturbed alcoholic into a father figure and role model without any hesitation.

For a while, he had been thinking of mentioning this to Rakel but had let the matter drop. It would only make him look like a helpless idiot. Or even make her wonder if he was the right man for them. And that was what he wanted: to be the right man. He was willing to be whoever he had to be to keep her. And to know who that was, he had to ask, of course. So he had: What was it about that policeman? And she had answered that it wasn't anything in particular. Except that she had loved him. And if she hadn't formulated it like that, perhaps he wouldn't have focused on the fact that she had never used that word about him.

Mathias Lund-Helgesen dismissed these idle thoughts, checked the name of the next patient on the computer and walked down the central aisle where the nurses first received them. But at this time of night it was deserted, so he went on to the waiting room.

Five people looked at him, eyes begging for it to be their turn. Apart from a man in the far corner, sleeping with his mouth open and his head on the wall. Had to be a drug addict. The blue jacket and the stench of stale urine coming in waves were sure signs. Just as sure as he would complain of pains and ask for pills.

Mathias went over to him and wrinkled his nose. Shook him hard and took a hasty step back. Quite a few addicts, after years of being robbed of drugs and money when they were out of it, had an automatic response if they were woken: thrashing out or stabbing with a knife.

The man blinked and regarded Mathias with surprisingly clear eyes.

"How can I help?" Mathias asked. Standard procedure, of course, was that you asked a patient this question only when you had privacy, but Mathias was exhausted and sick to death of junkies and drunks who took time and resources away from other patients.

The man pulled the jacket around him more tightly and said nothing.

"Hello! I'm afraid you have to tell me why you're here."

The man shook his head and pointed to one of the others as if explaining it wasn't his turn.

"This is not a lounge," Mathias said. "You're not allowed to sleep here. Scram. Now."

"I don't understand," the man said.

"Leave," Mathias said. "Or I'll call the police."

To his astonishment, Mathias could feel he had to control himself not to drag this stinking junkie out of the chair. The others had turned to watch.

The man nodded and staggered to his feet. Mathias stood watching him after the glass door had swung shut.

"It's good you chuck their kind out," a voice behind him said. Mathias gave an absent-minded nod. Perhaps he hadn't told her enough times. That he loved her. Perhaps that was it.

It was seven-thirty and still dark outside the neurosurgical ward and Room 19, where Officer Stranden was looking down at the neat yet unoccupied bed where Jon Karlsen had been lying. Soon another patient would be there. That was a strange thought. But now he needed to find a bed to lie in himself. For a long time. He yawned and checked that he hadn't left anything on the bedside table, took the newspaper from the chair and turned to leave.

A man was standing in the doorway. It was the inspector. Hole.

"Where is he?"

"Gone," Stranden said. "They came for him fifteen minutes ago. Drove him away."

"Oh? Who authorized that?"

"The social worker. They didn't want him here anymore."

"I meant who authorized the transport? And where to?"

"That was your new boss in Crime Squad. He called."

"Hagen? In person?"

"Yep. And they took Karlsen to his brother's flat."

Hole shook his head slowly. Then he left.

Dawn was breaking in the east as Harry trudged up the stairs of the reddish-brown brick building on Gørbitz Gate, a short stretch of asphalt full of potholes between Kirkeveien and Fagerborggata. He stopped on the first floor, as instructed via the door intercom. Embossed in white on a pale-blue strip of plastic on the door that had been left ajar was a name: ROBERT KARLSEN.

Harry entered and gave the flat a once-over. It was a tiny, messy studio that confirmed the impression one had upon seeing Robert's office—although the possibility could not be ruled out that Li and Li might have contributed to the mess while searching for letters and any other paperwork that could help them. A color print of Jesus dominated one wall, and it struck Harry that if the crown of thorns was exchanged for a beret, you would have Che Guevara.

"So Gunnar Hagen decided you should be brought here?" Harry addressed the back of the person sitting at the desk by the window.

"Yes," said Jon Karlsen, turning around. "Since the gunman knows the address of my flat, he said I would be safer here."

"Mm," Harry said, looking around. "Sleep well?"

"Not particularly." Jon Karlsen wore an embarrassed smile. "I lay listening for sounds that weren't there. And when in the end I did fall asleep, Stranden came and scared the living daylights out of me."

Harry moved a pile of comics off a chair and flopped down. "I can understand you being afraid, Jon. Have you thought any more about who would want to take your life?"

Jon sighed. "I haven't thought about anything else since last night. But the answer is the same: I really don't have a clue."

"Have you ever been to Zagreb?" Harry asked. "Or Croatia?"

Jon shook his head. "The farthest I've been from Norway is Sweden and Denmark. And then I was just a boy."

"Do you know any Croatians?"

"Only the refugees we give lodging to."

"Mm. Did the police say why they brought you here, of all places?"

Jon shrugged. "I said I had a key to the flat. And it's empty, of course, so . . ."

Harry ran a hand across his face.

"There used to be a computer here," Jon said, pointing to the desk.

"We picked it up," Harry said, standing up again.

"Do you have to go already?"

"I have to catch a flight to Bergen."

"Oh," Jon said with a blank stare.

Harry felt an inclination to lay a hand on the ungainly man's narrow shoulders.

The airport express was late. It was the third time in a row. "Because of a delay," came the brief and vague justification. Øystein Eikeland, Harry's taxi-driving pal from boyhood, had explained to Harry that a train's electrical motor was one of the simplest things in existence. His little sister could make it work, and if the technical staff of SAS and the Norwegian State Railways were to swap places for a day, all the trains would run on time and all the planes would still be on the ground. Harry preferred the situation as it was.

He called Gunnar Hagen's direct line after they emerged from the tunnel before Lillestrøm.

"Hole speaking."

"I can hear."

"I've authorized round-the-clock surveillance for Jon Karlsen. And I didn't authorize his removal from Ullevål Hospital."

"The hospital determines the latter," Hagen said. "And I determine the former."

Harry counted three houses in the white landscape before answering. "You put me in charge of this investigation, Hagen."

"Yes, but not of overtime expenses. Which, as you ought to know, went overbudget ages ago."

"The man's scared out of his wits," Harry said. "So you put him in the flat belonging to the killer's previous victim, his own brother. To save the few hundred kroner a day a hotel room would have cost."

The loudspeakers announced the next stop.

"Lillestrøm?" Hagen sounded surprised. "Are you on the airport express?"

Harry mouthed a silent curse. "Quick trip to Bergen."

"Is that so?"

Harry gulped. "I'll be back this afternoon."

"Are you out of your mind? We're under the spotlight here. The media—"

"A tunnel's coming," Harry said, pressing the red button.

Ragnhild Gilstrup awoke slowly from a dream. It was dark in the room. She knew it was morning, but she didn't know what the sound was. It was like a large mechanical clock. But they didn't have any clocks like that in the bedroom. She rolled over and recoiled. In the gloom she saw a naked figure standing by the foot of the bed watching her.

"Good morning, darling," he said.

"Mads! You frightened me."

"Oh?"

He had just taken a shower. Behind him the door to the bathroom was open and the ticking sound came from the soft, resonant drips of water from his body onto the parquet floor.

"Have you been standing like that for long?" she asked, pulling the duvet around her more tightly.

"What do you mean?"

She shrugged, but was taken aback. There was something about the way he said it. Cheery, almost teasing. And the tiny smile. He never used to be like that. She stretched and yawned—a sham, she acknowledged to herself.

"When did you get home last night?" she asked. "I didn't wake up."

"You must have been enjoying the sleep of the innocent." Again that little smile.

She studied him. Over recent months he had indeed changed. He had always been slim, but now he looked stronger and fitter. And there was something about his stance; he seemed to have become more erect. Of course she had wondered if he had a lover, but that had not bothered her too much. Or so she thought.

"Where were you?" she asked.

"Meal with Jan Petter Sissener."

"The stockbroker?"

"Yes. He thinks the market prospects are good. Also for property."

"Isn't it my job to talk to him?" she asked.

"Just like to keep myself up to date."

"You don't think I keep you up to date, dear?"

He looked at her. Held her gaze until she felt something that never happened when she was speaking to Mads: blood suffusing her face.

"I'm sure you tell me what I need to know, darling." He went into the bathroom, where she heard him turn on the tap.

"I've been examining a couple of interesting property

ideas," she shouted, mostly to say something, to break the strange silence that had followed the last thing he said.

"Me, too," Mads shouted. "I went to take a look at an apartment building on Gøteborggata yesterday. The one the Salvation Army owns, you know."

She froze. Jon's flat.

"Fine property. But do you know what? There was police tape over the door to one of the flats. A resident told me there had been a shooting there. Can you imagine?"

"You're kidding," she shouted. "What was the police tape for?"

"That's what the police do, secure the premises while they turn the flat upside down for fingerprints and DNA to find out who's been there. Anyway, the Salvation Army may be willing to lower the price if there's been a shooting in the building, don't you think?"

"They don't want to sell. I've told you."

"They didn't want to sell, darling."

A thought struck her. "Why would the police search the flat if the shooting came from the hallway outside?"

She heard Mads turn off the tap and looked up. He was standing in the doorway, with a yellow smile in the white shaving foam and a razor in his hand. And soon he would sprinkle on the expensive aftershave she could not bear.

"What are you talking about?" he said. "I didn't say anything about hallways. And why so pale, darling?"

There was still a layer of transparent, icy morning mist hanging over Sofienberg Park as Ragnhild hurried up Helgesens Gate, breathing into her beige Bottega Veneta scarf. Even wool bought in Milan for nine thousand kroner could not keep the cold out, but at least it covered her face.

Fingerprints. DNA. To find out who had been there. That must not happen; the consequences would be disastrous.

She rounded the corner to Gøteborggata. There weren't any police cars outside, anyway.

The key slid into the lock of the main entrance, and she scuttled in toward the elevator. It was a long time since she had been here, and the first time she was arriving unannounced, of course.

Her heart was pounding as the elevator was going up and she was thinking of her hair in his shower drain, clothing fibers in the carpet, fingerprints everywhere.

The hallway was empty. The orange tape across the door showed that no one was at home, but she knocked anyway and waited. Then she took out the key and tried it. It didn't fit. She tried again, but could only get the tip into the cylinder. Christ, had Jon changed the lock? She took a deep breath, turned the key around and said a silent prayer.

The key slipped in and the lock gave a gentle click as it opened.

She inhaled the smell of the flat that she knew so well and made for the closet where she knew he kept the vacuum cleaner. It was a black Siemens VS08G2040, the same model as they had at home, two thousand watts, the most powerful on the market. Jon liked for things to be clean. The vacuum cleaner gave a hoarse roar as she plugged it in at the wall. It was ten o'clock. She should be able to clean all the floors and wipe all the walls and surfaces within an hour. She regarded the closed bedroom door and wondered whether to start there. Where the memories, and the evidence, were strongest. No. She placed the nozzle of the vacuum cleaner against her forearm. It felt like a bite. She pulled it away and saw that blood had already gathered.

She had been cleaning for a few minutes when she remembered. The letters! God, she had almost forgotten they might find the letters she had written. The first ones, in which she had written about her innermost dreams and desires, and the last ones, the desperate, naked ones, where she had implored him to get in touch. She left the vacuum cleaner on, draped the hose over a chair and ran over to Jon's desk and began to pull out the drawers. The first contained pens, tape and a hole punch. The second telephone directories. The third was locked. Of course.

She grabbed the letter opener from the bureau, forced it in above the lock and leaned with all her strength against the shaft. The old, dry wood creaked. And while she was thinking the letter opener would break, the front of the drawer split along its length. She pulled out the drawer with a jerk, brushed away the wooden splinters and looked down at the envelopes. The piles of them. Her fingers flipped through them. Hafslund Energi. Den Norske Bank. Intelligent Finance. The Salvation Army. A blank envelope. She opened it. "*Dear Son*," it said at the top. She continued to flick through the pile. There! The envelope bore the investment fund's name—Gilstrup Invest—in a discreet pale blue, down in the right-hand corner.

Relieved, she took out the letter.

When she had finished reading, she laid the letter aside and felt the tears streaming down her cheeks. It was as though her eyes had been opened again, as though she had been blind and now she could see and everything was as it had been. As though everything she had believed in and had once rejected was true again. The letter had been brief, yet, after she'd read it, everything had changed.

The vacuum cleaner groaned without remorse and drowned out everything except the simple, unambiguous sentences on the writing paper, their absurd and at the same time self-evident logic. She didn't hear the traffic from the street, the creaking of the door or the person standing right behind her chair. It wasn't until she caught his aroma that the hairs on her neck stood up.

The SAS plane landed at Flesland Airport, buffeted by westerly gales. In the taxi to Bergen the windshield wipers hissed and the studded winter tires crunched on wet, black pavement as they cut their way between cliff faces with comb-overs of wet grassy tufts and bare trees. Winter in western Norway.

When they arrived in Fyllingsdalen, Skarre called.

"We've found something."

"Out with it."

"We've been through Robert Karlsen's hard drive. The only thing of doubtful character was cookies to a couple of porn sites on the Net."

"We would have found that on your computer, too, Skarre. Get to the point."

"We didn't find any persons of doubtful character in the papers or letters, either."

"Skarre . . ." Harry warned.

"On the other hand, we did find an interesting ticket stub," he said. "Guess to where."

"I'll clobber you."

"Zagreb," Skarre hurried to add. And then when Harry didn't answer: "In Croatia."

"Thank you. When was he there?"

"In October. Departure October 12, returning the same evening."

"Mm. Just the one October day in Zagreb. Doesn't sound like a vacation."

"I checked with his boss at Fretex on Kirkeveien, and she says that Robert didn't do any jobs abroad for them."

Harry hung up, wondering why he hadn't told Skarre he was pleased with his work. He could have done that. Was he becoming mean in his old age? No, he thought, as he took the four kroner in change from the taxi driver; he had always been mean.

Harry stepped out into a sad, gonorrheal discharge of a Bergen squall, which, according to myth, starts one afternoon in September and finishes one afternoon in March. He walked the few paces to the front door of Børs Café and stood inside scanning the room and wondering what the imminent smoking law would do to places like this. Harry had been to Børs twice before, and it was a place where he instinctively felt at home, yet like an outsider at the same time. The waiters bustled around wearing red jackets and expressions that said they were working at a high-class establishment while serving half-liters and bone-dry witticisms to local crabbers, retired fishermen, hardy wartime seamen and others whose lives had capsized. The first time Harry went there a washed-up celeb had been dancing the tango with a fisherman between the tables while an older lady dressed to the nines had sung German ballads to accordion accompaniment and reeled off rhythmic obscenities with heavily rolled r's during the instrumental breaks.

Harry's eyes found what they were looking for, and he headed for the table where a tall, thin man towered over one empty and one almost empty beer glass.

"Boss."

The man's head bobbed up at the sound of Harry's voice. His eyes followed after a slight delay. Behind the mist of intoxication his pupils were contracting.

"Harry." To his surprise, the voice was clear and distinct. Harry pulled over a free chair from a neighboring table.

"Passing through?" asked Bjarne Møller.

"Yes."

"How did you find me?"

Harry didn't answer. He had been prepared, but still he could hardly believe what he was seeing.

"So they're gossiping at the station? Well, well." Møller took another deep draft from the glass. "Strange change of roles, isn't it? It used to be me who found you like this. Beer?"

Harry leaned over the table. "What's happened, boss?"

"What's usually happened when a grown man drinks during working hours, Harry?"

"Either he's been given the sack or his wife's left him."

"I haven't been given the boot yet. As far as I know."
Møller laughed. His shoulders shook, but no sound came
out.

"Has Kari . . . ?" Harry stopped, not knowing quite how
to formulate the words.

"She and the kids didn't come with me. That's OK. That
was decided in advance."

"What?"

"I miss the boys—of course I do. I'm managing,
though. This is just . . . what do they call it . . . a passing
phase . . . but there's a more elegant word . . . trans . . . no."
Bjarne Møller's head had sunk down over his glass.

"Let's go for a walk," Harry said, waving his hand for
the bill. Twenty-five minutes later Harry and Bjarne Møller
were standing in the same rain cloud by a railing on Fløyen
Mountain, looking down on what might have been Bergen.
A cable car that looked like a slice of cake and was pulled by
thick steel wires had transported them up from downtown.

"Was that why you came here?" Harry asked. "Because
you and Kari were going to split up?"

"It rains here as much as they say," Møller said.

Harry sighed. "Drinking doesn't help, boss. Things get
worse."

"That's my line, Harry. How are you getting along with
Gunnar Hagen?"

"OK. Good lecturer."

"Don't make the mistake of underestimating him, Harry.
He's more than a lecturer. Gunnar Hagen was in FSK for
seven years."

"Special Forces?" Harry asked in surprise.

"Indeed. I was told that by the chief superintendent.
Hagen was redeployed in FSK in 1981 when it was set up
to protect our oil rigs in the North Sea. Because of security
clearances, it's never been on any CV."

"FSK," Harry said, conscious that the ice-cold rain was

seeping through his jacket onto his shoulders. "I've heard the loyalty there is uncommonly fierce."

"It's like a brotherhood," Møller said. "Impenetrable."

"Do you know anyone else who's been in it?"

Møller shook his head. He already looked sober. "Anything new in the investigation? I've been given some insider information."

"We don't even have a motive."

"The motive's money," Møller said, clearing his throat. "Greed, the illusion that things will change if you have money. That you can change."

"Money." Harry looked at Møller. "Maybe," he conceded.

Møller spat with disgust into the gray soup in front of them. "Find the money. Find the money and follow it. It will always lead you to the answer." Harry had never heard him talk like that before, not with this bitter certainty, as though he had an insight he would have preferred not to possess.

Harry breathed in and took the plunge. "Boss, you know I don't like to beat around the bush, so here it is. You and I are the types of people who don't have many friends. And even though you may not regard me as a friend I am something of the kind, anyway."

Harry watched Møller, but there was no response.

"I came here to find out whether there was anything I could do. Anything you wanted to talk about or . . ."

Still no response.

"Well, damned if I know why I came, boss. But I'm here now."

Møller leaned his head back to face the sky. "Did you know that Bergensians call what's behind us mountains? And in fact they are. Real mountains. Six minutes on the cable car from the center of the second-biggest city in Norway there are people who get lost and die. Funny, isn't it."

Harry shrugged.

Møller sighed. "The rain's not going to stop. Let's take the tin can back down."

At the bottom they walked to the taxi stand.

"It'll take twenty minutes to Flesland Airport now, before the rush hour," Møller said.

Harry nodded and waited before he got in. His jacket was drenched.

"Follow the money," Møller said, putting a hand on Harry's shoulder. "Do whatever you have to do."

"You, too, boss."

Møller raised a hand in the air and began to walk, but turned when Harry got into the taxi and shouted something that was drowned out by the traffic. Harry switched on his cell phone as they roared across Danmarksplass. A text message was waiting from Halvorsen telling him to call back. Harry dialed the number.

"We've got Stankic's credit card," Halvorsen said. "The cash machine in Youngstorget ate it last night around twelve."

"So that's where he was coming from when we raided the hostel," Harry said.

"Yes."

"Youngstorget is a good distance from there," Harry said. "He must have gone there because he was frightened we would trace the card to somewhere near the hostel. And it suggests he's in desperate need of money."

"But it gets better," Halvorsen said. "The cash machine's got a surveillance camera, of course."

"Yeah?"

Halvorsen paused for effect.

"Come on," Harry said. "He doesn't hide his face—is that it?"

"He smiled straight into the camera like a film star," Halvorsen said.

"Does Beate have the tape?"

"She's sitting in the House of Pain going through it now."

Ragnhild Gilstrup thought about Johannes. About how different everything could have been. If only she had followed her heart, which had always been wiser than her head. It was strange that she had never been that unhappy and yet she had never wanted to live as much as right now.

To live a bit longer.

Because she knew everything now.

She stared into a black muzzle and she knew what she saw. And what would happen.

Her scream was drowned out by the roar of the very simple motor of a Siemens VS08G2040. A chair fell to the floor. The muzzle with the powerful suction approached her eye. She tried to squeeze her eyelids shut, but they were held open by strong fingers that wanted her to see. And she saw. And knew, knew what was going to happen.

17

The Face

The wall clock over the counter in the big pharmacy showed eight-thirty. People sat around the room coughing, closed sleepy eyes or alternated glances between the red digital figure on the wall and their line number as though it were their lottery ticket for life and every *ping* a new draw.

He had not taken a number from the machine; he wanted to sit by the heaters in the shop, but he had a feeling the blue jacket was attracting unwanted attention, because the staff were beginning to send him looks. He gazed out the window. Behind the mist he could make out the contours of a feeble, impotent sun. A police car passed by. They had security cameras in here. He had to move on, but where to? Without any money he would be thrown out of cafés and bars. Now he didn't even have the credit card anymore. Last night he had decided he would withdraw money, even though he knew there was a risk the card would be traced. He had searched on his evening walk from the hostel, and in the end found an ATM some distance away. But the machine had just eaten his card without giving him anything, except for confirmation of what he already knew: They were circling him; he was under siege again.

*   *   *

The semi-deserted Biscuit restaurant was immersed in panpipe music. It was the quiet period after lunch and before evening meals, so Tore Bjørgen had positioned himself by the window and was staring dreamily out at Karl Johans Gate. Not because the view was so appealing, but because the radiators were under the windows and he couldn't seem to get warm. He was in a bad mood. He had to pick up the plane ticket to Cape Town within the next two days and he had just concluded what he had known for a long time: He didn't have enough money. Even though he had worked hard, it wasn't there. There was the rococo mirror he had bought for the flat in the autumn, of course, but there had been too much Champagne, cocaine and other expensive treats. Not that he had lost his grip on things, but, to be honest, it was time he escaped from the vicious circle of coke for parties, pills for sleep and coke to give him the energy to do enough overtime to finance his bad habits. And right now he didn't have a bean in his account. For the last five years he had celebrated Christmas and New Year's in Cape Town instead of going home to the village of Vegårdshei, to religious narrow-mindedness, his parents' silent accusations and his uncles' and his nephews' thinly disguised revulsion. He exchanged three weeks of unbearable freezing temperatures, dismal darkness and tedium for sun, beautiful people and pulsating nightlife. And games. Dangerous games. In December and January, Cape Town was invaded by European advertising agencies, film crews and models, female and male. And this was where he found like-minded individuals. The game he liked best was Blind Date. In a place like Cape Town there was always a certain risk involved, but to meet a man amid the shacks in Cape Flats you were risking your life. And yet that was what he did. He didn't always know why he did these idiotic things; all he knew was that he needed danger to feel he was alive. The game had to have a potential penalty to be interesting.

Tore Bjørgen sniffed. His daydreams had been disturbed by a smell he hoped did not come from the kitchen. He turned.

"Hello again," the man standing behind him said.

If Bjørgen had been a less professional waiter his face would have assumed a disapproving expression. The man in front of him was not only wearing the unbecoming blue jacket that was in fashion among the drug addicts on Karl Johans Gate, he was also unshaven and red-eyed and stank like a urinal.

"Remember me?" the man said. "In the men's room?"

Bjørgen thought he was referring to the nightclub of the same name before realizing that the guy meant the bathroom. It was only then that he recognized him. That is, he recognized the voice, while thinking that it was incredible what less than twenty-four hours without civilized necessities like a razor, a shower and a full night's sleep could do to a man's appearance.

It might have been the interrupted intense daydream that accounted for Bjørgen's two distinctly different reactions coming in the order they did: first of all the sweet sting of desire. The man's reason for coming back was obvious after the flirtation and the fleeting but intimate physical contact they had had. Then the shock as the image of the man with the soapy gun appeared on his retinas. Plus the fact that the policeman who had been here had connected it with the murder of the poor Salvation Army soldier.

"I need somewhere to stay," said the man.

Bjørgen blinked hard twice. He could not believe his ears. Here he was, standing opposite a man who might be a murderer, a man under suspicion of killing someone in cold blood. So why hadn't he already dropped everything and run out screaming for the police? The policeman had even said there was a reward for information leading to the man's arrest. Bjørgen glanced toward the end of the room where the headwaiter was leafing through the reservations book. Why was it that instead he felt this strange tingle of pleasure in his solar plexus, which spread through his body and made him shudder and shiver as he searched for something sensible to say?

"It's just for one night," the man said.

"I'm working today."

"I can wait."

Bjørgen eyed the man. It's insane, he thought, while his brain slowly and inexorably connected his love of risk with a potential solution to a problem. He swallowed and shifted weight from one foot to the other.

Harry jogged from the airport express in Oslo Central Station across Grønland to Police HQ, took the elevator up to the Robberies Unit and loped down the corridors to the House of Pain, the video room.

It was dark, warm and stuffy in the cramped, windowless room. He heard quick fingers scurrying across the computer keyboard.

"What can you see?" he asked the silhouette outlined against the flickering pictures on the wall screen.

"Something very interesting," Beate Lønn said without turning, but Harry knew her eyes were red-rimmed. He had seen Beate working before. Seen her staring at the screen for hours while she wound forward, stopped, focused, magnified, saved. Without knowing what she was looking for. Or what she could see. This was her territory.

"And maybe an explanation," she added.

"I'm all ears." Harry groped his way forward in the dark, hit his leg and sat down cursing.

"Ready?"

"Shoot."

"OK. Meet Christo Stankic."

On the screen a man stepped forward to an ATM.

"Are you sure?" Harry asked.

"Don't you recognize him?"

"I recognize the blue jacket, but . . ." Harry said, hearing the confusion in his own voice.

"Wait," Beate said.

The man put a card in the machine and stood waiting. Then he turned his face to the camera and grimaced. A pretend smile, the kind that meant the opposite.

"He's found out he can't withdraw any money," Beate said.

The man on camera kept pressing buttons, and in the end he smacked the keypad with his hand.

"And now he's found out he won't get his card back," Harry said. The man stared at the display on the machine for a long time.

Then he pulled back his sleeve, checked his wristwatch, turned and was gone.

"What make was the watch?" Harry asked.

"The glass was reflecting the light," Beate said. "But I magnified the negative. It says Seiko SQ-Fifty on the dial."

"Clever girl. But I didn't see an explanation."

"This is the explanation."

Beate typed, and two pictures of the man they had just seen appeared on the screen. One while he was taking out his card, the other while he was looking at his watch.

"I've chosen these two pictures because his face is in roughly the same position and this way it's easy to see. They've been taken with an interval of a little over a hundred seconds. Can you see that?"

"No," Harry said truthfully. "I can tell I'm no good at this. I can't even see if it's the same person in the two pictures. Or if he's the man I saw in Tøyen Park."

"Good. Then you've seen it."

"Seen what?"

"Here's the picture of him off the credit card," Beate said

and clicked. A picture of a man with short hair and a tie appeared.

"And here are the ones *Dagbladet* took of him in Egertorget." Two further pictures.

"Can you tell if this is the same person?" Beate asked.

"Well, no."

"Nor can I."

"*You* can't? If *you* can't, it means it's not the same person."

"No," Beate said. "It means here we have a case of what is known as hyperelasticity. Called *visage du pantomime* by professionals."

"What on earth are you talking about?"

"A person who can change his appearance without any need for makeup, disguise or plastic surgery."

Harry was waiting for all the investigative team to sit down in the red zone's meeting room before he spoke. "We know now that we're after one man and only one man. For the time being let's call him Christo Stankic. Beate?"

Beate switched on the projector and an image of a face with closed eyes and a mask of something like red spaghetti appeared on the screen.

"What you see here is an illustration of our facial musculature," she began. "Muscles we use to form expressions and thereby change our appearance. The most important are located in the forehead, around the eyes and around the mouth. For example, this is the *musculus frontalis*, which, along with the *musculus corrugator supercilii*, is used to raise and furrow the eyebrows. The *orbicularis oculi* is used to close the eyelids or create folds in the part of the face around the eyes. And so on."

Beate pressed the remote control. The image was replaced by one of a clown with large, inflated cheeks.

"We have hundreds of muscles like these in our faces, and even those whose job it is to make faces use just a tiny percentage of the options available. Actors and entertainers train facial muscles to achieve maximum movement, which we others ordinarily lose at a young age. However, even actors and mime artists tend to use the face for imitative movements to express certain emotions. And, important as they are, they are quite universal and few in number: anger, happiness, being in love, showing surprise, chuckling, roaring with laughter and so on. Nature, though, has given us this mask of muscles to make several million, indeed, an almost unlimited number of facial expressions. Concert pianists have trained the link between brain and finger musculature to such an extent that they can perform ten different simultaneous operations, independently of each other. And we don't even have many muscles in our fingers. So what is the face not capable of?"

Beate moved on to the clip of Christo Stankic outside the ATM.

"Well, we are capable of this, for example." The film advanced in slow motion.

"The changes are almost imperceptible. Tiny muscles are being tensed and slackened. The result of the small muscle movements is a changed expression. Does the face change that much? No, but the part of the brain that recognizes faces—the fusiform gyrus—is very, very sensitive to even minor changes, since its function is to distinguish among thousands of physiologically similar faces. Via the facial muscles' gradual adjustments, we end up with what seems to be a different person. Such as this."

The recording froze as it reached the last frame.

"Hello! This is Earth calling Mars."

Harry recognized the voice of Magnus Skarre. Someone laughed, and Beate blushed.

"Sorry," Skarre said, looking around with a self-satisfied chuckle. "That's still the Stankic dago. Science fiction is entertaining but guys who tense a bit here and slacken a bit there and become unrecognizable—that's a little far-fetched, if you ask me."

Harry was on the verge of breaking in, but changed his mind. Instead he observed Beate with interest. Two years ago a comment like that would have crushed her on the spot and he would have had to sweep up the pieces.

"As far as I know, no one was asking you," Beate said, her cheeks still bright red. "But since you feel that way let me give you an example I am sure you will understand."

"Whoa," exclaimed Skarre, holding his hands up in defense. "That wasn't meant personally, Lønn."

"When people die, something called rigor mortis sets in," Beate continued, undeterred, but Harry could see her nostrils were flared. "The muscles in the body, and in the face, too, stiffen. It's the same as tensing muscles. And what is the typical reaction when the next of kin has to identify the corpse?" In the ensuing silence all that could be heard was the hum of the projector fan. Harry was already smiling.

"They don't recognize them," said a loud, clear voice. Harry had not heard Gunnar Hagen enter the room. "Not an unusual problem in war when soldiers have to be identified. Of course, they're in uniform, but sometimes even comrades in their own unit have to check the dog tags to be sure."

"Thank you," Beate said. "Did that help the gray matter, Skarre?" Skarre shrugged, and Harry heard someone laugh out loud. Beate switched off the projector.

"The plasticity or mobility of the face is a very personal thing. To some extent it may be achieved through practice and to some extent, one has to assume, it's genetic. Some people cannot differentiate between the left and right sides of their face; others, with practice, can operate all the muscles independently of each other. Like the concert pianist. And that's called hyperelasticity, or *visage du pantomime*.

Known cases would suggest there is a strong genetic element. The ability was learned young or as a child and those who have an extreme degree of hyperelasticity often suffer from personality disorders—or have experienced terrible traumas while growing up."

"So what you're saying is that we're dealing with a crazy man here?" Gunnar Hagen said.

"My area of expertise is faces, not psychology," Beate said. "But at any rate it cannot be ruled out. Harry?"

"Thank you, Beate." Harry got to his feet. "So now you know what we're up against, guys. Questions? Yes, Li?"

"How do we catch a creature like this?"

Harry and Beate exchanged glances. Hagen coughed.

"I have no idea," Harry said. "All I know is that this will not be over until he has done his job. Or we have done ours."

There was a message from Rakel when Harry returned to his office. He called her immediately to be spared the brooding.

"How's it going?" she asked.

"Right to the Supreme Court," Harry said. It was an expression Rakel's father had used. An insider joke among Norwegian soldiers back from the Eastern Front after the war and facing trial. Rakel laughed. The gentle ripple—he once would have been willing to sacrifice everything to hear that every day. It still worked.

"Are you alone?" she asked.

"No. Halvorsen is sitting here listening, as always."

Halvorsen raised his head from the Egertorget witnesses' statements and grimaced.

"Oleg needs someone to talk to," Rakel said.

"Oh, yes?"

"Pssh, that was clumsy. Not someone. He needs to talk to you."

"Needs?"

"Another correction. He *said* he wants to talk to you."

"And asked you to call?"

"No. No, he would never have done that."

"No." Harry smiled at the thought.

"So . . . would you have time one evening, do you think?"

"Of course."

"Great. You could come and eat with us."

"Us?"

"Oleg and me."

"Mm."

"I know you've met Mathias—"

"Yes," Harry said quickly. "Seems like a nice guy."

"Yes."

Harry didn't know how to interpret her intonation.

"Are you still there?"

"I'm here," Harry said. "Look, we've got a murder case on our hands and things are heating up here. Could I think about it and call you later with a day?"

Pause.

"Rakel?"

"Yes, that would be fine. How are things otherwise?"

The question was so out of place that for a moment Harry wondered whether it was meant as irony.

"The days pass," Harry said.

"Nothing new has happened in your life since we last spoke?"

Harry breathed in. "I have to go, Rakel. I'll call you when I've found a day. Say hello to Oleg from me. OK?"

"OK."

Harry put down the receiver.

"Well?" Halvorsen said. "A convenient day?"

"It's a meal. Something to do with Oleg. What would Robert be doing in Zagreb?"

Halvorsen was about to say something when there was a soft knock at the door. They both turned. Skarre was standing in the doorway.

"The Zagreb police just called," he informed them. "The credit card was issued on the basis of a false passport."

"Mm." Harry leaned back in the chair and put his hands behind his head. "What would Robert be doing in Zagreb, Skarre?"

"You know what I think."

"Dope," Halvorsen said.

"Didn't you mention a girl asking for Robert in the Fretex on Kirkeveien, Skarre? In the shop they thought she was from Yugoslavia, didn't they?"

"Yes. It was the shop manager. She—"

"Call Fretex, Halvorsen."

The office was quiet as Halvorsen flicked through the Yellow Pages and dialed a number. Harry started to drum his fingers on the table, wondering how to phrase it: He was pleased with Skarre. He cleared his throat once. But then Halvorsen passed him the telephone.

Sergeant Major Rue listened, spoke and acted. An efficient woman, Harry was able to confirm two minutes later when he hung up and coughed again.

"It was one of her para 12 boys, a Serbian, who remembered the girl. He thinks her name was Sofia, but is not sure. He was certain she was from Vukovar."

Harry found Jon in bed in Robert's flat with an open Bible on his stomach. He looked anxious, as if he hadn't slept. Harry lit a cigarette, sat down on the fragile kitchen chair and asked Jon what he thought Robert had been doing in Zagreb.

"No idea. He said nothing to me. Maybe it had something to do with the secret project I'd lent him money for."

"OK. Do you know anything about a girlfriend—a young Croatian girl by the name of Sofia?"

"Sofia Miholjec? You're kidding!"

" 'Fraid not. Does that mean you know who she is?"

"Sofia lives in one of our buildings on Jacob Aalls Gate. Her family was among the Croatian refugees in Vukovar the commander brought here. But Sofia . . . Sofia is fifteen."

"Maybe she was just in love with Robert? Young girl. Good-looking young man. It's not exactly unusual, you know."

Jon was about to answer, but stopped himself.

"You said Robert liked young girls," Harry said.

Jon studied the floor. "I can give you the address of the family so you can ask her."

"OK." Harry glanced at his watch. "Anything you need?"

Jon looked around. "I should go back to my flat. Pick up some clothes and toiletries."

"Fine. I'll take you. Grab your coat and hat. It's got even colder."

The drive took twenty minutes. They passed the dilapidated old Bislett Stadium, which was due to be demolished, and Schrøder's restaurant, outside of which stood a familiar man in a thick wool coat and hat. Harry parked illegally in front of the entrance to 4 Gøteborggata, and they entered and then waited in front of the elevator. Harry saw from the red number over the door that the elevator was on the fourth floor, Jon's. Before they had time to press the button they heard the elevator start to move and could see from the numbers that it was on its way down. Harry rubbed his palms against his thighs.

"You don't like elevators," Jon said.

Harry eyed him in surprise. "Is it obvious?"

Jon smiled. "My father doesn't, either. Come on. Let's take the stairs."

They set off, and some way up Harry heard the elevator door open beneath them.

They let themselves into the flat and Harry stood by the door while Jon went to the bathroom and fetched a toiletry bag.

"Strange," Jon said with a frown. "It's as if someone has been here."

Jon slipped into the bedroom and returned with a bag.

"It smells funny," he said.

Harry took a look around. There were two glasses in the sink, but no milk or other visible signs of liquid on the rims that would reveal anything. No wet marks left by melted snow on the floor, just a few splinters of light wood in front of the desk, which must have come from one of the drawers. One drawer front looked as if it had split.

"Let's get moving," Harry said.

"Why's my vacuum there?" Jon asked, pointing. "Have your people been using it?"

Harry knew SOC procedures and none of them involved using the vacuum cleaner at the scene of the crime.

"Does anyone else have a key to this flat?" Harry asked.

Jon hesitated. "Thea, my girlfriend. But she would never have used the vacuum here of her own accord."

Harry studied the splinters of wood, which would have been the first thing a vacuum cleaner would have swallowed. Then he went over to the machine. The attachment had been removed from the plastic shaft at the end of the hose. Cold shivers ran down his spine. He lifted the hose and peered down it. Ran a finger around the circular black edge and looked at his fingertip.

"What's that?" Jon asked.

"Blood," Harry said. "Check that the door's locked."

Harry already knew. He was standing on the threshold to the room he hated and yet still never managed to keep away from. He removed the plastic lid in the middle of the machine. Loosened the yellow dust bag and lifted it out while thinking that *this* was in fact the House of Pain. The place where he was always forced to use his ability to empathize with evil. An ability that more and more often he thought he had overdeveloped.

"What are you doing?" Jon asked.

The bag was so full it bulged. Harry grabbed the soft, thick paper and ripped it open. The bag split and a fine cloud of black dust rose like a spirit from a lamp. It ascended weightlessly toward the ceiling as Jon and Harry examined the contents on the parquet floor.

"Mercy," Jon whispered.

18

The Chute

"My God," Jon groaned, groping for a chair. "What happened here? That's an . . . that's an . . ."

"Yes," Harry said, crouching beside the vacuum cleaner and concentrating on maintaining even breathing. "It's an eye."

The eyeball looked like a blood-streaked, stranded jellyfish. Dust was stuck to the white surface. On the blood-soaked back Harry could make out the base of muscles and the thicker, wormlike peg that was the optical nerve. "What I'm wondering is how it got through the filter unscathed and into the bag. If it *was* sucked in, that is."

"I took out the filter," Jon said in a tremulous voice. "It sucks better." Harry produced a pen from his jacket pocket and used it to turn the eye with great care. The consistency felt soft, but there was a hard center. He shifted position so that the light from the lamp in the ceiling fell on the pupil, which was large and black, with blurred edges, now that the eye muscles no longer kept it round. The light, almost turquoise iris encircling the pupil shone like the center of a marble. Harry heard Jon's quick breaths behind him.

"Unusually light-blue iris," Harry said. "Anyone you know?"

"No, I . . . I don't know."

"Listen, Jon," Harry said, without turning around. "I don't know how much practice you've had at lying, but you're not very good at it. I can't force you to tell me spicy details about your brother, but with this"—Harry pointed to the bloodstained eyeball—"I can force you to tell me who it is."

He swung around. Jon was sitting on one of the two kitchen chairs with his head bowed.

"I . . . she . . ." His voice was thick with emotion.

"A *she*, then," Harry said.

Jon gave a firm nod of his bowed head. "Her name's Ragnhild Gilstrup. No one else has eyes like her."

"And how did her eye end up here?"

"I have no idea. She . . . we . . . used to meet here. She had a key. What have I done, Harry? Why has this happened?"

"I don't know, Jon. But I have a job to do here, and we have to find you a place to go first."

"I can go back to Gørbitz Gate."

"No!" Harry shouted. "Do you have keys to Thea's flat?" Jon nodded.

"OK, go there. Keep the door locked and don't open up for anyone except me."

Jon walked toward the front door, then paused. "Harry?"

"Yes?"

"Does it have to come out, about Ragnhild and me? I stopped meeting her when Thea and I got together."

"Then it's not a problem."

"You don't understand," Jon said. "Ragnhild Gilstrup was married."

Harry inclined his head in acknowledgment. "The eighth commandment?"

"The tenth," Jon said.

"I can't keep that under wraps, Jon."

Jon regarded Harry with surprise in his eyes. Then he slowly shook his head from side to side.

"What is it?"

"I can't believe I just said that," Jon said. "Ragnhild's dead and all I can think about is saving my own skin."

There were tears in Jon's eyes. And for one vulnerable moment Harry felt nothing but sympathy. Not the sympathy he could feel for the victim or for the next of kin, but for the person who for one heartrending moment sees his own pathetic humanity.

There were times when Sverre Hasvold regretted giving up his life as a merchant seaman to be a caretaker in the brand-new apartment building at 4 Gøteborggata. Especially on freezing-cold days like this one, when they called to complain that the garbage chute was blocked again. It happened once a month, on average, and the reason was obvious: The openings on every floor were the same circumference as the shaft itself. The old apartment buildings were better. Even in the thirties, when the first garbage chutes appeared, the architects had had enough sense to make the diameter of the openings narrower so that people would not force in things that would get stuck farther down the shaft. Nowadays all they had on their minds was style and lighting.

Hasvold opened the chute door on the third floor, put his head in and switched on his flashlight. The light reflected off the white plastic bags and he established that, as usual, the problem lay between the ground floor and the second floor, where the shaft narrowed.

He unlocked the trash room in the basement and switched on the light. The cold was so raw that his glasses misted up. He shivered and grabbed the almost nine-foot-long iron rod he kept along the wall for exactly this purpose. There was even a plastic ball on the end so that he wouldn't puncture the bags when he prodded it up the chute. Drops were falling from the opening with a drip, drip onto the plastic bags in the trash container. The house rules made it very clear that the chute was to be used for dry matter inside sealed bags, but no one—not even the so-called Christians living in the building—took any notice of that kind of thing.

The eggshells and milk cartons crunched under his feet in the container as he moved toward the round opening in the ceiling. He peered up the hole, but all he could see was blackness. He poked the rod up. Waited until he hit the usual soft bulk of bags, but instead the rod met something solid. He poked harder. It wouldn't budge; something was wedged in there good and tight.

He took the flashlight hanging from his belt and shone the light up the shaft. A drop fell on his glasses. Blinded and cursing, he tore off his glasses and wiped the lenses on his blue coat while holding the flashlight under his arm. He shifted to the side and squinted nearsightedly up. Alarmed, he pointed the flashlight upward, his imagination beginning to work overtime. His heart was slowing as he stared. In disbelief, he put his glasses back on. Then his heart stopped beating.

The iron rod slid and scraped down the wall until it hit the floor with a clang. Sverre Hasvold found himself sitting in the trash container. The flashlight must have slipped down between the bags somewhere. Another drop dripped onto the plastic bag between his thighs. He jerked backward as though it were caustic acid. Then he got to his feet and sprinted out.

He had to have fresh air. He had seen things at sea, but nothing like this. This was . . . not normal. It had to be vomit. He pushed open the front door and staggered out onto the pavement without noticing the two tall men standing there or the cold air that met him. Dizzy and breathless, he leaned against the wall and took out his cell phone. Stared at it helplessly. They had changed the emergency numbers some years ago, made them easier to remember, but the old ones were the ones that occurred to him, of course. He caught sight of the two men. One of them was talking on his cell; the other he recognized as one of the residents.

"Sorry, but do you know how to call the police?" Hasvold asked and could hear that he had become hoarse as though from a long bout of screaming.

The resident glanced at the man beside him, who studied the caretaker for a moment before saying: "Hang on—we may not need Ivan and the tracker dogs after all." The man lowered his cell and turned to Sverre Hasvold. "I'm Inspector Hole, Oslo Police. Let me guess . . ."

In a flat by Vestkanttorget, Tore Bjørgen was looking down through the bedroom window onto the yard. It was as quiet outside as inside; no children running around screaming or playing in the snow. It must have been too cold and dark. And it was several years since he had seen children playing outside in the winter anyway. From the living room he could hear the TV news anchor warning about record low temperatures. The commissioner of social services was going to implement special measures to take the homeless off the streets and to encourage the elderly living on their own to turn up the heat in their flats. The police were looking for a Croatian national by the name of Christo Stankic. There was a reward for any tips leading to his arrest. The anchor didn't mention an amount, but Bjørgen assumed it would be more than enough for a return plane ticket to Cape Town and three weeks' food and accommodation.

Bjørgen dried his nostrils and rubbed the rest of the cocaine into his gums. It took away the last of the pizza taste.

He had told the manager of Biscuit that he had a headache and had gone home early. Christo—or Mike, as he had said his name was—was waiting for him on a bench in Vestkanttorget, as they had arranged. Christo had obviously enjoyed his Grandiosa frozen pizza and had wolfed it down without noticing the fifteen milligrams of Stesolid in chopped-up pill form.

Bjørgen surveyed the sleeping Christo, who was lying naked and facedown on his bed. Despite the ball gag, Christo's breathing was regular and deep. He hadn't shown any signs of waking while Tore was making his little arrangement. Tore had bought the sedatives off a frenetic junkie on the street right outside Biscuit for fifteen kroner a pill. The rest had not cost much, either. The handcuffs, ankle cuffs, the ball gag with head harness and the string of shiny anal beads had followed in a so-called beginners' pack that he had bought off a website for only 599 kroner.

The duvet was on the floor and Christo's skin glowed in the light from the flickering flames of the candles Tore had placed around the room. His body formed a Y shape against the white sheet; his hands were tied to the head of Tore's solid brass bed while his feet were attached to opposite rails at the end. Tore had managed to squeeze a cushion under Christo's stomach to raise his backside.

Tore removed the lid of the Vaseline container, scooped out a lump with his index finger and separated Christo's buttocks with the other hand. And the thought went through his mind again. This was rape. It would be difficult to call it anything else. And the thought, just the word *rape*, made him feel horny.

In fact, he was not sure whether Christo would have had any objection to being played with. The signals had been mixed. Nevertheless, it was dangerous to play with a murderer. Wonderfully dangerous. But not brainless. After all, the man beneath him would be locked up for the rest of his life.

He looked down at his erection. Then he took the anal beads from the box and pulled both ends of the thin but sturdy nylon string running through the beads like through a pearl necklace: The first beads were small but increased in volume, the largest the size of a golf ball. According to the instructions, the beads were to be inserted in the anal passage and then pulled out at leisure to achieve maximum stimulation of the nerves in and around the sensitive entrance to the anus. There were a variety of colors, and if you didn't know what anal beads were you could be excused for imagining they were something else. Tore smiled at his distorted reflection in the largest of the beads. Dad might be a bit taken aback when he opened Tore's Yuletide present with a greeting from Cape Town and his fervent hope that it would look nice on the Christmas tree. However, no one in the family from Vegårdshei would have the slightest idea what kind of beads were glinting in front of them as they jigged around the tree singing and dutifully holding hands. Or where they had been.

Harry led Beate and her two assistants down the stairs to the basement, where the caretaker unlocked the door to the garbage room. One of the assistants was new, a woman whose name Harry retained for no more than three seconds.

"Up there," Harry said. The other three, wearing outfits that looked like white beekeeper's outfits, stepped forward with care to stand beneath the chute opening, and the beams from their headlamps disappeared up into the dark. Harry studied the new assistant, waited for the reaction on her face. When it came, it reminded Harry of the coral life that instantly retracts when touched by divers' fingers. Beate gave an imperceptible nod of the head, like a plumber's dispassionate assessment of moderate to severe frost damage.

"Enucleation," she said. Her voice resounded in the chute. "Have you got that, Margaret?"

The female assistant was breathing hard as she groped for a pen and notebook inside the beekeeper costume.

"I beg your pardon," Harry said.

"The left eyeball has been removed. Margaret?"

"Got it," the assistant said, taking notes.

"The woman's hanging down headfirst. Stuck in the chute, I suppose. There's a little blood dripping from the eye socket and inside I can see some areas of white, which must be the inner cranium showing through the tissue. Dark-red blood, so it's a while since it coagulated. The pathologist will check temperature and rigidity when he comes. Too quick?"

"No, that's fine," Margaret said.

"We've found traces of blood by the chute door on the fourth floor, the same floor where the eye was found, so I assume the body was pushed in there. It's a tight opening and from here it looks as if the right shoulder has been dislocated. That may have happened when she was forced in or when her fall was broken. It's hard to know from this angle, but I think I can see bruising on the neck, which would suggest that she was strangled. The pathologist will check the shoulder and determine the cause of death. Otherwise there's not a lot we can do here. It's all yours, Gilberg."

Beate stepped aside and the male assistant took several flash photos of the chute.

"What's the yellowish-white stuff in the eye socket?" he asked.

"Fat," Beate said. "Clear the container and look for things that may be from the victim or the killer. Afterward you'll get some help from the officers outside to pull her down. Margaret, you come with me."

They went into the corridor and Margaret went to the elevator door and pressed the button.

"We're taking the stairs," Beate said in a light tone. Margaret regarded her with surprise and then followed her two older colleagues.

"Three more of my people will be here soon," Beate said in answer to Harry's unspoken question. Although Harry, with his long legs, was taking two steps at a time, the small woman kept up with ease. "Witnesses?"

"None so far," Harry said. "But we're doing the rounds. Three officers are ringing all the flats in the building. And after that the neighboring buildings."

"Do they have a photo of Stankic?"

Harry sent her a glance to see whether she was being ironic. It was difficult to say.

"What was your first impression?" Harry asked.

"A man," Beate said.

"Because whoever it was must have been strong to push her through the chute opening?"

"Maybe."

"Anything else?"

"Harry, are we in any doubt as to who this was?" She sighed.

"Yes, Beate, we are. As a matter of principle we profess doubt until we know."

Harry turned to Margaret, who was already out of breath from following them. "And your first impression?"

"What?"

They turned into the hallway on the fourth floor. A corpulent man in a tweed suit under an open tweed coat was standing in front of the door to Jon Karlsen's flat. He had obviously been waiting for them.

"I was wondering what you felt when you entered the building," Harry said. "And looked up into the chute."

"Felt?" Margaret asked with a puzzled smile.

"Yes, felt!" Ståle Aune bellowed, proffering a hand, which Harry shook without hesitation. "Come along and learn, folks, for this is the famous gospel according to Hole. Before entering a crime scene, empty your mind of all thoughts, become a newly born child, without language, open yourself to the sacred first impression, the vital first seconds that are your great, and only, chance to behold what happened without an ounce of a fact. It almost sounds like exorcism, doesn't it? Nice suit, Beate. And who is your charming colleague?"

"This is Margaret Svendsen."

"Ståle Aune," the man said, seizing Margaret's gloved hand and kissing it. "Goodness me, you taste of rubber, my dear."

"Aune is a psychologist," Beate said. "He often helps us."

"He often *tries* to help you," Aune said. "Psychology is, I'm afraid to say, a science that is still in its diapers and should not be accorded too much value for another fifty to a hundred years. And what is your response to Inspector Hole's question, my dear?"

Margaret looked to Beate for help.

"I . . . don't know," she said. "The eye was a bit off-putting, of course." Harry unlocked the door.

"You know I can't stand the sight of blood," Aune warned.

"Think of it as a glass eye," Harry said, opening the door and stepping to the side. "Walk on the plastic and don't touch anything."

Aune trod with care on the path of black plastic traversing the floor. He crouched down beside the eye, which still lay in the pile of dust next to the vacuum cleaner but now had a gray film over it.

"Apparently it's called enucleation," Harry said.

Aune raised one eyebrow. "Performed with a vacuum cleaner to the eye?"

"You can't suck an eye out of the head with just a vacuum cleaner," Harry said. "The perp must have sucked it out far enough for him to get a couple of fingers inside. Muscles and optic nerves are solid matter."

"What don't you know, Harry?"

"I once arrested a woman who had drowned her child in the bath. While she was in custody she tore out one of her eyes. The doctor acquainted me with the technique."

They heard a sharp intake of breath from Margaret behind them.

"Removing an eye does not have to be fatal," Harry said. "Beate thinks the woman may have been strangled. What's your first thought?"

"It goes without saying that this act has been committed by a person in a state of emotional or rational disequilibrium," Aune said. "The mutilation suggests uncontrolled anger. There may, of course, be practical reasons for the perpetrator to choose to send the body down the chute . . ."

"Unlikely," Harry said. "If the intention was that the body should not be found for a while, it would have been smarter to leave it in the empty flat."

"In that case to some extent this kind of thing tends to be a conscious symbolic act."

"Hm. Remove an eye and treat the rest as garbage?"

"Yes."

Harry looked at Beate. "It doesn't sound like the work of a professional killer."

Aune shrugged. "It could well be an angry professional killer."

"In general, pros have a method they rely on. Christo Stankic's method so far has been to shoot his victims."

"He may have a wider repertoire," Beate said. "Or perhaps the victim surprised him while he was in the flat."

"Perhaps he didn't want to shoot because it would have alerted the neighbors," Margaret said.

The other three faced her.

She flashed an intimidated smile. "I mean . . . perhaps he needed time and peace and quiet. Perhaps he was searching for something."

Harry noticed that all of a sudden Beate had begun to breathe hard through her nose and was even paler than usual.

"How does that sound?" he asked, addressing Aune.

"Like psychology," Aune said. "A mass of questions. And hypotheses by way of a response."

Outside again, Harry asked Beate if something was the matter.

"Just a bit of nausea," she said.

"Oh? You're refused permission to be sick right now. Understood?"

She answered him with a cryptic smile.

He woke up, opened his eyes and saw lights roaming across the white wall in front of him. His body and head ached, and he was frozen. There was something in his mouth. And when he tried to move he could feel that his hands and feet had been shackled. He raised his head. In the mirror next to the bed, in the light from the burning candles, he could see he was naked. And there was something on his head, something black, like a horse's harness. One of the straps went across his face, over his mouth, which was obstructed by a black ball. His hands were held by metal handcuffs, his feet by something black like bondage restraints. He stared into the mirror. On the sheet between his legs lay the end of a string that disappeared up between his buttocks. And there was something white on his back. It looked like semen. He sank back into the pillow and shut his eyes. He wanted to scream, but knew that the ball would effectively prevent any attempt.

He heard a voice from the living room.

"Hello? *Politi?*"

Politi? Polizei? Police?

He thrashed around on the bed, jerking his arms down and moaning with pain as the handcuffs cut into the back of his thumb, taking off the skin. He twisted his hands so that his fingers could get hold of the chain between the cuffs. Handcuffs. Steel bars. His father had taught him that building materials were almost always made to withstand pressure in one direction and that the art of bending steel was about knowing where and which way it would offer the least resistance. The chain between the handcuffs was there to prevent them from being pulled apart.

He heard the man speaking briefly on the living-room telephone, then all went quiet.

He pressed the point where the final link in the chain met one cuff against the bar of the head of the bed, but instead of pulling, he twisted. After a quarter-turn the link locked against the bar. He tried to twist further, but it wouldn't budge. He tried again, but his hands slipped.

"Hello?" came the voice from the living room.

He took a deep breath. Closed his eyes and saw his father, with his enormous forearms in a short-sleeved shirt, before the line of steel rods on the building site. He whispered to the boy: "Banish all doubt. There's only room for willpower. The steel has no willpower and that's why it always loses."

Tore Bjørgen drummed his fingers with impatience on the rococo mirror with the pearl-gray clam adornments. The owner of the antique shop had told him that "rococo" was often used in a derogatory sense, to mean the style was over the top, almost grotesque. Tore had realized afterward that that was what had tipped the balance, when he had made up his mind to take out a loan to be able to lay out the twelve thousand kroner that the mirror had cost.

The switchboard at Police HQ had tried to put him through to Crime Squad, but no one had picked up and now they were trying the uniformed police.

He heard sounds from the bedroom. The rattle of chains against the bed. Perhaps Stesolid had not been the most effective sedative after all.

"Duty officer." The deep, calm voice startled Tore.

"Um, this is . . . it's about the reward. For . . . erm, that guy who shot the guy from the Salvation Army."

"Who's speaking? And where are you calling from?"

"Tore. From Oslo."

"Could you be a little more specific, please?"

Tore gulped. He had—for several good reasons—exercised his right not to disclose his telephone number when phoning and he knew that now "unknown number" would be flashing on whatever display the duty officer had.

"I can help you." Tore's voice had gone up a register.

"First of all I need to know—"

"I've got him here. Chained to the bed."

"You've chained someone up, you say?"

"He's a killer, isn't he? He's dangerous. I saw him with a gun at the restaurant. His name's Christo Stankic. I saw the name in the paper."

The other end went quiet for a moment. Then the voice was back, but a little less unruffled. "Calm down now. Tell me who you are and where you are, then we'll come at once."

"And what about the reward?"

"If this leads to the arrest of the correct person I will confirm that you helped us."

"And I'll be given the reward right away?"

"Yes."

Tore thought. About Cape Town. About Father Christmas in the baking sun. The telephone creaked. He breathed in, ready to answer, and looked into the twelve-thousand-krone rococo mirror. At that moment Tore realized three things. The creaking sound had not come from the telephone. You don't get top-quality mail-order handcuffs in a beginners' pack for 599 kroner. And in all probability he had celebrated his last Christmas.

"Hello?" said the voice on the telephone.

Tore Bjørgen would have liked to answer, but a thin nylon string of shiny beads, looking every inch like a Christmas decoration, was blocking the airway essential for the production of sound from vocal cords.

The Container

Four people drove between high drifts of snow through the darkness.

"Østgård is up here to the left," Jon said from the backseat, where he had his arm around Thea's cowed figure.

Halvorsen turned off the main road. Harry observed the scattered farmhouses, lit up and flashing like lighthouses at the tops of hills or among clumps of trees.

Since Harry had said that Robert's flat was no longer a safe hideout, Jon had himself suggested Østgård. And insisted on Thea's joining him.

Halvorsen swung onto the drive between a white farmhouse and a red barn.

"We'll have to call the neighbor and ask him to clear away some snow with his tractor," Jon said as they waded through the fresh snow toward the farmhouse.

"Nothing doing," Harry said. "No one must know you're here. Not even the police."

Jon walked over to the house wall beside the steps, counted five boards and plunged his hand into the snow and under the boards.

"Here," he said, holding up a key.

It felt even colder indoors than outside, and the painted wooden walls seemed to have frozen into ice blocks, rendering their voices harsh. They stamped the snow off their footwear and entered a large kitchen with a solid table, kitchen cabinet, storage bench and Jøtul wood-burning stove in the corner.

"I'll get the fire going." Jon's breath was icy and he rubbed his hands for warmth. "There's probably some firewood inside the bench, but we'll need more from the woodshed."

"I can get it," Halvorsen said.

"You'll have to dig a pathway. There are two shovels on the porch."

"I'll join you," Thea mumbled.

It had stopped snowing and the weather was clearing. Harry stood by the window smoking and watching Halvorsen and Thea shoveling the light, fresh snow in the white moonlight. The stove was crackling and Jon was on his haunches staring into the flames.

"How did your girlfriend take the Ragnhild Gilstrup business?" Harry asked.

"She's forgiven me," he said. "As I said, it was before her time."

Harry watched his cigarette glow. "Still no ideas about what she might have been doing in your flat?"

Jon shook his head.

"I don't know whether you noticed," Harry said, "but it looked as though the bottom drawer of your desk had been broken into. What did you keep there?"

Jon shrugged. "Personal things. Letters, for the most part."

"Love letters? From Ragnhild, for example?"

Jon blushed. "I . . . don't remember. I threw away most of them, but I may have kept a few. I kept the drawer locked."

"So that Thea wouldn't find them if she was alone in the flat?"

Jon gave a slow nod.

Harry went out to the steps overlooking the farmyard,

took a few final drags on his cigarette, threw it into the snow and took out his cell phone. Gunnar Hagen answered on the third ring.

"I've moved Jon Karlsen," Harry said.

"Be specific."

"Not necessary."

"Pardon?"

"He's safer now than he was. Halvorsen will stay here tonight."

"Where, Hole?"

"Here."

Listening to the silence on the phone, Harry had an inkling of what was coming. Then Hagen's voice came through loud and clear.

"Hole, your commanding officer has just asked you a specific question. Refusing to answer is regarded as insubordination. Am I making myself clear?"

Harry often wished he had been wired in a different way and that he possessed a bit more of the social survival instinct most people have. But he didn't, and he never had.

"Why is it important for you to know, Hagen?"

Hagen's voice shook with fury. "I'll tell you when you can ask me questions, Hole. Have you got that?"

Harry waited. And waited. And then, hearing Hagen take a deep breath, he said: "Skansen Farm."

"What did you say?"

"It's east of Strømmen. The police training ground in Løren Forest."

"I see," Hagen said at length.

Harry hung up and punched in another number while watching Thea, who, illuminated by the moon, was standing and staring in the direction of the outhouse. She had stopped shoveling snow and her body was frozen in a strange pose.

"Skarre here."

"Harry. Anything new?"

"No."

"No tips?"

"Nothing serious."

"But people are calling in?"

"Christ, yes—they've realized there's a reward. Bad idea, if you ask me. Loads of extra work for us."

"What do they say?"

"What don't they say! They describe faces they've seen that are similar. The funniest one was a guy who called the duty officer claiming he had chained Stankic to his bed at home and asked if he was entitled to the reward."

Harry waited until Skarre's peal of laughter died away. "How did they establish that he hadn't?"

"They didn't need to. He put down the phone. Obviously confused. He claimed he had seen Stankic before. With a gun in the restaurant. What are you up to?"

"We— What did you say?"

"I asked if—"

"No, the part about seeing Stankic with a gun."

"Ha-ha—people have fertile imaginations, don't they."

"Put me through to the duty officer you spoke to."

"Well—"

"*Now*, Skarre."

Harry was put through, spoke to the officer in charge and after three sentences asked him to stay on the line.

"Halvorsen!" Harry's shout rang around the farmyard.

"Yes?" Halvorsen appeared in the moonlight in front of the barn.

"What's the name of that waiter who saw a guy in the bathroom with a gun covered in soap?"

"How am I supposed to remember that?"

"I don't care how, just do it."

In the night stillness the echoes rang out between the walls of the house and the barn.

"Tore something or other. Maybe."

"Bull's-eye! Tore's the name he gave on the phone. Good. And now the last name, please."

"Er . . . Bjørg? No. Bjørang? No . . ."

"Come on, Lev Yashin!"

"Bjørgen. That was it. Bjørgen."

"Drop the shovel. You have permission to drive like a maniac."

A police car stood waiting for them as, twenty-eight minutes later, Halvorsen and Harry drove past Vestkanttorget and turned in to Schives Gate to Tore Bjørgen's address, which the duty officer had been given by the headwaiter at Biscuit.

Halvorsen came to a halt next to the police car and rolled down the window.

"Third floor," the policewoman in the driver's seat said, pointing up to an illuminated window in the gray-brick façade.

Harry leaned across Halvorsen. "Halvorsen and I will go up. One of you stay here in contact with the station, and one of you come with us to the backyard and keep an eye on the kitchen stairs. Do you have a gun in the trunk I can borrow?"

"Yep," the woman said.

Her male colleague bent forward. "You're Harry Hole, aren't you?"

"That's right, Officer."

"Someone at the station said you don't have a gun license."

"*Didn't*, Officer."

"Oh?"

Harry smiled. "Overslept and missed the first shooting test in the autumn. But you will be pleased to know that in the second I was the third best in the whole force. OK?"

The two officers exchanged glances.

"OK," the man mumbled.

Harry jerked open the car door and the frozen rubber seal groaned. "OK—let's check if there's anything to this tip."

For the second time in two days Harry had an MP5 in his hands. He buzzed the intercom of someone called Sejerstedt and explained to a nervous lady's voice that they were from the police. She could go to the window and see the police car before she opened up. She did as he suggested. The female officer went into the backyard and took up position while Halvorsen and Harry went up the staircase.

The name Tore Bjørgen was written in black on a brass plate above a doorbell. Harry thought of Bjarne Møller, who the first time they had gone into action together had taught Harry the simplest and still the most effective method of finding out whether someone was at home. He pressed his ear against the glass in the door. There wasn't a sound from inside.

"Loaded and safety catch off?" Harry whispered.

Halvorsen had taken out his service revolver and was standing against the wall on the left of the door.

Harry rang.

Holding his breath, he listened. Then he rang a second time.

"To break in or not to break in," Harry whispered, "that is the question."

"In that case we should have phoned the prosecutor's office first for a search—"

Halvorsen was interrupted by the tinkle of glass as Harry's MP5 struck the door. Harry thrust his hand in and opened up.

They slipped into the hall and Harry pointed to the doors Halvorsen should check. He went into the living room. Empty. But he noticed at once that the mirror over the telephone table had been hit by something hard. A round piece of glass in the middle had fallen out and, as though from a black sun, black lines radiated out to the gilt ornamental frame. Harry concentrated on the door at the end of the room that stood ajar.

"No one in the kitchen or bathroom," Halvorsen whispered behind him.

"OK. Brace yourself."

Harry moved toward the door. He could sense it now. If there was anything here they would find it inside. A car with a defective muffler went by outside. The brakes of a tram squealed in the distance. Harry noticed that he had hunched up as if by instinct. To make himself the smallest target possible.

He pushed open the door with the muzzle of the machine gun and neatly stepped in and to the side so as not to be silhouetted. Hugged the wall and, keeping his finger on the trigger, he waited for his eyes to get used to the dark.

In the light that came through the doorway he saw a large bed with brass rails. A pair of naked legs protruded from under the duvet. He strode forward, took the duvet by the end and whipped it off.

"Wow!" Halvorsen exclaimed. He was standing in the doorway and slowly lowered his revolver as he stared at the bed in amazement.

He took stock of the fence. Then he began his run-up and launched himself, using the wormlike movements on his way up that Bobo had taught him. The gun in his pocket hit him in the stomach as he swung himself over. In the light of the street lamp, on the ice-covered pavement on the other side, he saw that there was a big tear in his blue jacket. White material billowed out.

A sound made him move away from the light, into the shadow of the containers that were lined up on top of one another in the huge port area. He listened and watched.

The wind whistled through the broken windows of a dark, derelict wooden hut.

He didn't know why, but he felt as if he were being observed. No, not observed—he had been discovered, caught. Someone knew he was there, but may not have seen him. His eyes searched the illuminated fence for possible alarms. Nothing.

He walked along two lines of containers before finding one that was open. Entered the impenetrable darkness and instantly knew this was no good; he would freeze to death if he slept here. Closing the door behind him, he felt the air move, as though he were standing in a block of something that was being transported.

There was a rustling sound as he stepped onto sheets of newspaper. He had to get warm.

Outside, he again had the feeling he was being observed. He went over to the hut, grabbed hold of one of the boards and pulled. It came away with a bang. He thought he glimpsed something move, and whirled around. But all he could see was the glimmer of lights from inviting-looking hotels around Oslo Central Station and the darkness in the doorway of his lodging here. After wrestling off two further boards, he walked back to the container. There were prints where the snow had drifted. Of paws. Big paws. A guard dog. Had the prints been there before? He broke chunks off the boards, which he placed against the steel wall inside the entrance to the container. He left the door ajar in the hope that some of the smoke would filter out. The box of matches from the room in the hostel was in the same pocket as his gun. He lit the newspaper, put it under the wood and held his hands over the heat. Small flames licked up the rust-red wall.

He thought about the waiter's terror-stricken eyes looking down the barrel of the gun as he had ransacked his pockets for change. That was all he had, he had explained. It had been enough for a burger and a subway fare. Not enough for a place to hide, keep warm or sleep. Then the waiter had been stupid enough to say the police had been alerted and were on their way. And he had done what he had to do.

The flames lit up the snow outside. He noticed more paw prints outside the door. Odd that he hadn't seen them when he first went to the container. He listened to his own breathing and its echo in the iron box where he was sitting, as though there were two of them inside, while following the prints with his eyes. He stiffened. His prints crossed the animal's. And in the middle of his shoe print he saw a paw mark.

He yanked the door to and the flames went out in the muffled thud. Only the edges of the newspaper glowed in the pitch dark. His breathing was heavy now. There was something out there, hunting him; it could smell him and recognize his smell. He held his breath. And that was when he knew that the something hunting him was not outside. That it was not an echo of his breathing he could hear. It was inside. As he made a lunge for his gun in his pocket, he caught himself thinking it was strange it hadn't growled, hadn't made a sound. Until now. And even that was no more than the soft scraping of claws on an iron floor as it launched itself. He just managed to raise his arm before the jaws snapped around his hand and the pain caused his mind to explode in a shower of fragments.

Harry scrutinized the bed and what he assumed was Tore Bjørgen.

Halvorsen came over and stood beside him: "Sweet Jesus," he whispered. "What is going on here?"

Without answering him, Harry unzipped the black face mask the man in front of him was wearing and pulled the flap to one side. The painted red lips and makeup around the eyes reminded him of Robert Smith, the singer with The Cure.

"Is this the waiter you talked to in Biscuit?" Harry asked, looking around the room.

"I think so. What on earth is this getup?"

"Latex," Harry said, running the tips of his fingers over some metal shavings on the sheet. Then he picked up something beside a half-full glass of water on the bedside table. It was a pill. He studied it.

Halvorsen groaned. "This is just sick."

"A kind of fetishism," Harry said. "And actually no sicker than you enjoying the sight of women in miniskirts and suspenders or whatever gets you going."

"Uniforms," Halvorsen said. "All kinds. Nurses, traffic cops . . ."

"Thank you," Harry said.

"What do you think?" Halvorsen asked. "Suicide pills?"

"Better ask him," Harry said, picking up the glass of water and emptying the contents over the face below. Halvorsen stared at the inspector, open-mouthed.

"If you hadn't been so full of prejudice you would have heard him breathing," Harry said. "This is Stesolid. Not much worse than Valium." The man on the bed was gasping for air. Then the face contracted and was seized with a fit of coughing.

Harry sat on the edge and waited for a pair of terrified, though still tiny, pupils to succeed in focusing on him.

"We're policemen, Bjørgen. Apologies for bursting in like this, but we were led to believe you had something we wanted. Which you no longer have, it seems."

The eyes in front of him blinked twice. "What are you talking about?" a thick voice said. "How did you get in?"

"Door," Harry said. "You had another visitor earlier this evening." The man shook his head.

"That's what you told the police," Harry said.

"No one has been here. And I have not called the police. My number is unlisted. You can't trace it."

"Yes, we can. And *I* didn't say anything about you calling. You said on the phone you had chained someone to the bed, and I can see bits of metal from the bed rails here on the sheet. Looks like the mirror out there has taken a beating, too. Did he get away, Bjørgen?"

The man gawked from Harry to Halvorsen and back.

"Did he threaten you?" Harry spoke in the same low monotone. "Did he say he would be back if you said a word to us? Is that it? You're frightened?"

The man's mouth opened. Perhaps it was the leather mask that made Harry think of a pilot who had strayed off-course. Robert Smith adrift.

"That's what they usually say," Harry said. "But do you know what? If he'd meant it, you'd be dead already."

The man stared at Harry.

"Do you know where he went, Bjørgen? Did he take anything with him? Money? Clothes?"

Silence.

"Come on. This is important. He's hunting a person here in Oslo he wants to kill."

"I have no idea what you're talking about," whispered Tore Bjørgen without taking his eyes off Harry. "Would you please go now?"

"Of course. But I ought to point out that you risk being charged for giving refuge to a murderer on the run. Which the court may, in a worst-case scenario, regard as being an accessory to murder."

"Based on what evidence? All right—maybe I did call. I was kidding. Wanted a laugh. So what?"

Harry got up from the bed. "As you like. We're going now. Pack a few clothes. I'll send a couple of guys to pick you up, Bjørgen."

"Pick me up?"

"As in arrest." Harry motioned to Halvorsen that they were going.

"*Arrest* me?" Bjørgen's voice was thick no longer. "Why? You haven't got a fucking thing on me."

Harry showed what he was holding between his thumb and first finger. "Stesolid is a prescription drug like amphetamines and cocaine, Bjørgen. So unless you produce a prescription I'm afraid we'll have to arrest you for possession. Two years."

"You're joking." Bjørgen hauled himself up in bed and made a grab for the duvet on the floor. Only now did he seem to be aware of the outfit he was wearing.

Harry walked to the door. "I agree with you, Bjørgen. In my personal opinion, Norwegian legislation is much too harsh on soft drugs. For that reason, under different circumstances, I might have turned a blind eye. Good night."

"Wait!"

Harry stopped. And waited.

"His b-b-brothers . . ." Bjørgen stammered.

"Brothers?"

"He said he would send his brothers after me if anything happened to him in Oslo. If he was arrested or killed, however it happened, they would come for me. He said his brothers like to use acid."

"He doesn't have any brothers," Harry said.

Bjørgen raised his head, looked up at the policeman and asked with genuine surprise in his voice: "He doesn't?"

Harry shook his head.

Bjørgen wrung his hands. "I . . . I took those pills because I was so upset. That's what they're for. Isn't it?"

"Where did he go?"

"He didn't say."

"Did he take any money?"

"Some change I had on me. Then he cleared out. And I . . . I just sat here and was so frightened . . ." A sudden sob interrupted the flow and he huddled under the duvet. "I *am* so frightened."

Harry eyed the weeping man. "If you like, you can sleep down at Police HQ tonight."

"I'll stay here." Bjørgen sniffled.

"OK. One of us will be by early tomorrow to talk further."

"All right. Wait! If you catch him . . ."

"Yes?"

"That reward's still on, isn't it?"

He had the fire going well now. The flames glinted in a triangular piece of glass he had used from the broken window in the hut. He had collected more wood and felt his body beginning to thaw. It would be worse in the night, but he was alive. He had cut strips off his shirt with the piece of glass and wound them around his bleeding fingers. The animal's jaws had closed around his hand holding the gun. And the gun.

The shadow of a black Metzner hanging between roof and floor flickered on the container wall. The jaws were open and the body stretched out and frozen in one last silent attack. The rear legs were tied with wire, which was threaded through a gap in one of the iron grooves in the roof. The blood trickling out of the mouth and the opening behind the ear where the bullet had exited dripped onto the floor with clocklike regularity. He would never know whether it was his forearm muscles or the dog's bite that squeezed the finger on the trigger, but he had the impression he could still feel the walls vibrating after the shot. The sixth since he had arrived in this accursed city. And now he had one bullet left in the gun.

One was enough, but how would he find Jon Karlsen now? He needed someone to lead him in the right direction. The policeman came to mind. Harry Hole. It didn't sound like a common name. Perhaps he wouldn't be so difficult to find.

PART THREE

Crucifixion

20

The Citadel

The neon sign outside Vika Atrium showed minus four and the clock inside 9:00 as Harry and Halvorsen stood in the glass elevator, watching the tropical plants becoming smaller and smaller beneath them.

Halvorsen pursed his lips, then changed his mind. Pursed them again.

"Glass elevators are fine," Harry said. "No problem with heights."

"Uh-huh."

"I want you to do the introductions and ask the questions. I'll join in after a while. OK?"

Halvorsen nodded.

They had just sat down in the car after the visit to Tore Bjørgen when Gunnar Hagen had called and asked them to go down to Vika Atrium, where Albert and Mads Gilstrup, father and son, were waiting for them in order to make a statement. Harry had pointed out that it was not normal practice to call the police to make a statement, and he had asked that Skarre deal with the matter.

"Albert is an old acquaintance of the Chief's," Hagen had explained. "He phoned to say they had decided they didn't want to make a statement to anyone except the officer leading the inquiry. On the positive side, there won't be a lawyer present."

"Well—"

"Great. I appreciate that."

So, no command this time.

A little man in a blue blazer was waiting for them outside the elevator.

"Albert Gilstrup," he said with minimal movement from a lipless mouth as he proffered a fleeting but firm handshake. Gilstrup had white hair and a furrowed, weather-beaten face but young, alert eyes, which studied Harry as he walked with him toward a door with a sign declaring that this was where Gilstrup Invest was housed.

"I would like you to be aware that my son has been hit hard by this," Albert Gilstrup said. "The body was in a terrible state, and Mads has a somewhat sensitive nature."

Harry concluded from the way Albert Gilstrup expressed himself that either he was a practical man who knew there was little to be done for the dead, or that his daughter-in-law had not occupied a special place in his heart.

In the small but expensively furnished reception area hung well-known Norwegian pictures with national-romantic motifs that Harry had seen countless times before. A man with a cat in the farmyard. Soria Moria Palace. The difference was that this time Harry was not so sure he was looking at reproductions.

Mads Gilstrup was sitting and staring through the glass wall facing the atrium as they came into the meeting room. The father coughed and the son slowly turned as if he had been disturbed in the middle of a dream he didn't want to relinquish. The first thing that struck Harry was that the son did not look like his father. His face was narrow, but the round, gentle features and the curly hair made Mads Gilstrup look younger than the thirty-something years Harry assumed he must be. Or perhaps it was his expression, the childlike helplessness in those brown eyes that finally focused on them when he stood up.

"I'm grateful that you were able to come," Mads Gilstrup whispered in a thick voice, squeezing Harry's hand with an intensity that made Harry wonder whether the son might have thought the priest had arrived and not the police.

"Not at all," Harry said. "We had wanted to talk to you anyway."

Albert Gilstrup coughed and his mouth barely opened, like a crack in a wooden face. "Mads means that he is grateful for your coming here at our request. We thought you might prefer the police station."

"And I thought you might have preferred to meet us at home, since it's so late," Harry said, addressing the son.

Mads looked at his father irresolutely, and on receiving a faint nod, answered: "I can't bear to be there now. It's so . . . empty. I'll sleep at home tonight."

"With us," the father added by way of explanation and sent him a look that Harry thought should have been sympathy. But it resembled contempt.

They sat down and father and son pushed their business cards across the table to Harry and Halvorsen. Halvorsen responded with two of his own. Albert Gilstrup looked at Harry in anticipation.

"Mine haven't been printed yet," Harry said. Which was true, as far as it went, and always had been. "But Halvorsen and I work as a team, so all you have to do is call him."

Halvorsen cleared his throat. "We have a few questions."

Halvorsen's questions sought to establish Ragnhild's movements earlier that day, what she was doing in Jon Karlsen's flat and possible enemies. Each one was met with a shake of the head.

Harry searched for milk for his coffee. He didn't take it black anymore, probably a sign that he was getting old. Some weeks ago he had put on the Beatles' indisputable masterpiece *Sgt. Pepper's Lonely Hearts Club Band* and was disappointed. It had got old, too.

Halvorsen was reading questions from his notepad and jotting down notes without making eye contact. He asked Mads Gilstrup to account for where he had been between nine and ten o'clock this morning, which was the doctor's estimate of the time of death.

"He was here," Albert Gilstrup said. "We've been working here all day, both of us. We're trying to turn around the firm." He addressed Harry. "We expected you to ask that question. I've read that the husband is always the first person the police suspect in murder investigations."

"With good reason," Harry said. "From a statistical point of view."

"Fine." Albert Gilstrup nodded. "But this isn't statistics. This is reality."

Harry met Albert Gilstrup's flashing blue eyes. Halvorsen glanced across at Harry as though in dread of something.

"So let's stick to reality," Harry said. "And shake our heads less and say more. Mads?"

Mads Gilstrup's head shot up as if he had dozed off. Harry waited until they had eye contact. "What did you know about Jon Karlsen and your wife?"

"Stop!" Albert's wooden-doll mouth snapped. "That kind of impudence may be acceptable with the clientele that you deal with on a day-to-day basis, but not here."

Harry sighed. "If it is your wish, your father may stay here, Mads. However, if I have to, I will throw him out."

Albert Gilstrup laughed. It was the seasoned victor's laugh from someone who has at last found a worthy opponent. "Tell me, Inspector, am I going to be obliged to call my friend the chief superintendent and tell him how his men treat someone who has just lost his wife?"

Harry was about to answer, but was interrupted by Mads, who raised his hand in a slow, strangely graceful movement. "We have to find him, Father. We have to help each other."

They waited, but Mads's gaze had returned to the glass wall and he said nothing further.

"All right," Albert said in English with superb pronunciation. "We'll talk on one condition: that we do this privately, Hole. Your assistant can wait outside."

"We don't work like that," Harry said.

"We're trying to cooperate here, Hole, but this is not up for debate. The alternative is to talk to us through our lawyer. Do you understand?"

Harry waited for the anger to rise. And when it still didn't come, he was no longer in any doubt: He was indeed getting old. He nodded to Halvorsen, who looked surprised but got to his feet. Albert Gilstrup waited until the officer had closed the door behind him.

"Yes, we have met Jon Karlsen. Mads, Ragnhild and I met him in his role as financial adviser for the Salvation Army. We made him an offer that would have been very advantageous and he rejected it. Doubtless a person of high morals and integrity. But, of course, he might have been courting Ragnhild anyway; he wouldn't have been the first. I am aware extramarital affairs are not front-page news anymore. What makes your intimations ridiculous, however, is Ragnhild herself. Believe me, I knew the woman for a long time. She was not only a much-loved member of the family; she was also a person with character."

"And if I tell you she had keys to Jon Karlsen's flat?"

"I don't want to hear any more about the case!" Albert snapped. Harry glanced at the glass wall and caught the reflection of Mads Gilstrup's face as his father continued.

"Let me get to the point of why we want a private meeting with you, Hole. You're leading the investigation, and we thought of offering you a prize if you catch the person guilty of the murder of Ragnhild. To be precise, two hundred thousand kroner. Absolute discretion."

"I beg your pardon?" Harry said.

"All right," Gilstrup said. "The sum can be discussed.

The vital thing for us is that this case is given top priority by the police."

"Are you trying to bribe me?"

Albert Gilstrup put on an acid smile. "That was very dramatic, Hole. Allow it to sink in. We won't quibble if you give the money to the fund for police widows."

Harry didn't answer. Albert Gilstrup smacked his hand down on the table.

"I think the meeting is over. Let's keep channels open, Inspector."

Halvorsen yawned as the glass elevator fell to the ground, gently, soundlessly, the way he imagined angels in Christmas carols descended to earth.

"Why didn't you throw out the father right away?" he asked.

"Because he's interesting," Harry said.

"What did he say while I was outside?"

"That Ragnhild was a lovely person who could not have had a relationship with Jon Karlsen."

"Do they believe that themselves?"

Harry shrugged.

"Anything else they talked about?"

Harry hesitated. "No," he said, peering down at the green oasis with the fountain in the marble desert.

"What are you thinking about?" Halvorsen asked.

"I'm not sure. I saw Mads Gilstrup smile."

"Eh?"

"I saw his reflection in the glass. Did you notice that Albert Gilstrup looks like a wooden doll? The sort ventriloquists use."

Halvorsen shook his head.

They walked down Munkedamsveien toward the Oslo Concert Hall, where fully laden Christmas shoppers were hurrying along the pavements.

"Nippy," said Harry, shivering. "Shame the cold makes exhaust fumes hug the ground. The whole town suffocates."

"Better that than the foul stench of aftershave in the meeting room, though," Halvorsen said.

At the staff entrance to the concert hall hung a poster for the Salvation Army's Christmas concert. On the pavement beneath it sat a kid with an outstretched hand and an empty paper cup.

"You lied to Bjørgen," Halvorsen said.

"Oh?"

"A two-year sentence for one Stesolid? And for all you know, Stankic may have nine vindictive brothers."

Harry shrugged and consulted his watch. He was too late for the AA meeting. He decided it was time he listened to God's words.

"But when Jesus comes back to Earth who will be able to recognize Him?" David Eckhoff shouted, and the flame in front of him flickered. "Maybe the Redeemer is among us now, in this town?"

A mumble passed through the crowd in the large, white, simply furnished auditorium. The citadel had neither an altarpiece nor a communion rail, but an "anxious bench" between the gathering and the podium, where you could kneel and confess your sins.

The commander looked down on those assembled and paused for effect before continuing. "For even though Matthew writes that the Redeemer shall come in all his glory, with all the angels, it is also written, 'I was a stranger and you did not invite me in, I needed clothes and you did not clothe me, I was sick and in prison and you did not look after me.'"

David Eckhoff breathed in, turned the page and raised his eyes to the congregation. And continued without looking down at the scriptures.

" 'Then they will answer: Lord, when did we see you hungry or thirsty or a stranger or needing clothes or sick or in prison, and did not help you? But he will reply: I tell you the truth, whatever you did not do for one of the humblest, you did not do for me. And they will be given eternal punishment, but the righteous will be given eternal life.' " The commander pounded the lectern. "What Matthew is saying here is a call to war, a declaration of war against selfishness and inhumanity!" he cried. "And we Salvationists believe there will be a universal judgment on the Last Day, that the righteous will receive eternal life and that the ungodly will receive eternal punishment."

When the commander's sermon was over, the floor was open for personal testimony. An elderly man talked about the battle of Oslo Cathedral square, which they had won with God's words spoken through Jesus and with openhearted sincerity. Then a younger man stepped forward, saying they should bring the evening to a close by playing Hymn No. 617 in the book. He stood in front of the uniformed band of eight wind musicians and Rikard Nilsen on the big bass drum and started counting. They played the introduction, then the conductor turned to the audience and they joined in. The hymn sounded powerful in the room: "*Let the flag of redemption wave, onward now to holy war!*"

When the hymn was finished David Eckhoff approached the lectern again. "Dear friends, let me conclude this evening's meeting by informing you that the prime minister's office has today confirmed that the prime minister will be attending the annual Christmas concert in Oslo Concert Hall."

The news was met with spontaneous applause. The congregation stood up and made its unhurried way to the exit as the room buzzed with lively conversation. Only Martine Eckhoff seemed to be in a hurry. Seated on the farthest bench to the back, Harry watched her come up the central aisle. She was wearing a wool skirt, black stockings,

Doc Martens like his and a white knitted cap. She looked straight at him without any sign of recognition. Then her face lit up. Harry got to his feet.

"Hi," she said, tilting her head and smiling. "Work or spiritual thirst?"

"Well, your father is quite a speaker."

"He would have been an international star of Pentecostalism."

Harry thought he caught a glimpse of Rikard in the crowd behind her. "Listen, I have a couple of questions. If you feel like walking in the cold I can accompany you home."

Martine looked doubtful.

"If that's where you want to go," Harry hastened to add.

Martine looked around before answering. "I can walk you home. Your place is on the way."

The air outside was raw and thick, and smelled of fried food and salty car exhaust.

"I'll get straight to the point," Harry said. "You know both Robert and Jon. Is it possible that Robert might have wanted to kill his brother?"

"What did you say?"

"Think a little before you answer."

They took tiny steps on the thick ice, past the Edderkoppen Theatre, through the deserted streets. The Christmas dinner season was coming to an end, but taxis were still shuttling passengers with festive clothes and aquavit eyes up and down Pilestredet.

"Robert was a little wild," Martine said. "But a killer?" She shook her head vigorously.

"Could he have gotten someone else to do it?"

Martine shrugged. "I didn't have much to do with Jon and Robert."

"Why not? You grew up together, so to speak."

"Yes, but I didn't have much to do with anyone, really. I liked my own company best. As you do."

"Me?" came the surprised response from Harry.

"One lone wolf recognizes another, you know." Harry glanced at her and met teasing eyes.

"You must have been the type of boy who went his own way. Exciting and unapproachable."

Harry smiled and shook his head. They passed the oil drums in front of the derelict though colorful façade of Blitz. He pointed.

"Do you remember when they occupied the property here in 1982 and there were punk gigs with Kjøtt, The Aller Værste and all the other bands?"

Martine laughed. "No. I had just started school then. And Blitz wasn't exactly the sort of place we in the Salvation Army would frequent."

Harry grinned. "No, well, I went there from time to time. At the beginning, at least, when I thought it might be somewhere for people like me, outsiders. But I didn't fit in there, either. Because when it came down to it, Blitz was about uniformity and thinking alike. The demagogues had a field day there, like . . ."

Harry paused, but Martine completed the sentence for him. "Like my father in the citadel this evening?"

Harry thrust his hands deeper into his pockets. "My point is that you soon become lonely if you want to use your own brain to find answers."

"And what answer has your lonely brain come up with so far, then?" Martine put her hand under his arm.

"It seems to me that both Jon and Robert had a number of lovers in their past. What's so special about Thea, since they both had their eyes on her?"

"Was Robert interested in Thea? That wasn't my impression."

"Jon says so."

"Well, as I said, I haven't had a lot to do with them. But I remember that Thea was popular with the boys during the summers we spent at Østgård. Competition starts early, you know."

"Competition?"

"Yes, boys who want to become officers have to find themselves a girl within the Army."

"Do they?" asked Harry in surprise.

"Didn't you know that? If you marry outside you immediately lose your job in the Army. The whole command chain is based on married officers living and working together. They have a joint calling."

"Sounds strict."

"We're a military organization." Martine said this without a hint of irony.

"And the boys knew that Thea wanted to be an officer? Even though she's a girl."

Martine smiled and shook her head. "I can see you don't know much about the Salvation Army. Two thirds of the officers are women."

"But the commander is a man? And the chief administrator?"

Martine nodded. "Our founder, William Booth, said his best men were women. Nevertheless, we are like the rest of society. Stupid, self-assured men ruling over smart women with a fear of heights."

"So the boys fought every summer to be the one who ruled over Thea?"

"For a while. But Thea stopped going to Østgård all of a sudden, so the problem was solved."

"Why did she stop?"

Martine shrugged. "Perhaps she didn't want to go. Or her parents didn't want her to go. So many boys around day and night at that age . . . you know."

Harry nodded. But he didn't know. He had never even been to a religious camp. They walked up Stensberggata.

"I was born here," Martine said, pointing to the wall that

used to run around Rikshospitalet before that building was pulled down. Before long the new residential project Pilestredet Park would be there.

"They've kept the building with the maternity ward and converted it into flats," Harry said.

"Do people really *live* there? Think of all the things that have happened there. Abortions and . . ."

Harry nodded. "Sometimes when you walk around here at midnight you can still hear the screams of children coming from there."

Martine stared at Harry. "You're joking! Are there ghosts?"

"Well," Harry said, turning in to Sofies Gate, "it might be because families with children have moved in."

Martine slapped him on the shoulder with a laugh. "No jokes about ghosts. I believe in them."

"Me, too," said Harry. "Me, too."

Martine stopped laughing.

"I live here," Harry said, pointing to a light-blue front door.

"Didn't you have any more questions?"

"Yes, but they can wait until the morning."

She cocked her head to the side. "I'm not tired. Do you have any tea?" A car crawled forward on creaking snow, but pulled toward the curb fifty yards lower down and blinded them with bluish-white light. Harry gave her a thoughtful look as he groped for his keys. "Just Nescafé. Listen, I'll call—"

"Nescafé's fine," Martine said. Harry went to put the key in the lock but Martine was a step ahead. She pushed open the light-blue front door. Harry watched it spring back and close against the frame, but it didn't snap shut.

"It's the cold," he mumbled. "The building's shrinking."

Harry slammed the door after them, then they went up the stairs.

"Tidy here," Martine said, taking off her boots in the hall.

"I don't have a lot of things," Harry said from the kitchen.

"What do you like best?"

Harry gave that some thought. "Records."

"Not the photo album?"

"I don't believe in photo albums," Harry said.

Martine went into the kitchen and slunk into one of the chairs. From the corner of his eye Harry watched her tuck her legs under her with the agility of a cat.

"You don't *believe*?" she asked. "What's that supposed to mean?"

"They destroy the ability to forget. Milk?"

She shook her head. "But you believe in records?"

"Yes. They lie in a more truthful way."

"But don't they destroy the ability to forget?"

Harry paused mid-pour. Martine was chuckling. "I don't believe in this surly, disillusioned inspector. I think you're a romantic, Hole."

"Let's go into the sitting room," Harry said. "I just bought a great new record. For the moment it comes without any memories attached." Martine slipped onto the sofa while Harry put on Jim Stärk's debut record. Then he sat in the green wing chair and caressed the coarse woolen material to the accompaniment of the first guitar notes. He remembered that the chair had been bought from Elevator, the Salvation Army's secondhand shop. He cleared his throat. "Robert may have been having a relationship with a girl who was much younger than him. What do you think about that?"

"What do I think about relationships between younger women and older men?" She chuckled but flushed deep red in the silence that followed. "Or do I think Robert liked underage girls?"

"I didn't say that, but a teenager, maybe. Croatian."

"*Izgubila sam se.*"

"Pardon?"

"That's Croatian. Or Serbo-Croatian. We used to spend the summer in Dalmatia when I was small, before the Salvation Army bought Østgård. When Daddy was eighteen he went to Yugoslavia to help with reconstruction after the Second World War. He got to know the families of a lot of the builders. That was why he committed us to taking refugees from Vukovar."

"With regard to Østgård, do you remember a Mads Gilstrup, the grandson of the people you bought it from?"

"Oh, yes. He was there for some days the summer we took it over. I didn't speak to him. No one spoke to him, I remember. He seemed so angry and introverted. But I think he liked Thea, too."

"What makes you think that? If he didn't speak to anyone, I mean."

"I saw him watching her. And when we were with Thea all of a sudden there he was. But he didn't say a word. He seemed weird, I thought. Almost a bit scary."

"Oh?"

"Yes. He slept at the neighbors' house on the days he was there, but one night I woke up in the room where a few of the girls slept. And I saw a face pressed against the window. Then it was gone. I'm almost positive it was him. When I told the other girls, they said I was seeing things. They were convinced there had to be something wrong with my eyesight."

"Why is that?"

"Haven't you noticed?"

"What?"

"Come and sit here, and I'll show you," Martine said, patting the sofa beside her. "Can you see my pupils?"

Harry leaned forward and felt her breath on his face. And then he saw it. The pupils inside the brown irises looked as though they had spilled into the iris, forming a keyhole shape.

"It's congenital," she said. "It's called iris coloboma. But you can still have normal eyesight."

"Interesting." Their faces were so close he could smell her skin and her hair. He breathed in and had the tremulous sensation of slipping into a hot bath. A short, firm buzz sounded.

It took Harry a moment to realize it came from the door. Not the intercom. Someone was standing outside his door on the landing.

"Must be Ali," Harry said, getting up from the sofa. "The neighbor." In the six seconds it took Harry to get off the sofa, go into the hall and open the door, it went through his mind that it was too late to be Ali. And he usually knocked, anyway.

It wasn't until the seventh second that he realized he shouldn't have opened up. He looked at the person standing there and had an intimation of what was in the offing.

"Now you're happy, I suppose," Astrid said with a slight slur. Harry didn't answer.

"I've just come from a Christmas dinner. Are you going to invite me in, Harry boy?" Her red lips tightened against her teeth as she smiled and her stiletto heels clattered on the floor as she stepped sideways to regain balance.

"It's not a good time," Harry said.

She scrunched up her eyes and studied his face. Then she peered over his shoulder. "Got a lady there, have you? Is that why you skipped the meeting today?"

"We can talk another time, Astrid. You're drunk."

"We discussed Step Three at the meeting today. *We made the decision to put our lives in God's care.* But I can't see any God—I can't, Harry." She took a halfhearted swipe at him with her bag.

"There is no third step, Astrid. Everyone has to look after himself."

She stiffened and looked at him as the tears welled in her eyes. "Let me in, Harry," she whispered.

"It won't help, Astrid." He put a hand on her shoulder. "I'll call for a taxi to take you home."

His hand was knocked away with surprising force. "Home?" she screeched. "I'm not fucking going home, you fucking impotent lech."

She swiveled around and started to stagger down the stairs.

"Astrid . . ."

"Get out of my sight! Fuck your other whore."

Harry watched her until she was gone, heard her fighting with the door, her curses, the creaking door hinges and then the silence.

When he turned, Martine was right behind him in the hall, slowly doing up her coat.

"I . . ." he began.

"It's late." She flashed a fleeting smile. "I was a bit tired, anyway."

It was three o'clock in the morning and Harry was still sitting in the wing chair. Tom Waits was singing in a low voice about Alice as the brushes swished on the snare drum.

"It's dreamy weather we're on / You waved your crooked wand / Along an icy pond . . ."

His mind ran unchecked. All the bars were closed now. He hadn't refilled his hip flask after emptying it down the dog's gullet in the container terminal. But he could phone Øystein. He drove a taxi almost every night and always kept a bottle of gin under the seat.

"It won't help."

Unless you believed in ghosts, of course. Believed in those encircling his chair and staring down at him with dark, hollow eye sockets. In Birgitta, who had come up from the sea with the anchor still around her neck; in Ellen, who was laughing with the baseball bat protruding from her head; in William, who hung like a galleon figurehead from the rotary dryer; and Tom, who had come to get his watch back, waving a bloody stump of an arm.

The booze couldn't free him; it could give only temporary relief. And right now he was willing to pay a lot for that.

He lifted the telephone and tapped in a number. It was answered on the second ring.

"How's it going, Halvorsen?"

"Cold. Jon and Thea are asleep. I'm sitting in the room with a view of the road. I'll have to take a nap tomorrow."

"Mm."

"We have to drive back to Thea's flat tomorrow to get more insulin. She's a diabetic."

"OK, but take Jon with you. I don't want him left on his own."

"I could get someone to come here."

"No!" Harry said sharply. "I don't want anyone else involved for the time being."

"Right."

Harry sighed. "Listen, I know babysitting isn't in the job description. You'll have to tell me if there's anything I can do in return."

"Well . . ."

"Come on."

"I promised to take Beate out one evening before Christmas to let her try lutefisk. She's never tasted it before, poor thing."

"That's a promise."

"Thanks."

"And, Halvorsen?"

"Yes?"

"You're . . ." Harry took a deep breath. ". . . OK."

"Thanks, boss."

Harry hung up. Waits was singing that the skates on the icy pond spelled Alice.

Zagreb

He sat shaking with cold on a piece of cardboard on the pavement by Sofienberg Park. It was rush hour and people were racing by. Some still had time to drop a few kroner in the paper cup in front of him. It would soon be Christmas. His lungs ached because he had been on his back breathing in smoke all night. He raised his eyes and looked up Gøteborggata.

That was all he could do now.

He thought about the Danube flowing past Vukovar. Patient, unstoppable. As he would have to be. Patient, waiting for the tank to come, for the dragon to stick its head out of the cave. For Jon Karlsen to come home. He looked at a pair of knees that had stopped right in front of him.

He peered up at a man with a red beard and a paper cup in his hand. The beard said something. Loud and angry.

"Excuse me?"

The man answered in English. Something about turf.

He could feel the gun in his pocket. One bullet. Instead he took out the large, sharp chunk of glass he kept in his other pocket. The beggar glowered at him but slunk off.

He dismissed the idea that Karlsen might not come. He had to come. And in the meantime he would be the Danube. Patient and unstoppable.

* * *

"Come in," ordered the happy, buxom woman in the Salvation Army flat on Jacob Aalls Gate. She pronounced the *n* with the tip of her tongue against her teeth, as is often the case when adults learn Norwegian later in life.

"Hope we're not disturbing you," Harry said as he and Beate Lønn entered the foyer. The floor was covered with shoes, big and small.

The woman shook her head while they started to take off their footwear.

"Cold," she said. "Hungry?"

"I've just had breakfast, thank you," Beate said. Harry shook his head with a friendly smile.

She led them into the sitting room. Around the table sat what Harry assumed was the Miholjec family: two men, a boy about Oleg's age, a small girl and a teenage girl Harry guessed would have to be Sofia. She hid her eyes behind a curtain of black hair and held a baby on her lap.

"*Zdravo*," the older man said. He was lean with thick, graying hair and black eyes that Harry recognized as the angry, frightened eyes of an outcast.

"This is my husband," the woman said. "He understands Norwegian, but doesn't speak much. This is Uncle Josip. He's visiting us for Christmas. My children."

"All four of them?" Beate asked.

"Yes." She laughed. "The last was a gift from God."

"A real sweetie," Beate said, making a face at the baby, who gurgled back with delight. And, as Harry had already suspected, she couldn't resist the temptation to tweak the chubby red cheeks. He gave Beate and Halvorsen one, maximum two, years before they produced one like it.

The man said something and the wife replied. Then she turned to Harry. "He wants me to say that you only like for Norwegians to work in Norway. He's tried to find work, but can't get any."

Harry met the man's eyes and sent him a nod, which went unanswered.

"Here," the wife said, pointing to two vacant chairs.

They sat down. Harry saw that Beate had taken out her notepad before he started speaking.

"We've come here to ask about—"

"Robert Karlsen," the wife said, looking at her husband, who was nodding assent.

"That's right. What can you tell us about him?"

"Not much. In fact, we'd only just met him."

"Just met him."

The wife's glance happened to catch that of Sofia, who was sitting with her nose buried in the baby's rumpled hair. "Jon asked Robert to help us when we moved from the little flat in the A building this summer. Jon is a good person. He saw to it that we got a bigger flat when we had him there, you know." She laughed at the baby. "But Robert stood around talking to Sofia most. And . . . well, she's fifteen."

Harry noticed the young girl's face change color. "Mm. We'd also like to talk to Sofia."

"Talk away," the mother said.

"Alone," Harry said.

The mother's and father's eyes met. The duel lasted two seconds, but Harry managed to read quite a bit into it. Perhaps once he had been the one who made the decisions, but in the new reality, in the new country, where she had turned out to be more adaptable, she was the decision-maker. She nodded to Harry.

"Sit in the kitchen. We won't disturb you."

"Thank you," Beate said.

"No need for thanks," the wife said gravely. "We want you to catch the man who did it. Do you know anything about him?"

"We believe he is a hired killer and lives in Zagreb," Harry said. "At least he phoned a hotel there from Oslo."

"Which one?"

Startled, Harry looked at the father, who had spoken in Norwegian.

"Hotel International," he said, and watched the father exchange glances with the uncle. "Do you know anything?"

The father shook his head.

"If so, I would be very grateful," Harry said. "The man is after Jon now. He peppered Jon's flat with bullets the day before yesterday."

Harry watched the father's expression change to incredulity. But he held his tongue.

The mother led the way into the kitchen, with Sofia dragging her feet behind her. As most teenagers would do, Harry assumed. As Oleg might well do in a few years' time.

Once the mother was gone, Harry took out his notepad and Beate positioned herself on a chair opposite Sofia.

"Hi, Sofia. My name's Beate. Was Robert your boyfriend?"

Sofia looked down and shook her head.

"Were you in love with him?"

Another shake of the head.

"Did he hurt you?"

For the first time since their arrival Sofia opened the curtain of black hair and looked straight into Beate's eyes. Harry guessed that behind the heavy makeup there was a pretty girl. Now he could see only the father, angry and frightened. And a bruise on her forehead that the makeup could not quite conceal.

"No," she said.

"Did your father tell you not to say anything, Sofia? That's what I can see."

"What can you see?"

"Someone has hurt you."

"You're lying."

"How did you get the mark on your forehead?"

"I walked into a door."

"Now you are lying."

Sofia snorted. "You sound clever and all that, but you know nothing. You're just an old policewoman who would prefer to be at home with children. I saw you in there." The anger was still there, but the voice had already started to thicken. Harry gave her one, two sentences at most.

Beate sighed. "You have to trust us, Sofia. And you have to help us. We're trying to stop a murderer."

"That's not my fault, is it?" Her voice cracked and Harry could see that she had managed only the one sentence. Then the tears came. A cloudburst of tears. Sofia hunched over and the curtain closed again.

Beate put a hand on her shoulder, but she shook it off.

"Go away!" she shouted.

"Did you know that Robert went to Zagreb this autumn?" Harry asked. Her head shot up and she looked at Harry with an expression of disbelief, coated in wet makeup.

"So he didn't tell you?" Harry went on. "Then he may not have told you that he was in love with a girl named Thea Nilsen, either?"

"No," she whispered tearfully. "And so what if he was?"

Harry tried to read her reaction to the information, but it was difficult with all the black cosmetics running.

"You were in Fretex asking about Robert. What did you want?"

"A cigarette!" Sofia snapped. "Go away!"

Harry and Beate looked at each other. Then they stood up.

"Think about it," Beate said. "Then call me at this number." She left her card on the table.

The mother was waiting for them in the hall.

"Sorry," Beate said. "I'm afraid she got a little upset. You might want to talk to her."

They stepped out into the December morning on Jacob Aalls Gate and headed for Suhms Gate, where Beate had found a lone parking spot.

"*Oprostite!*"

They turned. The voice came from the shadows of the arched entrance, where they saw the glow of two cigarettes. Then the glows dropped to the ground and two men came out to meet them. It was Sofia's father and Uncle Josip. They stopped in front of them.

"Hotel International, eh?" said the father. Harry nodded.

The father glanced at Beate from the corner of his eye.

"I'll go and get the car," Beate said quickly. Harry never ceased to be amazed by how a woman who had spent most of her short life alone with videos and forensic evidence could have developed a social intelligence that was so superior to his own.

"I worked first year by . . . you know . . . removal company. But back kaput. In Vukovar electrical engineer, see? Before the war. Here I have nothing."

Harry nodded. And waited. Uncle Josip said something.

"*Da, da*," the father mumbled, then turned to Harry. "When Yugoslav army take Vukovar in 1991, yes? There was boy who exploded twelve tanks with . . . land mines, yes? We called him *mali spasitelj*."

"*Mali spasitelj*," the uncle repeated with reverence.

"The little redeemer," the father said. "That was his . . . name they said on walkie-talkie."

"Code name?"

"Yes. After Vukovar capitulation Serbs tried to find him. But couldn't. Some said he was dead. And some didn't believe. They said he had never been . . . existed. Yes?"

"What does this have to do with Hotel International?"

"After the war people in Vukovar had no house. Everything rubble. So some came here. But most to Zagreb. President Tudjman—"

"*Tudjman*," the uncle repeated, rolling his eyes.

"—and his people gave them room in big old hotel where they could see them. Surveillance. Yes? They ate soup and had no job. Tudjman does not like people from Slavonia.

Too much Serb blood. Then Serbs who been in Vukovar dead. And there were rumors. That *mali spasitelj* was back."

"*Mali spasitelj*." Uncle Josip laughed.

"They said that Croatians could get help. In Hotel International."

"How?"

The father shrugged. "Don't know. Rumors."

"Mm. Does anyone else know about this . . . helper and Hotel International?"

"Others?"

"Anyone in the Salvation Army, for example?"

"Yes. David Eckhoff knows everything. And the others now. He said words . . . after meal at party in Østgård this summer."

"A speech?"

"Yes. He told about *mali spasitelj* and that some people always in war. War never finishes. For them, too."

"Did the commander really say that?" Beate said as she drove into the illuminated Ibsen Tunnel, slowed down and lined up behind the stopped traffic.

"According to Miholjec, he did," Harry pointed out. "And I suppose everyone was there. Robert, too."

"You think he could have given Robert the idea of using a hit man?" Beate drummed with impatience on the steering wheel.

"Well, at least we can establish that Robert has been to Zagreb. And since he knew Jon was seeing Thea, he also had a motive." Harry rubbed his chin. "Listen, can you see to it that Sofia is taken to a doctor for a thorough checkup? If I'm not much mistaken, there's more than that one bruise. I'll try to catch the next flight to Zagreb."

Beate sent him a swift, sharp glare. "If you travel abroad it ought to be to assist the national police. Or as a vacation. Our instructions clearly state—"

"The latter," Harry said. "A short Christmas break."

Beate sighed in desperation. "I hope you give Halvorsen a little Christmas break, too. We were planning to visit his parents in Steinkjer. Where are you planning to celebrate Christmas this year?"

At that moment Harry's cell phone went off, and as he searched his coat pocket he answered: "Last year I was with my dad and Sis. The year before with Rakel and Oleg. But this year I haven't had much time to think."

He was thinking about Rakel when he saw he must have pressed the phone's button in his pocket. And now he could hear her laughter in his ear.

"You can join me here," she said. "We have an open house on Christmas Eve and we always need volunteer helpers. At the Lighthouse." It took Harry two seconds to realize it wasn't Rakel.

"I was calling to say I'm sorry about yesterday," Martine said. "I didn't mean to run away like that. I was caught unawares. Did you get the answers you wanted?"

"Ah, it's you, is it?" Harry said in what he considered a neutral voice, but he still noticed Beate's lightning reaction. And superior social intelligence. "Can I call you back?"

"Of course."

"Thanks."

"Not at all." Her tone was serious but Harry could hear the suppressed laughter. "One tiny thing."

"OK?"

"What are you doing on Monday? The twenty-second."

"Don't know," Harry said.

"We've got a spare ticket for the Christmas concert at the concert hall."

"I see."

"Doesn't sound like you're swooning with excitement."

"Sorry. It's hectic here and I'm not much good at things you have to dress up for."

"And the artists are too bourgeois and boring."

"I didn't say that."

"No, *I* said it. And when I said we had a spare ticket I actually meant *I* had one."

"I see."

"It's a chance to see me in a dress. And I look good in it. All I'm missing is a tall, older guy. Think about it."

Harry laughed. "Thanks—I promise I will."

"Not at all."

Beate didn't say a word after he hung up, didn't comment on his grin that refused to go away, just mentioned that the snowplows were going to be busy, according to the weather forecasts. Now and then Harry wondered if Halvorsen appreciated the coup he had pulled off in getting together with Beate.

Jon Karlsen had not made an appearance yet. Stiff, he got up from the pavement by Sofienberg Park. The cold felt as though it came from the inside of the earth and had spread around his body. The blood in his legs began to circulate as he walked and he welcomed the pain. He hadn't counted the hours he had been sitting cross-legged with the paper cup in front of him while following the comings and goings in the building on Gøteborggata, but daylight was fading. He put his hand in his pocket.

His takings for the day would be enough for coffee, a bite to eat and, he hoped, a pack of cigarettes.

He hurried toward the intersection and the café where he had got the paper cup. He had seen a telephone on the wall, but dismissed the idea. In front of the café he paused, pulled back the blue hood and saw his reflection in the glass. No wonder people took him for a poor destitute soul. His beard was growing fast and there were sooty stripes over his face from the fire in the container.

In the reflection he saw the lights change to red and a car

stopped beside him. He glanced inside as he held the door to the café. And froze. The dragon. The Serbian tank. Jon Karlsen. In the passenger seat. Six feet away from him.

He entered the café, hurried to the window and watched the car. He thought he had seen the driver before, but couldn't remember where. At the hostel. Yes, he was one of the policemen who had been with Harry Hole. A woman was sitting in the back.

The lights changed. He charged out and saw the white smoke from the exhaust pipe as the car accelerated along the road by the park. Then he began to run. Farther ahead he saw the car turn in to Gøteborggata.

He fumbled in his pockets. Felt the piece of glass from the hut window with almost numb fingers. His legs wouldn't obey him—they were dead prostheses, and one false step and they would break like icicles, he feared.

The park, with the trees and the nursery and the head-stones, flickered in front of his eyes like a moving screen. His hand found the gun. He must have cut himself on the glass because the handle felt sticky.

Halvorsen parked outside 4 Gøteborggata, and he and Jon got out of the car to stretch their legs while Thea went in to pick up her insulin.

Halvorsen checked the deserted street from top to bottom. Jon seemed uneasy, too, as he walked around in the cold. Through the car window Halvorsen could see the center console with the holster containing his service revolver—he had taken it off because it was digging into his ribs while he was driving. If anything happened he would be able to grab it within two seconds. He switched on his cell and saw he had received a message on the journey. He tapped and a familiar voice repeated that he had a message. Then came the beep and an unfamiliar voice began to speak. Halvorsen listened with increasing amazement. He saw that Jon had become aware of the voice on the phone and had come closer. Halvorsen's amazement passed into incredulity.

As he hung up Jon looked at him with a question on his lips, but Halvorsen said nothing, just quickly punched in a number.

"What was that?" Jon asked.

"It was a confession," Halvorsen snapped.

"And what are you doing now?"

"I'm reporting to Harry."

Halvorsen looked up and saw Jon's distorted face: His eyes had grown big and black and seemed to be staring through him, past him.

"Is something the matter?" he asked.

Harry walked through customs and into Pleso's modest terminal building; he put his Visa card in a cash machine, which gave him a thousand kroner's worth of kune without a word of protest. He put half in a brown envelope before walking outside and climbing into a Mercedes with a blue taxi sign.

"Hotel International."

The taxi driver put the car in gear and drove off without a word. Rain fell from low cloud cover onto brown fields dotted with patches of gray snow as they cut northwest through the rolling landscape toward Zagreb.

After fifteen minutes he could see Zagreb taking shape: concrete apartment buildings and church towers outlined against the horizon. They passed a quiet, dark river that Harry figured had to be the Sava. Their entrance into the town was along a broad avenue that seemed out of all proportion to the low level of traffic; they passed the train station and a vast, open, deserted park with a large glass pavilion. Bare trees spread out their winter-black fingers.

"Hotel International," the taxi driver said, pulling up in

front of an impressive gray-brick colossus of the type communist countries used to build for their itinerant leaders.

Harry paid. One of the hotel doormen, dressed as an admiral, had already opened the car door and stood ready with an umbrella and a broad smile. "Welcome, sir. This way, sir."

Harry stepped onto the pavement at the same moment as two hotel guests came through the revolving doors and got into a Mercedes that had just driven up. A crystal chandelier sparkled behind the doors. Harry didn't move. "Refugees?"

"Sorry, sir?"

"Refugees," Harry repeated. "Vukovar."

Harry felt raindrops on his head as the umbrella and the broad smile were snatched away and the admiral's gloved index finger pointed to a door some way down from the main entrance.

The first thing that struck Harry as he entered a large, bare lobby with a vaulted ceiling was that it smelled like a hospital. And that the forty to fifty people sitting or standing by the two long tables placed in the middle, or standing in the soup line by the reception desk, reminded him of patients. It may have been something about their clothes; shapeless tracksuits, threadbare sweaters and tattered slippers suggested some indifference to appearance. Or it may have been the heads bowed over soup bowls and the sleep-deprived, dejected looks that did not take in his existence.

Harry's eyes swept across the room and stopped at the bar. It looked more like a hot-dog stand, and for the moment it was not serving customers; there was only a barman, who was doing three things at once: cleaning a glass, making loud comments to the men at the nearest table about the soccer match on the TV suspended from the ceiling and watching Harry's every move.

Harry had a feeling he was in the right place and went over to the counter. The barman ran a hand through his greasy, swept-back hair.

"*Da?*"

Harry tried to ignore the bottles on the shelf at the back of the hot-dog stand. But he had already spotted his old friend and foe Jim Beam. The barman followed Harry's gaze, and with raised eyebrows pointed to the four-sided bottle with the brown contents.

Harry shook his head. And breathed in. There was no reason to make this complicated.

"*Mali spasitelj.*" He said it low enough for the barman to hear above the racket from the TV. "I'm looking for the little redeemer."

The barman studied Harry before answering in English with a hard German accent. "I don't know any redeemers."

"I've been told by a friend from Vukovar that *mali spasitelj* can help me." Harry produced the brown envelope from his jacket pocket and placed it on the counter.

The barman looked down at the envelope without touching it. "You're a policeman," he said.

Harry shook his head.

"You're lying," the barman said. "I saw it the minute you walked in."

"What you saw was someone who was with the police for twelve years, but is not anymore. I quit two years ago." Harry met the barman's scrutiny. And wondered to himself what the man had been inside for. The size of his muscles and tattoos suggested he had been given a long sentence.

"No one calling themselves a redeemer lives here. And I know everyone." The barman was about to turn away when Harry leaned over the counter and grabbed his upper arm. The barman looked down at Harry's hand, and Harry could feel the man's biceps swelling. Harry let go. "My son was shot by a dealer standing outside his school selling shit. Because he told him he would report him to the head teacher if he continued."

The barman didn't answer.

"He was eleven when he died," Harry said.

"I have no idea why you're telling me this, mister."

"So that you understand why I'm going to sit here and wait until someone comes to help me."

The barman nodded slowly. The question came lightning-fast. "What was your boy's name?"

"Oleg," Harry said.

They stood facing each other. The barman screwed up one eye. Harry could feel his cell phone vibrating in his pocket, but ignored it.

The barman rested his hand on the envelope and pushed it back to Harry. "This is not necessary. What's your name and where are you staying?"

"I've come straight from the airport."

"Write your name on this napkin and go to the Balkan Hotel, by the train station. Over the bridge and straight ahead. Wait in your room. Someone will contact you."

Harry was about to say something, but the barman had turned back to the TV and resumed his commentary.

When he went outside, Harry saw he had a missed call from Halvorsen.

"Do vraga!" he groaned. Shit!

The snow on Gøteborggata looked like red sorbet.

He was confused. Everything had happened so fast. The last bullet, which he had fired at the fleeing Jon Karlsen, had hit the outside of the building with a soft thud. Jon Karlsen had fled through the door and was gone. He crouched down and heard the bloodstained glass tear the material of his jacket pocket. The policeman was lying facedown in the snow, which was drinking in the blood flowing from the slashes to his neck.

The gun, he thought, and grabbed the man's shoulder and turned him over. He needed a weapon to shoot with. A gust of wind blew the hair away from the unnaturally pale face. In haste, he searched through the coat pockets. The blood flowed and flowed, thick and red. He barely had time to sense the acidic taste of bile before his mouth was full. He turned, and the yellow contents of his stomach splashed over the blue ice. He wiped around his mouth. The trouser pockets. Found a wallet. Trouser waistband. For Christ's sake, cop, you've got to have a gun if you're going to protect someone!

A car swung around the corner and came toward them. He took the wallet, stood up, crossed the road and began to walk. The car stopped. Don't run. He began to run.

He slipped on the pavement by the corner shop and landed on his hip, but was up in a second without feeling any pain. Headed for the park, the same way he went last time. This was a nightmare, with an unending succession of meaningless events. Had he gone crazy or were these things really happening? Cold air and bile stung his throat. He had reached Markveien when he heard the first police sirens. And he knew. He was frightened.

22

The Miniatures

The police station was lit up like a Christmas tree in the afternoon gloom. Inside, in Interview Room 2, Jon Karlsen sat with his head in his hands. On the other side of the small round table in the cramped room sat Officer Toril Li. Between them two microphones and a copy of Jon's statement. Through the window Jon could see Thea waiting for her turn in the adjacent room.

"So he attacked you?" the policewoman said while reading the statement.

"The man with the blue jacket came running toward us with a gun."

"And then?"

"It happened so fast. I was so frightened I can only remember fragments. Maybe I have a concussion."

"I see," said Toril Li, with an expression that indicated the opposite. She glanced at the red light that told her the machine was still recording.

"But Halvorsen ran to the car?"

"Yes, his gun was there. I remember he put it in the center console before we set out from Østgård."

"And what did you do?"

"I was confused. At first I thought of hiding in the car,

but then I changed my mind and ran to the front door of the nearby building."

"And the gunman fired a shot at you?"

"I heard a bang, anyway."

"Go on."

"I made it inside, and when I looked out he had attacked Halvorsen."

"Who hadn't got into the car?"

"No. He had been complaining the door was stuck because of the cold."

"And the man attacked Halvorsen with a knife, not a gun?"

"It looked like that from where I was standing. He jumped on Halvorsen from behind and stabbed him several times."

"How many times?"

"Four or five. I don't know . . . I . . ."

"And then?"

"Then I ran down to the basement and called the police."

"But the gunman didn't go after you?"

"I don't know. The door was locked."

"But he could have smashed the glass. I mean, he had already stabbed a policeman."

"Yes, you're right. I don't know."

Toril Li looked down at the statement. "Vomit was found beside Halvorsen. We assume it belongs to the gunman, but can you confirm that?"

Jon shook his head. "I stayed on the basement stairs until you came. Perhaps I ought to have helped . . . but I . . ."

"Yes?"

"I was scared."

"You probably did the right thing." Again the expression said something different from the words.

"What do the doctors say? Will he . . . ?"

"He'll be in a coma until his condition improves. But

whether his life can be saved, they don't know yet. Let's move on."

"It's like a recurring nightmare," Jon whispered. "It just keeps happening. Again and again."

"Please don't make me repeat myself. You have to speak into the microphone," Toril Li intoned.

Harry stood by the hotel-room window surveying the rooftops, on which maimed and mangled TV antennae made strange signs and gestures to the yellow-brown sky. The sound of Swedish from the TV was muted by the thick, dark carpets and curtains. Max von Sydow was playing Knut Hamsun. The minibar door was open. The hotel's brochure lay on the coffee table. On the front page was a picture of the statue of Josip Jelačić in Jelačić Square, and on top of Jelačić were four miniature bottles: Johnnie Walker, Smirnoff, Jägermeister and Gordon's. As well as two bottles of Ožujsko beer. None of the bottles had been opened. Yet. Skarre had phoned an hour ago to tell him what had happened on Gøteborggata.

He wanted to be sober when he made this call. Beate answered on the fourth ring.

"He's alive," she said before Harry could ask. "They put him on a respirator and he's in a coma."

"What do the doctors say?"

"They don't know, Harry. He could have died on the spot because it looks as though Stankic tried to sever his main artery, but he managed to get his hand in between. He has a deep cut on the back of his hand and bleeding from smaller arteries on both sides of the neck. Then Stankic stabbed him several times in the chest above the heart. The doctors say the knife may have caught the tip."

Apart from an almost imperceptible tremor in the voice, she could have been talking about any victim at all. Harry knew it was the only way she could talk about this right now—as a part of the job. In the silence Max von Sydow roared with indignation. Harry was searching for words of comfort.

"I've been talking to Toril Li," he said instead. "She reported back on Karlsen's statement. Do you have anything to add?"

"We found the bullet in the front of the building, to the right of the door. The ballistics guys are checking it out now, but I'm pretty sure it will match the bullets in Egertorget, Jon's flat and outside the hostel. This is Stankic."

"What makes you so sure?"

"A couple driving by stopped when they saw Halvorsen lying on the pavement. They said they saw someone resembling a beggar crossing the street in front of them. The girl said he slipped on the pavement a bit farther down. We checked the place. My colleague Bjørn Holm found a foreign coin buried so deep in the snow that at first we thought it must have been there for a few days. He didn't know where it was from, either, since all we could see was 'Republika Hrvatska' and 'five kune.' So he checked."

"Thanks—I know the answer," Harry said. "So it is Stankic."

"We took samples of the vomit on the ice to make sure. The pathologists are checking the DNA against hairs we found on the pillow in his hostel room. We'll get the results tomorrow, I hope."

"Then we know we have DNA, anyway."

"Well, funnily enough, a pool of vomit is not the ideal place to get DNA. Surface cells from the mucous membranes are scattered when there is such volume. And under the open sky—"

"They are exposed to pollution from innumerable other DNA sources. I know all that, but at least we have something to go on now. What are you doing at the moment?"

Beate sighed. "I received a strange text message from the

Veterinary Institute and have to call and find out what they mean."

"The Veterinary Institute?"

"Yes, we found some half-digested meat in the vomit, so we sent it for DNA analysis. The idea was they would check it against the meat archive that the Agricultural High School in Ås uses to trace meat to its place of origin and the producer. If it has any special qualities maybe we can link it to a restaurant in Oslo. It's a shot in the dark, but if Stankic has found a place to hide in the last twenty-four hours he must be moving as little as possible. And if he has eaten somewhere close by it's probable he would go there again."

"Well, why not? What was the text message?"

" 'In which case it must be a Chinese restaurant.' Bit cryptic."

"Mm. Call back when you know any more. And . . ."

"Yes?"

Harry could hear that what he was going to say would sound ridiculous: Halvorsen was strong; they could do the most extraordinary things nowadays and everything would be fine.

"Nothing."

After Beate had hung up, Harry addressed himself to the table and the bottles. Eenie, meenie . . . Mo was the bottle of Johnnie Walker. Harry held the miniature with one hand and unscrewed—or to be more precise, twisted—the top with the other. He felt like Gulliver. Trapped in a foreign land with Pygmy bottles. He breathed in the familiar, sweet smell from the narrow opening. It was just a mouthful, but his body was already alarmed by the prospect of a toxic attack and was on full alert. Harry dreaded the inevitable first fit of puking, but knew this would not stop him. On the TV, Knut Hamsun said he was tired and could not write anymore.

Harry inhaled as though preparing for a long and deep dive. The telephone rang.

Harry hesitated. The telephone went quiet after one ring.

He was raising the bottle when the telephone rang again. And went quiet.

He realized they were calling from reception.

He put the bottle down on the bedside table and waited. When there was a third ring, he picked up the receiver.

"Mr. Hansen?"

"Yes."

"There is somebody in the lobby for you."

Harry stared at the gentleman in the red jacket on the label. "Say I'm on my way."

"Yes, sir."

Harry held the bottle with three fingers. Then he leaned back and emptied the contents down his throat. Four seconds later he was bent over the toilet bowl throwing up his airline lunch.

The receptionist pointed to the cluster of furniture by the piano, where a small, gray-haired woman with a shawl over her shoulders was sitting erect in a chair. She observed Harry with calm brown eyes as he walked toward her. He stopped in front of the table, on which there was a small battery-powered radio. Excited voices were commenting on a sports event, perhaps a soccer match. The sound merged with a potpourri of classic-film Muzak-type tunes that the pianist behind her was concocting as his fingers glided across the keys.

"*Doctor Zhivago*," she said in English with a nod in the direction of the pianist. "Nice, isn't it, Mr. Hansen?"

Her pronunciation and intonation were precise. She smirked as if she had said something amusing and signaled with a discreet but firm flick of the hand that he should sit down.

"Do you like music?" Harry asked.

"Doesn't everyone? I used to teach music." She leaned forward and turned up the volume of the radio.

"Are you afraid that we're being monitored?"

She sat back in her chair. "What do you want, Hansen?"

Harry repeated the story of his son and the man outside the school, while the bile burned in his throat and the pack of hounds in his stomach snapped and howled for more.

"How did you find me?" she asked.

"I was tipped off by a person from Vukovar."

"Where do you come from?"

Harry swallowed. His tongue felt dry and swollen. "Copenhagen." She studied him. Harry waited. He felt a drop of sweat roll down between his shoulder blades and another forming on his top lip. To hell with this. He needed his medicine. Now.

"I don't believe you," she said at length.

"OK," Harry said, getting up. "I have to go."

"Wait!" The small woman's voice was firm and she motioned for him to sit down again. "This does not mean that I don't have eyes in my head," she said.

Harry sat down.

"I can see hatred," she said. "And grief. And I can smell booze. I believe the bit about your dead son." She evinced a brief smile. "What is it you want done?"

Harry tried to collect himself. "How much does it cost? And how quickly can it be done?"

"That depends, but you won't find any professional operatives more reasonable than us. We start at five thousand euros plus expenses."

"OK. Next week?"

"That . . . may be rather short notice."

The woman had hesitated for only a fraction of a second, but it had been enough. Enough for him to know. And now he could see that she knew he knew. The voices on the radio were screaming with excitement and the crowd in the background was cheering. Someone had scored.

"You're not sure your operative will return in time?" Harry said.

She looked at him long and hard. "You're still a policeman, aren't you."

Harry nodded. "I'm an inspector in Oslo." The skin around her eyes recoiled.

"But I'm no danger to you," Harry said. "Croatia is not under my jurisdiction, and no one knows I'm here. Neither the Croatian police nor my own bosses."

"So what do you want?"

"To strike a deal."

"About what?" She leaned across the table and turned down the volume on the radio.

"Your operative in exchange for my target."

"What do you mean?"

"A swap. Your man for Jon Karlsen. If he gives up his hunt for Karlsen, we'll let him go."

She raised an eyebrow. "All of you protecting one man against an operative, Mr. Hansen? And you're frightened?"

"We're frightened of a bloodbath. Your operative has already taken the lives of two people and stabbed one of my colleagues."

"Has . . ." She paused. "That can't be right."

"There will be more dead bodies if you don't call him back. And one of them will be his."

She closed her eyes. Sat like that for some time. Then she breathed in. "If he's killed one of your colleagues you'll be out for revenge. How can I rely on you to keep your part of the deal?"

"My name's Harry Hole." He placed his passport on the table. "If it comes out that I've been here without permission from the Croatian authorities there will be a diplomatic incident. And I'll be without a job."

She produced a pair of glasses. "So you're putting yourself forward as a hostage? Do you think that sounds credible, Mr. . . ." She placed the glasses on her nose and read the passport: "Harry Hole."

"That's my stake in the deal."

She nodded. "I understand. And do you know what?" She took off her glasses. "I might have been willing to do a deal, but what good is it if I can't call him back?"

"What do you mean?"

"I don't know where he is."

Harry studied her. Saw the pain in her eyes. Heard the tremor in her voice.

"Well," Harry said, "you'll have to negotiate with what you have. Give me the name of the person who contracted the murder."

"No."

"If the policeman dies," Harry said, taking a photograph from his pocket and placing it on the table between them, "the chances are that your operative will be killed. It may well be made to look as if the policeman was forced to shoot in self-defense. That's the way it is. Unless I prevent it. Do you understand? Is this the person?"

"Threats don't work very well with me, Mr. Hole."

"I'm going back to Oslo early tomorrow morning. I'll write my telephone number on the back of the photo. Call me if you change your mind."

She took the photograph and put it in her bag.

Harry spoke in a hurried whisper. "It's your son, isn't it?"

She stiffened. "What makes you think that?"

"I have eyes in my head, too. I can also see pain."

She sat hunched over her bag. "And what about you, Hole?" She raised her eyes and looked into his face. "Is this policeman one you don't know? Since you can forgo revenge so easily?"

Harry's mouth was so dry that his breath burned inside. "Yes," he said. "I don't know him."

Harry thought he could hear a cock crowing as, through

the window, he watched her walk away on the opposite side of the road until she turned left and disappeared from view.

In his room he drained the rest of the miniatures, vomited again, drank beer, vomited, looked at himself in the mirror and took the elevator down to the bar.

23

The Dogs

He sat in the dark container trying to think. The policeman's wallet contained 2,800 Norwegian kroner, and if he remembered the exchange rate correctly that meant he had enough for food, a new jacket and a plane ticket to Copenhagen.

The problem now was ammunition.

The shot on Gøteborggata had been the seventh and the last. He had been down to Plata and inquired where he could buy nine-millimeter bullets, but had received blank looks in reply. If he kept on asking random faces, the odds of him bumping into an undercover cop were pretty high.

He smacked his empty Llama Mini-Max down on the floor.

A man smiled up at him from the ID card. Halvorsen. They were bound to have formed a protective cordon around Jon Karlsen now. There was just one possibility left: a Trojan horse. And he knew who the horse would have to be. Harry Hole. Number 5 Sofies Gate, according to the woman at directory assistance, who told him there was only one Harry Hole in Oslo. He checked his watch. And froze.

There was the sound of footsteps outside.

He jumped up, grabbed the chunk of glass with one hand and the gun with the other and stood beside the opening.

The door opened. He saw a silhouette against the lights of the town. Then the figure came in and sat down on the floor with crossed legs.

He held his breath. Nothing happened.

Then there was the hiss of a match, and the corner and the face of the intruder were lit up. He was holding a teaspoon in the same hand as the match. With the other hand and his teeth he tore open a plastic bag. He recognized the boy in the light-blue denim jacket.

As he breathed out with relief, the boy's swift, effective movements came to a sudden halt.

"Hello?" The boy peered into the dark while stashing away the bag in his pocket.

He cleared his throat and stepped into the outer circle of light from the match. "Remember me?"

The boy stared at him in terror.

"I talked to you outside the railway station. I gave you money. Your name's Kristoffer, isn't it?"

Kristoffer gaped. "Is that you? The foreigner who gave me five hundred kroner? Christ. Well, OK, I recognize your voice—ow!" Kristoffer dropped the match, which went out on the floor. His voice sounded closer in the pitch darkness: "Is it all right if I share this place with you tonight, pal?"

"You can have it all to yourself. I was on my way out."

Another match flickered into life. "Better if you stay here. Warmer with two. I mean it, man." He was holding a spoon and filling it with liquid from a small bottle.

"What's that?"

"Water and ascorbic acid." Kristoffer opened the bag and poured the powder into the spoon without contaminating a single grain, then deftly moved the match into the other hand.

"You're good at that, Kristoffer." He watched the junkie hold the flame under the teaspoon while flipping out another match and holding it ready.

"They call me 'Steadyhand' in Plata."

"I can see why. Listen, I've got to be going. Let's change jackets and you might survive the night."

Kristoffer looked first at his thin denim jacket and then at the other man's thick blue one. "Wow. Do you mean that?"

"Yes, of course."

"Shit, that's kind of you. Hang on until I've fixed this shot. Could you hold the match?"

"Wouldn't it be easier if I held the syringe?"

Kristoffer scowled at him. "Hello, I may be green but I'm not falling for the oldest junkie trick in the world. Come on, hold the match."

He took the match.

The powder dissolved in the water and became a clear brown liquid, and Kristoffer put a cotton ball in the spoon.

"To get rid of the crap," he answered before the other asked, then sucked the liquid up into the syringe through the cotton ball and placed the tip against his arm. "Can you see how wonderful my skin is? Hardly a mark—can you see that? Wonderful, thick veins. Pure virgin territory, they say. But in a couple of years it will be yellow with inflamed scabs, like theirs. And no more Steadyhand, either. I know that but I still keep doing it. Crazy or what?"

While Kristoffer was talking he shook the syringe to cool the liquid. He had tightened the rubber strap around his upper arm, inserted the needle into the vein that wound like a blue snake under his skin. The metal slid through the skin. Then he injected the heroin into his bloodstream. His eyelids half-closed and his mouth half-opened. Then his head fell back and his eyes found the hovering dog's corpse.

He watched Kristoffer for a while. Then he threw away the burned match and unzipped the blue jacket.

When Beate Lønn did get through at last, she could hardly hear Harry because of the disco version of "Jingle Bells" reverberating in the background. But she heard enough to know that he was not sober. Not because his speech was slurred; quite the contrary, he was very articulate. She told him about Halvorsen.

"Cardiac tamponade?" Harry shouted.

"Internal bleeding that fills the area around the heart so that it can't beat properly. They had to drain a lot of blood. The situation has stabilized now, but he's still in a coma. We just have to wait. I'll call you if there are any developments."

"Thanks. Anything else I ought to know?"

"Hagen sent Jon Karlsen and Thea Nilsen back to Øst-gård with two babysitters. And I spoke to Sofia Miholjec's mother. She promised to take Sofia to a doctor today."

"Mm. What about the Veterinary Institute report about the meat in the vomit?"

"They said they suggested Chinese restaurants because China is the only country in the world where they eat that kind of thing."

"Eat what kind of thing?"

"Dog."

"Dog? Hold on."

The music was gone and in its place she heard traffic noise. Then Harry's voice was there again. "But they don't serve dog meat in Norway, for Christ's sake."

"No, this is special. The Veterinary Institute managed to pinpoint the breed, so I'll call the Norwegian Kennel Club tomorrow. They have a database of all pedigreed dogs and their owners."

"I don't quite see how that will help us. There must be hundreds of thousands of dogs in Norway."

"Four hundred thousand. At least one for every house-hold. I've checked it. The point is that this one is rare. Have you ever heard of a black Metzner?"

"Please repeat that."

She repeated. And for a couple of seconds all she heard was the traffic noise in Zagreb until Harry shouted: "Of course! That makes sense. A man looking for shelter. Why didn't I think of that before?"

"Think of what?"

"I know where Stankic is hiding."

"What?"

"You must get hold of Hagen and have him authorize an armed operation by Special Forces."

"Where? What are you talking about?"

"The container terminal. Stankic is hiding in one of the containers."

"How do you know that?"

"Because there aren't many fucking places in Oslo where you can eat black Metzner. Make sure Special Forces and Falkeid have surrounded the terminal by the time I arrive on the first plane tomorrow. But no arrests before I get there. Is that clear?"

After Beate hung up, Harry stood in the street looking at the hotel bar. Where the plastic music was pounding away. And the half-finished glass of poison was awaiting him.

He had him now, the *mali spasitelj*. All that was needed was a clear head and a steady hand. Harry thought about Halvorsen. Of a heart drowning in blood. He could go straight up to his room, where there was no more alcohol, lock the door and throw the key out the window. Or he could go in and finish off his drink. Harry shivered and took a deep breath and switched off his cell. Then he went into the bar.

The staff at the Salvation Army's headquarters had long since switched off the lights and gone home, but the light in Martine's office was still on. She dialed Harry Hole's number while asking herself the same questions: Was it because he was older that it was so exciting? Or because there seemed to be so many repressed emotions? Or because he looked so helpless? The incident where Harry snubbed the woman outside his flat should have frightened her off, but for some reason or other the opposite was the case; she had become more intent than ever to . . . yes, what did she want, actually? Martine groaned when the voice announced that the person she was calling either had switched the phone off or was in an area with poor coverage. She called directory assistance, got the number of his landline on Sofies Gate and called. Her heart leapt when she heard his voice, but it was only an answering machine. She had the perfect excuse for popping by on her way home from the office and now he wasn't there! She left another message, saying she had to give him the ticket for the Christmas concert in advance because she would be helping at the concert hall from the morning onward.

She put down the phone and at that moment became aware that someone was standing in the doorway observing her.

"Rikard! Don't do that. You frightened me."

"Sorry. I was on my way home and just poked my head in to see if I was the last one here. Can I drive you home?"

"Thank you, but—"

"You've got your jacket on. Come on and then you don't have to bother with the alarm." Rikard laughed his staccato laugh. Martine had managed to set off the new alarm twice last week when she had been last to leave, and they'd had to pay the security company to come out.

"OK," she said. "Thank you."

"Not at all . . ." Rikard sniffled.

His heart was pounding. He could smell Harry Hole now. With infinite care he opened the door and groped for the light switch on the wall. In his other hand he held the gun, pointing it at the bed he could more or less make out in the dark. He breathed in and flicked the light switch; the bedroom was flooded in light. The room was bare—just a basic bed, which was tidy and unoccupied. Like the rest of the flat. He had already searched the other rooms. And now he was in the bedroom and could feel his pulse beginning to calm down. Harry Hole was not at home.

He put his gun in the pocket of the filthy denim jacket and felt it crush the urinal block he had taken from the bathroom in Oslo Central Station, which was next to the public telephone he had used to find out Hole's Sofies Gate address.

It had been easier to enter the building than he had thought. After ringing twice at the main door without receiving an answer, he had been about to give up. But then he pushed the door, and although it was closed it had not snapped shut. Must have been the cold. On the third floor Hole's name was scribbled on a strip of masking tape. He had put his cap against the glass pane above the lock and hit it with the barrel of his gun; it had yielded with a crisp crack.

The sitting room faced the backyard, so he took the risk of switching on a lamp. He looked around. Simple and spartan. Tidy.

But his Trojan horse, the man who could lead him to Jon Karlsen, was not there. For the time being. But he hoped he had a weapon or ammunition. He started with the places it would be natural to imagine a policeman might keep a gun, in drawers or cupboards or under the pillow. On finding nothing, he carried out a systematic room-to-room search, but without any success. Then he began the random search that is manifest proof that you have in fact given up and are desperate. Under a letter on the telephone table he found a police ID card with a photo of Harry Hole. He pocketed it. He moved books and records, which he noticed were arranged in alphabetical order on the shelves. There was a stack of papers on the coffee table. He flicked through them and stopped at a photograph with a motif he had seen in many variants: dead man in a uniform. Robert Karlsen.

He saw the name Stankic. One form had Harry's name at the top; his eyes ran down it and stopped at a check mark by a familiar expression: Smith & Wesson .38. The signatory had written his name with grandiose flourishes. A gun license? A request form?

He gave up. So Harry Hole had the gun on him.

He went into the cramped but clean bathroom and turned on the tap. The hot water made him tremble. The soot from his face turned the sink black. Then he turned on the cold tap and the coagulated blood on his hands dissolved and the sink went red. He dried himself and opened the cabinet above the sink. Found a roll of gauze, which he tied around his hand and the wound from the glass.

There was something missing.

He saw a short bristle beside the tap. As if after a shave. But there was no razor, no shaving foam. Or a toothbrush, toothpaste or a toiletry bag. Was Hole away, in the middle of a murder investigation? Or perhaps he lived with a girlfriend?

In the kitchen, he opened the fridge, which contained a milk carton with a sell-by date six days away, a jar of jam, white cheese, three containers of stew and a freezer compartment with sliced rye bread in a plastic wrapper. He took the milk, the bread, two of the containers and switched on the stove. There was a newspaper with today's date lying beside the toaster. Fresh milk, latest newspaper. He began to lean toward the travel theory.

He had taken a glass from the high wall cupboard and was about to pour some milk when a sound made him drop the carton on the floor.

The telephone.

He watched the milk spread across the red terra-cotta tiles while listening to the insistent ringing in the hall. Three mechanical clicks followed five beeps and a woman's voice filled the room. The words came fast and the tone seemed cheerful. She laughed, then put down the phone. There was something about that voice.

He placed the opened cans of stew in the hot frying pan, as they had done during the siege. Not because they didn't have plates, but so that everyone knew they had equal portions. Then he went into the hall. The small black answering machine was flashing red and showed a number 2. He pressed PLAY. The tape started.

"Rakel," a woman's voice said. She sounded a little older than the one who had just spoken. After a couple of sentences she handed the phone over to a boy, who excitedly chatted away. Then the last message came again. And he knew for certain he had not been imagining that he had heard the voice before. It was the girl on the white bus.

When the messages were finished, he stood looking at the two color photographs stuck to the wall under the mirror. In one, Hole, a dark-haired woman and a boy were standing on skis in the snow, squinting at the camera. The other was faded and old, and showed a small girl and boy, both in bathing suits. She seemed to have Down syndrome; he was Harry Hole.

He sat in the kitchen eating at his leisure and listening to the sounds in the stairwell. The glass pane was patched up with the transparent tape he found in the drawer of the telephone table. After eating he went to the bedroom. It was cold. He sat on the bed and ran a hand over the soft sheets. Smelled the pillow. Opened the closet. He found a pair of gray boxer shorts and a folded white T-shirt with a drawing of a kind of eight-armed Shiva with the word FRELST! underneath and JOKKE & VALENTINERNE above. The clothes smelled of soap. He undressed and put them on. Lay down on the bed. Closed his eyes. Thought of the photograph of Hole. Of Giorgi. Put the gun under the pillow. Even though he was absolutely exhausted, he could feel an erection on the way. His dick pressed against the tight-fitting but soft cotton. And he went to sleep in the secure knowledge that he would wake up if anyone opened the front door.

"Expect the unexpected."

That was the motto of Sivert Falkeid, the leader of Delta, the police Special Forces Unit. Falkeid stood on a ridge behind the container, holding a walkie-talkie, his ears full of the roar of taxis, cars and trucks heading home for Christmas on the highway. Beside him stood POB Gunnar Hagen with the collar of his green flak jacket turned up. Falkeid's boys were in the cold, ice-bound darkness beneath them. He checked his watch. Five to three.

It was nineteen minutes since one of the dog patrol's German shepherds had indicated that a person was inside a red container. Nevertheless, Falkeid did not like the situation—even though the task seemed easy enough.

So far everything had gone like clockwork. It had taken a mere forty-five minutes from the time he received Hagen's call for the five selected soldiers to appear primed and ready at the police station. Delta consisted of seventy people, mostly highly motivated, well-trained men with an average age of thirty-one. Details were drawn up according to need, and their spheres of activity included so-called difficult armed actions, the category into which this job fell. In addition to the five men from Delta there was one person from FSK, Forsvarets Spesialkommando, the military Special Forces. And this was where his misgivings began. The man was an ace marksman personally drafted in by Gunnar Hagen. He called himself Aron, but Falkeid knew that no one in FSK operated under his real name. In fact, the whole force had been secret since its inception in 1981, and it was only during the famous Operation Enduring Freedom in Afghanistan that the media had managed to get hold of any specific details at all about this crack unit, which, in Falkeid's opinion, was more reminiscent of a secret brotherhood.

"Because I trust Aron," had been Hagen's brief explanation to Falkeid. "Do you recall the rifle shot in Torp in '94?"

Falkeid remembered the hostage drama at Torp airfield very well. He had been there. No one was told afterward who had fired the shot that saved the day, but the bullet had gone through the armpit of a bulletproof vest hanging in front of the car window and into the bank robber's head, which had then exploded like a pumpkin in the backseat of a brand-new Volvo, which the car dealer took back, washed and resold. That wasn't what bothered him. Nor that Aron was carrying a rifle that Falkeid had not seen before. The letters MÄR on the gunstock did not mean a thing to him. At this moment Aron was lying somewhere outside the target area with laser sights and night-vision goggles, and had reported in that he had a clear view of the container. Otherwise Aron confined himself to grunts when Falkeid asked for updates on the radio. But that didn't bother him, either. What Falkeid did not like about the situation was that Aron was there at all. They had no need whatsoever of a marksman.

Falkeid hesitated for a moment. Then he raised the walkie-talkie to his mouth. "Flash the light if you're ready, Atle."

A light next to the container moved up and down.

"Everyone in position," Falkeid said. "We're ready to move in."

Hagen nodded. "Good. Before we go into action I would just like to have confirmation that you share my view, Falkeid—that it's best to make the arrest now and not to wait for Hole."

Falkeid shrugged. It would be light in six hours, Stankic would come out and they could arrest him with the dogs on open ground. They said Gunnar Hagen was being groomed for the job of chief super when the time came.

"Seems sensible enough, yes."

"Good. And that's what will be in my report. This was a

joint decision. In case anyone maintains that I put the arrest forward to claim the kudos."

"I don't think anyone will suspect you of that."

"Good."

Falkeid pressed the TALK button on the walkie-talkie. "Ready in two minutes."

Hagen's and Falkeid's white frosty breath merged into the same cloud before disappearing again.

"Falkeid . . ." It was the walkie-talkie. Atle. He whispered, "A man just came out through the door of the container."

"Stand by, everyone," Falkeid said. In a firm, calm voice. Expect the unexpected. "Is he going out?"

"No. He's standing still. He's . . . it looks like . . ."

A single shot resounded across the darkness of Oslo Fjord. Then it went still again.

"What the hell was that?" Hagen asked. The unexpected, thought Falkeid.

24

The Promise

It was early Saturday morning, and he was still asleep. In Harry's flat, in Harry's bed, in Harry's clothes. And he was having Harry's nightmares. About returning ghosts, always about returning ghosts.

There was a tiny sound, a mere scratching outside the front door. But it was more than enough. He woke up, put his hand under the pillow and was on his feet in an instant. The freezing floor burned his bare feet as he crept into the hall. Through the wavy glass he could see the silhouette of someone. He had switched off all the lights and knew that no one could see him from the outside. The person seemed to be bending down and fidgeting with something. Couldn't he get the key in the lock? Was Harry Hole drunk? Perhaps he hadn't been traveling after all. He had been out drinking all night.

He stood close to the door now and stretched out his hand for the cold metal door handle. Held his breath and felt the comforting friction of the gunstock against his other palm. The person outside also seemed to be holding his breath.

He hoped it didn't mean there would be unnecessary trouble; he hoped that Hole would be sensible enough to realize he had no choice: He had to take him to Jon Karlsen, or if that proved to be impossible, to bring Karlsen here to the flat.

With his gun raised so that it was immediately visible, he yanked open the door. The person outside gasped and retreated two paces.

There was something stuck to the outside door handle. A bunch of flowers wrapped in paper and cellophane. With a large envelope glued to the paper.

He recognized her at once, despite her horrified expression.

"Come in here," he growled.

Martine Eckhoff hesitated until he raised the gun again.

He waved her into the sitting room with the barrel and followed. Asked her politely to sit in the wing chair while he sat on the sofa.

She dragged her eyes away from the gun and looked at him.

"Sorry about the clothes," he said. "Where's Harry?"

"What do you want?" she asked in English.

He was surprised by her voice. It was calm, almost warm.

"To get hold of Harry Hole," he said. "Where is he?"

"I don't know. What do you want from him?"

"Let me ask the questions. If you don't tell me where he is I will have to shoot you. Do you understand?"

"I don't know. So you'll have to shoot me. If you think that will help you."

He searched for fear in her eyes. Without success. Perhaps it was her pupils; there was something wrong with them.

"What are you doing here?" he said.

"I brought Harry a concert ticket."

"And flowers?"

"Just a whim."

He seized the bag that she had set down on the table,

rummaged through it until he found a wallet and a bank card. Martine Eckhoff. Born in 1977. Address: Sorgenfrigata, Oslo.

"You're Stankic," she said. "You're the man who was on the white bus, aren't you?"

He looked at her again and she held his gaze. Then she nodded slowly.

"You're here because you want Harry to lead you to Jon Karlsen, aren't you? And now you don't know what to do, do you?"

"Shut up," he said. But he didn't achieve the tone he had intended. Because she was right: Everything was falling apart. They sat without speaking in the darkened room as dawn filtered through.

In the end she broke the silence.

"I can take you to Jon Karlsen."

"What?" he said in amazement.

"I know where he is."

"Where?"

"On a farm."

"How do you know?"

"Because the Salvation Army owns the farm and I have the list of those who use it. The police called me to check that they could have sole use of it for the next few days."

"I see. But why would you take me there?"

"Because Harry won't tell you where it is," she stated simply. "And then you'll shoot him."

He observed her. And he realized she meant what she was saying. He nodded slowly. "How many of them are there at the farm?"

"Jon, his girlfriend and a policeman."

One policeman. A plan began to form in his mind.

"How far away is it?"

"Forty-five minutes to an hour at peak times, but this is the weekend," she said. "My car's outside."

"Why are you helping me?"

"I told you. I just want it to be over."

"You realize I'll shoot you through the head if you're bluffing?"

She nodded.

"Let's get going now," he said.

At 7:14 Harry knew he was alive. He knew that because the pain could be felt in every nerve fiber. And because the hounds wanted more. He opened one eye and looked around him. Clothes were scattered all over the hotel room. But at least he was alone. His hand aimed at the glass on the bedside table and struck lucky. Empty. He ran a finger around the bottom and licked it. Sweet. All the alcohol had evaporated.

He dragged himself out of bed and took the glass into the bathroom. Avoided the mirror and filled the glass with water. Drank slowly. The hounds protested, but he held firm. Then another glass. The plane. He focused on his wrist. Where the hell was his watch? And what was the time? He had to get out, get home. One drink first . . . He found his trousers, put them on. Fingers felt numb and swollen. The bag. There. The toiletry bag. His shoes. Where was his cell phone, though? Gone. He dialed 9 for reception and heard the printer belching out a bill behind the receptionist, who answered Harry's question four times without his registering it.

Harry stammered something in English he struggled to understand himself.

"Sorry, sir," the receptionist replied. "The bar doesn't open until three o'clock. Do you want to check out now?"

Harry nodded and searched for the plane ticket in the jacket at the foot of the bed.

"Sir?"

"Yes," Harry said, putting down the phone. He leaned back in bed to continue his search through his trouser pockets, but found only a Norwegian twenty-krone coin. And then remembered what had happened to his watch. When the bar was closing and it was time to settle up, he had been short a few kune and had put a Norwegian twenty-krone coin on top of the notes and left. But before he had got as far as the door he'd heard an angry shout and felt a stinging pain at the back of his head; he had looked down as the coin bounced around the floor and spun between his feet with a ringing noise. So he had gone back to the bar and the barman, with a grunt, had accepted the wristwatch as final payment.

Harry knew the inside pockets of his jacket were torn; he fumbled and located the ticket inside the lining, coaxed it out and found the departure time. At that moment there was a knock at the door. One knock at first and then another, harder.

Harry could not remember much of what had happened after the bar closed, so if the knock had anything to do with that, there was little reason to believe there was anything pleasant in store for him. On the other hand, someone may have found his cell phone. He staggered to the door and opened it a fraction of an inch.

"Good morning," said the woman outside. "Or maybe not?"

Harry essayed a smile and leaned against the door frame. "What do you want?"

She looked even more like an English teacher now with her hair up.

"To strike a deal," she said.

"Oh? Why now and not yesterday?"

"Because I wanted to know what you would do after our meeting. Whether you would meet anyone from the Croatian police, for example."

"And you know that I didn't?"

"You were drinking in the bar until it closed. Then you tottered up to your room."

"Do you have spies, too?"

"Come on, Hole. You've got a plane to catch."

There was a car outside waiting for them. Behind the wheel sat the barman with the prison tattoos.

"To Saint Stephen's, Fred," the woman said. "Step on it. His flight leaves in an hour and a half."

"You know a lot about me," Harry said. "And I know nothing about you."

"You can call me Maria," she said.

The tower of the mighty St. Stephen's Cathedral vanished in the morning mist sweeping over Zagreb.

Maria led Harry in through the large, almost deserted, central nave. They passed confessionals and a selection of saints with appurtenant prayer benches. Recorded mantra-like choral singing issued from hidden speakers, low and heavy with reverberations, presumably to stimulate contemplation, but for Harry all it did was remind him of Muzak in some kind of Catholic supermarket. She took him into a side aisle and through a door to a small room with double prayer benches. The morning light, red and blue, streamed in through the stained-glass windows. Two candles burned on either side of Jesus Christ on the cross. In front, a waxen figure knelt with upturned face and outstretched arms in desperate supplication.

"Saint Thomas the Apostle, the patron saint of builders," she explained, bowing her head and making the sign of the cross. "Who wanted to die with Jesus."

Doubting Thomas, Harry thought, as she stooped over her bag, took out a small wax candle displaying a picture of a saint, lit it and placed it in front of the apostle.

"Kneel," she said.

"Why?"

"Just do as I say."

With reluctance, Harry knelt down on the tatty red velvet prayer bench and placed his elbows on the slanting wooden arm rail, black with sweat, grease and tears. It was an oddly comfortable position.

"Swear by the Son of God that you will keep your part of the bargain."

Harry hesitated. Then he bowed his head.

"I swear . . ." she began.

"I swear . . ."

"In the name of the Son, my Redeemer . . ."

"In the name of the Son, my Redeemer . . ."

"To do whatever is in my power to save the one they call *mali spasitelj*."

Harry repeated it.

She sat erect. "This is where I met the client's go-between," she said. "This is where he set up the job. However, let's go. This is not the place to negotiate human destinies."

Fred drove them to the large, open King Tomislav Square and waited in the car while Harry and Maria found a bench. Withering blades of brown grass tried to stand but were flattened by the cold, wet wind. A tram bell rang on the other side of the old Exhibition Pavilion.

"I didn't see him," she said. "But he sounded young."

"Sounded?"

"He phoned Hotel International in October the first time. If there are any calls about refugees they go through to Fred. He passed it on to me. The man told me he was calling on behalf of an anonymous person who wanted a job done in Oslo. I remember there was a lot of traffic in the background."

"Public telephone."

"I assume so. I told him I never do business over the phone and never with anonymous individuals and hung up. Two days later he called again and asked me to go to Saint Stephen's in three days' time. I was given a precise time for when I was to appear and in which confessional."

A crow landed on a branch in front of the bench, cocked its head and looked down on them gloomily.

"There were lots of tourists in the church that day. I entered the confessional at the appointed time. There was a sealed envelope on the chair. I opened it. Inside were detailed instructions about where and when Jon Karlsen was to be dispatched, an advance in dollars, way beyond our usual fee, and a suggested final figure. I was also informed that the go-between I had already spoken to on the phone would contact me to hear my answer and agree to details of the financial arrangement, if I accepted. The go-between would be our sole point of contact, but for security reasons he had not been initiated into the details of the task. Hence I was not allowed to divulge anything, under any circumstances. I took the envelope, walked out of the confessional and the church and went back to the hotel. Half an hour later the go-between called."

"The same person who had called you from Oslo?"

"He didn't introduce himself, but as an ex-teacher I tend to notice how people speak English. And this person had a very idiosyncratic accent."

"And what did you talk about?"

"I told him we were refusing the job for three reasons. First of all, because we make it our principle to know why a client wants a job done. Second, for security reasons we never let others determine the time or place. And, third, because we don't work with anonymous clients."

"What did he say?"

"He said he was responsible for making the payment, so I would have to put up with having only his identity. And he asked how much the price would have to increase for me to ignore the other objections. I answered that it was more than he could pay. So he told me how much he could pay. And I . . ."

Harry watched her as she searched for the right English words.

". . . was not prepared for a sum of that size."

"What did he say?"

"Two hundred thousand dollars. That's fifteen times our standard fee."

Harry nodded slowly. "So the motive wasn't that important anymore?"

"You don't have to understand this, Hole, but we have had a plan the whole time. When we had enough money we would stop and move back to Vukovar. Start a new life. I knew this offer was our ticket out. This would be the last job."

"So the principle of an ethical murder business had to give way?" Harry asked, rummaging for his cigarettes.

"Do you run ethical murder investigations, Hole?"

"Yes and no. You have to live."

She flashed a smile. "So there's not much difference between you and me, is there?"

"I doubt it."

"Aha. If I'm not much mistaken, you hope, as I do, that you deal only with those who deserve your attentions. Isn't that correct?"

"That goes without saying."

"But it's not quite like that, is it? You've discovered that guilt is not as black-and-white as you thought when you decided to become a policeman and redeem humankind from evil. As a rule there's little evil but a lot of human frailty. Many sad stories you can recognize in yourself. However, as you say, one has to live. So we start lying. To those around us and to ourselves."

Harry couldn't find his lighter. If he didn't get the cigarette lit soon, he would explode. He didn't want to think about Birger Holmen. Not now. There was a dry crunch as he bit through the filter: "What did you say his name was—the go-between's, that is?"

"You ask as though you already know," she said.

"Robert Karlsen," Harry said, rubbing his face hard with

his palms. "And he gave you the envelope with the instructions on October twelfth." She raised one of her elegantly plucked eyebrows.

"We found his plane ticket." Harry was frozen. The wind was blowing through him as though he were a mere apparition. "And on his return he unwittingly took the place of the person he had helped to sentence to death. You could kill yourself laughing, couldn't you."

She did not answer.

"What I don't understand," Harry said, "is why your son didn't abort the mission when he saw on the TV or read in the paper that he had in fact killed the person who was to hand over the cash."

"He is never told who the client is, nor what the victim's crime is," she said. "It's best like that."

"So he can't reveal anything if he's caught?"

"So he doesn't have to think. So he can just do the job and rely on me having made the correct judgment."

"Moral as well as financial?"

She shrugged. "In this case, of course, it would have been an advantage if he had known names. The problem is that my son hasn't contacted us since the killing. I don't know why."

"He doesn't dare," Harry said.

She closed her eyes, and Harry saw the muscles in her narrow face moving.

"You wanted me to withdraw the operative as my part of the deal," she said. "Now you know it isn't possible. However, I have told you the name of the person who gave us the contract. Will you still keep your part of the deal, Harry? Will you save my boy?"

Harry did not answer. The crow took off from the branch and drops of water rained down onto the gravel in front of them.

"Do you think your boy would have stopped if he had known the odds were stacked against him?" Harry asked.

She gave a wry smile. Then shook her head gloomily.

"Why not?"

"Because he is fearless and stubborn. He takes after his father." Harry studied the lean woman with the erect posture and concluded he wasn't so sure about the latter. "Say good-bye to Fred. I'll take a taxi to the airport."

She examined her hands. "Do you believe in God, Harry?"

"No."

"Yet you swore in His sight that you would save my son."

"Yes," Harry said, standing up.

She remained seated and looked up at him. "Are you the kind of man who keeps his promises?"

"Not always."

"You don't believe in God," she said. "Nor in your own word. What's left, then?"

He pulled his jacket around him more tightly.

"Tell me what you believe in, Harry."

"I believe in the next promise," he said, turning to squint down the broad avenue of weekend Sunday traffic. "People can keep a promise even though they broke the last one. I believe in new starts. I may not have said this . . ." He waved down a car cruising with a blue sign. "But that's why I'm in this business."

In the taxi Harry realized that he had no cash on him. He was told that there were ATMs that took Visa cards at Pleso Airport. Harry sat fingering the twenty-krone coin the whole way. Thoughts of the spinning coin on the floor of the bar and the first drink onboard wrestled for supremacy.

It was daylight outside when Jon awoke to the sound of a car turning in to Østgård. He lay contemplating the ceiling. It had been a long, cold night and he had not slept much.

"Who's that?" asked Thea, who had been fast asleep a moment ago. He could hear the anxiety in her voice.

"Probably relief for the policeman," Jon said. The motor died and two car doors were opened and closed. Two people, then. But no voices. Silent police. From the sitting room, where the policeman had set himself up, they heard a knock on the front door. Once. Twice.

"Isn't he going to open up?" Thea whispered.

"Shh," Jon said. "Maybe he's outside. Maybe he went to the outhouse."

There was a third knock. Loud.

"I'll go," Jon said.

"Wait!" she said.

"We have to let them in," Jon said, scrambling over her and putting on his clothes.

He opened the sitting-room door. In the ashtray on the coffee table there was a smoking cigarette and on the sofa a discarded blanket. Another knock. Jon peered out the window, but couldn't see the car. Strange. He stood in front of the door.

"Who is it?" he shouted, no longer so sure of himself.

"Police," said a voice from outside.

Jon might have been mistaken, but he thought he detected an unusual accent.

He jumped when there was another knock. He stretched out a trembling hand to the door handle. Then he took a deep breath and wrenched open the door.

It was like being hit by a wall of water as an icy wind swept in and the sharp, blinding light of the low morning sun made him squint at the two silhouettes on the steps.

"Are you the relief?" Jon asked.

"No," said a woman's voice he recognized. "It's over now."

"It's over?" Jon asked in surprise, shielding his eyes with his hand. "Ah, it's you, is it?"

"Yes, you can pack. We'll drive you home," she said.

"Why?"

She told him why.

"Jon!" Thea shouted from the bedroom.

"Just a moment," Jon said, leaving the door open while going in to see Thea.

"Who is it?" Thea asked.

"It's the one who questioned me," Jon said. "Toril Li. And a guy called Li, too, I think. They said Stankic was dead. He was shot last night." The policeman who had kept an eye on them last night returned from the outhouse, packed his things and left. And ten minutes later Jon swung his bag up onto his shoulder, shut the door and turned the key in the lock. He trod in his own footprints in the deep snow over to the wall of the house, counted five boards and hung the key on the hook inside. Then he ran after the others to the red Golf that stood idling and snorting white exhaust fumes. He forced his way in next to Thea on the backseat. After they set off, he put his arm around her and squeezed, then leaned forward between the seats.

"What did happen down at the container terminal last night?"

Toril Li, the driver, glanced across at her colleague Ola Li, beside her.

"They say Stankic went for his weapon," Ola Li said. "That is, the marksman from the Special Forces thought he saw that."

"Didn't Stankic go for his weapon?"

"Depends what you mean by weapon," Ola said, glancing at Toril Li, who was having trouble keeping a straight face. "When they turned him over, his fly was open and his dick was hanging out. Seems like he was standing in the doorway taking a leak."

Toril Li, suddenly gruff, cleared her throat.

"This is off the record," Ola Li hastened to add. "But you understand that, don't you?"

"Do you mean you shot him, just like that?" Thea exclaimed in disbelief.

"*We* didn't," Toril Li said. "The FSK marksman did."

"They think Stankic must have heard something and turned his head," Ola said. "Because the bullet went in behind his ear and came out where the nose had been. Snip-snap-snout. Snout—ha-ha."

Thea looked at Jon.

"That must have been some ammo," Ola reflected. "Well, you'll soon see for yourself, Karlsen. Miracle if you could identify the guy."

"That wouldn't have been easy anyway," Jon said.

"Yes, we heard about that," Ola said with a shake of the head. "Rubbery face and all that. Bullshit, if you ask me. But that's off the record, OK?"

They drove in silence for a while.

"How are you so sure it's him?" Thea asked. "If his face is smashed to pieces, I mean."

"They recognized the jacket," Ola said.

"Is that all?"

Ola and Toril exchanged looks.

"No," Toril said. "There was dried blood on the inside of the jacket and on the piece of glass they found in the pocket. They're checking that for Halvorsen's blood now."

"It's over, Thea," Jon said, pulling her closer. She rested her head on his shoulder, and he inhaled the fragrance of her hair. Soon he would be asleep. For a long time. Through the front seats he saw Toril Li's hand on the top of the steering wheel. She moved over to the right of the narrow country road when they met a small white electric car. Jon recognized it as the same model as the one the Salvation Army had been given by the royal family.

25

Forgiveness

The charts and numbers on the screen and the regular sonar beep of the EKG bestowed an illusion of control.

Halvorsen was wearing a mask that covered mouth and nose and what looked like a helmet on his head, which, the doctor had explained, registered changes in cerebral activity. His eyelids were dark with a network of fine blood vessels. It struck Harry that he had never seen this before. He had never seen Halvorsen with closed eyes. They were always open. The door creaked behind him. It was Beate.

"At last," she said.

"I came straight from the airport," Harry whispered. "He looks like a sleeping jet pilot."

It was only when he saw Beate's strained smile that he understood how ominous the metaphor was. If his brain had not been so numb he might have chosen a different one. Or just kept his mouth shut. The reason he had been able to put up some kind of façade was that the plane between Zagreb and Oslo is in international airspace for a mere one and a half hours and the stewardess with the alcohol had seemed to serve everyone else in the plane before she noticed the light illuminated above Harry's seat.

They went outside and found a sitting area at the end of the corridor.

"Anything new?" Harry asked,

Beate ran a hand across her face. "The doctor who examined Sofia Miholjec called me late last night. He was unable to find anything apart from the bruise on her forehead, which could well have been due to a door, he thought, as Sofia had explained. He said his professional oath was a grave matter for him, but his wife had persuaded him to talk, since this concerned the investigation of such a serious case. He took a blood sample from Sofia, but it showed nothing abnormal until—he had had a gut instinct—he asked for the sample to be checked for the hormone HCG. The level leaves little doubt, he says."

Beate bit her lower lip.

"Interesting gut instinct," Harry said. "But I have no idea what the hormone HCG is."

"Sofia has had a recent pregnancy, Harry."

Harry tried to whistle, but his mouth was too dry. "You'd better drop by and talk to her."

"Yes, because we became such great friends last time," Beate said drily.

"You don't need to be friends. You want to know if she was raped."

"Raped?"

"Gut instinct."

She sighed. "OK, but there's no hurry anymore, is there?"

"What do you mean?"

"After what happened last night."

"What happened last night?"

Beate gaped at him. "Don't you know?"

Harry shook his head.

"I left at least four messages on your phone."

"I lost my phone yesterday. Come on, tell me." He saw Beate swallow.

"Oh, shit," he said. "Don't say it's what I think it is."

"They shot Stankic last night. He died on the spot."

Harry closed his eyes and heard Beate's voice in the distance. "Stankic made a sudden movement and, according to the report, warnings were shouted."

Report, Harry thought. Already.

"I'm afraid the only weapon they found was a piece of glass in the jacket pocket. There was blood on it, which the pathologist has promised will have been checked by this morning. He must have hidden the gun until it was required again. It would have been material evidence if he had been caught with it. He didn't have any papers on him, either."

"Did you find anything else?" Harry's question came as if from a machine because his mind was elsewhere. To be precise, in St. Stephen's Cathedral. *I swear in the name of the Son, my Redeemer.*

"There was some drug paraphernalia left in one corner. Syringe, spoon and so on. More interesting was the dog hanging from the ceiling. A black Metzner, the harbor watchman told me. Chunks had been cut off it."

"Glad to hear that," Harry mumbled.

"What!"

"Nothing."

"That explains, as you suggested, the pieces of meat in the vomit on Gøteborggata."

"Anybody else take part in the action, apart from Delta?"

"Not according to the report."

"Who wrote the report?"

"The officer in charge of the raid, of course. Sivert Falkeid."

"Of course."

"It's all over now, anyway."

"No, it isn't!"

"You don't need to shout, Harry."

"It's not over. Where there's a prince, there's a king."

"What's up with you?" Beate's cheeks were flushed. "A contract killer is dead and you behave as if he were . . . a pal."

Halvorsen, Harry thought. She was about to say Halvorsen. He closed his eyes and saw the red flickering light inside his eyelids. Like candles, he thought. Like candles in a church. He had been a boy when his mother was buried. In Åndalsnes, with a view of the mountains—that was what she had asked for on her sickbed. And they had all stood there: his father, Sis and himself listening to the priest talking about a person he had never known. Because his father had not been able to do it. And perhaps Harry had known even then that without her they were no longer a family. Grandfather, from whom Harry had inherited his height, had leaned down with a strong smell of alcohol and said that was how it should be. Parents should die first. Harry gulped.

"I found Stankic's boss," he said. "And she confirmed that the murder had been set up by Robert Karlsen."

Beate gaped at him.

"But it doesn't stop there," Harry said. "Robert was only a go-between. There is someone hiding behind him."

"Who?"

"Don't know. All I know is that someone can afford to pay two hundred thousand dollars for a murder."

"And Stankic's boss told you all this just like that?"

Harry shook his head. "We made a deal."

"What kind of deal?"

"You don't want to know."

Beate blinked twice in quick succession. Then she nodded. Harry watched an elderly woman stumping along on crutches and wondered whether Stankic's mother and Fred followed Norwegian newspapers on the Net. Whether they already knew Stankic was dead.

"Halvorsen's parents are eating in the cafeteria. I'm going down to them now. Will you join me? Harry?"

"What? Sorry. I ate on the plane."

"They would appreciate it. They say he talked about you with affection. Like a big brother."

Harry shook his head. "Later, maybe."

When she had gone Harry went back to Halvorsen's room. He sat perched on the edge of the chair beside the bed and looked down at the pale face on the pillow. In his bag he had an unopened bottle of Jim Beam from duty-free.

"Us against the rest of the world," he whispered.

Harry snapped his fingers above Halvorsen's forehead. His middle finger hit Halvorsen hard between the eyes, but his eyelids didn't stir.

"Yashin," Harry whispered, hearing his voice thicken. His jacket banged against the bed. Harry felt inside. There was something in the lining. The missing cell phone.

He was gone by the time Beate and the parents returned.

Jon was lying on the sofa with his head in Thea's lap. She was watching an old film on TV and, as he stared up at the ceiling, Jon could hear Bette Davis's distinctive voice cut through his thoughts: He knew this ceiling better than his own. And if he stared hard enough he would, in the end, see something familiar, something different from the smashed face they had shown him in the cold basement at Rikshospitalet. He had shaken his head when they asked whether this was the man he had seen in the doorway of his flat and who later attacked the policeman with a knife.

"But that doesn't mean it isn't him," Jon had answered, and they had nodded, taken notes and led him out.

"Are you sure the police won't let you sleep in your own flat?" Thea asked. "There'll be so much gossip if you stay here tonight."

"It's a crime scene," Jon said. "It's sealed until they've finished the investigation."

"Sealed," she said. "It sounds like a letter."

Bette Davis ran toward the younger woman, and the violins upped the volume and the drama.

"What are you thinking about?" Thea asked.

Jon didn't answer. He didn't answer that he was thinking

about the moment he had lied to her when he said it was all over. It wouldn't be over until he had done what he had to do. And what he had to do was take the bull by the horns, block the enemy, be a courageous little soldier. Because now he knew. He had been standing so close to Halvorsen when he played back the message from Mads Gilstrup that he had heard the confession.

The doorbell rang. She stood up as though it were a welcome interruption. It was Rikard.

"Am I disturbing you?" he asked.

"No," Jon said. "I was on my way out."

Jon put on his outdoor clothing in the threefold silence. After closing the door behind him he stood for a few seconds listening to the voices inside. They were whispering. Why were they whispering? Rikard sounded angry.

He caught the tram to town and took the Holmenkollen line from there. Normally, with snow on the fields on the weekend, the train would have been full of cross-country skiers, but it must have been too cold for most today. He got off at the last station and observed Oslo nestling a long way below.

Mads and Ragnhild's home was situated on a hill. Jon had never been there before. The gate was quite narrow and so was the drive, curving around a clump of trees, which hid most of the house from the road. The house itself was low and built in such a way that you didn't notice how big it was until you were inside and walking around. At least that was what Ragnhild had said.

Jon rang and after a few seconds he heard a voice from a speaker he could not see. "Well, what do you know? Jon Karlsen."

Jon looked at the camera over the door.

"I'm in the living room." Mads Gilstrup's voice sounded slurred and he was chuckling. "I assume you know the way."

The door opened automatically and Jon Karlsen stepped into a foyer the size of his flat.

"Hello?"

He received a short, harsh echo by way of an answer.

He began to walk down a hallway that he assumed would end in a living room. Unframed canvases covered in vivid oil colors hung on the walls. And there was a particular smell that got stronger the farther he advanced. He passed a kitchen with a cooking island and a dining table surrounded by a dozen chairs. The sink was full of plates, glasses and empty bottles of booze. There was a sickly smell of stale food and beer. Jon continued. Clothes lay strewn along the hallway. He peered through the door to a bathroom. There was a stench of vomit.

He rounded a corner and was presented with the kind of panorama of Oslo and the fjord that he had seen when he and his father had gone for walks in Nordmarka.

A screen had been set up in the middle of the room and images from what was evidently an amateur video of a wedding rolled silently across the white canvas. The father led the bride up the aisle as she nodded and smiled to guests on both sides. The gentle hum of the projector fan was all that could be heard. Facing the screen he saw a black high-backed armchair and two empty—and one half-empty—bottles on the floor beside it.

Jon announced himself with a loud cough and went closer. The chair swiveled around slowly.

And Jon came to an abrupt halt.

A man he half-recognized as Mads Gilstrup was sitting in the chair. He was wearing a clean white shirt and black trousers, but he was unshaven and his face was bloated, his eyes blanched with a chalky gray film over them. In his lap was a double-barreled rifle with intricate carvings of animals on the burgundy gunstock. The way he sat, it was pointing at Jon.

"Do you hunt, Karlsen?" Gilstrup asked gently in a hoarse, alcohol-drenched voice.

Jon shook his head, unable to take his eyes off the rifle.

"In our family we hunt everything," Gilstrup said. "No game too small, none too big. I think you could say that is our family motto. My father has shot everything on four legs. Every winter he travels to a country where there are animals he has not yet shot. Last year it was Paraguay, where there was said to be a rare forest puma. I am no great shakes myself. Not according to Father. He says I don't have the necessary cold-bloodedness. He used to say that the only animal I was capable of catching was her." Gilstrup flicked his head toward the screen. "Although I suspect he thought she was the one who caught me."

Gilstrup placed the rifle on the coffee table beside him and opened his palm. "Take a seat. We're due to sign a contract with your boss David Eckhoff this week. Transferring the properties on Jacob Aalls Gate, first of all. Father will thank you for recommending the sale."

"Nothing to thank me for, I'm afraid," Jon said, taking a seat on the black sofa. The leather was soft and ice-cold. "A completely professional assessment."

"Oh, yes? Tell me."

Jon swallowed. "The benefits of having money tied up in property versus the ways it could benefit the other work we do."

"However, other sellers might have floated the properties on the open market?"

"We would have liked to do that, too. But you drove a hard bargain and made it pretty clear that if you were making an offer for the whole property package you would not permit an auction."

"Nevertheless, it was your recommendation that swung the balance."

"I considered it a good offer."

Mads Gilstrup smiled. "Bullshit. You could have got double."

Jon shrugged. "We might have got a bit more if we'd

split up the package, but this way we save ourselves the long, arduous process of selling the properties. And the board has stressed that it trusts you with regard to rent. After all, there are a number of residents we have to consider. We wouldn't like to know what more unscrupulous purchasers would have done with them."

"The clause freezing rents and allowing present tenants to stay runs for eighteen months."

"Trust is more important than clauses."

Gilstrup leaned forward in his chair. "That's fucking right, Karlsen. Do you know I knew about you and Ragnhild all the time? You see, she always had these rosy cheeks after she'd been screwed. And she had them whenever your name was mentioned in the office. Did you read the Bible to her while you were fucking her? Because you know what? I think she would have liked that . . ." Mads Gilstrup slumped back in his chair with a brief snort of laughter and ran a hand over the rifle on the table. "I've got two cartridges in this gun, Karlsen. Have you ever seen what cartridges like these can do? You don't even need to aim very well, just pull the trigger and—bang—you'd be blasted up against that wall. Fascinating, isn't it?"

"I've come here to tell you I don't want you as my enemy."

"Enemy?" Mads Gilstrup laughed. "You people will always be my enemies. Do you remember the summer you bought Østgård and I was invited by the commander himself, Eckhoff? You felt sorry for me. I was the poor boy you'd deprived of childhood memories. You're sensitive about things like that. My God, how I hated you all!" Gilstrup laughed. "I stood watching you playing and enjoying yourselves as though the place belonged to you. Especially your brother, Robert. He had a way with the girls. Tickled them and took them into the barn and . . ." Gilstrup shifted his foot and hit the bottle, which toppled over with a clunk. Brown alcohol gurgled out onto the parquet floor. "You didn't see me. None of you saw me. It was as though I didn't exist. You were absorbed in one another. So I thought, Well, OK, then I must be invisible. I'll show you what invisible people can do."

"Is that why you did it?"

"Me?" Mads laughed. "But I'm innocent, Jon Karlsen, aren't I? We, the privileged, always are. Surely you must know that. We always have a clear conscience because we can afford to buy it from others. From those who are employed to serve us, to do the dirty work. That's the law of nature."

Jon nodded. "Why did you call the policeman and confess?"

Gilstrup shrugged. "I thought of calling the other one, Harry Hole, in fact. But the asshole didn't have a business card, so I called the one whose number I did have. Halvorsen something or other. I don't remember because I was drunk."

"Have you told anyone else?" Jon asked.

Gilstrup shook his head, picked up the bottle off the floor and took a swig.

"My father."

"Father?" Jon said. "Ah, yes, of course."

"Of course?" Mads chortled. "Do you love your father, Jon Karlsen?"

"Yes. Very much."

"And do you not agree that love for a father is a curse?" Jon did not answer and Mads went on. "Father was here right after I phoned the policeman, and when I told him, do you know what he did? He fetched his ski pole and hit me. And he can still hit hard, the bastard. Hatred gives you strength, you know. He said that if I mentioned a word of this to anyone, if I dragged the family's name into the dirt, he would kill me. Those were his exact words. And do you know what?" Mads's eyes filled with tears and a sob caught his voice. "I still love him. And I think that's what makes him hate me with such passion. The fact that I, his only son, am so weak that I can't even return his hatred."

The room echoed as he banged the bottle down hard on the floor. Jon folded his hands. "Listen to me. The policeman who heard your confession is in a coma. If you promise me you will never come after me or mine, I promise I will never reveal what I know about you."

Mads Gilstrup did not appear to be listening to Jon. Instead his gaze had turned to the screen, where the happy couple were standing with their backs to them. "Look—now she's saying yes. I play that exact part again and again because I can't understand it. She swore, didn't she? She . . ." He shook his head. "I thought it might make her love me again. If I managed to carry out this . . . crime, then she would see me as I am. A criminal must be brave. Strong. A man, isn't that right? Not . . ." He snorted through his nose and spat out the words: "The son of one."

Jon rose to his feet. "I have to go."

Gilstrup nodded. "I have something that belongs to you. Let's call it"—he bit his top lip as he reflected—"a farewell present from Ragnhild." On the Holmenkollen train Jon sat staring at the black bag he had been given by Mads Gilstrup.

It was so raw that those who had ventured out for a ramble were walking with hunched shoulders and bowed heads, swathed in hats and scarves. Standing on Jacob Aalls Gate and pressing the Miholjec family doorbell, however, Beate Lønn did not feel the cold. She had not felt a thing since the latest message they had received from the hospital.

"It's not his heart that's the biggest problem now," the doctor had said. "The other organs have problems, too. Above all, his kidneys."

Fru Miholjec was waiting in the doorway above the stairs and showed Beate into the kitchen, where Sofia sat, fidgeting with her hair. Then she filled the kettle and put out three cups.

"It might be best if I talk to Sofia on my own," Beate said.

"She wants me to be present," Fru Miholjec said. "Coffee?"

"No, thanks. I have to get back to Rikshospitalet. This doesn't have to take long."

"Fine," Fru Miholjec said, emptying the kettle.

Beate sat opposite Sofia. Tried to catch her eyes, which were studying split ends.

"Are you sure we shouldn't do this on our own, Sofia?"

"Why should we?" she said in the contrary tone that irritated teenagers use with amazing efficacy to achieve their purpose: to irritate.

"This is a very personal thing, Sofia."

"She's my mother!"

"Fine," said Beate. "Did you have an abortion?"

Sofia recoiled. She grimaced, a mixture of anger and pain. "What are you talking about?" she snapped, without quite hiding the surprise in her voice.

"Who was the father?" Beate asked.

Sofia continued to smooth out nonexistent knots. Fru Miholjec's jaw had dropped.

"Did you have sex with him of your own free will?" Beate went on. "Or did he rape you?"

"How dare you say that to my daughter?" the mother exclaimed. "She's just a child, and you dare to talk to her as if she were a . . . a whore."

"Your daughter was pregnant, Fru Miholjec. I need to know if this has any relevance for the murder case we're working on."

The mother seemed to have control of her jaw again, and her mouth closed. Beate leaned toward Sofia.

"Was it Robert Karlsen, Sofia? Was it?"

She could see the girl's lower lip quivering.

The mother got up from her chair. "What is this she's saying, Sofia? Tell me it isn't true."

Sofia rested her face on the table and covered her head with her arms.

"Sofia!" the mother shouted.

"Yes," Sofia whispered, stifling a sob. "It was him. It was Robert Karlsen. I didn't think . . . I had no idea that . . . he was like that."

Beate stood up. Sofia was sobbing and the mother looked as though someone had struck her. All Beate felt was numbness. "The man who killed Robert was caught last night," she said. "Special Forces shot him at the container terminal. He's dead."

She watched for reactions, but saw none.

"I'll be going now."

No one heard her and she walked to the door unaccompanied.

He was standing by the window, staring across the billowing white countryside. It resembled a sea of milk frozen in mid-movement. On the crests of some waves he glimpsed houses and red barns. The sun hung low over the ridge, drained.

"They're not coming back," he said. "They're gone. Or maybe they were never here? Maybe you were lying?"

"They've been here," Martine said, taking the casserole out of the oven. "It was warm when we arrived and you saw the prints in the snow yourself. Something must have happened. Sit down—the food's ready." He put the gun beside the plate and ate the stew. He noticed the containers were the same brand as the ones in Harry Hole's flat. There was an old blue transistor radio on the windowsill playing comprehensible pop music interrupted by incomprehensible Norwegian chat. Right now it was a tune he had once heard in a film, one his mother had played now and then on the piano in front of the window, which was "the only one in the house with a view of the Danube," as his father used to joke when he wanted to tease her. And if the teasing nettled her he always used to bring the squabble to an end by asking how such a beautiful, intelligent woman could marry a man like him.

"Is Harry your lover?" he asked.

Martine shook her head.

"Why were you taking him a concert ticket, then?"

She didn't answer.

He smiled. "I think you're in love with him."

She raised her fork and pointed it at him as though wanting to emphasize something, but then changed her mind.

"What about you? Do you have a girl back home?"

He shook his head while drinking water from a glass.

"Why not? Too busy working?"

He sprayed water all over the tablecloth. Must be the tension, he thought. That was why he burst into hysterical laughter. She laughed with him.

"Or perhaps you're gay?" she said, wiping away a tear. "Maybe you've got a boy back home?"

He laughed even louder. And continued to laugh long after she had stopped speaking.

She served both of them more stew.

"Since you like him so much you can have this," he said, throwing a photo onto the table. It was the one on the hall mirror with Harry, the dark-haired woman and the boy. She picked it up and studied it.

"He looks happy," she said.

"Maybe he was having a good time. At that moment."

"Yes."

A grayish darkness had seeped in through the window and settled over the room.

"Maybe he'll have good times again," she said softly.

"Do you think that's possible?"

"To have good times again? Of course."

He studied the radio behind her. "Why are you helping me?"

"I told you, didn't I? Harry wouldn't have helped you and—"

"I don't believe you. There must be something else."

She shrugged.

"Can you tell me what this says?" he said, unfolding the form he had found in the pile of papers on Harry's coffee table and passing it to her.

She read while he examined Harry's photograph on the ID card from his flat. The policeman was staring above the camera lens, and he guessed Harry was looking at the photographer instead of the camera. And he thought that said something about the man in the picture.

"It's a requisition form for something called a Smith and Wesson thirty-eight," Martine said. "He's been asked to show this signed form and collect the gun from Police HQ."

He nodded slowly. "And it has been signed?"

"Yes. By . . . let me see . . . Chief Inspector Gunnar Hagen."

"In other words Harry hasn't collected his gun. And that means he is not dangerous. Right now he is defenseless."

Martine blinked twice in quick succession.

"What is it you have in mind?"

The Magic Trick

The streetlights went on on Gøteborggata.

"OK," Harry said to Beate. "So this is where Halvorsen was parked?"

"Yes."

"They got out. And were attacked by Stankic. Who first shot at Jon fleeing into the flats. And then went for Halvorsen, who was moving to get his gun from the car."

"Yes. Halvorsen was found lying beside the car. We found blood on Halvorsen's coat pockets, trouser pockets and waistband. It isn't his, so we assume it's from Stankic, who must have been searching him. And he took his wallet and cell phone."

"Mm," Harry said, rubbing his chin. "Why didn't he just shoot Halvorsen? Why use a knife? He didn't need to be quiet; he'd already woken up the neighborhood when he shot at Jon."

"We were asking ourselves the same question."

"And why stab Halvorsen and then flee? The only reason for tackling Halvorsen must be to get him out of the way so that he can grab Jon afterward. But he doesn't even try."

"A car came, didn't it?"

"Yes, but we're talking here about a guy who has stabbed

a policeman in broad daylight. Why would he be frightened off by a car coming past? And why use a knife when he already had his gun out?"

"Yes, that's the point."

Harry closed his eyes. For a long time. Beate stamped her feet on the snow.

"Harry," she said. "I want to go. I . . ."

Harry slowly opened his eyes. "He'd run out of bullets."

"What?"

"That was Stankic's last bullet."

Beate heaved a weary sigh. "He was a pro, Harry. You don't exactly run out of ammunition, do you?"

"Yes, that's exactly why," Harry said, enthusiastically. "If you have a detailed plan of how you intend to kill a man and you need one or, maximum, two bullets, you don't take a huge ammo supply with you. You have to enter a foreign country, all baggage is X-rayed and you have to hide it somewhere, don't you?"

Beate didn't answer.

Harry went on. "Stankic fires his last bullet at Jon and misses. So he attacks Halvorsen with a sharp instrument. Why? Well, to get his service revolver off him and chase Jon. That's why there's blood on Halvorsen's waistband. You don't look for a wallet there—you look for a gun. But he doesn't find one because he doesn't know it's in the car. And now Jon has locked himself in the house and Stankic has only a knife. So he gives up and makes a run for it."

"Great theory," Beate said with a yawn. "We could have asked Stankic, but he's dead. So it doesn't matter."

Harry observed Beate. Her eyes were small and red from lack of sleep. She had been tactful enough not to mention that he stank of recent and not-so-recent booze. Or wise enough to know there was no point in confronting him. But he also understood that at this moment she had no confidence in him.

"What did the witness in the car say?" Harry asked. "That Stankic made off down the left-hand side of the road?"

"Yes, she watched him in the mirror. Then he fell on the corner. Where we found a Croatian coin."

He focused on the corner. That was where the beggar with the beard had been standing the last time he had been here. Maybe he had seen something? But now it was minus eight and no one was around.

"Let's go to Forensics," Harry said.

Without a word they drove up Toftes Gate to Ring 2. Past Ullevål Hospital. They were passing white gardens and English-style brick houses on Sognsveien when Harry broke the silence.

"Pull in."

"Now? Here?"

"Yes."

She checked her mirror and did as he said.

"Put the hazard lights on," Harry said. "And then concentrate on me. Do you remember the association game I taught you?"

"You mean the one about speaking before you think?"

"Or saying what you think before thinking that you shouldn't think that. Empty your mind."

Beate closed her eyes. Outside, a family passed them on skis.

"Ready? OK. Who sent Robert Karlsen to Zagreb?"

"Sofia's mother."

"Mm," Harry said. "Where did that come from?"

"No idea," Beate said, opening her eyes. "She has no motive, as far as we're aware. And she is definitely not the type. Maybe because she is a Croatian like Stankic. My subconscious doesn't have such complicated thoughts."

"All of that may be correct," Harry said. "Apart from the last part about your subconscious. OK. Ask me."

"Do I have to ask . . . aloud?"

"Yes."

"Why?"

"Just do it," he said, closing his eyes. "I'm ready."

"Who sent Robert Karlsen to Zagreb?"

"Nilsen."

"Nilsen? Who's Nilsen?"

Harry opened his eyes again.

He blinked into the lights of the oncoming traffic, a little dazed. "I suppose it must be Rikard."

"Funny game," Beate said.

"Drive," Harry said.

Darkness had fallen over Østgård. The radio on the windowsill jabbered away.

"Is there really no one who can recognize you?" Martine asked.

"There are some who can," he said. "But it takes time to learn my face. Not many have taken the time."

"So it's not about you. It's the others?"

"Maybe. But I don't want them to recognize me. That's . . . something I do."

"You flee."

"No, on the contrary—I infiltrate. I invade. I make myself invisible and sneak into places I want to be."

"But if no one sees you, what's the point?"

He looked at her in surprise. There was a jingle on the radio and then a woman's voice began to speak with the neutral gravity of a newscaster.

"What is she saying?" he asked.

"It's going to get even colder. Nursery schools closing. Old people warned to stay inside and not to save electricity."

"But you saw me," he said. "You recognized me."

"I'm a people-watcher," she said. "I see them. That's my one talent."

"Is that why you're helping me?" he asked. "Is that why you haven't tried to run away even once?"

She studied him. "No, that's not why," she said at length.

"Why?"

"Because I want Jon Karlsen to die. I want him to be even deader than you are."

He gave a start. Was she out of her mind?

"Me, dead?"

"That's what they have been claiming on the news for the past few hours," she said, nodding toward the radio.

She breathed in and put on the grave, imperious voice of the newscaster. "The man suspected of the Egertorget murder died last night, shot by police Special Forces during a raid on the container terminal. According to Sivert Falkeid, the Special Forces commander, the suspect refused to surrender and went for his gun. Oslo Crime Squad head Chief Inspector Gunnar Hagen has said the case will be put in the hands of SEFO, the internal-affairs division, as a matter of routine. Chief Inspector Hagen commented that this case is another example of the police having to deal with ever more brutal organized crime and that discussion of whether to arm the police should not only be about effective law enforcement but also the safety of our police officers."

He blinked twice. Three times. Then it dawned on him. Kristoffer. The blue jacket.

"I'm dead," he said. "That's why they left before we arrived. They think it's over." He placed his hand on Martine's. "You want Jon Karlsen to die."

She stared into space. Breathed in as if she were going to speak, then released the air with a groan as though the words she had found were not the correct ones, and tried again. At the third attempt she succeeded.

"Because Jon Karlsen knew. He's known for all these years. And that's why I hate him. And that's why I hate myself."

*   *   *

Harry eyed the naked corpse on the table. It almost didn't affect him anymore to see them like this. Almost.

Room temperature was around fifty-seven degrees and the smooth cement walls returned a short, harsh echo as the female pathologist answered Harry's question.

"No, we weren't thinking of doing an autopsy on him. The line's long enough as it is, and the cause is fairly obvious in this case, don't you think?" She motioned toward the face with the big black hole that had taken with it most of the nose and the top lip, leaving the mouth and the upper set of teeth open.

"Bit of a crater," Harry said. "Doesn't look like the work of an MP-Five. When will I have the report?"

"Ask your boss. He asked for it to go straight to him."

"Hagen?"

"Yup. So you'd better ask him for a copy if you're in a hurry."

Harry and Beate exchanged glances.

"Listen," said the pathologist, the corners of her mouth stretched in what Harry realized was meant to be a smile. "We're understaffed this weekend and I have a lot on my plate, so if you wouldn't mind?"

"Of course," Beate said.

The pathologist and Beate made for the door, but both stopped when they heard Harry's voice.

"Has anyone noticed this?"

They turned to Harry, who was bent over the body.

"He's got syringe marks. Have you checked his blood for drugs?"

The pathologist sighed. "He came in this morning, and all we have managed to do is put him in the freezer."

"When can you have it done?"

"Is it vital?" she asked, and seeing Harry's hesitation,

went on. "An honest answer would be nice, because if we make it a priority, that will mean all the other cases you're nagging us for will be even more delayed. It's hell right now, coming into Christmas."

"Well," Harry said, "maybe he had the odd fix." He shrugged. "But he's dead. And so I suppose it's not that vital. Did you take his watch?"

"Watch?"

"Yes, he was wearing a Seiko SQ-Fifty when he was withdrawing money from the ATM the other day."

"He didn't have a watch."

"Mm," Harry said, looking at his own bare wrist. "Must have lost it."

"I'll hop down to the intensive care unit," Beate said when they were outside.

"OK," Harry said. "I'll catch a taxi. Will you get the identity confirmed?"

"What do you mean?"

"So that we're one hundred percent certain that's Stankic lying in there."

"Of course—that's the usual procedure. The body has blood type A, which matches the blood we found on Halvorsen's pockets."

"It's the most common blood type in Norway, Beate."

"Yes, but they're checking the DNA profile as well. Are you not convinced?"

Harry shrugged. "It has to be done. When?"

"Tuesday at the earliest, all right?"

"Three days? Not all right."

"Harry . . ."

Harry held up his hands in defense. "Fine. I'll go. Get some sleep, OK?"

"To be frank, you look like you need it more than I do."

Harry rested a hand on her shoulder. Felt how thin she was under the jacket. "He's tough, Beate. And he wants to be here. OK?"

Beate bit her lower lip. Gave the impression she was going to say something, but flashed a quick smile and nodded.

In the taxi Harry took out his cell phone and called Halvorsen's cell. But, as expected, there was no answer.

Then he punched in the number of Hotel International. He got reception and asked to be put through to Fred in the bar. Fred? Which bar?

"The other bar," Harry said.

"It's the policeman," Harry said when he had the barman on the line. "The one who was in yesterday asking about *mali spasitelj*."

"*Da?*"

"I have to talk to her."

"She's had bad news," Fred said. "Good-bye."

Harry sat listening to the severed connection for a while. Then he put his cell in his inside pocket and gazed out the side window at the dead streets. Imagined her in the cathedral lighting another candle.

"Schrøder's," the taxi driver announced, pulling in.

Harry sat at his usual table, staring into his half-full beer glass. The so-called restaurant was in fact a plain, shabby café serving alcohol, but it had an aura of pride and dignity that may have been due to the clientele, or perhaps the staff, or perhaps the impressive and out-of-place paintings adorning the smoke-stained walls.

There weren't many people just before closing time. But in came a new customer, who glanced around the room while unbuttoning the coat he wore over his tweed jacket, and then hastened toward Harry's table.

"Good evening, my friend," said Ståle Aune. "This appears to be your regular corner."

"It's not a corner," Harry said without a hint of a slur. "It's an angle. Corners are on the outside. You walk around a corner, you don't sit in one."

"What about the expression 'a corner table'?"

"That's not a table in a corner, but a table with corners. As in 'a corner sofa.'"

Aune gave a smile of pleasure. This was his type of conversation. The waitress arrived and gave him a brief, suspicious glance when he ordered tea.

"So dunces are not sent to the corner, then, I assume?" he said, straightening his red-and-white-dotted bow tie.

Harry smiled. "Are you trying to tell me something, Mr. Psychologist?"

"Well, I assume you called me because you wanted me to tell you something."

"How much do you charge to tell people that right now they should be ashamed of themselves?"

"Be careful, Harry. Drinking makes you not only irritable but irritating. I have not come here to divest you of your self-respect, your balls or your beer. But your current problem is that all three are in that glass."

"You are eternally right," Harry said, raising his glass. "And that's why I have to hurry up and finish this drink."

Aune stood up. "If you want to talk about your drinking, we can do this as usual in my office. This consultation is over and you're paying for the tea."

"Wait," Harry said. "Look." He turned around and put the rest of his beer on the empty table behind him. "This is my magic trick. I control my boozing by ordering half a liter, which I take an hour to drink. A little sip every alternate minute. Like a sleeping pill. Then I go home and from the very next day I'm on the wagon. I wanted to talk to you about the attack on Halvorsen."

Aune hesitated. Then he sat down again. "Terrible thing. I heard the details."

"And what can you see?"

"Glimpse, Harry. Glimpse, and hardly that." Aune nodded amiably to the waitress, who brought his tea. "But, as you know, I glimpse better than the other good-for-nothings in my line of work. What I can see is that there are similarities between this attack and the murder of Ragnhild Gilstrup."

"Tell me."

"Deep, heartfelt anger being vented. Violence caused by sexual frustration. As you know, bouts of fury are typical of borderline personalities."

"Yes, except that this individual seems to be able to control the fury. If not, we would have had more clues at the crime scenes."

"Good point. It may be a fury-driven assailant—or a 'person who commits violence,' as the old maids in my profession would have us call them—who on a day-to-day basis may seem sedate, almost defensive. There was a recent article in the *American Journal of Psychology* about such people with what they call 'slumbering rage.' What I call Dr. Jekyll and Mr. Hyde. And when Mr. Hyde wakes up"—Aune brandished the forefinger of his left hand while taking a sip of tea—"it's Judgment Day and Armageddon at once. But once the fury has been released he cannot control it."

"Sounds like a handy personality trait for a professional contract killer."

"Not at all. What are you referring to?"

"Stankic loses points for style in the murder of Ragnhild Gilstrup and the attack on Halvorsen. There's something . . . unclinical about it. Quite different from the murders of Robert Karlsen and the others in the reports Europol sent us."

"An angry, unstable contract killer? Well, I suppose there are unstable airplane pilots and unstable managers of nuclear power stations, too. Not everyone is in a job he ought to be in, you know."

"I'll drink to that."

"In fact, I wasn't thinking about you just now. Do you know you have certain narcissistic qualities, Inspector?"

Harry smiled.

"Will you tell me why you're ashamed?" Aune asked. "Do you think it's your fault Halvorsen was stabbed?"

Harry cleared his throat. "Well, it was me who gave him the task of looking after Jon Karlsen. And it was me who should have taught him where you keep your gun when on babysitting duties."

Aune nodded. "So it's all your fault. As usual."

Harry looked to the side and across the room. The lights had begun to flash and the few customers left were obediently drinking up and putting on scarves and hats. Harry put a hundred-krone note on the table and kicked a bag out from under his chair. "Next time, Ståle. I haven't been home since Zagreb and now I need some shut-eye."

Harry followed Aune to the door, but was unable to stop himself from glancing back at the glass of beer on the table behind them.

As Harry was unlocking the door to his flat he noticed the smashed glass and swore aloud. It was the second time his flat had been broken into within a year. He noted that the intruder had taken the time to tape the glass so as not to arouse the curiosity of passing residents. Yet had not taken the time to depart with the stereo or the TV. Easy enough to understand, since neither was this year's model. Or the previous year's. And there were no other marketable items of value.

Someone had moved the pile of papers on the coffee table. Harry went into the bathroom and saw the mess in the medicine cabinet above the sink, so it was not difficult to work out that a drug addict had been on the loose.

He was puzzled by a plate on the countertop and the empty stew containers in the garbage bag under the sink. Had the unfortunate intruder been overwhelmed by a need for comfort food?

Once in bed Harry could feel the pain coming on and hoped he would be able to sleep while still somewhat under the effects of the alcohol. Through the crack between the curtains the moon laid a white stripe along the floor to his bed. He tossed and turned as he waited for the ghosts. He could hear the rustling; it was only a question of time. Even though he was aware it was alcoholic paranoia, he thought he could smell death and bloodshed on the sheets.

27

The Disciple

Someone had hung a Christmas wreath outside the meeting room in the red zone.

Behind the closed door the last morning meeting of the investigative team was drawing to an end.

Harry stood sweating in front of the assembled group in a tight-fitting, dark suit.

"Since the contract killer, Stankic, and the go-between, Robert Karlsen, are both dead, the investigative team, in its present form, will be dissolved as of this meeting," Harry said. "And that means most of us can look forward to a Christmas holiday this year. However, I will ask Hagen to make a few of you available for further detective work. Any questions before we wrap things up? Yes, Toril?"

"You say that the Stankic link in Zagreb confirmed our suspicion that Robert Karlsen contracted the murder of Jon. Who spoke to the link and how?"

"I'm afraid I can't go into any details on that," Harry said, ignoring Beate's eloquent eyes and feeling the sweat running down his back. Not because of the suit or the question, but because he was sober.

"OK," he continued. "The next job is to find out who Robert was working with. In the course of today I will contact the fortunate few who will be allowed to be involved.

Hagen is holding a press conference later today and will take care of whatever has to be said." Harry shooed with his hands. "Run along to your piles of paperwork, guys."

"Hey!" shouted Skarre over the scraping of chairs. "Shouldn't we celebrate?"

The noise died away and the group looked at Harry.

"Well," Harry said quietly, "I don't know quite what we should celebrate, Skarre. That three people are dead? That the man behind Robert Karlsen is still free? Or that we still have an officer in a coma?"

Harry watched them and did nothing to ease the painful silence that followed.

When the room was empty, Skarre went over to Harry, who was sorting through the notes he had written at six o'clock that morning.

"Sorry," Skarre said. "Rotten suggestion."

"That's all right," Harry said. "You meant well."

Skarre coughed. "Rare to see you in a suit."

"Robert Karlsen's funeral is at twelve," Harry said without looking up. "Thought I would see who turned up."

"Right." Skarre rocked back on his heels.

Harry stopped flicking through his papers. "Anything else, Skarre?"

"Well, yes. I was thinking that quite a few people in Crime Squad have got families and are looking forward to Christmas, whereas I'm single . . ."

"Mm?"

"Well, I'd like to volunteer."

"Volunteer?"

"I mean I'd like to keep working on the case. If you want me, that is," Skarre hastened to add.

Harry studied Magnus Skarre.

"I know you don't like me," Skarre said.

"It's not that," Harry said. "I've already decided who will stay. And it's those I consider the best, not the ones I like."

Skarre shrugged, and his Adam's apple bobbed up and down. "Fair enough. Merry Christmas, then." He moved toward the door.

"That's why," Harry said, putting the notes in the brief-case, "I want you to start checking Robert Karlsen's bank account. See what's gone in and out over the last six months and note any irregularities."

Skarre stopped and turned in amazement.

"Do the same for Albert and Mads Gilstrup. Have you got that, Skarre?"

Magnus Skarre nodded with enthusiasm.

"Check with Telenor if there have been any phone conversations between Robert and either Gilstrup during that period. Yes, and since it looks as though Stankic took Halvorsen's cell, check if there have been any conversations on that number. Talk to the prosecutor about access to bank accounts."

"No need," Skarre said. "According to new regulations, we have permanent access."

"Mm." Harry sent Skarre a serious look. "Thought it would be a good idea to have someone on the team who reads instructions. Yup."

Then he strode out the door.

Robert Karlsen didn't have the rank of an officer, but since he had died on duty it was decided that he would still be entitled to a grave in the area the Army reserved for offi-cers in Vestre Cemetery. After the burial, there was to be a memorial service with the corps in Majorstuen.

As Harry entered the chapel, Jon, sitting alone on the front bench with Thea, turned his head. Harry noted the absence of Robert and Jon's parents. He and Jon made eye contact and Jon gave a quick, somber nod, but there was gratitude in his expression.

The chapel was, as expected, full to the last bench.

Most people were wearing the Salvation Army uniform. Harry saw Rikard Nilsen and David Eckhoff. And beside them, Gunnar Hagen. There were also a few vultures from the press. At that moment Roger Gjendem slipped onto the bench next to him and asked whether he knew why the prime minister was not coming, as previously announced.

"Ask the prime minister's office," Harry answered, knowing that the office had that very morning received a discreet telephone call from the top echelons of the police to talk about Robert Karlsen's possible role in the murder case. The prime minister's office had subsequently remembered that the premier had other, more pressing engagements.

Commander David Eckhoff had also received a call from Police HQ, and it had created panic in the Salvation Army headquarters, particularly since one of the key figures in the preparations for the burial, his daughter, Martine, had called in early that morning to say she was sick and would not be coming to work.

The commander, however, had announced in a resolute voice that a man is innocent until the contrary has been proven beyond any shadow of doubt. Besides, he had added, it was too late to change the arrangement now. The show had to go on. And the prime minister had assured the commander his attendance at the Christmas concert was definite, whatever happened.

"Anything else?" Gjendem whispered. "Anything new on the murders?"

"I understand you've all been told," Harry said. "The press have to go through Gunnar Hagen or the spokesperson."

"They're not saying anything."

"Sounds like they know their jobs."

"Come on, Hole—I know something's going on. The officer that was stabbed on Gøteborggata—is there any connection between him and the gunman you shot down last night?"

Harry shook his head in a way that could mean both "No" and "No comment."

The organ music stopped at that moment, the mumbling went silent and the girl with the debut album stepped forward and sang a well-known psalm with an alluring amount of air and the suggestion of a groan and brought it to an end by taking the final syllable on a roller-coaster ride that Mariah Carey would have envied. For a second Harry experienced an overwhelming yearning for a drink, but at long last she closed her mouth and bowed her head in sorrow to an imaginary storm of camera flashes. Her manager smiled with pleasure. It was obvious he hadn't received a telephone call from Police HQ.

Eckhoff spoke to the congregation about courage and sacrifice.

Harry was unable to concentrate. He looked at the coffin and thought about Halvorsen. And he thought about Stankic's mother. And when he closed his eyes, he thought about Martine.

Afterward six Salvation Army officers carried out the coffin. Jon and Rikard went first.

Jon slipped on the ice as they turned on the gravel path.

Harry left the others still gathered around the grave. He walked through the deserted part of the cemetery toward Frogner Park, where he heard the creak of shoes on the snow behind him.

At first he thought it was a journalist but when he heard the fast, agitated breathing he reacted without thinking and spun around.

It was Rikard—who came to a sudden halt.

"Where is she?" he wheezed.

"Where is who?"

"Martine."

"I heard she was ill today."

"Ill, yes." Rikard's chest was heaving. "But home in bed, no. And she wasn't at home last night, either."

"How do you know?"

"Don't . . . !" Rikard's shout sounded like a scream of pain and his face went into contortions as though he were no longer in charge of his own expressions. But then he caught his breath, and with what seemed like a huge exertion pulled himself together. "Don't try that on me," he whispered. "I know. You've duped her. Defiled her. She's in your flat, isn't she? But you won't get . . ."

Rikard took a step toward Harry, who automatically took his hands out of his coat pockets.

"Listen," Harry said, "I have no idea where Martine is."

"You're lying!" Rikard clenched his fists and Harry realized he needed to find the correct words to calm him down in a hurry. He took a punt on these: "There are a couple of things you ought to reflect on right now, Rikard. I'm not very quick but I weigh over two hundred pounds and I have punched my fist through an oak front door. And paragraph one twenty-seven of the Penal Code gives a minimum punishment of six months for violence against a public servant. You're risking a hospital visit. *And* prison."

Rikard's eyes smoldered. "See you, Harry Hole," he said airily, turned and ran back between the graves to the chapel.

Imtiaz Rahim was in a bad mood. He had just had a fight with his brother about whether to put Christmas decorations on the wall behind the cash register. Imtiaz thought it was enough to sell pork, Advent calendars, and other Christian paraphernalia without desecrating Allah by bowing to this kind of heathen custom. What would their Pakistani customers say? His brother, however, thought that they had to think of the other customers. For example, those from the apartment building on the other side of Gøteborggata. It wouldn't hurt to give the grocer's shop a tiny touch of

Christianity during the holiday period. Although Imtiaz had won the heated discussion, it gave him no pleasure.

So it was with a heavy sigh that he heard the irascible ring of the bell over the door. A tall, broad-shouldered man in a dark suit entered and came over to the cash register.

"Harry Hole, police," the man said, and for one small moment of panic Imtiaz wondered whether there was a law in Norway stipulating that all shops had to display Christmas decorations.

"A few days ago there was a beggar sitting outside this shop," the policeman said. "A guy with red hair and a beard like this." He ran a finger over his top lip and down the side of the mouth.

"Yes," Imtiaz said. "I know him. He brings empty bottles here to get the deposit."

"Do you know his name?"

"The Tiger. Or the Cheetah."

"Pardon?"

Imtiaz laughed. He was back in a good mood. "Tiger, after *tigger*, your Norwegian word for beggar. And Cheetah because he pinches the empties from . . . we don't know where."

Harry nodded.

Imtiaz shrugged. "It's my nephew's joke . . ."

"Mm. Very good. So . . ."

"No, I don't know his name. But I do know where you can find him."

Espen Kaspersen was sitting with a pile of books in front of him, as usual, in the Deichmanske Public Library on Henrik Ibsens Gate when he felt a figure loom above him. He looked up.

"Hole, police," the man said and sat down at the long table in the chair opposite. Espen saw the girl reading at the end of the table look over. New employees in reception did ask to check his bag when he left. And twice he had been asked to leave because he stank so much they couldn't concentrate on their work. This was the first time the police had talked to him, though. Well, except when he was begging in the street, that is.

"What are you reading?" the detective asked.

Kaspersen shrugged. He could see right away it would be a waste of time telling this policeman about his project.

"Søren Kierkegaard?" said the detective, peering at the spine. "Schopenhauer. Nietzsche. Philosophy. You're a thinker."

Espen Kaspersen sniffed. "I'm trying to find the right path. And that implies thinking about what it is to be human."

"Isn't that being a thinker?"

Kaspersen observed the man. Maybe he had misjudged him.

"I was talking to the grocer on Gøteborggata," the detective said. "He says you sit here every day. And when you're not sitting here, you're begging in the street."

"This is the life I've chosen, yes."

The detective took out a notepad, and, when asked, Espen Kaspersen gave his full name and his address at his great-aunt's on Hagegata.

"And profession?"

"Monk."

Kaspersen watched with satisfaction as the detective took notes without a murmur.

The detective nodded. "Well, Espen, you're no drug addict, so why do you beg?"

"Because it's my mission to be a mirror for mankind so that they can see which actions are great and which small."

"And which are great?"

Espen sighed in despair, as though weary of repeating the obvious. "Charity. Sharing and helping your neighbor. The Bible deals with nothing else. In fact, you have to search extremely hard to find anything about sex before marriage, abortion, homosexuality or a woman's right to speak in public. But, of course, it is easier for Pharisees to talk aloud about subordinate clauses than to describe and perform the great actions that the Bible leaves us in no doubt about: You have to give half of what you own to someone who has nothing. Thousands of people are dying every day without hearing the words of God because these Christians will not let go of their earthly goods. I'm giving them a chance to reflect."

The detective nodded.

Kaspersen was puzzled. "How did you know, by the way, that I am not a drug addict?"

"Because I saw you a few days ago on Gøteborggata. You were begging and I was walking with a young man who gave you a coin. But you picked it up and threw it at him in a rage. A drug addict would never have done that, however insignificant the coin."

"I remember."

"And then the same thing happened to me in a bar in Zagreb two days ago, and I began to think. That is, something made me think, but I didn't. Until now."

"There was one reason I threw the coin," Kaspersen said.

"That was what suddenly struck me," Harry said, placing an object in a plastic bag on the table. "Is this the reason?"

28

The Kiss

The press conference was held in the lecture hall on the fourth floor. Gunnar Hagen and the chief superintendent were sitting on the podium, their voices reverberating around the large, bare room. Harry had been summoned to attend in case Hagen needed to confer with him over details of the investigation. However, the journalists' questions were mostly about the dramatic shooting incident at the container terminal, and Hagen's answers varied between "No comment," "I can't go into that" and "We'll have to leave it to SEFO to answer that."

To the question about whether the police knew if the gunman was in cahoots with anyone, Hagen answered: "Not for the moment, but this is the subject of intense investigation."

When the press conference came to an end and the hall was emptying, Hagen called Harry over. He looked down from the podium at his tall inspector. "I gave clear instructions that I wanted to see all my inspectors carrying weapons this week. You received a requisition order from me, so where's yours?"

"I've been involved in the investigation and did not make it a priority, boss."

"Make it a priority." The words echoed around the hall. Harry nodded slowly. "Anything else, boss?"

In his office, Harry sat staring at Halvorsen's empty chair. Then he called the passport office on the second floor and asked them to get him a list of passports issued to the Karlsen family. A nasal female voice asked if he was kidding, there being quite a number of Karlsens in Norway, and he gave her Robert's national identity number. Using the national registration office and a medium-fast computer, the search was soon narrowed down to Robert, Jon, Josef and Dorthe.

"The parents, Josef and Dorthe, have passports, renewed four years ago. We haven't issued a passport to Jon. And let's see . . . the machine's a bit slow today . . . there, yes. Robert Karlsen has a ten-year-old passport that will soon be invalid, so you can tell him to—"

"He's dead."

Harry dialed Skarre's number and asked him to join him at once.

"Nothing," said Skarre, who, by chance or in a sudden fit of tact, sat on the edge of the desk instead of Halvorsen's chair. "I've checked the Gilstrups' accounts and there is no link anywhere with Robert Karlsen or with Swiss bank accounts. The only unusual transaction was a cash withdrawal of five million kroner, in dollars, from one of the company accounts. I called Albert Gilstrup and asked, and he said without any hesitation that they were the Christmas bonuses for the harbor masters in Buenos Aires, Manila and Bombay whom Mads visits in December. Quite a business those people are in."

"And Robert's account?"

"Incoming wages and minor withdrawals throughout."

"What about calls from the Gilstrups?"

"None to Robert Karlsen. But we came across something else while going through the itemized telephone bills.

Guess who called Jon Karlsen heaps of times and on occasion in the middle of the night?"

"Ragnhild Gilstrup," Harry said, looking into Skarre's disappointed face. "Anything else?"

"No," Skarre said. "Apart from a familiar number making an appearance. Mads Gilstrup called Halvorsen the day he was attacked. Unanswered call."

"I see," Harry said. "I want you to check one more account."

"Whose?"

"David Eckhoff's."

"The commander? What should I look for?"

"Don't quite know. Just do it."

After Skarre had gone, Harry phoned Forensics. The female pathologist promised without any delay or fuss to fax a photograph of Christo Stankic's body to a number at Hotel International in Zagreb.

Harry thanked her, put down the telephone and dialed the number of the same hotel.

"There's also the question of what to do with the body," he said when he had been put through to Fred. "The Croatian authorities don't know anything about a Christo Stankic and therefore have not requested his extradition."

Ten seconds later he heard her schooled English.

"I would like to suggest another deal," Harry said.

Klaus Torkildsen in the Telenor operations center for the Oslo region had one aim in life: to be left in peace. And since he was very overweight, always perspiring and for the most part grumpy, by and large his wish was fulfilled. With regard to the contact he was forced to have with others, he made sure there was maximum distance. That was why he sat alone a lot, enclosed in a room in the operations section with several hot machines and cooling fans, where few, if any, knew exactly what he was up to; all they knew was that he was indispensable. The need for distance may also have been the motivation for him to expose himself and thus on the odd occasion achieve satisfaction with a partner who was five to fifty yards away. However, Klaus Torkildsen's utmost desire was to be left in peace. And he had had enough hassle for this week. First it was that Halvorsen, who wanted a line to a hotel in Zagreb monitored. Then Skarre needed a list of the conversations between a Gilstrup and a Karlsen. Both had referred to Harry Hole, whom Klaus Torkildsen still owed a certain debt of gratitude. And that was the only reason he did not put down the telephone when Harry Hole himself called.

"There's something called the Police Answering Service," Torkildsen said in a sulky tone. "If you go by the book you should call them if you need help."

"I know," Harry said. He didn't need to say any more. "I've called Martine Eckhoff four times without getting an answer," Hole said. "No one in the Salvation Army knows where she is, not even her father."

"They're the last to know," said Klaus, who knew nothing about that kind of thing, but it was the sort of knowledge you could acquire if you were a regular moviegoer. Or, in Klaus Torkildsen's case, an extremely regular moviegoer.

"She may have switched off her cell, but I was wondering whether you could try to locate it for me. So that I know whether she's in town or not, at any rate."

Torkildsen sighed. A pose, pure and simple, because he adored these little police jobs. Especially when they were of the shady variety.

"May I have her number?"

Fifteen minutes later Klaus called back to say that her SIM card was definitely not in Oslo. Two base stations, both to the west of the E6, had received signals. He explained where the base stations were, and what range they had. Since Hole thanked him and hung up at once, Klaus presumed he had been of some help and returned with relish to the list of the day's movie times.

Jon let himself into Robert's flat.

The walls still smelled of smoke, and there was a dirty T-shirt lying on the floor in front of the cupboard. As though Robert had been in and then popped out to the shop to buy coffee and cigarettes.

Jon put the black bag Mads had given him next to the bed and turned up the radiator. Threw off all his clothes, went into the shower and let the hot water beat down on his skin until it was red and nubbly. He dried himself, left the bathroom, sat down naked on the bed and stared at the bag.

He hardly dared open it. For he knew what was inside, behind the thick, smooth material. Perdition. Death. Jon thought he could smell the stench of decay already. He closed his eyes. He needed to think.

His cell rang.

Thea must be wondering where he was. He didn't feel like talking to her now. But it kept ringing, insistent and inescapable, like Chinese water torture, and in the end he snatched the phone and said in a voice he could hear was shaking with anger: "What is it?"

But there was no answer. He read the display but didn't recognize the number. Jon realized it was not Thea calling.

"Hello, this is Jon Karlsen," he said, guardedly. Still nothing.

"Hello, who is it? Hello, I can hear someone is there. Who . . . ?" Panic tiptoed up his spine.

"Hello?" he heard himself say in English. "Who is this? Is that you? I need to speak to you. Hello!"

There was a click and the connection was cut.

Ridiculous, thought Jon. Probably a wrong number. He swallowed. Stankic was dead. Robert was dead. And

Ragnhild was dead. They were all dead. Just the policeman was still alive. And him. He stared at the bag, felt the cold come creeping in and pulled the duvet over him.

After turning off the E6 and driving some way down the narrow roads in the snow-covered rural landscape, Harry looked up and saw the stars were out.

He had a strange trembling feeling that something was going to happen soon. And when he saw a shooting star tear a parabola through the base of the sky ahead of him he thought if omens existed, this had to mean something.

He saw light in the windows on the ground floor of Østgård. Turning in to the drive, he saw the electric car, and the feeling that something was looming was reinforced.

He walked toward the house, observing the footprints in the snow. Stood by the door with his ear to it. There was the sound of low voices.

He knocked. Three quick taps. The voices died away. Then he heard steps and her soft voice. "Who is it?"

"It's Harry," he said. "Hole." He added the latter so as not to awaken a third party's suspicion that he and Martine Eckhoff had too personal a relationship.

There was some fumbling with the lock, then the door opened.

His first and only thought was that she was pretty. She was wearing a soft, thick white cotton blouse open at the neck, and her eyes were radiant.

"I'm glad," she said with a laugh.

"I can see." Harry smiled. "And I'm glad, too."

Then her arms were around his neck and he could feel her accelerated pulse.

"How did you find me?" she whispered in his ear.

"Modern technology."

The heat from her body, the gleam in her eyes, the whole ecstatic welcome gave Harry an unreal sense of happiness, a pleasant dream he, for his part, had no desire to wake from in the immediate future. But he had to.

"Is anyone here?" he asked.

"Er, no . . ."

"I thought I heard voices."

"Oh, that," she said, letting him go. "That was just the radio. I switched it off when I heard the knocking. I got a little frightened. And then it was you . . ." She patted him on the arm. "It was Harry Hole."

"No one knows where you are, Martine."

"Wonderful."

"Some of them are worried."

"Oh?"

"Especially Rikard."

"Oh, forget Rikard." Martine took Harry's hand and led him into the kitchen. She took down a blue coffee cup from the cupboard. Harry noticed there were two plates and two cups in the sink.

"You don't look that ill to me," he said.

"I just needed a day off after all that's happened." She poured the coffee and passed him the cup. "Black, wasn't it?"

Harry shrugged. She had the heat on high, and he took off his jacket and sweater before sitting at the table.

"But tomorrow it's the Christmas concert and I have to go back." She sighed. "Are you coming?"

"Well, I was promised a ticket . . ."

"Say you're coming!" Then Martine bit her lower lip. "Oh, dear—in fact I had tickets for us in the VIP box. Three rows behind the prime minister. But I had to give yours to someone else."

"That doesn't matter."

"You would have been left on your own, anyway. I have to work backstage."

"So it really doesn't matter."

"No!" She laughed. "I want you to be there."

She took his hand. Harry looked at her small hand, which was squeezing and stroking his large paw. It was so quiet he could hear his blood rushing like a waterfall in his ears.

"I saw a shooting star on the way here," Harry said. "Isn't that strange? A meteor is supposed to bring good luck."

Martine gave a silent nod. Then she stood up without letting go of Harry's hand, walked around the table and sat astride his lap, facing him. Put her hand around his neck.

"Martine . . ." he began.

"Shh." She ran her index finger over his lips.

And without taking her finger away, she leaned forward and placed her lips gently against his.

Harry closed his eyes and waited, feeling his heart pound, heavily, pleasurably, though he was sitting quite still. It occurred to him he was waiting for her heart to beat in tune with his, but knew for certain only this: He would have to wait. Then he felt her lips part and automatically he opened his mouth and his tongue lay flat in his mouth, against his teeth, ready to receive hers. Her finger had an exciting, bitter taste of soap and coffee that burned the tip of his tongue. Her hand squeezed his neck tighter. Then he felt her tongue. It pressed against her finger so that he had contact on both sides and it made him think it was split, like a snake's tongue. That they were giving each other two half-kisses.

She let go.

"Keep your eyes closed," she whispered by his ear.

Harry leaned back and resisted the temptation to put his hands on her hips. The seconds passed. Then he felt the soft cotton material on the back of his hand as her blouse slipped to the floor.

"Now you can open them," she whispered.

Harry did as instructed. And sat watching her. Her face expressed a mixture of anxiety and anticipation.

"You're so beautiful," he said in a voice that had become constricted and odd. Also bewildered.

He noticed her swallow. Then a triumphant smile spread across her face.

"Raise your arms," she commanded. She grabbed hold of his T-shirt at the bottom and pulled it over his head.

"And you're ugly," she said. "Wonderful and ugly."

Harry felt an intoxicating stab of pain as she bit into his nipple. One of her hands had moved behind her back and between his legs. Her breathing against his neck began to race and her other hand grabbed his belt. He held his arm against her lithe back. That was when he felt it. An involuntary quiver of her muscles, a tension she had managed to hide. She was frightened.

"Wait, Martine," Harry whispered. Her hand froze.

Harry lowered his mouth to her ear. "Do you want this? Do you know what you're getting yourself into here?"

He could feel her breathing, quickened and moist against his skin, as she gasped: "No—do you?"

"No. Then perhaps we shouldn't . . ."

She sat up. Looking at him with wounded, desperate eyes. "But I . . . I can feel that you . . ."

"Yes," Harry said, caressing her hair. "I want you. I have wanted you from the first moment I saw you."

"Is that the truth?" she said, taking his hand and laying it against a hot, flushed cheek.

Harry smiled. "The second, anyway."

"The second time?"

"OK, the third, then. All good music takes a little time."

"And I'm good music?"

"I'm lying. It was the first time. But that doesn't mean I'm a pushover, OK?"

Martine smiled. Then she started laughing. Harry, too. She leaned forward and rested her forehead against his chest. Shook with laughter and banged against his shoulder, and it was only then that Harry felt her tears running down his stomach and realized she was crying.

*   *   *

Jon was woken by the cold. He thought. Robert's flat was dark and there could be no other explanation. But then his brain rewound and he knew that what he assumed were the final fragments of a dream were not. He *had* heard a key in the lock. And the door opening. Now someone was in the room, breathing.

With a sense of déjà vu, that everything in this nightmare was repeating itself, he whirled around.

A figure stood over the bed.

Jon gasped for air as the fear of death attacked, its teeth sinking into his flesh and striking the nerves beneath. For he had total certainty, was quite sure that this person wished him dead.

"*Stigla sam*," the figure said.

Jon didn't know many Croatian words, but the ones he had picked up from the tenants from Vukovar were enough for him to be able to work out what the voice had said: "I have come."

"Have you always been lonely, Harry?"

"I think so."

"Why?"

Harry shrugged. "I've never been the sociable type."

"Is that all?"

Harry blew a ring of smoke up to the ceiling and could feel Martine sniffing at his sweater and his neck. They were in the bedroom, he on top of the duvet, she beneath.

"Bjarne Møller, my former boss, says people like me always choose the line of most resistance. It's in what he calls our 'accursed nature.' That's why we always end up on our own. I don't know. I like being alone. Perhaps I have grown to like my self-image of being a loner, too. What about you?"

"I want you to talk."

"Why?"

"I don't know. I like listening to you. How can anyone like the self-image of a loner?"

Harry took a deep breath. Held the smoke in his lungs, thinking how good it would be if you could blow smoke patterns to explain everything. Then he released the smoke in one long exhalation.

"I think you have to find something about yourself that you like in order to survive. Some people say being alone is unsociable and selfish. But you're independent and you don't drag others down with you, if that's the way you're headed. Many people are afraid of being alone. But it made me feel free, strong and invulnerable."

"Strong from being alone?"

"Yep. As Dr. Stockmann said: 'The strongest man in the world is he who stands most alone.' "

"First Süskind and now Ibsen?"

Harry grinned. "That was a line my father used to quote." He sighed and then added, "Before my mother died."

"You said it *made* you invulnerable. Is that no longer the case?"

Harry felt the ash fall from his cigarette onto his chest. He left it where it was. "I met Rakel and . . . well, Oleg. They attached themselves to me. It opened my eyes to the fact that there could be other people in my life. People who were friends and who cared about me. And that I needed them." Harry blew on his cigarette, making it glow. "And, even worse, that they might need me."

"So you weren't free any longer?"

"No. No, I wasn't free any longer." They lay staring into the dark.

Martine nestled her nose into his neck. "You really like them, don't you?"

"Yes." Harry pulled her close. "Yes, I do."

After she had fallen asleep, Harry slipped out of the bed and tucked the duvet in around her. He checked the time.

Two o'clock on the dot. He walked into the hall, put on his boots and opened the door to the starry night. Heading for the outhouse, he studied the footprints while trying to remember whether it had snowed since Saturday morning.

The outhouse was not lit, so he struck a match and oriented himself. As it was about to go out he spotted two letters carved into the wall under a fading picture of Princess Grace of Monaco. In the dark Harry mused that someone had been sitting here, as he was, diligently forming the simple declaration: R+M.

Coming out of the outhouse, he caught a quick movement by the corner of the barn. He stopped. There was a set of footprints going that way.

Harry hesitated. There it was again. The feeling that something was about to happen, right now, something fated, which he could not prevent. He put a hand inside the outhouse door and found the spade he had seen standing there. Then he began to follow the prints to the barn.

At the corner he paused and took a firm grip on the spade. His breathing thundered in his ears. He stopped breathing. Now. It was going to happen now. Harry plunged around the corner with the spade at the ready.

Ahead of him, in the middle of the field shining so bewitchingly and so white in the moonlight that he was dazzled, he saw a fox running toward the woods.

He slumped back against the barn door and inhaled trembling lungfuls of air.

There was a knock at the door, and he backed away out of instinct.

Had he been seen? The person on the other side of the door must not come inside.

He cursed his carelessness. Bobo would have scolded him for breaking cover in such an amateurish way.

The door was locked, but he still cast around for an

object he could use in case whoever it was managed to make his way in.

A knife. Martine's bread knife that he had just been using. It was in the kitchen.

There was another knock.

And then there was his gun. Empty, it was true, but enough to scare off a sensible man. The problem was that he doubted if this one was.

The person had arrived in a car and parked outside Martine's flat on Sorgenfrigata. He hadn't seen him until he chanced by the window and scanned the cars parked by the curb. That was when he had seen the motionless silhouette inside one of them. On seeing it move, leaning forward to see better, he knew it was too late. He had been seen. He had come away from the window, waited for half an hour, then lowered the blinds and switched off all the lights in Martine's flat. She had said he could leave them on. The radiators all had thermostats, and since 90 percent of the energy of a lightbulb is heat, the electricity you save by turning them off would be counterbalanced by the radiators compensating for the heat loss.

"Simple physics," she had explained. If only she had explained to him what this was instead. A demented suitor? A jealous ex-lover. It wasn't the police, anyway, because he had started up again: a desperate, pained howl that made his blood run cold.

"Mar-tine! Mar-tine!" Then a few tremulous words in Norwegian. And then almost a sob: "Martine . . ."

He had no idea how the guy had got in through the front door, but now he could hear one of the other doors opening and a voice. Among the snatches of foreign words there was one he recognized now: *politi*.

Then the neighbor's door was slammed shut.

He heard the person outside groaning in despair and fingers scratching at the door. Then footsteps finally dying away. He heaved a sigh of relief.

It had been a long day. Martine had driven him down to the station in the morning and he had caught the local train to town. The first thing he had done was go to the travel agent at Oslo Central, where he had bought a ticket for the last flight to Copenhagen the following evening. They hadn't reacted to the Norwegian-sounding surname he had given them. Halvorsen. He had paid with the cash in Halvorsen's wallet, thanked them and left. From Copenhagen he would call Zagreb and have Fred fly there with a new passport. If he was lucky, he would be back for Christmas Eve.

He had been to three hairdressers, who had all shaken their heads and said they had no appointments left before the holiday. The fourth had nodded to a gum-chewing teenage girl sitting in a corner and looking lost—he guessed she was an apprentice. After several attempts at explaining what he wanted, he had finally shown her the photograph. She had stopped chewing, looked up at him with eyes thick with mascara and asked in MTV English: "You sure, man?"

Afterward he had taken a taxi to the address on Sorgenfrigata, unlocked the doors with the keys he had been given by Martine and begun the wait. The telephone had rung several times, but otherwise it had been peaceful. Until, that is, he had been stupid enough to go to the window of an illuminated room.

He walked back to the living room.

At that moment there was a bang. The air quivered and the ceiling lamp shook.

"Mar-tine!"

He heard the person make another attempt, sprinting up and charging at the door, which seemed to bulge into the room.

Her name was called out twice, followed by two bangs. Then he heard feet running down the stairs.

He went to the living-room window and watched the

person race out. As the guy paused to unlock the car and the streetlight fell on him, he recognized him.

It was the young man who had helped him at the hostel. Niclas, Rikard . . . something like that. The car started up with a roar and accelerated away into the winter night.

An hour later he was asleep, dreaming about landscapes he had once known, and only woke up when he heard the patter of feet and the sound of newspapers landing on doorsteps in the stairwell.

Harry woke up at eight. He opened his eyes and smelled the wool blanket half-covering his face. The smell reminded him of something. Then he threw it off. His sleep had been profound, without dreams, and he was in a curious mood. Exhilarated. Happy—no other word for it.

He went into the kitchen, put on the coffee, washed his face in the sink and hummed Jim Stärk's "Morning Song." Over the low ridge to the east the sky was reddening like a young maiden, the last star blanching and fading. A new, mysterious, unsullied world lay outside the kitchen window and, white and optimistic, it was surging toward the horizon.

He sliced some bread, found some cheese, poured water into a glass and steaming coffee into a clean cup, put it all on a tray and carried it into the bedroom.

Her black untidy hair spilled over the duvet and she made no sound. He placed the tray on the bedside table, sat on the edge of the bed and waited.

The aroma of coffee slowly wafted through the room.

Her breathing became irregular. She blinked. Caught sight of him, rubbed her face and stretched with exaggerated, embarrassed movements. It was like someone operating a dimmer switch, and the light shining out of her eyes grew stronger and stronger until the smile reached her lips.

"Good morning," he said.

"Good morning."

"Breakfast?"

"Mmm." Her smile grew broader. "Don't you want any?"

"I'll wait. I'll make do with one of these if that's all right." He produced a packet of cigarettes.

"You smoke too much," she said.

"I always do after I've been boozing. Nicotine curbs the craving."

She tasted the coffee. "Isn't that a paradox?"

"What?"

"You, who were so frightened of losing your freedom, becoming an alcoholic."

"True." He opened the window, lit a cigarette and lay down beside her on the bed.

"Is that what frightens you about me?" she asked, snuggling up to him. "That I will deprive you of your freedom? Is that why . . . you don't want . . . to make love to me?"

"No, Martine." Harry took a drag of the cigarette, grimaced and eyed it with disapproval. "It's because you are frightened."

He felt her stiffen.

"Am I frightened?" she asked with surprise in her voice.

"Yes. And I would have been, too, if I were you. I've never been able to understand how women have the courage to share roof and bed with those who are, physically, their complete masters." He stubbed out his cigarette in the plate on the bedside table. "Men would never dare."

"What makes you think I'm frightened?"

"I can sense it. You take the initiative and want to be in charge. But mostly because you're frightened about what might happen if you let me take charge. And that's fine, but I don't want you to do it if you're frightened."

"But it's not up to you to decide whether I want it or not!" she burst out. "Even if I *am* frightened."

Harry looked at her. Without warning she flung her arms around him and hid her face in his neck.

"You must think I'm very strange," she said.

"Not at all," said Harry.

She held him tight. Squeezed him.

"What if I was always frightened?" she whispered. "What if I never . . ." She paused.

Harry waited.

"Something happened," she said. "I don't know what." And waited.

"Yes, I know what," she said. "I was raped. Here on this farm, many years ago. And I kind of went to pieces."

The cold scream of a crow in the woods rent the silence.

"Do you want . . . ?"

"No, I don't want to talk about it. There's not very much to talk about, anyway. It's a long time ago and I'm in one piece now. I'm just"—she snuggled up to him again—"a tiny bit frightened."

"Did you report it?"

"No. I wasn't up to it."

"I know it's tough, but you should have."

She smiled. "Yes, I've heard you should. Because another girl's next—isn't that right?"

"This is no joke, Martine."

"Sorry, Daddy."

Harry shrugged. "I don't know if crime pays, but I do know it repeats itself."

"Because it's in your genes, right?"

"That I don't know."

"Have you read the research into adoption? It shows that children with criminal parents who grow up in a normal family with other children, unaware that they're adopted, have a much greater chance of turning out to be criminals than the other children in the family. So there has to be a criminal gene."

"Yes, I've read that," Harry said. "Behavioral patterns may be hereditary. But I prefer to believe that in our own way, each of us is distinct."

"You think we're programmed creatures of habit?" She curled a finger and tickled Harry under the chin.

"I think we throw everything into one great calculation, lust and fear and excitement and greed and all that kind of thing. And the brain is brilliant. It computes away and almost never makes a mistake; that's why it produces the same answers every time."

Martine propped herself up on one elbow and gazed down at Harry. "And morality and free choice?"

"They're in the great calculation, too."

"So you think a criminal will always—"

"No—otherwise I couldn't do my job."

She ran a finger across his forehead. "So people can still change?"

"That's what I hope, anyway. That people learn."

She rested her forehead on his. "And what can you learn?"

"You can learn"—he was interrupted by her lips touching his—"not to be lonely. You can learn"—the tip of her tongue caressed the bottom of his lower lip—"not to be frightened. And you can—"

"Learn to kiss?"

"Yes. But not if the girl has just woken up and has a disgusting white coating on her tongue that—"

Her hand hit his cheek with a smack and her laughter tinkled like ice cubes in a glass. Then her hot tongue found his and she covered him with the duvet; she pulled up his sweater and T-shirt and the skin on her stomach glowed bed-warm and soft against his.

Harry's hand wandered under her top and up her back, felt the shoulder blades that moved under the skin and the muscles that tensed and relaxed as she wriggled toward him.

He unbuttoned her top and held her gaze as he moved his hand over her stomach, over her ribs, until the soft skin of his thumb and forefinger was holding her stiff nipple. She panted hot air over him as her open mouth closed on him and they kissed. As she forced her hand down between their hips, he knew that this time he would not be able to stop. Nor did he want to.

"It's ringing," she said.

"What?"

"The phone in your trousers—it's vibrating." She began to laugh. "Feel—"

"Sorry." Harry dragged the silent phone up from his pocket, leaned over her and put it on the bedside table. But it was on its side and the throbbing display faced him. He tried to ignore it, but it was too late. He had seen that it was Beate.

"Shit," he breathed. "Just a moment."

He sat up and studied Martine's face, which studied his as he listened to Beate. And her face was like a mirror; they seemed to be playing a mime game. Apart from seeing himself, Harry could see his fear, his pain and in the end his resignation reflected in her face.

"What is it?" she asked after he hung up.

"He's dead."

"Who?"

"Halvorsen. He died in the night. Nine minutes past two. While I was out by the barn."

PART FOUR

Mercy

29

The Commanding Officer

It was the shortest day of the year, but for Inspector Harry Hole the day seemed impossibly long before it had even started.

After hearing the news of Halvorsen's death he had first gone for a walk outdoors. Trudged through the deep snow to the woods and sat there watching day break. He had hoped the cold would freeze, alleviate or, at least, numb his feelings.

Then he had walked back. Martine had watched him with questions in her eyes, but said nothing. He had drunk a cup of coffee, kissed her on the cheek and got into the car. In the mirror, Martine had seemed even smaller standing on the step with her arms crossed.

Harry drove home, took a shower, changed clothes and flicked through the papers on the coffee table three times before giving up, bewildered. For the umpteenth time since the day before yesterday he would check his watch only to see his bare wrist. He fetched Møller's watch from the drawer in the bedside table. It was still working and would have to do for the time being. He drove to Police HQ and parked in the garage beside Hagen's Audi.

Walking up the stairs to the sixth floor he could hear voices, footsteps and laughter resounding in the atrium. But when the Crime Squad department door closed behind him it was as though the volume had been switched off. In the corridor he met an officer who observed him, shook his head in silence and walked on.

"Hi, Harry."

He turned. It was Toril Li. He could not recall her using his first name before.

"How are you doing?" she asked.

Harry was about to answer, opened his mouth, but realized all of a sudden that he had no voice.

"We thought we might assemble after the briefing to pay our respects," Toril Li said with brisk delicacy, as though to cover for him.

Harry nodded in silent gratitude.

"Maybe you could get in touch with Beate?"

"Of course."

Harry stood in front of his office door. He had been dreading this moment. Then he entered.

In Halvorsen's chair sat a person leaning back and bobbing up and down, as if he had been waiting.

"Good morning, Harry," said Gunnar Hagen.

Harry hung his jacket on the coatrack without replying.

"Sorry," Hagen said. "Poor choice of words."

"What do you want?" Harry sat down.

"To express my regret about what has happened. I'll do the same at the morning meeting, but first I want to do it face-to-face with you. Jack was your closest colleague, wasn't he?"

"Halvorsen."

"I beg your pardon."

Harry rested his head in his hands. "We called him Halvorsen."

Hagen nodded. "Halvorsen. One more thing, Harry—"

"I thought I had the requisition order at home," Harry said between his fingers. "But it's gone."

"Oh, that . . ." Hagen shifted; he seemed uncomfortable in the chair. "I wasn't thinking about the gun. With regard to travel expense cutbacks, I've asked Accounts to present me with all receipts for approval. It turns out you've been to Zagreb. I don't recall having authorized any foreign travel. And if the Norwegian police have carried out any investigations there, it is a flagrant breach of instructions."

They've finally found it, thought Harry, his face still buried in his hands. The blunder they have been waiting for. The formal reason for kicking the alcoholic inspector back to where he belongs, among the uncivilized civilians. Harry tried to sound out what he felt. But the only thing he was conscious of was relief.

"You'll have my notice on your desk tomorrow, boss."

"I have no idea what you're talking about," Hagen said. "I assume there has been *no* investigation in Zagreb. That would have been very embarrassing for all concerned."

Harry looked up.

"The way I read it," Hagen said, "you've been on a little study trip to Zagreb."

"Study trip, boss?"

"Yes, an unspecified study trip. And here is my written consent to your oral inquiry about a study trip to Zagreb." A printed sheet of paper sailed over the desk and landed in front of Harry. "And so this business should be a thing of the past." Hagen stood up and went to the wall where the photo of Ellen Gjelten hung. "Halvorsen is the second partner you've lost, isn't he?"

Harry inclined his head. It went quiet in the cramped, windowless room.

Then Hagen coughed. "You've seen the little piece of carved bone on my desk, haven't you? I bought it in Nagasaki. It's a copy of the little finger belonging to Yoshito Yasuda, a well-known Japanese battalion commander." He turned to Harry. "The Japanese usually cremate their dead, but in Burma they had to bury them because there were so many and it can take up to two hours for a body to burn up. So instead they would cut off a little finger, cremate it and send the ashes home to the family. After a decisive battle by Pegu in the spring of 1944 the Japanese were forced to retreat and hide in the jungle. The battalion commander begged his superior officer to attack that same evening so that they could recover the bones of their dead men. His request was rejected—the victors' numbers were too large— and that evening he stood weeping before his men in the light of the campfire and told them of the CO's decision. On seeing the hopelessness in his men's faces, he dried his tears, drew his bayonet, laid his hand on a tree stump, cut off his little finger and threw it on the fire. The men cheered. It got back to the CO and the next day the Japanese attacked in full force."

Hagen went to Halvorsen's desk and picked up a pencil sharpener, which he studied in minute detail.

"I made a number of mistakes in my first days here as boss. For all I know one of them may have indirectly caused Halvorsen's death. What I'm trying to say . . ." He put down the sharpener and breathed in. "Is that I wish I could do as Yoshito Yasuda did and inspire all of you. But I don't know how."

Harry was nonplussed, so he kept his mouth shut.

"So let me just put it like this, Harry. I want you to find the person or persons behind these murders. That's all."

The two men avoided each other's eyes. Hagen clapped his hands together to break the silence. "But you would be doing me a favor if you would carry a weapon, Harry. You know, in front of the others . . . at least until the New Year. Then I'll rescind the instruction."

"Fine."

"Thank you. I'll write you a new requisition order." Harry nodded, and Hagen moved toward the door.

"How did it turn out?" Harry asked. "The Japanese counter-attack?"

"Oh, that." Hagen turned with a lopsided grin. "It was crushed."

*   *   *

Kjell Atle Orø had been working at the bottom of Police HQ for nineteen years, and this morning he was sitting with the betting slip in front of him, wondering whether he had the nerve to go for an away win for Fulham against Southampton on Boxing Day. He wanted to give the slip to Oshaug when he went for lunch, so he was in a hurry. That was why he cursed when he heard someone strike the metal bell.

He got to his feet with a groan. In his time Orø had played first-division soccer for Skeid and had had a long and injury-free career; he was therefore eternally bitter that what had seemed an innocent strain in a game for the police team had resulted in his still dragging his right leg ten years later.

A man with a blond crew cut was standing in front of the counter. Orø took the requisition order he was passed and squinted at the letters that seemed to be getting smaller and smaller. Last week, when he had told his wife he would like a bigger TV for Christmas, she had suggested he book an appointment with the optician.

"Harry Hole, Smith and Wesson thirty-eight, yes," Orø groaned, limping back to the armory, where he found a service revolver that looked like the previous owner had been gentle. It struck him that they would soon be receiving the weapon belonging to the officer who had been stabbed to death on Gøteborggata. He got down the holster and the standard three boxes of ammunition and went back to the counter.

"Sign here," he said, pointing to the order sheet. "Can I see some ID?" The man, who had already put his ID card on the counter, took the pen Orø passed him and signed as instructed. Orø peered at Harry Hole's ID card and the scribbles. He wondered if Southampton could stop Louis Saha.

"And remember to shoot at the bad guys," Orø said, but received no response.

Hobbling back to the betting slip, he reflected that the policeman's sulkiness was perhaps not so surprising. The ID card said he was in Crime Squad. Wasn't that where the dead officer had been working?

Harry parked the car by the Henie-Onstad Art Center on Høvikodden and walked from the beautiful, low brick building down the slight slope to the fjord.

On the ice stretching to Snarøya he could see a lone black figure. He tested a sheet of ice adjacent to the shore with one foot. It broke with a loud crack. Harry shouted David Eckhoff's name, but the figure on the ice did not stir.

Then he swore, and, realizing that the commander could not weigh much less than his own two hundred ten pounds, balanced on the stranded ice sheets and gingerly placed his feet on the treacherous snow-camouflaged ice field. It took his weight. He made his way across the ice with short, quick steps. It was farther than it had seemed from land, and when at last Harry was so near that he could say with certainty that the figure wearing the wolf pelt, sitting on a folding chair and bent over a hole in the ice with a jig in his mittens, was indeed the Salvation Army commander, he could see why he hadn't heard him.

"Are you sure this ice is safe, Eckhoff?"

David Eckhoff turned and looked down at Harry's boots first.

"Ice on Oslo Fjord in December is never safe," he said, with frozen breath issuing from his mouth. "That's why you fish alone. But I always use these." He motioned toward the skis he was wearing. "They spread the weight."

Harry nodded slowly. He seemed to hear the ice cracking beneath his feet. "They told me at headquarters I would find you here."

"Only place you can hear yourself think." Eckhoff grabbed the jig. He had put a box of bait and a knife on some newspaper beside the opening in the ice. The front page predicted mild weather from Christmas Day onward. Nothing about Halvorsen's death. It must have gone to print too early.

"A lot to think about?" Harry asked.

"Hm. My wife and I have to host the prime minister during the concert this evening. And then there's Gilstrup's contract that has to be signed this week. Yes, there are a few things."

"I wanted to ask just one question," Harry said, concentrating on spreading his weight equally between both feet.

"Uh-huh?"

"I asked Skarre, one of my men, to check if there were any sums of money passing between your account and Robert Karlsen's. There weren't. But he found another Karlsen who transferred regular sums of money: Josef Karlsen."

David Eckhoff stared into the circle of dark water without batting an eyelid.

"My question," Harry said, focusing on Eckhoff, "is why you've received eight thousand kroner from Robert and Jon's father every quarter for the last twelve years."

Eckhoff jerked as though he had a big fish on the hook.

"Well?" Harry said.

"Is this of any importance?"

"I think so, Eckhoff."

"In that case it will have to remain between the two of us."

"I can't promise that."

"Then I can't tell you."

"Then I'll have to take you to the station and ask you to make a statement there."

The commander looked up with one eye closed and scrutinized Harry to gauge the strength of his potential adversary. "And you think Gunnar Hagen will approve of that? Dragging me down there?"

"Let's find out."

Eckhoff was about to say something, but paused, as though scenting Harry's determination. Harry was reflecting that a man does not become the leader of a flock through brute strength but through his ability to read situations correctly.

"Fine," said the commander. "But it's a long story."

"I have time," Harry lied, feeling the cold from the ice through his soles.

"Josef Karlsen, father of Jon and Robert, was my best friend." Eckhoff fixed his gaze on a point on Snarøya. "We studied together, we worked together and were both ambitious and promising, as they say. But most important of all we shared a vision of a strong Salvation Army that would do God's work on earth. That would prevail. Do you understand?"

Harry nodded.

"We also came up through the ranks together," Eckhoff continued. "And, yes, after a while Josef and I were seen as rivals for the job I have now. I didn't think the position was that important; it was the vision that was driving us. But when I was chosen something happened to Josef. He seemed to crumble. And who knows—we don't know ourselves inside out—I might have reacted in the same way. Anyway, Josef was given the trusted post of chief administrator, and even though our families kept in touch as before, there was not the same"—Eckhoff groped for words—"confidentiality. Something was oppressing Josef, something unpleasant. It was the autumn of 1991 when I and our chief accountant, Frank Nilsen—Rikard and Thea's father—discovered what. Josef had been misappropriating funds."

"What happened?"

"We have little experience of that sort of thing at the Salvation Army, so until we knew what to do, Nilsen and I kept it to ourselves. Of course I was disappointed by Josef's behavior, but at the same time I could see a cause-and-effect scenario of which I was a part. I could have handled the situation when I was chosen and he was rejected with greater . . . sensitivity. However, the Army was going through a period of poor recruitment at that time and did not enjoy anywhere near the widespread goodwill it enjoys today. We simply could not afford to have a scandal. I had been left a summer house by my parents in Sørlandet that we seldom used, and we intended to vacation in Østgård. So I sold it in a hurry and received enough to cover the shortfall before it was discovered."

"You?" Harry said. "You patched over Josef Karlsen's embezzlement with your own capital?"

Eckhoff shrugged. "There was no other solution."

"It's not exactly commonplace in business for the boss to—"

"No, but this is no commonplace business, Hole. We do God's work. Then it's personal, whatever happens."

Harry nodded slowly. He thought about the carved little finger on Hagen's desk. "So Josef packed it in and traveled abroad with his wife. And no one was any the wiser?"

"I offered him a job, less high-powered," Eckhoff said. "But of course he couldn't accept it. That would have raised all sorts of questions. They live in Thailand, I gather. Not far from Bangkok."

"So the story about the Chinese peasant and the snake bite was made up?"

Eckhoff smiled and shook his head. "No. Josef was a real doubter. And that story made a deep impression on him. Josef doubted, as indeed we all do at times."

"You, too, Commander?"

"Me, too. Doubt is faith's shadow. If you are unable to doubt you can't be a believer. It's the same as with courage, Inspector. If you are unable to feel fear, you cannot be courageous."

"And the money?"

"Josef insists on paying me back. Not because he wants redress. What happened happened, and he will never earn enough money to pay me back living where he is. But I think he feels the penance does him good. And why should I deny him that?"

Harry nodded slowly. "Did Robert and Jon know about this?"

"I don't know," Eckhoff said. "I've never mentioned it. The one thing I've been at pains to ensure is that whatever their father did does not stand in the way of his sons' careers in the Army. Above all Jon's. He has become one of our most important professional resources. Take this property sale, for instance. First of all, on Jacob Aalls Gate, but others, too, in time. Gilstrup may even buy back Østgård. If this sale had taken place ten years ago, we would have had to employ all sorts of advisers to accomplish it. But with people like Jon we have the skills in our own ranks."

"Do you mean Jon has steered the sale through?"

"No, not at all—the sale was approved at board level. But without his spadework and persuasive conclusions I really don't believe we would have dared to do it. Jon is a man of the future for us. Not to say a man of the present. And the best proof that his father has not stood in his way is that he and Thea Nilsen will be sitting on the other side of the prime minister in the VIP box tonight." Eckhoff frowned. "By the way, I tried to get hold of Jon today, but he's not answering his phone. You haven't spoken to him, by any chance?"

"I'm afraid not. Suppose Jon weren't there . . ."

"Pardon?"

"Suppose Jon had been killed—as the gunman had intended—who would take his place?"

David Eckhoff raised not one but both eyebrows. "Tonight?"

"I was thinking more of the post."

"Oh, I see. Well, I won't be giving away any secrets if I say it would be Rikard Nilsen." He chuckled. "People have been muttering about parallels between Jon and Rikard and Josef and me all those years ago."

"The same competition?"

"Wherever you find people you will find competition. Also in the Salvation Army. We have to hope that, on the whole, trials of strength place people where they do the best for themselves and serve the common cause. Well, well." The commander pulled up the fishing line.

"I hope that's answered your question, Harry. Frank Nilsen can confirm the story about Josef for you, if you wish, but I hope you understand why I would not like it to get out."

"I have one last question while we're into Salvation Army secrets."

"Out with it then," the commander said, impatient now and packing his fishing tackle into a bag.

"Do you know anything about a rape that took place at Østgård twelve years ago?"

Harry went on the assumption that a face like Eckhoff's was limited in its ability to express surprise. And since this limit appeared to have been exceeded, he considered it fairly certain that his question was news to the commander.

"That must be a mistake, Inspector. If not, it would be terrible. Who was involved?"

Harry hoped his face would not give anything away. "Professional discretion prevents me from saying."

Eckhoff scratched his chin with the mitten. "Of course. But . . . hasn't the statute of limitations passed on this crime?"

"Depends on how you look at it," Harry said, scanning the shore. "Ready to go?"

"Maybe it's better if we return separately. The weight . . ."

Harry swallowed and nodded.

On reaching the beach without a soaking, Harry turned around. The wind had risen and snow was drifting across the ice, making it look like a flying smokescreen. Eckhoff seemed to be walking on clouds.

In the parking lot, the windows of Harry's car were

already covered with a fine layer of white frost. He got in, started the engine and put the heat on full blast. The hot air streamed up against the cold glass. While waiting for the windshield to clear, he was reminded of something Skarre had said. Mads Gilstrup had called Halvorsen. He took out the business card he still had in his pocket and dialed the number. No answer. As he was putting the phone back in his pocket it rang. He saw from the number that it was Hotel International.

"How are you?" the woman said in her clipped English.

"So-so," Harry said. "Did you get . . . ?"

"Yes, I did."

Harry took a deep breath. "Was it him?"

"Yes," she sighed. "It was him."

"Are you absolutely sure? I mean, it's not so easy to identify someone from just—"

"Harry?"

"Yes?"

"I'm quite sure."

Harry had an inkling that this English teacher had mastered stress and intonation to such an extent that she meant what she said. She was absolutely sure.

"Thank you," he said and hung up. Hoping with all his heart that she was right. For it would all start now.

And it did.

As Harry activated the windshield wipers and they pushed the melting frost crystals to both sides, his cell rang for the second time.

"Harry Hole."

"This is Fru Miholjec. Sofia's mother. You said I could call this number if . . ."

"Yes?"

"Something has happened. To Sofia."

30

The Silence

The shortest day of the year.

It was on the front page of the *Aftenposten* lying on the table in front of Harry in the doctor's waiting room on Storgata. He checked the clock on the wall. Then realized he had a watch of his own.

"He'll see you now, Herr Hole," called a woman's voice from the window where he had explained that he wanted to speak to the doctor who had seen Sofia Miholjec and her father a few hours ago.

"Down the corridor, third door on the right," the woman called out. Harry jumped up and left behind him the silent, drooping band of people in the waiting room.

Third door on the right. Of course, chance might have sent Sofia to the second door on the left. Or the third door on the left. But no, third door on the right.

"Hi—I heard it was you." Mathias Lund-Helgesen smiled and stood up to proffer his hand. "What can I help you with this time?"

"It's about a patient you saw this morning. Sofia Miholjec."

"Really? Take a seat, Harry."

Harry did not allow himself to be irritated by the other man's friendly tone, but this was an invitation he was reluctant to accept. Not because he was too proud but because it was going to be embarrassing for them both.

"Sofia's mother called me to say she had been woken up this morning by Sofia crying in her room," Harry said. "She went in and found her daughter bruised and bleeding. Sofia said she had been out with friends and had slipped on the ice on the way home. The mother woke the father and he brought her here."

"It may be true," Mathias said. He had leaned forward on his elbows as if to show how much this interested him.

"However, the mother maintains she's lying," Harry went on. "She checked the bed after Sofia and her father had gone. And there was blood not only on the pillow, but also on the sheet. 'Down there,' as she put it."

"Mm-hm." The sound Mathias made was neither support nor denial, but a sound that Harry knew for a fact they rehearsed in the therapy section of the psychology department. Rising intonation on the final syllable was meant to encourage patients to continue. Mathias's intonation had gone up.

"Sofia has locked herself in her room now," Harry said. "She's crying and refuses to say a word. And according to her mother she won't, either. The mother has called Sofia's girlfriends. Not one of them saw her yesterday."

"I see." Mathias pinched the bridge of his nose. "And now you're asking me to ignore patient confidentiality for you?"

"No," said Harry.

"No?"

"Not for me. For them. For Sofia and her parents. And for others he may have raped and will rape."

"Those are strong words." Mathias smiled, but the smile faded with the silence. He coughed. "You understand, I'm sure, that I have to mull this over first, Harry."

"Was she raped last night or not?"

Mathias sighed. "Harry, patient confidentiality is—"

"I know what confidentiality is," Harry interrupted. "I'm subject to it as well. When I ask you to make an exception in this case it's not because I take patient confidentiality lightly, but because I have made an assessment of the brutal nature of this crime and the potential danger of its recurrence. If you would trust me and rely on my assessment I would be grateful. If you don't you will have to try to live with it as best you can."

Harry wondered how many times he had given this spiel in similar situations.

Mathias blinked and his face fell.

"It's good enough if you nod or shake your head," Harry said. Mathias Lund-Helgesen nodded.

It had done the trick again.

"Thank you," Harry said, getting up. "Things going well with Rakel and you and Oleg?"

Lund-Helgesen nodded again with a wan smile. Harry leaned forward and placed a hand on the doctor's shoulder. "Merry Christmas, Mathias." The last thing Harry saw as he went out the door was Mathias Lund-Helgesen sitting in the chair with slumped shoulders, looking as though someone had given him a slap.

The last daylight leaked out between orange clouds over the spruce trees and rooftops to the west of Norway's largest cemetery. Harry walked past the stone monument for Yugoslavia's war dead, the Norwegian Labor Party's plot, the gravestones for prime ministers Einar Gerhardsen and Trygve Bratteli, to the Salvation Army's own plot. As expected, he found Sofia by the freshest grave. She was sitting erect in the snow wrapped up in a large down jacket.

"Hi," said Harry, settling down beside her.

He lit a cigarette and exhaled into the icy breeze, which carried the blue smoke away.

"Your mother said you'd just left," Harry said. "And you

took the flowers your father had bought you. It wasn't hard to guess."

Sofia didn't answer.

"Robert was a good friend, wasn't he? Someone you could rely on. And talk to. Not a rapist."

"Robert was the one who did it," she whispered lethargically.

"Your flowers are on Robert's grave, Sofia. I believe someone else raped you. And he did it again last night. And he may have done it several times."

"Leave me in peace!" she screamed and struggled to her feet in the snow. "Don't you people listen?"

Harry held his cigarette in one hand, grabbed her arm with the other and pulled her down hard into the snow.

"This one's dead, Sofia. You're alive. Do you hear me? You're alive. And if you intend to continue living, we'd better catch him now. If not, he'll keep going. You weren't the first and you won't be the last. Look at me. Look at me, I'm telling you!"

His vehemence startled Sofia, and she obeyed.

"I know you're scared, Sofia. But I promise you I'll get him. Whatever happens. I swear."

Harry saw something stir in her eyes. And if he was right, it was hope. He waited. And then she breathed something inaudible.

"What did you say?" Harry asked, leaning forward.

"Who will believe me?" she whispered. "Who will believe me now . . . that Robert is dead?"

Harry placed a careful hand on her shoulders. "Try. Then we'll see." The orange clouds had begun to turn red.

"He threatened to destroy everything for us if I didn't do as he ordered," she said. "He would make sure we were thrown out of the flat and would have to go back. But we have nothing to go back to. And if I had told them, who would have believed me? Who . . . ?"

She paused.

"Except for Robert," Harry said. Waiting.

Harry found the address on Mads Gilstrup's business card. He wanted to pay him a call. And, first of all, ask him why he had called Halvorsen. From the address he saw he would have to drive past Rakel and Oleg, who also lived on Holmenkollen Ridge.

As he passed he didn't slow down, but he did glance up the drive. The last time he drove past he had seen a Jeep Cherokee outside the garage and had assumed it was the doctor's. Now there was only Rakel's car. The window in Oleg's room was lit.

Harry drove up through the hairpin bends between the most expensive houses in Oslo until the road straightened and climbed farther to a brow and past the capital's white obelisk, the Holmenkollen ski jump. Beneath him lay the town and the fjord, with a thin layer of icy mist floating between snow-covered islands. The short day that really consisted of just a sunrise and a sunset blinked, and down there lights were already being switched on, like Advent candles in the countdown to Christmas.

He had almost all the pieces of the jigsaw puzzle now.

After ringing Gilstrup's doorbell four times without any success, Harry gave up. On his way back to the car a man jogged over from a neighboring house and asked Harry if he was a friend of Gilstrup's. Well, he didn't want to intrude into Gilstrup's private life, but he had heard a loud bang inside the house this morning and Mads Gilstrup had lost his wife, hadn't he? Perhaps they ought to call the police? Harry went back to the house, smashed the window beside the front door and an alarm went off.

While the alarm howled its two hoarse tones again and again Harry made his way to the living room. For the benefit of the report he checked his watch and subtracted the two minutes Møller had wound it forward: 3:37.

Mads Gilstrup was naked and the back of his head was missing.

He lay on his side on the parquet floor in front of a lit screen and the rifle with the burgundy stock seemed to be growing out of his mouth. It had a long barrel, and from what Harry could see Mads Gilstrup must have used his big toe to press the trigger. That not only required certain motor coordination skills but also a strong will to die.

Then the alarm stopped and Harry could hear the buzz of the projector, which showed a quivering still of a bride and bridegroom in close-up on their way down the aisle. The faces, the white smile and the white dress were spattered with blood, which had dried on the canvas in a grille pattern.

Stuffed under an empty bottle of Cognac lay the suicide note. It was brief.

Forgive me, Father. Mads.

31

The Resurrection

He regarded himself in the mirror. When one day, maybe next year, they walked out of the little house in Vukovar in the morning, might this face be one the neighbors would greet with a smile and a *zdravo*? The way you greet familiar, safe faces. And good faces.

"Perfect," said the woman behind him.

He assumed she meant the dinner suit he was parading in the mirror of the combined suit-rental and dry-cleaning store.

"How much?" he asked.

He paid her and promised the suit would be returned before twelve o'clock the next day.

Then he walked out into the gray gloom. He had found a café where he could have a coffee and the food wasn't too expensive. Now it was just a question of waiting. He looked at his watch.

The longest night had begun. Dusk was turning houses and fields gray as Harry drove from Holmenkollen, but well before he reached Grønland the gloom had invaded the parks.

He had called the uniforms from Mads Gilstrup's house and told them to send a patrol car. Then he had left without touching anything.

He parked in the garage at Police HQ and went up to his office. From there he phoned Torkildsen.

"Halvorsen's cell has disappeared and I want to know whether Mads Gilstrup left a message on it."

"And if he did?"

"I want to hear the message."

"That's wiretapping and I can't do it." Torkildsen sighed. "Call the Police Answering Service."

"I need a court order for that, and I don't have time. Any suggestions?"

Torkildsen pondered. "Does Halvorsen have a computer?"

"I'm sitting next to it."

"No, no, forget it."

"Why's that?"

"You can access all the messages on a cell via the web page for Telenor Mobil, but of course you'll need his password to do that."

"Is it a password we choose?"

"Yes, but if you don't have it you'll need a lucky break to—"

"Let's try it," Harry said. "What's the address of the web page?"

"You'll need a big break," Torkildsen said, with the tone of someone who was not used to having many of them.

"I have a feeling I know it," Harry said.

With the page up on his screen Harry typed in LEV YAS-HIN. And was informed that the password was incorrect. So he shortened it to YASHIN. And there they were. Eight messages. Six of them from Beate. One from a number in Trøndelag. And one from the cell number on the business card Harry was holding in his hand. From Mads Gilstrup.

Harry clicked on the PLAY button and the voice of the person he had seen less than an hour ago lying dead in his house spoke to him with a metallic twang through the computer's plastic speakers.

When the message was over Harry had the last piece of the puzzle.

"Does anyone know where Jon Karlsen is?" Harry said on his phone to Skarre as he was walking down to the ground floor of Police HQ. "Have you tried Robert's flat?"

Harry went through the door and smacked the bell on the counter in front of him.

"I called there, too," Skarre said. "No answer."

"Go and take a look. If no one opens up, go in, OK?"

"The keys are at Krimteknisk and it's past four now. Beate usually stays until late afternoon, but today, what with Halvorsen and—"

"Forget the keys," Harry said. "Take a crowbar with you."

Harry heard the shuffling of feet and a man in blue overalls, with a very wrinkled face and a pair of glasses on the tip of his nose, hobbled in. Without gracing Harry with a glance he picked up the requisition order Harry placed on the counter.

"Court order?" Skarre questioned.

"Not necessary. The one we've got is still valid," Harry lied.

"Is it?"

"If anyone asks, this was a direct order from me, all right?"

"All right."

The man in blue grunted. Then he shook his head and passed the requisition slip back to Harry.

"I'll call you later, Skarre. Looks like there's a problem

here . . ." Harry put the cell in his pocket and stared quizzically at the blue overalls.

"You can't collect the same gun twice, Hole," the man said.

Harry didn't understand what Kjell Atle Orø meant, but he had a hot prickling sensation at the back of his neck. It was not the first time he had felt it. And he knew it meant the nightmare was not over yet. In fact, it had just begun.

Gunnar Hagen's wife straightened her dress and came out of the bathroom. In front of the hall mirror her husband was trying to do up the black bow tie to go with his dinner jacket. She stood and waited because she knew that soon he would snort with irritation and ask her to help.

This morning, when they called from Police HQ to say that Jack Halvorsen had died, Gunnar had not felt like going to the concert, nor had he thought he would be able to go. She knew it was going to be a week of brooding. Sometimes she wondered whether anyone apart from her knew how hard such incidents hit Gunnar. In any case, later in the day the chief superintendent had asked Gunnar to make an appearance at the concert, since the Salvation Army had decided they were going to mark Jack Halvorsen's death with a minute of silence, and it went without saying that the police should be represented by Halvorsen's superior officer. But she could see he was not looking forward to going; the solemnity of it enveloped his brow like a tight-fitting helmet.

He snorted and ripped off the bow tie. "Lise!"

"I'm here," she said calmly, walked over, stood behind him and stretched out her hand. "Give it to me."

The phone on the table under the mirror rang. He leaned over to pick it up. "Hagen."

She heard a distant voice at the other end.

"Good evening, Harry," Gunnar said. "No, I'm at home.

My wife and I are going to the performance at the concert hall tonight, so I came home early. Anything new?"

Lise Hagen watched the metaphorical, imaginary helmet tightening further as he listened in total silence.

"Yes," he said at length. "I'll call the station and put everyone on full alert. We'll have every officer available involved in the search. I'm going to the concert soon and will be there for a couple of hours, but my cell will be on vibrate mode the whole time, so all you have to do is call."

He hung up.

"What's up?" Lise asked.

"One of my inspectors, Harry Hole, has just come from downstairs at HQ, where he was supposed to be picking up a gun with the requisition order I signed for him today. He needed a replacement for one that went missing after someone broke into his flat. It seems that earlier today someone else picked up the gun and ammunition with the first order slip."

"Well, if that isn't the limit . . ." Lise said.

"Afraid it isn't." Gunnar Hagen sighed. "Unfortunately, there's worse. Harry had a suspicion who it might have been. So he called Forensics and had his suspicion confirmed."

To her horror, Lise saw her husband's face go ashen. As though the repercussions of what Harry had said were only just sinking in as he heard himself telling his wife: "The blood sample of the man we shot at the container terminal shows he is not the man who threw up beside Halvorsen. Or spread blood over his coat. Or left a hair on the pillow at the hostel. In a nutshell, the man we shot is not Christo Stankic. If Harry's right, that means Christo Stankic is still out there. And he's armed."

"But then . . . he might still be after that poor man—what was his name again?"

"Jon Karlsen. Yes. And that's why I have to call the station now and mobilize every officer available to search for both Jon Karlsen and Christo Stankic." He pressed the backs of his hands against his eyes, as though that were the source of the pain. "And Harry received a call from an officer who broke into Robert Karlsen's flat to find Jon."

"Yes?"

"Seems there had been a tussle there. The bed linens . . . were soaked in blood, Lise. And no sign of Jon Karlsen, just a jackknife under the bed with dried black blood on the blade."

He took his hands away from his face and she could see in the mirror that his eyes were red.

"This is bad news, Lise."

"I know, Gunnar, my love. But . . . but who was the person you shot down by the harbor, then?"

Gunnar Hagen swallowed hard before answering. "We don't know, Lise. All we know is that he was living in a container and had heroin in his blood."

"My God, Gunnar . . ."

She squeezed his shoulder and tried to catch his eye in the mirror.

"He was resurrected on the third day," Hagen whispered.

"What?"

"The Redeemer. We killed him on Friday night. Today is Monday. It's the third day."

Martine Eckhoff was so beautiful that she took Harry's breath away.

"Hello, is that you?" she said in that deep alto voice Harry remembered from the first time he had seen her at the Lighthouse. At that time she had been wearing a uniform. Now she stood in front of him in a plain, elegant, sleeveless black dress that glistened like her hair. Her eyes seemed larger and darker than usual. Her skin was white in a delicate, almost transparent, way.

"I'm dolling myself up," she said with a laugh. "Look." She raised her hand in what Harry considered an unimaginably supple movement, like part of a dance, an extension of another equally graceful sequence. In her hand she was holding a white tear-shaped pearl that reflected the frugal light in the hallway outside her flat. The other pearl hung from her ear.

"Come in," she said, retreating a step and letting go of the door. Harry crossed the threshold into her arms. "So good that you came," she said, pulling his face down to hers, breathing hot air into his ear as she whispered, "I've been thinking about you all the time."

Harry closed his eyes, held her tight and felt the warmth emanating from the small, feline body. It was the second time in less than a day that he had stood like this with his arms around her. And he didn't want to let go. Because he knew it would be the last time.

The pearl drop lay against his cheek under one eye, like a frozen tear. He freed himself.

"Is something the matter?" she asked.

"Let's sit down," Harry said. "We have to talk."

They went into the living room and she sat down on the sofa. Harry stood by the window, looking down onto the street below.

"Someone is sitting in a car looking up here," he said.

Martine sighed. "It's Rikard. He's waiting for me. He's driving me to the concert hall."

"Mm. Do you know where Jon is, Martine?" Harry concentrated on the reflection of her face in the windowpane.

"No," she said, meeting his eyes. "Are you trying to say there is a specific reason why I should know? Since you ask in that way, I mean?" The sweetness was gone from her voice.

"We've just broken into Robert's flat, which we think Jon has been using," Harry said, "and found a bed covered in blood."

"I didn't know," Martine said in a tone of surprise that sounded genuine.

"I know you didn't know," Harry said. "Forensics is checking the blood type now. That is to say, it has already been identified. And I'm pretty sure I know their conclusion."

"Jon's?" she said in breathless suspense.

"No," said Harry. "But perhaps that's what you had been hoping?"

"Why do you say that?"

"Since it was Jon who raped you."

The room went quiet. Harry held his breath in order to hear her gasp for air and then, long before it had entered her lungs, exhale it again with a wheeze.

"Why do you think that?" she asked with the tiniest tremor in her voice.

"Because you said it happened in Østgård and there are not so many men who rape. But Jon Karlsen does. The blood in Robert's bed is from a girl named Sofia Miholjec. She went to Robert's flat last night because Jon Karlsen had ordered her to. As agreed, she let herself in with a key she had been given earlier by Robert, her best friend. After raping her, Jon beat her up. She said he often did that."

"Often?"

"According to Sofia, he raped her for the first time one afternoon last summer. It happened in the Miholjec family home while her parents were out. Jon went there under the pretext of examining the flat. After all, that was his job. Just as it was his job to decide who would be allowed to keep the flats."

"You mean . . . he threatened her?"

Harry nodded. "He said the family would be evicted and sent home if Sofia did not do as he ordered and keep their secret. The Miholjecs' fate rested on his, Jon's, discretion. And her compliance. The poor girl didn't dare do anything else. But when she became pregnant she had to find someone to help her. A friend she could trust, someone older who could arrange an abortion without too many questions being asked."

"Robert," Martine said. "My God. She went to Robert."

"Yes. And even though she didn't say anything to him, she thought Robert knew it was Jon. I think so, too. Robert knew Jon had raped before, didn't he?"

Martine did not answer. Instead she coiled up on the sofa, drew her legs in beneath her and wrapped her arms around her bare shoulders, as if she were cold or wanted to disappear inside herself.

When Martine finally began to talk, her voice was so low that Harry could hear the ticking of Møller's watch.

"I was fourteen. While he was doing it I lay there thinking that if I concentrated on the stars I would be able to see them through the roof." Harry listened as she spoke about the hot day in Østgård, the game with Robert and Jon's reproving eyes that were dark with jealousy. And about when the door of the outhouse opened and Jon stood there with his brother's jackknife. The rape and the pain afterward as she was left crying while he went back to the house. And how incomprehensible it was that the birds soon began to sing outside.

"But the worst was not the rape," Martine said with a tear-filled voice but dry cheeks. "The worst was that Jon knew. Knew he didn't even have to make threats to keep me silent. I would never squeal. He knew I knew that even if I produced my shredded clothes and was believed, there would always be a shadow of doubt regarding motive and guilt. And that it was about loyalty. Would I be the one, the daughter of the commander, to drag my parents and the whole Army into a ruinous scandal? All these years, whenever I've observed Jon, he's given me a look that says: 'I know. I know how you shook with terror and cried quietly afterward so that no one would hear you. I know and can see your mute cowardice every single day.'" The first tear rolled down her cheek. "And that's why I hate him so much. Not for raping me; I would have been able to forgive that. But for always going around showing me he knew."

Harry went into the kitchen, tore off a paper towel from the roll, went back and sat down beside her.

"Watch your makeup," he said, passing her the towel. "Prime minister and all that."

She dabbed carefully.

"Stankic has been to Østgård," Harry said. "Was it you who took him there?"

"What are you talking about?"

"He's been there."

"Why do you say that?"

"Because of the smell."

"Smell?"

Harry nodded. "A sweet, perfumelike smell. I recognized it the first time I opened the door to Stankic in Jon's flat. The second time when I was standing in his room in the hostel. And the third time when I woke up in Østgård this morning. The smell was in the blanket." He studied Martine's keyhole-shaped pupils. "Where is he, Martine?"

Martine stood up. "Now I think you should go."

"Answer me first."

"I don't need to answer for something I haven't done."

She had reached the living-room door when Harry caught up with her. He stood in front of her and gripped her shoulders. "Martine . . ."

"I have to go to a concert."

"He killed one of my best friends, Martine."

Her face was closed and hard as she replied. "Perhaps he shouldn't have got in the way."

Harry took his hands away as if burned. "You can't just let Jon Karlsen be killed. What about forgiveness? Isn't that an intrinsic part of the business you're all in?"

"You're the one who thinks that people can change," Martine said. "Not me. And I don't know where Stankic is."

Harry let her go; she went into the bathroom and closed the door. Harry stood waiting.

"And you're wrong about our line of business," Martine called from behind the door. "It's not about forgiveness. We're in the same business as everyone else. Redemption, right?"

Despite the cold, Rikard was standing outside the car leaning against the hood with his arms crossed. He didn't return Harry's nod as the police officer passed.

32

The Exodus

It was six-thirty in the evening, but there was feverish activity in Crime Squad.

Harry found Ola Li by the fax machine. He glanced at the sheet coming through. Sent by Interpol.

"What's going on, Ola?"

"Gunnar Hagen called around and collected the department. Absolutely everyone is here. We're going to get the guy who got Halvorsen."

There was a determination in Li's tone that Harry knew by instinct reflected the atmosphere on the sixth floor that evening.

Harry went into his office, where Skarre was standing behind the desk speaking on the telephone, fast and in a loud voice.

"We can make more trouble for you and your boys than you imagine, Affi. If you don't help me by getting your boys on the street, you will shoot right up to first place on our most-wanted list. Have I made myself clear? So: Croatian, medium height—"

"Blond, crew cut," Harry said.

Skarre looked up and sent Harry a nod. "Blond crew cut. Call me back when you've got something."

He put down the receiver. "Total Band-Aid atmosphere

out there. Everything on two legs is ready to roll. I've never seen anything like it."

"Mm," Harry said. "Still no sign of Jon Karlsen?"

"Zilch. All we know is that his girlfriend, Thea, says they agreed to meet this evening at the concert hall. They're supposed to be sitting in the VIP box."

Harry consulted his watch. "Then Stankic has an hour and a half to see if he can finish off the job."

"How do you figure that?"

"I phoned the concert hall. All the tickets were sold out four weeks ago, and they won't let anyone in without a ticket, not even to the foyer. In other words, once Jon is inside he's safe. Call and check whether Torkildsen is on tap at Telenor. If he is, ask him to trace Karlsen's cell phone. Oh, and make sure we have enough police outside the concert hall, armed and with a description of Stankic. Then call the prime minister's office and make them aware of the extra security measures."

"Me?" Skarre said. "The . . . prime minister's office?"

"Do it," Harry said. "You're a big boy now."

From the office telephone Harry called one of the six numbers he knew by heart.

The other five were: Sis's, his parents' house in Oppsal, Halvorsen's cell, Bjarne Møller's old private number and Ellen Gjelten's disconnected number.

"Rakel here."

"It's me."

He heard an intake of breath. "I thought so."

"Why?"

"Because I was thinking about you." She chuckled. "That's just the way it is. Don't you think?"

Harry closed his eyes. "I wondered about meeting Oleg tomorrow," he said. "As we discussed."

"Great!" she said. "He'll be so pleased. Will you come here and pick him up?" On hearing his hesitation, she added, "We're alone."

Harry both wanted and didn't want to ask what she meant by that.

"I'll try to be there around six," he said.

According to Klaus Torkildsen, Jon Karlsen's cell phone was located to the east of Oslo, in Haugerud or Høybråten.

"That's not much help," Harry said.

After pacing the floors for an hour, from office to office, to hear how the others were doing, Harry put on his jacket and said he was off to the concert hall.

He parked in a restricted area down one of the small streets around Victoria Terrasse, walked past the Ministry for Foreign Affairs and down the broad steps to Ruseløkk-veien and took a right to the concert hall.

People dressed in formal attire hurried through the biting sub-zero temperatures in the large, open square in front of the glass façade. By the entrance stood two broad-shouldered men wearing black coats and earpieces. And there were six uniformed policemen standing at intervals in front of the building and receiving curious looks from shivering concertgoers unaccustomed to seeing Oslo policemen with machine guns.

Harry recognized Sivert Falkeid in one of the uniforms and went over to him.

"I didn't know Delta had been drafted in."

"We haven't been," Falkeid said. "I called the police station and asked if we could be of help. He was your partner, wasn't he?"

Harry nodded, took out a packet of cigarettes from his inside pocket and offered one to Falkeid, who shook his head.

"Jon Karlsen hasn't turned up yet?"

"No," Falkeid said. "And when the prime minister's here we won't be letting anyone else in the VIP box." At that moment two black cars swung in to the square. "Speak of the devil."

Harry watched the prime minister emerging and being led briskly inside. As the front door opened Harry caught a glimpse of the reception committee. He saw David Eckhoff with a broad smile and Thea Nilsen with not such a big smile, both wearing Salvation Army uniforms.

Harry lit his cigarette.

"Fuck, it's cold," Falkeid said. "I've lost feeling in both legs and half my head."

I envy you, thought Harry.

With the cigarette half smoked, the inspector said aloud: "He's not coming."

"Looks like that. We'll have to hope he hasn't already found Karlsen."

"It's Karlsen I'm talking about. He knows the game's up."

Falkeid glanced at the tall detective, whom, at one time, before the rumors of drinking and unruliness reached him, he had considered Delta material. "What sort of game?" he asked.

"Long story. I'm going in. If Jon Karlsen turns up, arrest him."

"Karlsen?" Falkeid looked perplexed. "What about Stankic?"

Harry let go of his cigarette, which fell in the snow at his feet with a hiss.

"Yes," he drawled, as though to himself. "What about Stankic?"

He sat in the dark fingering the coat he had spread across his lap. Hushed harp music issued forth from the speakers. Small cones of light from the spotlights in the ceiling swept across the audience, the purpose of which he assumed was to create a quiver of anticipation for what was to take place onstage in a short while.

The rows in front of him began to stir as a group of a dozen or so guests appeared. A few people attempted to get to their feet but after some whispering and mumbling they sat down again. In this country it seemed you didn't show respect for elected leaders in that particular way. The company was ushered to seats three rows in front of him, which had been unoccupied for the half hour he had been sitting and waiting.

He saw a man in a suit with a wire leading to one ear, but no uniformed police. The police presence outside had not given rise to alarm, either. In fact he had been expecting a greater show of force. After all, Martine had told him the prime minister would be attending the concert. On the other hand, what difference did the number of police make? He was invisible. Even more invisible than usual. Pleased with himself, he cast his eyes around the auditorium. How many hundreds of men were here in dinner suits? He could already imagine the chaos. And the simple but effective getaway. He had popped in the day before and found the escape route. The last thing he did before entering this evening was to check that no one had locked the windows in the men's room. The plain, frosted windows could be pushed outward and were large enough and low enough for a man to escape onto the ledge outside without any problems. From there it was a jump of nine feet onto one of the car roofs in the parking lot. Then on with the coat, onto busy Haakon VII's Gate and two minutes and forty seconds of rapid walking later, he would be on the platform of the National Theatre station, where the airport express stopped every twenty minutes. The train he was aiming for left at 8:19. Before leaving the bathroom, he had put two urinal blocks in his jacket pocket.

He had had to show his ticket a second time to enter the auditorium. He had shaken his head with a smile when the lady had pointed to his coat and asked him something in

Norwegian. She had examined his ticket and shown him to a seat in the VIP box, which, in fact, turned out to be four normal rows in the center of the auditorium cordoned off with red tape for the occasion. Martine had explained where Jon Karlsen and his girlfriend, Thea, would be sitting.

And there they were at last. He glanced at his watch. Six minutes past eight. The concert hall was in semidarkness and the light on the stage was too strong for him to be able to identify anyone in the delegation, but all of a sudden one of the faces was illuminated by a small spotlight. He caught a brief glimpse of a pained, wan face, but he had no doubt: This was the woman he had seen in the back of the car with Jon Karlsen on Gøteborggata.

Ahead of him there seemed to be some confusion regarding seat numbers, but then the situation was resolved and the wall of bodies sank into place. He squeezed the stock of the gun under his coat. There were six bullets in the drum. It was an unfamiliar weapon, with a heavier trigger than a pistol, but he had been practicing all day and had found the threshold for the trigger to release the bullet.

Then, as if in response to an invisible signal, silence descended on the auditorium.

A man in a uniform appeared, welcomed everyone, he supposed, and said something that made everyone stand up. He followed suit and watched the people around him lower their heads in silence. Someone must have died. Then the man at the front said something and everyone sat down.

And then, at long last, the curtain went up.

Harry was standing in the wings, in the dark, watching the curtain rise. The footlights prevented him from seeing the audience, but he felt its presence, like a large animal breathing.

The conductor raised his baton and the Oslo 3rd Corps Choir burst into the song Harry had heard in the citadel.

"Let the flag of redemption wave, onward now to holy war!"

"Excuse me," he heard a voice say, turned and saw a young woman wearing glasses and a headset. "What are you doing here?" she asked.

"Police," Harry said.

"I'm the stage manager and I must ask you not to stand in the way."

"I'm looking for Martine Eckhoff," Harry said. "I was told she was here."

"She's *there*," the stage manager said, pointing to the choir. Harry located her. She was at the back, on the top step, singing with a serious expression, almost one of suffering. As though it were lost love and not fighting and victory she was singing about.

At her side was Rikard. Who, unlike her, had a beatific smile on his lips. His face looked quite different when he was singing. The harsh, repressed features were gone; there was a radiance in his young eyes as though he meant what he was singing from the bottom of his heart: that they would conquer the world for their God, for the cause of compassion and charity.

Harry noticed, to his surprise, that the melody and the lyrics were having an impact.

After they had finished, they received the applause and came toward the side of the stage. Rikard looked at Harry in astonishment, but said nothing. Martine, on catching sight of him, lowered her eyes and tried to skirt around him. But Harry was quick off the mark and stood in front of her.

"I'll give you a last chance, Martine. Please don't throw it away."

She heaved a great sigh. "I don't know where he is. I told you."

Harry grabbed her shoulders and in a hoarse whisper said: "You'll be arrested for aiding and abetting. Do you want to give him the pleasure?"

"Pleasure?" She put on a weary smile. "He won't have any pleasure where he's going."

"And the song you sang? 'Who always shows compassion and is the sinner's true friend.' Does that mean nothing? Are they just words?"

She did not answer.

"I know this is more difficult," Harry said, "than the cheap forgiveness you in your self-glorification hand out at the Lighthouse. A helpless junkie who steals from anonymous people to satisfy his needs, what is that? What is that compared to forgiving someone who does need your forgiveness? A real sinner on the path to hell?"

"Stop it," she sobbed, weakly trying to push him away.

"You can still save Jon, Martine. Then he'll have another chance. Then you'll have another chance."

"Is he bothering you, Martine?" It was Rikard.

Without turning, Harry clenched his right fist and prepared himself while looking into Martine's tear-wet eyes.

"No, Rikard," she said. "It's fine."

Harry listened to Rikard's footsteps dying away as he watched her. Someone began to strum a guitar on the stage. Then a piano came in. Harry recognized the song. The night in Egertorget. And the radio in Østgård. "Morning Song." It seemed like an eternity ago.

"They'll both die if you don't help me stop this," Harry said.

"Why do you say that?"

"Because Jon has a borderline personality disorder and is controlled by his anger. And Stankic is not afraid of anything."

"Are you trying to tell me you're so anxious to save them because it's your job?"

"Yes," Harry said. "And because I promised Stankic's mother."

"Mother? Have you spoken to his mother?"

"I swore I would try to save her son. If I don't stop Stankic now, he'll be shot. Same as at the container terminal. Believe me."

Harry looked at Martine, then turned his back on her and walked away. He had reached the steps when he heard her voice behind him:

"He's here."

Harry froze mid-stride. "What?"

"I gave Stankic your ticket."

At that moment the remaining stage lights came up.

The silhouettes of those in front of him stood out against the shimmering white cascade of light. He sank deeper into his chair, raised his hand slowly, placed the short barrel on the seat in front so that he had a clear line of fire at the dinner-jacket back of the person to the left of Thea. He would shoot twice. Then stand up and fire a third, if necessary. Although he already knew it wouldn't be.

The trigger felt lighter than before, but he knew that was the effect of adrenaline. Nevertheless, he was no longer afraid. Tighter and tighter he squeezed, and now he had reached the point where there was no more resistance, the .5 of a millimeter in the trigger's no-man's-land, where you relaxed and squeezed because there was no way back, you were subject to the inexorable laws and vagaries of the gun's mechanism.

The head on top of the back soon to receive a bullet turned to Thea and said something.

In that instant his brain formed two observations. It was odd that Jon Karlsen was wearing a dinner suit and not the Salvation Army uniform. And the physical distance between Thea and Jon did not make sense. In a concert hall, with loud music playing, two lovers would be nestling up to each other.

In desperation his brain tried to reverse the train

of events he had already set in motion, the finger curled around the trigger.

There was a loud bang.

So loud Harry's ears were ringing from where he was standing.

"What?" he shouted at Martine over the sound of the drummer's sudden attack on the crash cymbal, making Harry temporarily deaf.

"He's sitting in row nineteen, three rows back from Jon and the prime minister. Seat twenty-five. In the middle." She tried to smile, but her lips were trembling too much. "I got you the best seat in the house, Harry."

Harry looked at her. Then he began to run.

Jon Karlsen was trying to make his legs move like the beat of drumsticks on the platform of Oslo Central, but he had never been much of a sprinter. The automatic doors let out protracted sighs, closed again and the shimmering silver airport express set off as Jon arrived. He groaned, put down his suitcase, relinquished the small backpack and slumped down on one of the designer benches on the platform. He kept the black bag on his lap. Ten minutes to the next train. No problem; he had plenty of time. Oceans of time, he had. So much he almost wished he had a bit less. He peered down the tunnel from which the next train would emerge. When Sofia had left Robert's flat and he had finally fallen asleep toward the morning, he had had a dream. A bad dream, in which Ragnhild's eye had transfixed him.

He checked his watch.

Now the concert would have started. And poor Thea would be sitting there without him, and she didn't know a thing. Nor did the others, for that matter. Jon blew on his hands, but the cold temperatures cooled down the moist air so fast that his hands became colder. It had to be done like this—there was no other way. Everything had spiraled out of control; he couldn't risk staying any longer.

It was all his own fault. He had lost control with Sofia last night and he should have foreseen that. All his tensions came spilling out. What made him so mad was the way Sofia had taken everything without a word, without a sound. Just watched him with the same closed, introverted gaze. Like a dumb, sacrificial lamb. Then he had hit her in the face. With a clenched fist. He had grazed the skin on his knuckles and had punched her again. Stupid. So that he wouldn't see her he had turned her face to the wall, and had only calmed down after he had ejaculated. But it was too late. Looking at her before she left, he realized that this time she would not be able to get away with excuses like walking into a door or slipping on ice.

The second reason for his having to escape was the silent phone call he had received yesterday. He had checked. It came from a hotel in Zagreb. Hotel International. He had no idea how they had got hold of his cell number; it wasn't registered anywhere. But he did have a premonition about what it meant: Even though Robert was dead they still had unfinished business. That was not the plan, and he couldn't understand it. Perhaps they would send another man to Oslo. He would have to get away, whatever happened.

The plane ticket he had bought in a desperate hurry was for Bangkok via Amsterdam. And in the name of Robert Karlsen. Like the one he had bought in October. Now, as then, he had his brother's ten-year-old passport in his inside pocket. No one could refute the similarity between him and the person in the photo. All passport officials were aware that things happened to a young person's appearance over ten years.

After buying the ticket, he had gone to Gøteborggata to pack a suitcase and a backpack. There were still ten hours before the plane was scheduled to take off, and he needed to go into hiding. So he had headed for one of the Army's "partly furnished" flats in Haugerud for which he had a key. The flat had been empty for two years and, besides its mold problems, it had a sofa, an armchair with the stuffing coming out of the back and a bed with a stained mattress. This was where Sofia had been ordered to appear every Thursday at 6 p.m. Some of the stains were hers. Others he had made when he was alone. And at those times he had always thought about Martine. It had been like a hunger that had only been satisfied once, and it was that satisfaction he had been searching for ever since. And now he had found it, with the fifteen-year-old Croatian girl.

Then one autumn day an angry Robert had visited him and said Sofia had taken him into her confidence. Jon had been so furious he had almost lost control of himself.

It had been so . . . humiliating. Just like the time when he was thirteen and his father had beaten him with his belt because his mother had found semen stains on his bedsheets.

When Robert had threatened to tell all to the high command of the Salvation Army if he so much as looked in Sofia's direction again, Jon had realized there was one option left. And it was not to stop meeting Sofia. For what neither Robert nor Ragnhild nor Thea understood was that he had to have her; it was the only way he could achieve redemption and true satisfaction. In a couple of years Sofia would be too old and he would have to find someone else. However, until then she would be his little princess, the light of his soul and the flame of his loins, as Martine had been when the magic had worked for the first time in Østgård.

More people arrived on the platform. Perhaps nothing would happen. Perhaps he would just have to wait for a couple of weeks and then could return. Return to Thea. He took out his cell and texted her. DAD's ILL. FLYING TO BANGKOK TONIGHT. I'LL CALL TOMORROW.

He pressed SEND and patted the black bag. Five million

kroner in dollar notes. Dad would be so happy to hear he could pay off the debt and be free at last. I'm carrying the sins of others, he thought. I'll set them free.

He stared into the tunnel, the black eye socket. Eighteen minutes past eight. Where was it?

Where was Jon Karlsen? He scanned the rows of backs in front of him while slowly lowering the revolver. The finger had obeyed and slackened the pressure on the trigger. How close he had been to firing the gun he would never know, but now he knew this: Jon Karlsen was not here. He had not come. That was the reason for the confusion when they were taking their seats.

The music became quieter; the brushes flitted across the drums and the guitar strumming slowed to a stroll.

He saw Jon Karlsen's girlfriend duck down and her shoulders move as if searching for something in her bag. She sat still for a few seconds with bowed head. Then stood up, and he followed her with his eyes as, with jerky, impatient movements, she danced along the row of people standing up and making room. He knew what he had to do.

"Excuse me," he said, getting up. He barely noticed the glares of the people standing up with affected effort and sighs; all he was concerned about was that his last chance to find Jon Karlsen was leaving the auditorium.

Emerging into the foyer, he stopped and heard the padded auditorium door slip back into place as the music died, as if by a flick of the fingers. The woman had not gone far. She was standing by a pillar in the middle of the foyer, texting. Two men in suits stood talking by the other entrance to the auditorium, and two cloakroom attendants were sitting behind the counter staring absentmindedly into the distance. He checked that the coat hanging over his arm still hid the revolver and was about to approach her when he heard the sound of running to his right. He turned in time to see a tall man with reddened cheeks and wild eyes charging toward him. Harry Hole. He knew it was too late; the coat was in the way and he would not be able to get a clear shot. He staggered backward against the wall as the policeman's hand hit him in the shoulder. And watched in amazement as Hole grabbed the handle to the auditorium door, tore it open and was gone.

He leaned back against the wall and squeezed his eyes shut. Then he slowly straightened up, saw the woman pacing with the phone to her ear and a desperate expression on her face, and walked toward her. He faced her, pulled the coat to one side so that she could see the revolver and said in a slow, clear voice: "Please come with me. Otherwise I will have to kill you."

He could see her eyes darken as her pupils dilated with terror and she dropped her cell phone.

It fell and hit the railway track with a thud. Jon looked at the phone, which continued to ring. For a moment, before he saw that it was Thea on the line, he had thought it was the voiceless person from last night calling again. She hadn't said a word, but it had been a woman—he was sure of that now. It had been her; it had been Ragnhild. Stop! What was going on? Was he going crazy? He concentrated on breathing. He mustn't lose control now.

He clung to the black bag as the train glided into the station.

The train doors opened with a puff of air, he boarded, put the suitcase and backpack in the luggage compartment and found an empty seat.

There was a gap in the row of seats like a missing tooth. Harry studied the faces on either side of the empty seat, but they were too old, too young or the wrong gender. He ran to the first seat in row nineteen and crouched down by the old white-haired man sitting there.

"Police. We're—"

"What?" the man shouted with a hand behind his ear.

"Police," Harry said, louder this time. In a row a bit farther forward he noticed a man with a wire behind his ear move and talk to his lapel.

"We're on the lookout for someone who was supposed to be sitting in the middle of this row. Have you seen anyone leave or—"

"What?"

An elderly lady, obviously his companion for the evening, leaned over. "He just left. The auditorium, that is. During the performance . . ." She said the latter in such a way that it was clear she assumed that this was the reason the police wanted to talk to him.

Harry ran up the aisle, pushed open the door, stormed through the foyer and down the stairs to the front doors. He saw the uniformed back outside and shouted from the stairs. "Falkeid!"

Sivert Falkeid turned, saw Harry and opened the door.

"Did a man just come out here?"

Falkeid shook his head.

"Stankic is in the building," Harry said. "Sound the alarm." Falkeid nodded and raised his lapel.

Harry raced back into the foyer, spotted a small red cell phone on the floor and asked the women in the cloakroom if they had seen anyone leaving the auditorium. They looked at each other and answered no in unison. He asked if there were other exits apart from down the stairs to the front doors.

"The emergency exit," one suggested.

"Yes, but the doors make such a noise when they shut we would have heard it," the other one said.

Harry stood by the auditorium door, surveying the foyer from left to right as he tried to figure out escape routes. Had

Stankic really been here? Had Martine told him the truth this time? At that very instant he knew she had. There was that sweet smell in the air again. The man who had been standing in the way when Harry arrived. He knew in an instant where Stankic must have made his getaway.

Harry tore open the door to the men's bathroom and was met by a gust of ice-cold wind from the open window on the far side. He went to the window, looked down at the cornice and the parking lot beneath and thumped the sill with his fist. "Fuck, fuck, fuck."

A sound came from one of the toilet stalls.

"Hello!" Harry shouted. "Is there anyone in there?"

There was that sound again. A sort of sobbing. Harry's eyes ran along the locks on the stall doors and found one with red for "occupied." He threw himself down on his stomach and saw a pair of legs and pumps.

"Police," Harry shouted. "Are you hurt?"

The sobbing ceased. "Has he gone?" asked a tremulous woman's voice.

"Who?"

"He said I had to stay here for fifteen minutes."

"He's gone."

The stall door slid open. Thea Nilsen was sitting on the floor, between the bowl and the wall, with makeup running down her face.

"He said he would kill me if I didn't say where Jon was," she said through her tears. As though to apologize.

"And what did you say?" Harry asked, helping her up onto the toilet lid.

She blinked twice.

"Thea, what did you tell him?"

"Jon texted me," she said, staring without focus at the bathroom walls. "His father's ill, he said. He's flying to Bangkok tonight. Imagine. This evening of all evenings."

"Bangkok? Did you tell Stankic?"

"We were supposed to meet the prime minister this evening," Thea said as a tear rolled down her cheek. "And he didn't even answer me when I called, the . . . the—"

"Thea! Did you tell him Jon was catching a plane this evening?"

She nodded, like a somnambulist, as though none of this had anything to do with her.

Harry rose to his feet and strode into the foyer, where Martine and Rikard were talking to a man Harry recognized as one of the prime minister's bodyguards.

"Call off the alarm," Harry shouted. "Stankic is no longer in the building."

The three of them turned toward him.

"Rikard, your sister is sitting in there. Could you look after her? And, Martine, could you come with me?"

Without waiting for an answer, Harry took her arm and she had to jog to keep up with him down the steps toward the exit.

"Where are we going?" she asked.

"Gardermoen Airport."

"And what are you going to do with me there?"

"You will be my eyes, dear Martine. You will see the invisible man for me."

He studied his facial features in the reflection from the train window. The forehead, the nose, the cheeks, the mouth, the chin, the eyes. Tried to see what it was, where the secret lay. But he couldn't see anything special above the red neckerchief, just an expressionless face with eyes and hair that, against the walls of the tunnel between Oslo Central and Lillestrøm, were as black as the night outside.

33

The Shortest Day

It took Harry and Martine exactly two minutes and thirty-eight seconds to run from the concert hall to the platform of the National Theatre Station, where, two minutes later, they boarded an inter-city train stopping at Oslo Central and Gardermoen Airport on its way to Lillehammer. True, this was a slower train, but it was still faster than waiting for the next airport express. They dropped into the two free seats left in a car full of soldiers on their way home for Christmas leave and groups of students with boxes of wine and Santa hats.

"What's going on?" Martine asked.

"Jon's making his getaway," Harry said.

"Does he know Stankic is alive?"

"He's not fleeing Stankic, but us. He knows his cover is blown."

Martine's eyes widened. "What do you mean?"

"I hardly know where to begin."

The train drew into Oslo Central. Harry scrutinized the passengers on the platform, but did not see Jon Karlsen.

"It all started when Ragnhild Gilstrup offered Jon two million kroner to help Gilstrup Invest buy some of the Salvation Army's properties," Harry said. "He turned her down because he wasn't convinced she was scrupulous enough to keep a secret. Instead he went behind her back and spoke to Mads and Albert Gilstrup. He demanded five million, and they were instructed not to tell Ragnhild about the deal. They agreed."

Martine's mouth fell open. "How do you know this?"

"After Ragnhild's death Mads Gilstrup more or less broke down. He decided to come clean about the whole business. So he called the police—a telephone number on Halvorsen's business card. Halvorsen didn't answer, but Mads left the confession as a voicemail. A few hours ago I played the message. Among many other things, he said Jon demanded a written agreement."

"Jon likes things to be neat and tidy," Martine muttered. The train pulled out of the station, past the stationmaster's Villa Valle and into east Oslo's gray landscape of backyards with wrecked bikes, bare clotheslines and soot-black windows.

"But what does this have to do with Stankic?" she asked. "Who took out the contract? Mads Gilstrup?"

"No."

They were sucked into the tunnel's black void, and in the dark her voice was barely audible above the rattle of the train on the rails. "Was it Rikard? Say it wasn't Rikard . . ."

"Why do you think it's Rikard?"

"The night Jon raped me Rikard found me in the outhouse. I said I had tripped in the dark, but I could see he didn't believe me. He helped me get to bed without waking any of the others. Even though he has never said anything, I've always had the feeling that he saw Jon and knows what happened."

"Mm," Harry said. "So that's why he's so protective. Rikard seems to like you, and it's genuine."

She nodded. "I suppose that's why I . . ." she began, then paused.

"Yes?"

"Why I don't want it to be him."

"In that case your wish is granted." Harry checked his watch. Fifteen minutes until they arrived.

With a look of alarm, Martine suddenly said, "You . . . you don't think?"

"What?"

"You don't think that my father knew about the rape, do you? That he . . ."

"No, your father has nothing to do with any of this. The person who took out the contract on Jon Karlsen . . ."

They were out of the tunnel; a black, starry sky hung over white, phosphorescent fields.

". . . is Jon Karlsen."

Jon entered the vast departures hall. He had been here before, but had never seen as many people as there were now. The noise of voices, feet and announcements rose to the steeple-high vaulted ceiling. An excited cacophony, a hodgepodge of languages and fragments of opinions he didn't understand. Home for Christmas. Going away for Christmas. Seemingly motionless lines at the check-in counters coiled around and between the barriers like over-fed boa constrictors.

Take a deep breath, he told himself. Plenty of time. They don't know anything. Not yet. Maybe they never will. He stood behind an elderly lady and bent down to help her move her suitcase as the line shuffled forward five inches. When she turned to him with a smile of gratitude he could see that her skin was only a thin, deathly pale fabric stretched over a bony skull.

He returned the smile, and at length she looked away again. But through the noise of living people he could always hear her scream. The unbearable, unending scream struggling to drown out the roar of an electric motor.

After being taken to the hospital and finding out that the police were searching his flat, he had realized they might stumble on the contract with Gilstrup Invest in his desk. The one that stated that Jon would receive five million kroner if the Salvation Army board of directors supported the offer, signed by Albert and Mads Gilstrup. After the police had driven him to Robert's flat he had gone to Gøteborggata to collect the contract. But when he arrived, someone was already there: Ragnhild. She hadn't heard him because of the vacuum cleaner. She was sitting down reading the contract. She had seen. Seen his sins, as his mother had seen the semen stains on the bedding. And, like his mother, Ragnhild would humiliate him, destroy him, tell everyone. Tell his father. She mustn't see. I took her eye, he thought. But she is still screaming.

"Beggars don't say no to charity," Harry said. "It's in the very nature of things. That was what struck me in Zagreb. Quite literally. A Norwegian twenty-krone coin that was hurled at me. And as I watched it spinning on the floor I remembered the Crime Scene Unit had found a Croatian coin trodden into the snow outside the shop on the corner of Gøteborggata. They automatically connected it with Stankic, who had been escaping that way while Halvorsen lay bleeding farther up the street. I am by inclination a doubter, but when I saw this coin in Zagreb it was as though a higher authority wanted to make me aware of something. The first time I met Jon, a beggar threw a coin at him. I remember because I was surprised that a beggar would reject charity. Yesterday I tracked down the beggar at the Deichmanske Library and showed him the coin the Crime Scene Unit had found. He confirmed he had hurled a foreign coin at Jon and that it could well have been the one I showed him. Yes, it could indeed have been that one, he said."

"So Jon must have been to Croatia at some point. But that's not illegal."

"Not at all. Yet he told me he had never been abroad

in his life, except to Denmark and Sweden. I checked with the passport office, and no passport has ever been issued in Jon Karlsen's name. However, a passport had been issued to Robert Karlsen almost ten years ago."

"Maybe Jon got the coin from Robert?"

"You're right," Harry said. "The coin proves nothing. But it makes sluggish brains like mine think a little. What if Robert never went to Zagreb? What if it had been Jon who went? Jon had keys to all the Salvation Army's rental flats, including Robert's. What if he had borrowed Robert's passport, traveled to Zagreb in his name and pretended to be Robert Karlsen when he arranged the hit on Jon Karlsen? And the plan had always been to kill Robert?"

Martine chewed a nail, deep in thought. "But if Jon wanted to kill Robert, why take out a contract on yourself?"

"To give yourself the perfect alibi. Even if Stankic was arrested and confessed, Jon would never be suspected. He was the intended victim. Jon and Robert swapping shifts on that day of all days would be seen as the hand of fate. Stankic was merely following instructions. And when Stankic, and Zagreb, discovered later that they had killed their own customer, there would be no reason for them to fulfill the contract by killing Jon. After all, there was no one to pay the bill. In fact that was part of the genius of the plan. Jon could promise Zagreb as much money as they wanted after the event, as there would be no billing address. And the one person who could have refuted that Robert was in Zagreb that day or who might have had an alibi for the date the contract was signed—Robert Karlsen—was dead. The plan was like a circle of logic that worked, the illusion of a snake eating itself, a self-destructing creation that would guarantee nothing would be left afterward, no loose threads."

"A man of ordered habits," Martine said.

Two of the male students had started singing a drinking song: a two-voice experiment, accompanied by the loud snoring of one of the recruits.

"But why?" Martine asked. "Why would he kill Robert?"

"Because Robert represented a threat. According to Sergeant Major Rue, Robert supposedly threatened Jon that he would 'destroy' him if he ever approached a certain woman again. The first thing that came to my mind was that they were talking about Thea. But you were right when you said that Robert did not entertain any special feelings for her. Jon claimed Robert had a sick obsession with Thea so that it would seem as though Robert had a motive for wishing to kill Jon. The threat that Robert made, however, concerned Sofia Miholjec. A Croatian girl of fifteen who has just told me everything. How Jon forced her to have sex with him on regular occasions, saying he would evict her family from the Salvation Army flat and have them thrown out of the country if she put up any resistance or told anyone. When she became pregnant, however, she went to Robert, who helped her and promised to stop Jon. Unfortunately Robert did not go straight to the police or those in command in the Salvation Army. He must have considered it a family affair and wanted to solve the problem within the organization. I gather there's a bit of a tradition of that in the Salvation Army."

Martine was staring out at the snow-covered, night-faded fields rolling by like the swell of the sea.

"So that was the plan," she said. "What went wrong?"

"What always goes wrong," Harry said. "The weather."

"The weather?"

"If the flight to Zagreb had not been canceled because of snow that night, Stankic would have traveled home, found out that they had killed their go-between by mistake and the story would have finished there. Instead Stankic had to spend a night in Oslo and he discovered he killed the wrong person. But he didn't know that Robert Karlsen was also the name of the go-between, so he continued his hunt."

The loudspeaker announced: "Gardermoen Airport,

Gardermoen. Passengers, please disembark on the right-hand side."

"And now you're going to catch Stankic."

"That's my job."

"Will you kill him?"

Harry looked at her.

"He killed your colleague," Martine said.

"Did he say that to you?"

"I said I didn't want to know anything, so he didn't say a word."

"I'm a policeman, Martine. We arrest people and the court sentences them."

"Is that so? Then why haven't you sounded a full alarm? Why haven't you called the airport police? Why isn't the Special Forces Unit on its way, with all its sirens blaring? Why are you on your own?"

Harry didn't answer.

"No one else even knows what you've just told me, do they?"

Harry saw the designer-smooth, gray cement platform of Gardermoen Airport approach through the train window.

"Our stop," he said.

34

The Crucifixion

There was one person between him and the check-in counter when he smelled it. A sweet soap smell that vaguely reminded him of something. Something that had happened not too long ago. He closed his eyes and tried to pinpoint what.

"Next, please!"

Jon shuffled forward, put the suitcase and backpack on the conveyor belt and placed his ticket and passport on the counter in front of a suntanned man wearing the airline's white short-sleeved shirt.

"Robert Karlsen," the man said, eyeing Jon, who confirmed with a nod. "Two bags. And that's carry-on luggage?" He gestured toward the black bag.

"Yes."

The man flipped through the pages, typed, and a hissing printer spat out tags marked BANGKOK for the luggage. That was when Jon remembered the smell. For one second in the doorway of his flat, the last second he had felt safe. The man standing outside who said in English he had a message, then raised a black pistol. He forced himself not to look.

"Have a good trip, Herr Karlsen," the man said with an ultra-swift smile, handing over his boarding pass and the passport.

Jon walked without delay to security. Putting the ticket in his inside pocket, he snatched a glimpse over his shoulder.

He looked straight at him. For one desperate instant he wondered whether Jon Karlsen had recognized him, but then Jon's gaze moved on. What worried him, however, was that Karlsen appeared frightened.

He had been a little too slow to catch Karlsen at the check-in desk. And now he was in a hurry because Karlsen was already lining up at security, where everything and everyone was screened and a revolver was impossible to conceal. It had to happen on this side.

He breathed in and tightened and slackened his grip on the gunstock inside his coat.

His instinct was to shoot the target on the spot, his usual practice. But even though he could soon disappear into the crowd, they would close the airport and check everyone's identities, and he would not only miss his flight to Copenhagen in forty-five minutes but lose his freedom for the next twenty years.

He moved toward Jon Karlsen's back. It had to happen with speed and decisiveness. He would go up to him, thrust the gun in his ribs and give him the ultimatum in plain, concise terms. Thereafter lead him calmly through the jam-packed departures hall into the parking garage, behind a car, a shot to the head, body under the car, lose the gun between there and security, Gate 32, plane to Copenhagen.

He already had the gun out halfway and was two steps away, when Karlsen stepped out of the line and with long strides made for the other end of the departures hall. *Do vraga!* He turned to follow, forcing himself not to run. He hasn't seen you, he kept repeating to himself.

Jon told himself not to run, that it would make it obvious he knew he had been seen. He had not recognized the face, but he didn't need to. The man was wearing the red neckerchief. On the stairs down to the arrivals hall Jon felt the sweat coming. At the bottom he turned back on himself, and when he was out of sight from those on the staircase, he placed the bag under his arm and began to run. The faces in front of him flashed past, with Ragnhild's empty eye socket and unstoppable screams. He ran down another staircase, and now there was no one around him anymore, just cold, damp air and the echo of his own footsteps and breathing in a broad corridor sloping downward. He realized he was in the corridor leading to the parking garage and hesitated for a moment to stare into the black eye of a surveillance camera, as if that could give him the answer. Farther ahead he saw a neon sign over a door like a living image of himself: a man standing erect and helpless. The men's restroom. A hiding place. Out of sight. He could lock himself in. Wait until the plane was about to leave before coming out.

He heard an echo of rapid footsteps coming closer. He ran to the restroom, opened the door and stepped inside. The white light that was reflected toward him was how he imagined heaven would reveal itself to a dying man. Bearing in mind the isolated location of the restroom, he thought it absurdly spacious. Rows of unoccupied white bowls stood in line, waiting along one wall, while stalls of the same white hue lined the other. He heard the door glide to behind him and close with a metallic click.

The air in the cramped monitoring room at Gardermoen Airport was unpleasantly warm and dry.

"There," Martine said, pointing.

Harry and the two security guards in the chairs faced her first, then the wall of screens she was pointing at.

"Which one?" Harry asked.

"There," she said, walking over to the monitor showing an empty corridor. "I saw him pass by. I'm positive it was him."

"That's the surveillance camera in the corridor to the parking garage," one of the guards said.

"Thanks," Harry said. "I'll handle this from here."

"Hang on," the guard said. "This is an international airport and you may have police ID but you need authorization to . . ."

He stopped in his tracks. Harry had drawn a revolver from his waistband and was weighing it in his hand. "Can we say this authority is valid until further notice?"

Harry didn't wait for an answer.

Jon had heard someone enter the restroom. But all he could hear now was the flush of water in the white tear-shaped bowls outside the stall in which he had locked himself.

Jon was sitting on the toilet lid. The stalls were open at the top, but the doors went right down to the floor so he didn't have to pull up his legs.

Then the flush stopped and he heard a splash. Someone was peeing.

Jon's first thought was that it couldn't have been Stankic. No one could be so cold-blooded that they would think about urinating before committing murder. His second was that Sofia's father may have been right about the little redeemer you could hire for peanuts at Hotel International in Zagreb: He was fearless.

Jon clearly heard the swish of a fly being zipped up, and then the white porcelain orchestra's water music started up again.

It stopped as if at the command of a baton, and he heard running water from a tap. A man was washing his hands. With scrupulous care. The tap was turned off. Then more steps. The door creaked. The metallic click.

Jon slumped in a heap on the toilet lid with the bag in his lap. There was a knock at the stall door.

Three light taps, but with the sound of something hard.

Like steel. The blood seemed to refuse to enter his brain. He didn't stir, just closed his eyes and held his breath. But his heart was pounding. He had read somewhere that some predators have ears that can pick up the sound of a victim's frightened heart—in fact that was how they found them. Apart from his heartbeat, the silence was total. He shut his eyes tight and thought that if he concentrated he would be able to see through the roof and catch sight of the cold, clear starry sky, see the planet's invisible but comforting plan and logic, see the meaning of everything.

Then came the inevitable crash.

Jon felt the air pressure against his face and for a moment believed it was from a gunshot. He opened his eyes with caution. Where the lock had been were now splinters of wood, and the door was hanging at an angle.

The man before him had opened his coat. Underneath he was wearing a dinner jacket and a shirt that was the same dazzling white as the walls behind him. Around his neck was a red neckerchief.

Dressed for a party, thought Jon.

He inhaled the smell of urine and freedom as he looked down at the skulking figure before him. An ungainly young man scared out of his wits, sitting and shaking as he waited for death. Under any other circumstances he would have wondered what this man with the turbid blue eyes might have done. But for once he knew. And for the first time since the Christmas dinner in Dalj, this would give him personal satisfaction. And he was no longer frightened.

Without lowering the revolver he glanced at his watch. Thirty-five minutes before the departure of the plane. He had seen the camera outside. Which meant there were probably surveillance cameras in the parking garage, too. It would have to be done here. Pull him out and into the next stall, shoot him, lock the stall from the inside and climb out. They wouldn't find Jon Karlsen before the airport was closed for the night.

"Come out!" he said.

Karlsen seemed to be in a trance and did not move. He cocked the gun and took aim. Karlsen inched out of the stall. Stopped. Opened his mouth.

"Police. Drop the gun."

Harry held the revolver with both hands and pointed it at the man with the red silk neckerchief as the door closed with a metallic click behind him.

Instead of putting down the gun, the man held it to Jon Karlsen's head and said in accented English that Harry recognized: "Hello, Harry. Do you have a good line of fire?"

"Perfect," Harry said. "Right through the back of your head. Drop the gun, I said."

"How can I know if you're holding a gun, Harry? I've got yours, don't I."

"I've got one that belonged to a colleague." Harry saw his finger squeezing the trigger. "Jack Halvorsen's. The one you stabbed on Gøteborggata."

Harry saw the man stiffen.

"Jack Halvorsen," Stankic repeated. "What makes you think it was me?"

"Your DNA in the vomit. Your blood on his coat. And the witness standing in front of you."

Stankic nodded slowly. "I see. I killed your colleague. But if you believe that, why haven't you already shot me?"

"Because there's a difference between you and me," Harry said. "I'm not a murderer but a policeman. So if you put that revolver down I'll only take half of your remaining life. About twenty years. Your choice, Stankic." Harry's arm muscles were already beginning to ache.

"Tell him!"

Harry realized Stankic had shouted this to Jon when he saw Jon start.

"Tell him!"

Jon's Adam's apple bobbed up and down like a float. Then he shook his head.

"Jon?" Harry said.

"I can't . . ."

"He'll shoot you, Jon. Talk."

"I don't know what you want me to—"

"Listen, Jon," Harry said without taking his eyes off Stankic. "None of what you say with a pistol to your head can be used against you in a court of law. Do you understand? Right now you have nothing to lose." The hard, smooth surfaces of the room created an unnaturally clear and loud sound reproduction of metal in motion and the tensing of springs as the man in the dinner jacket cocked the revolver.

"Stop!" Jon held up his arms in front of him. "I'll tell you everything." Jon met the policeman's eyes over Stankic's shoulder. And saw that he already knew. Perhaps he had known for a long time. The policeman was right: He had nothing to lose. None of what he said could be used against him. And the strange thing was that he wanted to talk. In fact, there was nothing he would rather do.

"We were standing by the car waiting for Thea," Jon said. "The policeman was listening to a message left on his cell phone. I could hear it was from Mads. And then I knew when the policeman said it was a confession and he was going to call you. I knew my number would be up. I had Robert's jackknife on me and I reacted out of instinct."

In his mind's eye he could see himself struggling to hold the policeman's arms in a lock behind his back, but the policeman had managed to get one hand free and place it between the knife blade and his throat. Jon had slashed and slashed at the hand without getting near the carotid artery.

Furious, he had swung the policeman to the left and the right like a rag doll as he kept stabbing, and in the end the knife had sunk into his chest, and a sigh had seemed to run through the policeman's body and his arms went limp. He had picked up the cell phone from the ground and stuffed it into his pocket. All that remained was to give him the coup de grâce.

"But Stankic got in the way, didn't he?" Harry asked.

Jon had raised the knife to cut the throat of the unconscious policeman when he heard someone shouting in a foreign language, looked up and saw a man in a blue jacket running toward him.

"He had a pistol, so I had to get away," Jon said, feeling the purging effect of his confession, the lifting of a burden. And he saw Harry nod, saw that the tall blond man understood. And forgave him. And he was so moved that he felt his throat constrict with emotion as he continued. "He fired a shot at me as I ran inside. Almost hit me as well. He was going to kill me, Harry. He's a crazy murderer. You have to shoot him, Harry. We have to take him out, you and I . . . we . . ."

He watched Harry lower his revolver and put it in his trouser waistband.

"What . . . what are you doing, Harry?"

The tall policeman buttoned up his coat. "I'm taking my Christmas leave, Jon. Thank you for the confession."

"Harry? Wait . . ." The certainty of his imminent fate had absorbed all the moisture in his throat and mouth, and the words had to be forced out by dry mucous membranes. "We can share the money, Harry. Listen, all three of us can share it. No one will need to know."

But Harry had already turned to address Stankic in English. "I think you'll find there's enough money in the bag for several of you at Hotel International to build a house in Vukovar. And your mother may want to donate some to the apostle in Saint Stephen's Cathedral, too."

"Harry!" Jon's scream was hoarse, like a death rattle. "Everyone deserves another chance, Harry!"

With his hand on the door handle, the policeman paused.

"Look into the depths of your heart, Harry. You must find some forgiveness there!"

"The problem is . . ." Harry rubbed his chin. "I'm not in the forgiveness business."

"What!" exclaimed Jon, in astonishment.

"Redemption, Jon. Redemption. That's what I go in for. Me, too."

After hearing the door close behind Harry with a metallic click and seeing the man in the dinner jacket raise the gun, Jon stared into the black eye of the muzzle and the fear had become a physical pain, and he no longer knew whose the screams were: Ragnhild's, his own or those of others. But before the bullet smashed through his forehead Jon Karlsen had time to arrive at one realization that had hatched after years of doubt, shame and desperate prayer: that no one would hear either his screams or his prayers.

PART FIVE

Epilogue

35

Guilt

Harry emerged from the subway in Egertorget. It was the day before Christmas Eve and people were hurrying past him in search of the last presents. Nevertheless, Yuletide serenity seemed to have settled over the town already. You could see it in people's faces, the smiles of contentment because Christmas preparations were over or the smiles of weary resignation. A man in matching down jacket and trousers waddled past like an astronaut, grinning and blowing frosted breath from round, pink cheeks. Harry saw one desperate face, though. A pale woman dressed in a thin, black leather jacket with holes in the elbows standing by the jeweler's and hopping from one foot to the other.

The face of the young man behind the counter lit up when he caught sight of Harry; he hurriedly dealt with his customer and darted into the back room. He came back with Harry's grandfather's watch, which he placed on the counter with an expression of pride.

"It's working," Harry said, impressed.

"Everything can be repaired," the young man said. "Just make sure you don't overwind it. That wears down the mechanisms. Try and I'll show you."

As Harry wound the watch he could feel the rough friction against the metal parts and the resistance of the spring. And he noticed the rapt attention of the young man.

"Excuse me," the young man asked, "but may I ask where you got hold of that watch?"

"I was given it by my grandfather," Harry answered, taken aback by the sudden reverence in the watch repairer's voice.

"Not that one. *That* one." The young man pointed to Harry's wrist.

"I was given it by my former boss when he resigned."

"My goodness." The young watch repairer leaned over Harry's left arm and examined the wristwatch with great care. "It's genuine, no doubt about it. That was a generous gift."

"Oh? Is there anything special about it?"

The watch repairer looked at Harry in disbelief. "Don't you know?"

Harry shook his head.

"It's a Lange One Tourbillon made by A. Lange and Söhne. On the back you'll find a serial number that tells you how many units of this model were made. If my memory serves me well, there were a hundred and fifty. You're wearing one of the most beautiful timepieces that has ever been made. In fact, the question is whether it is wise to wear it. With the market price the way it is now, strictly speaking, it should be in a bank vault."

"Bank vault?" Harry eyed the anonymous-looking watch that a few days ago he had thrown out the bedroom window. "It doesn't seem very exclusive."

"But that's what it is. It's only available with the standard black watch strap and the gray face, and there's not a single diamond or ounce of gold in the watch. It does look like standard steel, platinum—it's true. However, its value lies in the fact that this is workmanship that has been elevated to the level of art."

"I see. How much would you say this watch is worth?"

"I don't know. At home I have some catalogs of auction prices for rare watches. I could bring them in sometime."

"Just give me a round figure," Harry said.

"A round figure?"

"An idea."

The young man stuck out his lower lip and moved his head from side to side. Harry waited.

"Well, I wouldn't sell it for less than four hundred thousand."

"Four *hundred* thousand kroner?" Harry exclaimed.

"No, no," said the young man. "Four hundred thousand dollars."

Back outside the jeweler's shop, Harry no longer felt the cold. Nor the heavy drowsiness that remained in his body after twelve hours of sound sleep. Nor did he notice the hollow-eyed woman with the thin leather jacket and the junkie glaze come over to ask him whether he was the policeman she had spoken to a few days before, and whether he knew anything about her son, whom no one had seen for four days.

"Where was he last seen?" Harry asked mechanically.

"Where do you think?" the woman said. "In Plata, of course."

"What's his name?"

"Kristoffer. Kristoffer Jørgensen. Hello! Is anyone at home?"

"What?"

"You look like you're on a trip, man."

"Sorry. You'd better take a photo of him to the main police station, ground floor, and report him missing."

"Photo?" She gave a shrill laugh. "I've got a photo of him from when he was seven. Do you think that will do?"

"Don't you have anything more recent?"

"And who do you think would have taken it?"

Harry found Martine at the Lighthouse. The café was closed, but the receptionist at the hostel had let Harry in around the back.

She was standing with her back to him in the clothing

store, emptying the washing machine. He coughed quietly so as not to frighten her.

Harry was watching her shoulder blades and neck muscles when she turned around and he wondered where she had this suppleness from. And whether she would always have it. She stood up, tilted her head, brushed away a wisp of hair and smiled.

"Hi, the one they call Harry."

She was standing a step away from him with her arms down by her sides. He had a good look at her. At the winter-pale skin that still had this strange glow. The sensitive, flared nostrils, the unusual eyes with pupils that had spilled over, making them resemble partial lunar eclipses. And at the lips that she unconsciously curled inside, moistened and then pressed against each other, soft and wet, as though she had just kissed herself. The drum of the tumble dryer rumbled.

They were alone. She took a deep breath and leaned back her head a tiny bit. She was a step away.

"Hi," Harry said. Without moving.

She blinked twice in quick succession. Then she sent him a fleeting, somewhat bewildered smile, turned to the countertop and started folding clothes.

"I'll be finished soon. Will you wait?"

"I have reports to finish before the holidays start."

"We're putting on a Christmas dinner here tomorrow," she said, half-turning. "Would you like to come and help?"

He shook his head.

"Other plans?"

Today's *Aftenposten* lay open on the countertop beside her. They had devoted a whole page to the Salvation Army soldier who had been found dead in the restroom at Gardermoen Airport last night. The newspaper quoted Chief Inspector Gunnar Hagen, who said the gunman and the motive were as yet unknown, but they thought the case was connected with the previous week's killing in Egertorget.

Since the two murder victims were brothers and police

suspicions were now concentrated on an unidentified Croatian, the day's newspapers had already begun to speculate whether the background could be a family feud. *Verdens Gang* drew attention to the fact that many years ago the Karlsen family had taken their vacations in Croatia, and with the Croatian tradition of blood vengeance this explanation seemed a possibility. The article in *Dagbladet* warned against prejudices and lumping Croatians with criminal elements among Serbians and Kosovar Albanians.

"I've been invited by Rakel and Oleg," he said. "I've just been up there with a present for Oleg and they asked then."

"They?"

"She."

Martine continued to fold clothes while nodding, as though he had said something that needed to be thought through.

"Does that mean that you two . . . ?"

"No," Harry said. "It doesn't mean that."

"Is she still with that other guy, then? The doctor."

"As far as I know."

"Haven't you asked?" He could hear that a wounded anger had crept into her voice.

"That's nothing to do with me. I'm told he's going to celebrate Christmas with his parents. That's all. And you're going to be here?"

She nodded in silence, and went on folding.

"I came to say good-bye," he said. She nodded, but didn't turn.

"Good-bye," he said.

She stopped folding. He could see her shoulders heaving.

"You will understand," he said. "You might not think so now, but in time you'll understand that it couldn't have been . . . any different."

She turned. Her eyes brimmed with tears. "I know, Harry. But I wanted it anyway. For a while. Would that have been asking so much?"

"No." Harry gave a wry smile. "A while would have been great. But it's better to say good-bye now than to wait until it hurts."

"It already hurts, though, Harry." The first tear rolled.

Had Harry not known what he did about Martine Eckhoff he would have considered it impossible for such a young woman to know what it was to hurt. Instead he reflected on what his mother had once said when she was in the hospital. There was only one thing emptier than having lived without love, and that was having lived without pain.

"I'm going now, Martine."

And so he did. He walked to the car parked by the curb and banged on the side window. It slid down.

"She's a big girl now," he said. "So I'm not sure she needs such close attention anymore. I know you'll continue anyway, but I wanted to say that. And wish you a Merry Christmas and good luck."

Rikard seemed to be about to say something, but made do with a nod.

Harry started walking toward the Akerselva. He could already feel that the weather was becoming milder.

Halvorsen was buried on December 27. It was raining; melted snow ran in fast-flowing streams down the streets and the snow in the cemetery was gray and heavy.

Harry was a pallbearer. In front of him was Jack's younger brother. Harry recognized the gait.

Afterward they gathered in Valkyrien, a popular pub better known as Valka.

"Come here," Beate said, taking Harry away from the others and over to a table in the corner. "Everyone was there," she said.

Harry nodded. Refraining from saying what was on his mind: Bjarne Møller wasn't there. No one had even heard from him.

"There are a couple of things I have to know, Harry. Since this case has not been solved."

He looked at her. Her face was pale and lined with grief. He knew she wasn't a teetotaler, but she had Farris mineral water in her glass. Why? he wondered. If he could have stood it, he would have anesthetized himself with anything he could have got his hands on today.

"The case isn't closed, Beate."

"Harry, don't you think I've got eyes in my head? The case has been passed over to an idiot and an incompetent Kripos officer, who shift piles of papers and scratch heads they haven't got."

Harry shrugged.

"But you solved the case, didn't you, Harry? You know what happened; you just don't want to tell anyone."

Harry sipped his coffee.

"Why, Harry? Why is it so important no one knows?"

"I had decided to tell you," he said. "When some time had passed. It wasn't Robert who took out the contract in Zagreb. It was Jon."

"Jon?" Beate gaped at him in amazement.

Harry told her about the coin and Espen Kaspersen.

"But I had to know for sure," he said. "So I did a deal with the only person who could identify Jon as the person who had been in Zagreb. I gave Stankic's mother Jon's cell phone number. She called him the evening he raped Sofia. She said that Jon spoke Norwegian at first, but when she didn't answer, he spoke English and said, 'Is that you?' obviously thinking it was the little redeemer. She called me afterward and confirmed it was the same voice that she had heard in Zagreb."

"Was she absolutely certain?"

Harry nodded. "The expression she used was 'quite sure.' Jon had an unmistakable accent, she said."

"And what was your part of the deal?"

"To make sure her son was not shot dead by our guys."

Beate took a large swig of Farris as though the information needed to be washed down.

"Did you promise that?"

"I did," Harry said. "And here's the part I was going to tell you. It wasn't Stankic who killed Halvorsen. It was Jon Karlsen."

She stared at him open-mouthed. Then tears filled her eyes and she whispered with bitterness in her voice: "Is that true, Harry? Or are you saying that to make me feel better? Because you believe I couldn't have lived with the knowledge that the perpetrator had got away?"

"Well, we have the jackknife that was found under the bed in Robert's flat the day after Jon raped Sofia there. If you ask someone on the q.t. to examine the blood to see if it matches Halvorsen's DNA, I think you'll have peace of mind."

Beate gazed into her glass. "I know it says in the report that you were in the restroom and that you didn't see anyone there. Do you know what I think? I think you did see Stankic, but you didn't make a move to stop him."

Harry didn't answer.

"I think the reason you didn't tell anyone you knew that Jon was guilty was you didn't want anyone to intervene before Stankic had carried out his mission. To kill Jon Karlsen." Beate's voice quivered with anger. "But if you think I'm going to thank you for that, you're wrong." She slammed the glass down on the table, and a couple of the others peered over in their direction. Harry kept his mouth shut and waited.

"We're police officers, Harry. We maintain law and order—we don't judge. And you're not my personal fucking redeemer—have you got that?" Her breathing was labored and she ran the back of her hand across her cheeks, where tears were beginning to flow.

"Are you finished?" asked Harry.

"Yes," she said with a stubborn glare.

"I don't know all the reasons for why I did what I did," Harry said. "The brain is a singular piece of machinery. You may be right. I may have set everything up to happen as it did. But, if that was the case, I want you to know that I didn't do it for your redemption, Beate." Harry drained his coffee in one swig and stood up. "I did it for mine."

In the time between Christmas Day and New Year's Eve the streets were washed clean by the rain, the snow disappeared entirely and when the New Year dawned a few degrees below freezing with feathery snow, the winter seemed to have been given a new and better start. Oleg had received slalom skis for Christmas and Harry took him up to the Wyller downhill slope and started with snowplow turns. On the way home in the car after the third day on the slope Oleg asked Harry if they couldn't do the gates soon.

Harry saw Lund-Helgesen's car parked in front of the garage so he dropped Oleg at the bottom of the drive, headed home, lay on the sofa staring at the ceiling and listened to records. Old ones.

In the second week of January, Beate announced that she was pregnant. She would be giving birth to her and Halvorsen's baby in the summer. Harry thought back and wondered how blind you could be.

Harry had a lot of time to think in January, since the part of humanity that lives in Oslo had decided to take a break from killing one another. So he considered whether to let Skarre move in with him in 605, the Clearing House. He considered what he should do with the rest of his life. And he considered whether you ever found out if you had made the right decisions while you were still alive.

It was the end of February before Harry bought a plane ticket to Bergen.

In the town of the seven mountains it was still autumn and snow-free, and on Fløyen Mountain, Harry had the impression that the cloud enveloping them was the same as on the previous visit. He found him at a table in the Fløyen Folkerestaurant.

"I was told this is where you sit these days," Harry said.

"I've been waiting," said Bjarne Møller, drinking up. "You took your time."

They went outside and stood by the railing at the vantage point. Møller seemed even paler and thinner than last time. His eyes were clear, but his face was bloated and his hands trembled. Harry guessed it was because of pills rather than alcohol.

"I didn't understand what you meant at first," Harry said. "When you said I should follow the money."

"Wasn't I right?"

"Yes," Harry said. "You were right. But I thought you were talking about my case. Not about you."

"I was talking about all cases, Harry." The wind blew long strands of hair in and out of Møller's face. "By the way, you didn't tell me if Gunnar Hagen was pleased with the outcome of your case. Or, to be more precise, the lack of outcome."

Harry shrugged. "David Eckhoff and the Salvation Army were spared an embarrassing scandal that could have damaged their reputation and their work. Albert Gilstrup lost his only son and a daughter-in-law and had a contract canceled that might have saved the family fortune. Sofia Miholjec and her family are going back to Vukovar. They have received support from a newly established local benefactor to build a house down there. Martine Eckhoff is going out with a man named Rikard Nilsen. In short, life goes on."

"What about you? Are you seeing Rakel?"

"Now and then I do."

"What about the doctor guy?"

"I don't ask. They have their own problems to deal with."

"Does she want you back—is that it?"

"I think she wishes I was the kind of person who could live the sort of life he does." Harry turned up his collar and peered down at what it was claimed was the town beneath. "And for that matter, I wish that, too, sometimes."

They fell silent.

"I took Tom Waaler's watch to a jeweler's and had it checked out by a young man who understands that kind of thing. Do you remember I once told you I was having nightmares about the Rolex watch that kept ticking on Waaler's severed arm?"

Møller nodded.

"Now I have the explanation," Harry said. "The world's most expensive watches have a Tourbillon system with a frequency of twenty-eight thousand vibrations an hour. This has the effect of making the second hand look as if it's flying around in one movement. And with a mechanical escapement the ticking sound is more intense than in other watches."

"Wonderful watches, Rolex."

"The Rolex brand was added by a watchmaker to disguise what kind of watch it really is. It's a Lange One Tourbillon. One of a hundred and fifty specimens. In the same series as the one I got from you. The last time a Lange One Tourbillon was sold at an auction the price was a little under three million kroner."

Møller nodded, a tiny smile playing on his lips.

"Was that how you paid yourselves?" Harry asked. "With watches costing three million?"

Møller buttoned up his coat and turned up the collar. "Their value is more stable and they're less conspicuous than cars. Less flamboyant than expensive art, easier to smuggle than cash and they don't need to be laundered."

"And watches are something you give as a present."

"That's it."

"What happened?"

"It's a long story, Harry. And like many tragedies it

started with the best intentions. We were a small group of people who wanted to play our part. Put things right that a society governed by law was not able to do unaided."

Møller put on a pair of black gloves.

"Some say the reason so many criminals go free is that the legal system is a net with a large mesh. But that gives a completely false picture. It's a thin, fine-meshed net that catches the small fry but tears when the big fish crash into it. We wanted to be the net behind the net, the one that could bring the sharks up short. There weren't only people from the police in the group, but also lawyers, politicians and bureaucrats who could see that the structure of our society, legislation and the legal system were not ready for the international organized crime that invaded our country when the borders came down. The police did not have the authority to play by the same rules as the lawbreakers. Until legislation had caught up. Therefore, we had to operate in a covert fashion."

Møller, staring into the mist, shook his head.

"But in those places that are closed and secret and cannot be ventilated the rot sets in. A culture of microorganisms grew in the police, who first declared we would have to smuggle in weapons to match those our adversaries had at their disposal. Then we would have to sell them so as to finance our work. It was a bizarre paradox, but those who opposed this soon found out that the microorganisms had taken over. And then came the gifts. Trivialities, to start with. Encouragement to spur you on, as they said. Thereby signaling that not accepting a gift would be seen as not showing solidarity. But in fact it was just the next stage in the rotting process, in the corruption that assimilated you almost without your noticing until you were sitting in crap up to your neck. And there was no way out. They had too much on you. The worst thing was that you didn't know who 'they' were. We had organized ourselves into small cells that communicated with each other via a contact person who was pledged to secrecy. I didn't know that Tom Waaler was one of us, that he was the one organizing the arms smuggling or that a person with the code name Prince even existed. Not until you and Ellen Gjelten discovered it. And then I also knew that we had lost sight of our real goal. That it was a long time since we had had any other goal except lining our own pockets. That I was corrupt. And that I was an accessory in"—Møller took a deep breath—"the murder of police officers like Ellen Gjelten."

Wisps and wafers of cloud whirled up past them as though Fløyen were flying.

"One day I couldn't take it anymore. I tried to get out. They gave me alternatives. Which were simple. But I'm not afraid for myself. The only thing I'm afraid of is that they will hurt my family."

"Is that why you fled?"

Bjarne Møller nodded.

Harry sighed. "And so you gave me this watch to put an end to it."

"It had to be you, Harry. It couldn't be anyone else."

Harry nodded. He felt a lump growing in his throat. He was reminded of something Møller had said the previous time they had stood here at the top of the mountain. It was funny to think that six minutes on the cable car from the center of the second-biggest town in Norway there were people who got lost and died. And to imagine you are at the heart of what you think is justice and then suddenly lose all sense of direction and become the very thing you oppose. He thought of all the mental calculations he had gone through, all the major and minor decisions that had led to the last minutes in Gardermoen Airport.

"And what about if I am not so different from you, boss? What about if I said I could be standing where you are now?"

Møller shrugged. "It's chance and nuances that separate the hero from the villain. That's how it's always been. Righteousness is the virtue of the lazy and the visionless. Without lawbreakers and disobedience we would still be living in a feudal society. I lost, Harry; it's as simple as that. I believed in something, but I was blinded, and by the time I regained my sight I had been corrupted. It happens all the time."

Harry shivered in the wind and searched for words. When he finally found some his voice sounded alien and tormented. "Sorry, boss. I can't arrest you."

"That's fine, Harry. I'll sort out the rest myself from here." Møller's voice sounded calm, almost consoling. "I just wanted you to see everything. And understand. And perhaps learn. There was no more to it than that."

Harry stared into the impenetrable mist and tried in vain to do as his boss and friend had asked him to do: "to see everything." Harry kept his eyes open until the tears came. When he turned around, Bjarne Møller had gone. He called his name in the mist even though he knew that Møller was right: There was no more to it than that. But he thought someone ought to call his name anyway.

A NOTE ABOUT THE TRANSLATOR

Don Bartlett lives in Norfolk, England, and works as a freelance translator of Scandinavian literature. He has translated, or cotranslated, Norwegian novels by Lars Saabye Christensen, Roy Jacobsen, Ingvar Ambjørnsen, Kjell Ola Dahl, Gunnar Staalesen and Pernille Rygg.

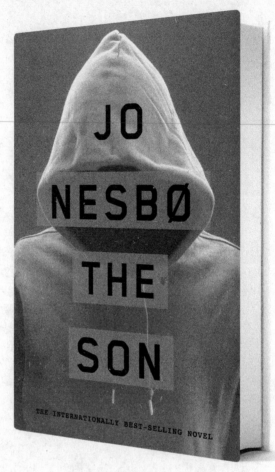

The Son is an electrifying stand-alone novel in which one very unusual young man is about to propel himself into a mission of brutal revenge.